John Hervey Bristol, Thomas Hervey

Letter-books; With Sir Thomas Hervey's letters during courtship and poems during widowhood

Vol. 1: 1651 to 1750

John Hervey Bristol, Thomas Hervey

Letter-books; With Sir Thomas Hervey's letters during courtship and poems during widowhood
Vol. 1: 1651 to 1750

ISBN/EAN: 9783337206185

Printed in Europe, USA, Canada, Australia, Japan

Cover: Foto ©Andreas Hilbeck / pixelio.de

More available books at **www.hansebooks.com**

LETTER-BOOKS of JOHN HERVEY,

FIRST EARL OF BRISTOL.

John Hervey, 1st Earl of Bristol.
1665 ~ 1751.

LETTER-BOOKS

OF

JOHN HERVEY,

FIRST EARL OF BRISTOL.

WITH SIR THOMAS HERVEY'S LETTERS DURING COURT-SHIP & POEMS DURING WIDOWHOOD.

1651 TO 1750.

IN THREE VOLUMES.

VOL. I.—1651 TO 1715.

WITH FIVE PORTRAITS.

Wells:

ERNEST JACKSON, 5, HIGH STREET.

—

1894.

ILLUSTRATIONS.

CONTENTS OF VOL. I.

———:o:———

———

ALPHABETICAL LIST OF THOSE TO WHOM LORD BRISTOL'S LETTERS ARE WRITTEN.

Vol. I. *(b)*

PREFACE.

THESE volumes are by way of containing a selection of Lord Bristol's letters.
But the selecting has consisted in accepting 1372 and rejecting about 6; and
even those 6 I now wish had been accepted too. I dare say it will be thought that
many more might well have been rejected, because there was nothing in them; but it
seemed to me that there was something, however little, in them, and so I included
them. They had something for somebody at some time, if they had not something for
everybody at all times. No doubt a volume of more condensed interest might have
been produced by rejecting many more; but my object was not to produce a volume
of condensed interest; it was to secure what I thought was worth securing. And
printing is the only possible way of securing. What is printed is secured, because it
is multiplied; what is not printed is not secured, no, and will not and cannot be till it
is printed. Nothing that exists only in manuscript is secure; it is liable to destruction,
wilful or accidental, at any moment. What is worth preserving is worth securing;
and as the only way to secure is to print, therefore it follows that what is worth
preserving is worth printing. And things printed should be wholly printed. The
printing of extracts and selections is in most cases an abomination. The extractor and
selector probably only gives what interests him or somebody else at one particular
moment, and what might interest other people and at other moments is left out. He
has therefore done more harm than good. He has not secured the whole thing himself,
and by what he has done has, perhaps, prevented anybody else from doing so. Away
with such a fellow!

The manuscript volumes now printed and secured are three in number.

I. A thick folio volume with clasp and lock, containing 483 pages. This book
originally belonged to Sir Thomas Hervey; 24 pages contain his letters to Isabella
May written in 1651—1653 during their long courtship, and the verses that he wrote
on six successive anniversaries of her death. The remaining 459 pages are filled by

his son, John Lord Bristol. Immediately after Sir Thomas Hervey's Anniversary poems come 3 pages of letters to John Hervey from the Duke of Marlborough; these letters are 8 in number, and are written from abroad between 1703 and 1716. Then turning the book over and beginning at the other end are John Hervey's letters to various correspondents. These are in strict chronological order, and were evidently copied into the book at the time when the original letter was written. A few of them are in Lord Bristol's own large, clear hand; a few are in the hand of Mary, Lady Hervey, and one or other of her children; but the bulk of them are in another hand, which may have been that of William Oliver, his steward. They have been read over by Lord Bristol from time to time, and his pencil has made marginal notes, and those other mysterious marks and symbols which are so common in his printed books. These letters range from 1692 to 1750.

II. III. Two quarto volumes with clasps, containing only letters between Lord and Lady Bristol. Some of these have been copied by Lord Bristol's hand. They range from July 1695 (when the future Lady Bristol was still Mrs. Felton, though she was within a week of becoming Mrs. Hervey,) to Dec. 1737, when by the death of Queen Caroline Lady Bristol's duties at Court came to an end. A few poems are copied in at the beginning and end of them, and these I have printed in an Appendix to Lord Bristol's Diary.

So much for the books. Now for the man and his forefathers and his family.

In 1858 Lord Arthur Hervey printed a History of the Hervey family, the result of much research, labour and ingenuity on his part and on that of his eldest brother, Lord Bristol. Therein many errors in the old Heralds' Visitations and pedigrees were exposed, and some sort of a succession was made out from very early times. We are there shown a family of Hervey settled in Bedfordshire in the 13th and two following centuries. Three successive John Herveys, father, son and grandson, were seated at Thurleigh in that county, and filled up the greater part of the 15th century. The first John married Margery Parles (afterwards Margery Argentine), and died somewhere about 1415. He lies buried at Thurleigh, and you yet may see his effigy in brass. The second John married Joan Niernuyt, and died soon after 1475. He also lies buried at Thurleigh. The third John married Agnes Morley, and died in 1474, before his father. His only son George, 6 months old at the time of his father's death, was knighted by Henry VIII at Tournay, was present at the Battle of Spurs in 1513, at the Field of the Cloth of Gold in 1520, and died in 1521. He disinherited his only daughter, and the Bedfordshire estates went to his natural son Gerard, from whom was descended the Major Hervey with whom Lord Bristol corresponded. See Letters 187, 243, 270.

But a younger son of the second John Hervey was Thomas Hervey, who somewhere about 1460 married Jane Drury, and by that marriage Ickworth and Wordwell were brought into the possession of his children, though not till after his and his wife's death. He died about 1468, and she before 1475. She married secondly Sir William Carew. Where Thomas Hervey lived and died is not known.

His son and heir, William, was born in 1464, married Joan Cockett of Ampton in 1485, and died in 1528 or 1538. He lies buried in St. Mary's, Bury St. Edmunds.

His son, John, married Elizabeth Pope of Mildenhall in 1510, and died in 1556.

His son, William, married about 1555 Elizabeth Poley of Boxted, died in 1592, and is buried at Ickworth.

His son, John, married Frances Bocking of Ash-Bocking in Suffolk in 1582, died in 1630, and lies buried at Ickworth. I have printed his will in an Appendix to Lord Bristol's Diary, a simple and pathetic will, in which the lawyer and his intolerable confusion of words find no place.

His son, William, knighted in 1608, married firstly Susan Jermyn of Rushbrooke, and secondly Lady Penelope Gage, and died in 1660; he lies buried at Ickworth. By Lady Penelope he had no children.

His eldest son, John, the uncle Hervey of these letters, married his cousin, Elizabeth, daughter of Lord Hervey of Kidbrook, and died without children in 1680.

A second son, William, died of small pox while an undergraduate at Cambridge in 1642; an ode on his death will be found among Cowley's Poems.

A third son, Sir Thomas, born in 1625, married Isabella May, daughter of Sir Humphrey May, Knt., succeeded his brother John in 1680, and died in 1694. As I have already shown he has some part and lot in these letter-books.

Of Sir William's daughters, Judith married James Reynolds of Bumpsted in Essex ; Mary was the first of the five wives of Sir Edward Gage of Hengrave ; Susan married Sir Thomas Hanmer of Hanmer, Co. Flint; and Kezia married Thomas Tyrell of Gipping in Suffolk. Descendants of all these marriages will be found mentioned in the Letter-books.

This brings us to John, son and heir of Sir Thomas Hervey. 1200 letters and a Diary written by him will of course supply some of the facts of his life, and it would be very strange if they did not also give us some insight into his character. But beyond what is to be learnt from them I know little. He was born Aug. 27, 1665, and baptized in St. Mary's Church, Bury St. Edmunds, on Sept. 29. In due time he went to the Grammar School at Bury. The Master was Mr. Edward Leeds, to whom two letters will be found, Nos. 189, 254, written long afterwards, wherein the old scholar makes the usual penitential allusion to his "fatal idleness" at School. I do not see his name in the Graduati Cantabrigienses, 1659 to 1824 ; but the Dictionary of National Biography says that he matriculated at Clare Hall, Cambridge, on July 5, 1684, and was admitted to the degree of LL.D. on April 16, 1705. After his matriculation I lose sight of him till Nov. 1, 1688, on which day he married Isabella, daughter of Sir Robert Carr, Bart. of Aswarby, Co. Lincoln. With his married life begin also his Diary and Expenses. It is more than possible that between 1684 when he matriculated at Cambridge and 1688 when he married he may have travelled abroad, as both his sons, Carr and John, did afterwards. In recording the death of Sir Henry Bond (Diary, Aug. 1721,) he calls him "my friend and fellow-traveller"; and I can see no interval at any other time of his life long enough for him to have travelled in. The Diary and Letters not only make no mention of his going abroad, but show him constantly and continually in England from 1688 to 1750.

He tells us what was his income at the beginning of his married life. He had an allowance of £1000 a year from his father ; and there would be another £1000 when Aunt Hervey died. His wife had £912 a year, besides an annuity of £100 which was not actually being received, but was running on as a debt. His calculation of his annual expenditure will be found in the Volume containing his Diary, p. 88. His wife brought him a house and estate at Aswarby in Lincolnshire. His time must have been divided between London, Aswarby and Bury. Ickworth at this time was not in a habitable state. [See notes to Diary, p. 277.] His London house up to the time of his first wife's death was first "at ye Pall-Mall," and afterwards in King St. His wife's mother, Lady Carr, a sister of Henry Bennet, Lord Arlington, who was one of the Cabal, apparently shared this house with them. Three children were born; first Isabella in 1689; then Carr in 1691; and then Elizabeth. But the moment of Elizabeth's coming in was the moment of her mother's going out. She died on March 7, 1693. There is not much to go upon in forming an estimate of her character, but what there is is satisfactory. There is the testimony of her portrait at Ickworth, which seems to tell of a simple and amiable mind. And there is the testimony of her husband, and the very great love which he had for her, and which he ever retained for her memory. His grief at her death seems to have been unbounded, not silently borne, not borne with very much of that resignation on which he afterwards prided himself, but displayed in letters of such terrific length and vehemence as to call forth rebukes from his father.

In March, 1694, just a year after his wife's death, John Hervey was first sent to Parliament to represent Bury St. Edmunds. His speech to the Corporation on that occasion will be found among his letters. (No. 94.) He continued to represent Bury (or rather its Corporation, for they alone returned the members; see Diary Appendix, No. 7,) till he was raised to the Peerage in 1703.

In the following year, 1695, the Diary records several visits to Boxted. What was the attraction at Boxted and what was the object of those visits is soon made clear. Lady Poley, wife of Sir John Poley of Boxted, had a niece, Elizabeth, only child of her brother Sir Thomas Felton; and on July 25, 1695, that niece became Mrs. Hervey in Boxted Church, Dr. Henry Felton, uncle of the bride and Rector of Long Melford, being the officiating clergyman.

Two quarto volumes, as already stated, contain the correspondence between John Hervey and Elizabeth his second wife. In 1718 she was appointed one of the Ladies of the Bedchamber to Caroline, Princess of Wales, and so continued till her mistress's death in 1737. Letter 1065 contains a touching account of the King's bidding farewell to the late Queen's household. Her duties at Court caused periodical seperations from her husband, as did her visits to Bath, nominally for her health sake, but more likely for the sake of the diversions to be met with there. During these and other shorter separations, however short they may have been, never a post was missed by either one or the other; letters passed to and fro every day, filled with the most extravagant expressions of affection, and describing the miserable, intolerable condition that each was in by reason of the absence of the other. Mr. Croker, who went through these volumes at the time of his editing Lord Hervey's Memoirs, thus describes them in his Biographical notice of Lord Hervey: *the whole correspondence between Lord and Lady Bristol during their occasional separations from their marriage in 1695 to 1737 has been preserved, and it exhibits a series of love letters, by almost every post, of a passionate fondness that would seem excessive after a few month's matrimony. Lord Bristol was—in all tender emotions at least—something of an enthusiast, and the Countess was vehement in all her feelings.* Vol. I. p. xxii. That there was some interruption to this affectionate correspondence, I have shown in a note to Letter 971. Nominally this interruption was caused by Lady Bristol's interference in Bury politics; but probably there were other irritating causes to help. Possibly rumours of her flirtations at Bath or elsewhere may have been among them. Certainly Lord and Lady Bristol were in many respects diametrically opposed to each other. He was a plain countryman, hating Courts and Towns, and delighting in country pursuits and domestic life and the improvement of his estate; she was a courtier, miserable in the country. He took a solemn vow against gaming, which he recorded in his Diary; (See June, 1703;) she gamed herself and taught her children to do the same. He was always preaching, and no doubt practiced also, the wisdom of looking for health from temperance and exercise and country air: she was content to rely on the continual swallowing of drugs and potions, and the frequent visits of physicians and apothecaries. Why wont you take air and exercise,? was the burden of his advice; Why wont you take your rhubarb,? was the burden of hers. There could not have been two people more unlike in many respects than they were; and the fact of their living so harmoniously together for so many years would seem to support the theory that those who are unlike get on better together than those who are like.

Lady Bristol was certainly clever in her way, and full of wit and vivacity; her letters, without the smallest pretence to literary excellence, are admirable; easy, natural, light, pointed and graphic. Her temper from all accounts, including her husband's, was none of the best; tears in great abundance would flow for little or no reason; and the blessed gift of calmness, and the still more blessed gift of reasonableness, were certainly not hers.

She was a considerable heiress. As heiress to her father, she brought to her husband the Felton property at Playford and thereabouts. As heiress to her mother, who was co-heiress to James, Earl of Suffolk and Lord Howard de Walden, she brought to him a part of Lord Audley's inheritance, and to her descendants in the second generation the Barony of Howard de Walden. She also inherited from the Howards a share in an estate in Staffordshire or Shropshire, frequent allusion to which will be found in the Letters.

It was not long after John Hervey's second marriage that his Aunt Hervey died abroad, viz. in 1700, with whom both he and his father before him had been continually engaged in lawsuits. By her death he came into possession of the house in St. James' Square, which he had been renting of her, and of the uninhabitable Manor house at Ickworth. He seems immediately to have enlarged and improved one of the farm-houses at Ickworth, about half a mile from the old Hall, and thither he brought his wife, as he records in his Diary, on April 14, 1702. I will not repeat here what I have said in a note to that passage. It is enough to say that from that date began his long residence of 50 years at Ickworth. It was the renewal of a dropped family acquaintance, the taking up of a dropped thread; for although the two generations before him had scarcely slept a night at Ickworth, although for 80 years or so old Ickworth Hall had been left to the owls and bats, yet the four generations before that had all lived and died there. Henceforth he poured on Ickworth all the affection of a warm heart, and never mentions it without adding an expression of his love. The farm-house which he fitted up there was only meant for a temporary arrangement; he intended building a new house; the architect was to have been Sir John Vanbrugh, the architect of Blenheim, who came to Ickworth, chose the site, and made a plan. At one moment there seems to have been an idea of buying Rushbrook, the seat of the Davers' family,

Vol. I. *(c)*

which afterwards came by marriage to his grandson Frederick, and settling there. But that idea was given up in favour of Ickworth. Writing to Sir John Vanbrugh in 1703 (Letter 228) he speaks of Rushbrook "declining in its unequal competition with Ickworth." But somehow the house at Ickworth was never built. Heavy taxes, the expenses of a long family, one thing and another, kept him from fulfilling his purpose, and it was left to his grandson Frederick, Bishop of Derry, to do what he had intended doing. He to the end of his long life, and his two immediate successors, George and Augustus, were content to remain at the adapted farm-house, making improvements in it from time to time. Illustrations of this house as it was and as it is will be found in the volume containing the Diary.

A word or two must be added about his family. Of the three children by his first wife none were married. Isabella died in 1711 aged 22 years, and Elizabeth in 1695 in her second year, and Carr in 1723 aged 32 years. Carr was educated at Clare Hall, Cambridge, took his degree of M.A. in 1710, and then went abroad for nearly three years. In 1713, during his absence abroad, he was chosen to represent Bury St. Edmunds in Parliament, and continued to do so till 1722. He was a Gentleman of the Bedchamber to the Prince of Wales. His manner of life ruined him and shortened his days, and helped to increase his father's hatred of Courts. He inherited Aswarby and a part of the Lincolnshire property from his mother; but after a few years, being in pecuniary difficulties, he sold it, greatly against his father's wishes, to Sir Francis Whichcote. The purchase money seems to have been unpaid, or only partly paid, at the time of his death. I imagine that that part of the Lincolnshire property still remaining to the owner of Ickworth represents those shares of the Carr property which went to Isabella Hervey's aunts, and which the first Lord Bristol bought up, and which, therefore, never came to Carr Hervey.

Lord Bristol's children by his second wife were very numerous. In his clear, methodical way he has left a memorandum giving their names, and the names of their gossips, and the day and hour of their births.* They are seventeen in number, including one stillborn. Besides them there were triplets born at Bath in 1701, but

* I have printed this memorandum in the volume containing the Diary: Appendix No. 2.

not living. Of the sixteen ten were boys and six were girls. Of the ten boys four died in infancy. The other six, John, Thomas, William, Henry, Charles and Felton all grew up, and figure in the Letters.

I. John, 1696—1743, was educated at Westminster School and Clare Hall, Cambridge. He is a well-known political character, and nothing more need be said of him here than that the letters show throughout the greatest affection borne to him by his father: borne to him when a boy, and still borne to him when a statesman taking a contrary part in politics. No mother of the most anxious type could have shown greater anxiety for a delicate or a supposed-to-be-delicate child than the old Earl shows for his son when a man of 40. His driving in a chaise in Ickworth park without a great coat, his travelling to London in a single day, his attention to his duties or his studies, these and such like are all matters causing the greatest anxiety to his father, and making him forget his own threescore and ten years. A slight coolness arose between father and son when George was put into the army, standing armies being one of the old Earl's greatest horrors; but this was got over by a promise that George should come out of the accursed thing as soon as he decently could. Of the parentage of Mary, Lady Hervey, I have given some account in the Diary, note 27, p. 287, and have transferred her from the Island of Sark to the middle of Russia. Of their four sons, George, Augustus and Frederick became successively Earls of Bristol, and William entered the army, attained to the rank of a General, and died unmarried in 1815. Of their four daughters, Lepel married Constantine Phipps, afterwards Lord Mulgrave, and was the mother of an Arctic explorer; Mary married George Fitzgerald of Turlough, and was the mother of the notorious George Robert Fitzgerald; Amelia and Caroline were amongst the early patrons of Brighton, and died there unmarried. William, Mary, Amelia and Caroline all inherited something of their grandfather's tenacity of life, and exceeded the fourscore years. In the next generation the first Marquis of Bristol reached the age of 89, and in the next generation again his children Lady Augusta Seymour and Lord Arthur Hervey reached the ages of 81 and 85 respectively.

II. Of Thomas Hervey, 1699—1775, the less said the better. He was sent to Westminster School, and then to Christ Church College, Oxford, which he left without taking a degree ; he afterwards had chambers at Lincoln's Inn, and presumably was a barrister. He has been admitted into the new Dictionary of National Biography;* one scarcely sees why. He published several Letters and pamphlets, which afford the material for his biography there. He had some offices at Court, and represented Bury St. Edmunds from 1733 to 1747. He married Ann Coghlan, an Irish lady, but the marriage was an unhappy one. He lived in Bond St. His only legitimate son, William, died without issue in 1791. By eloping with Lady Hanmer, by his gaming and general conduct, Thomas greatly incensed his father.

III. William Hervey, 1699—1776, was sent to Westminster School, and then went into the navy. He married in 1729 Elizabeth, daughter of Thomas Ridge of Portsmouth, who died a year afterwards in giving birth to a daughter. This daughter, Elizabeth, was living single in London in 1800. In 1742 William Hervey was court-martialled and cashiered, complaints having been made against him for undue rigour towards his officers and crew. An account of him will be found in Charnock's Biographia Navalis, Vol. IV.

IV. Henry Hervey, 1701—1748, was sent to Westminster School and then to Christ Church, Oxford, where he only stayed about a year. He then went into the army, and after some years service there went into the Church, changing his title but not his character. He seems to have been not without heart or talent, but absolutely without head or ballast. His debts and general conduct greatly incensed his father. He died Rector of Shotley. He married Catherine, daughter of Sir Thomas Aston of Aston in Cheshire ; she on the death of her brother inherited Aston Hall, and her husband took the name of Aston. In the male line their descendants, the Hervey Astons, have died out, but the present owner of Aston, Mr. Hervey Talbot, is a descendant in the female line.

V. Charles, 1703—1783, was sent to a school at Hampstead, then, I think, to the Bury School, and then to Queen's College, Cambridge, where he spent 8 years. He

---

* Three errors in the account of him there may be corrected. (1) He was born Jan. 1696, not 1698. (2) He was sent to Oxford, not Cambridge. (3) His son William was not killed at Ticonderoga : that must have been a natural son. William is mentioned in an Act of Parliament, 1807, to enable Lord Bristol to sell certain lands, and is there said to have died in 1791.

then was ordained, and was Rector of Ickworth cum Chedburgh, and afterwards of Sproughton and Shotley. He was also a Prebendary of Ely. He married Martha Maria Howard, but died without issue. He seems to have been a singularly dull, quiet, inoffensive man, as unlike the rest of his brothers as he well could be. See Diary, Note 30, p. 295.

VI. Felton, 1712—1773, was sent to Eton, where he got into a scrape, and was also a page at Court, where he got into another scrape and was dismissed. After that he does not seem to have given any more trouble. He represented Bury in 1747 and for some years afterwards. He married Dorothy, daughter of Solomon Ashley and widow of Charles Pitfield, and had a son Lionel, who shot himself. Lionel's eldest son was Sir Felton Hervey, Bart. who was at the battle of Waterloo, and who was succeeded in the Baronetcy by his brother Sir Frederick Ann Hervey, who took the name of Bathurst.

Lord Bristol's six daughters were Elizabeth, Henrietta (1), Ann, Barbara, Louisa, and Henrietta (2).

1. Elizabeth, 1697—1727, married Hon. Bussy Mansel, younger son of 1st Baron Mansel, of Margam, Co. Glamorgan, and died without issue. She was buried in Ickworth Church, the lines on her tombstone being written by her brother John.

2. Henrietta (1), twin sister of Charles, died in 1712 aged 9 years.

3. Ann, 1707—1771, died at Bury St. Edmunds unmarried. She was manifestly a favourite child of her father. There is a portrait of her belonging to Lord Cork at Marston, and a miniature belonging to Mr. Brookes of Eltham; but none at Ickworth.

4. Barbara, 1709—1727, died unmarried. There are two portraits of her at Rushbrooke.

5. Louisa, 1715—1770, married Sir Robert Smith or Smyth, and lies buried in West Ham Church. For the inscription on her tombstone see the volume containing the Ickworth Registers, p. 82. She had a son Hervey, who was aide-de-camp to General Wolfe at the seige of Quebec, and succeeded his father in 1773, and died unmarried in 1811, when the baronetcy become extinct.

6. Henrietta (2) 1716—1732.

So much for his forefathers, and so much for his children. With regard to himself, I need not say much more, but leave his Letters and Diary to speak for themselves. In 1703 he was raised to the peerage as Baron Hervey, and in 1714 was created Earl of Bristol. At the Coronation of George I. in Oct. 1714, he tells us rather proudly "I walked in ye procession as Earle of Bristol." As the Duchess of Marlborough tells us in her Account of her conduct, and as he himself acknowledges, this promotion was due to her recommendation. He was a strong supporter of the Hanoverian and Protestant succession, a great admirer of the Duke of Marlborough, and had a very poor opinion of the Tories. While holding strong opinions on political matters, as his letters to Sir Richard Cocks and others show, he took little or no part in public political affairs. In the earlier part of his married life his visits to New-market were frequent, and horse racing had no more enthusiastic patron than he. He kept a stud of running horses at Marham in Norfolk, and occasionally rode a race himself. A portrait of one of his racers will be found in the volume containing his Diary. But later on in life the care of his family and the improvement of his estate were enough to take up all his thought and time. His solemn renunciation of gaming is recorded in his Diary, June 14, 1703, though his matches at Newmarket still went on. He was well read, in the Classics, in Historical and in Theological works. The quotations and allusions with which his letters abound, and the list of books bought by him, which is printed in the volume containing his Diary, p. 91, will show what he read.

In May. 1711, Lady Bristol died, being seized with a fit as she was in St. James' Park in her sedan chair. Whether the sedan chair that now stands idle in the entrance hall of No. 6, St. James' Square, is the one in which she was taking the air, I know not. In August, 1713, John, Lord Hervey, died. His eldest son, George, succeeded to his barony, and also to his place in the old Earl's affections. I think it would have been hardly possible for Lord Bristol to have existed at any time of his life without some one upon whom he could pour out all his affection, and whom he could believe to be almost perfection. So he went on, never now stirring from Ickworth. His losses and disappointments seem to have been borne with a considerable amount of philosophical resignation. The time when grief could make him write such vehement letters as those which he wrote on the death of his first wife was long past. The sight of his eyes and the hearing of his ears were failing him; the infirmities of age and the undutifulness of sons were pressing upon him; but he still kept up a stout heart, and in the care of his grandchildren found something to distract him from himself. His daughter-in-law, Mary, Lady Hervey, did much to comfort his latter years, frequently visiting him at Ickworth, writing his letters for him, and listening to his prophecies of the impending ruin of the country. His last letters that we have were written in December, 1750. In January, 1751, he was gathered to his fathers and to his children in Ickworth Church, having reached the age of 85 years and 5 months.

Of his personal appearance, I think the three portraits of him which will be found in these volumes will give us some idea. Each is characteristic in its way. The first shows him in all the fulness and pride of early youth, a very handsome man, if the portrait is not unduly flattering. The second shows him in his newly acquired robes, and shows more of them than it does of him; he is proud with the pride of a new peer. The third shows the old man, no longer proud with the pride of youth, no longer proud with the pride of a new peer, but still possessing a will and a character which age has not diminished or weakened. A contemporary writer, John Mackay, whom I quote at secondhand from Doyle's Official Baronage, thus describes him: *A handsome man in his person, fair complexion, middle stature. (Macky's Memoirs etc., with characters of the Courtiers of Great Britain, 1733.)*

To sum up, I think we see in these pages a right worthy man; hot-tempered, imperious, impatient of contradiction or opposition, pompous, with an exaggerated idea of his own importance; perhaps, he was all that; but with it there was a warm heart capable of sincere and constant affection; that simplicity of character and that capacity for happiness which can find all the happiness it wants in domestic life and rural scenes, and needs not continual gas and glitter and glare to satisfy it; that true piety and devoutness, which is satisfied with a very few principles and formulas, and they of the simplest kind; he had moreover a good head for figures, and was a good man of business. His handwriting was large and clear. His style of writing was bad, his sentences being often long and intricate. It often happens, such is the length of his sentences, that long before he has got to the end of them, he has forgotten how they begun ; so that the two halves do not fit. It all comes of trying to say everything in the same sentence, instead of saying one thing in one sentence, and the next thing in another sentence. But in spite of it he can sometimes put a thing forcibly and well. He had humour and he had feeling, but I think indignation was his favourite mood.

With regard to my own part of the work, I have aimed simply to copy. The stopping is mine, as the stops which are very numerous in the original are also very perplexing, and apparently without any method in them ; and I have not copied in the matter of capital letters, and have sometimes written out full a contracted word ; but the spelling is as I found it. I think that spelling is not always the spelling of the original letter writer, but it is the spelling of the transcriber whom Lord Bristol employed ; and in the case of Lady Bristol's letters, the transcriber's spelling is much the better of the two. I have sometimes, but very seldom, had occasion to omit a sentence which seemed to me to be better omitted.

The ten portraits in the three volumes of Letters, as well as the portrait of Wenn, the race-horse, in the volume containing the Diary and expenses, are all, by Lord Bristol's leave, from the original pictures at Ickworth.* The portrait of Wenn was the work of a Bury artist named Brook ; Newmarket town lies in the background, though hard to see on account of the bad condition in which the picture is. The four topographical illustrations in the Diary and Expenses will be found explained at pp. 277—284 of that volume.

There remains for me to express my thanks to Lord Bristol for allowing me to have the original volumes in my custody for as long a time as I needed them.

And I cannot close this preface without one word to acknowledge the help that I have received from my father. His printed papers on the Hervey family, on Playford and the Feltons, and on Boxted and the Poleys, have told me much that I needed to know. Yet more he has told me personally, by word of mouth. Yet more I was

---

* Excepting that of Lady Bristol, which is from the engraving by Simon of a picture by Dahl. Where that picture is now, I know not. It belonged to the late Lord Howard de Walden, and it was sold at Christie's soon after his death in 1868.

expecting to learn from him when the time should come for these prefaces and notes to be written. But when that time came, he was not here. Just about the time when the work of copying was finished, and notes and prefaces had to be written, he was called away. So great was his interest in all matters of family history, so often had he asked me during the past year, When is the book coming out? that I could feel sure of his intelligent appreciation of it; and that appreciation was one of the rewards I looked for. The book is out at last, but that appreciation cannot be had.

Arthur Charles Hervey, 4th son of Frederick William, 5th Earl and 1st Marquis of Bristol, was born Aug. 20, 1808, when they were yet living who had seen John, the first Earl. I have often heard my father say that he could recollect seeing three, if not four, of John, Lord Hervey's children; viz. Lady Mary Fitzgerald, Ladies Emily and Caroline Hervey, and William, the General, old Gwog as he was familiarly called. All those four enter as children into their grandfather's Letters and Diary and Expenses, and were amongst the comforts that he found in the sorrows of his old age.

In his book of Expenses he makes this entry on Sept. 5, 1741. *Gace my grand-daughters Emely and Caroline for singing a duo on my birthday to each a piece of 5 Moydores Portugal coin, in all £13..10..0.*

Seventy or eighty years passed by after that, and those two little girls singing a duo had been transformed into two elderly ladies ending their days at the new watering place, Brighton; and amongst those of the youngest generation who were taken to see them were Augusta Hervey (afterwards Lady Augusta Seymour) and Arthur Charles Hervey (afterwards Bishop of Bath & Wells), grandchildren of their brother Frederick. One of the two old ladies lay in bed, and I have heard Lady Augusta tell how terrified she was, because the old lady looked so like the wolf in the picture that illustrated the story of Little Red Riding Hood.

Yet another eighty years passed by, and then Arthur Charles Hervey, the last of his generation, is gathered to his fathers, and laid in the burial ground of Wells Cathedral. So there is but one link between one born in 1665, in the early years of Charles II, and one who dies in 1894, in the latter years of Queen Victoria. The two little girls singing a duo to their grandfather, the two elderly ladies residing at Brighton, and visited by a great nephew, are the single link that is needed to join the early days of Charles II. to the latter days of Queen Victoria. Three lives end on end, or at least overlapping a little, cover a length of 230 years. Something of form and feature and character must needs be carried on from those in Charles the Second's reign to those in Queen Victoria's, and it is interesting to try and make out what and how much.

S. H. A. H.

Wedmore Vicarage,
Somerset,
September, 1894.

LETTER-BOOKS OF JOHN HERVEY,

FIRST EARL OF BRISTOL.

Copies of ye letters my chast & virtuous Father * wrote to ye most pious & charitable of her sex, my most dear mother, during ye 10 years contract between them before marriage, which was consummated ye 21 July, 1658.

> Notitiam primosque gradus vicinia fecit ;
> Tempore crevit Amor, tædæ quoque forte coissent ;
> Sed vetuere patres, quod non potuere vetare,
> Ex æquo captis ardebant mentibus ambo.—*Ovid de Pyr : & Thisbe.*

1.   My dearest life

Having declared how delightfull this is to me, I hope it will not be unpleasant to you ; tho I have no more to say then what I have a thousand times told you, that I am yours with a most intire affection. How shall I tell you how ye time passes with me when I am from

---

* This title and the quotation from Ovid are in the writing of John 1st Earl of Bristol, added by him after the letters had been copied. That the letters were copied by the direction of Sir Thomas himself and were read by him after being copied is proved by his pencil marks, for one of which see letter 41 and note.   In the following letters of Sir Thomas, "Town" always means Bury St. Edmunds, not London : Lady Penn : means Lady Penelope Gage, his stepmother : Kez : is his sister Kezia who married Thomas Tyrell of Gipping : Jud & Jude mean his sister Judith who married James Reynolds of Bumpstead. The letters are dated according to the old style, the year beginning on March 28. It is not clear what is the date of No. 23. If it stands in its right place, then there is a mistake in the dating of it. If its date is right, then its place is wrong.

Vol. I.   A

you; why truly ye night is to me as welcome as ye day, my thoughts are my only recreations, and these ye darkness hinders not; when that comes, tho' I sleep not, yet I do not complain; I love you no common way, for I shoud account it so much time lost, shoud not a kind dream represent you to me. Wonder not I like our company here no better, so seldom it is I hear you named amongst them; tis impossible I should; but when you are, (so much I must say for them) so handsome & friendly a mention is made of you as I am again reconciled to them, and that almost to a possibilitie of of being persuaded to mix with them. But why should I go abroad, & but rarely tast these dainties, when if I stay at home I fail not of a constant feast. I am interrupted, and can say no more but desire you, if you have heard anything of ye grand affaire, to communicate it to Yours etc.

2.   My dearest life

My confusion renders me uncapable of advising, therefore God in mercy direct you in this great occation. But I desire you to put down in writing what has already, or shall pass between you & your mother, and convey it as you did that which occasions this, which will not be hard to do, if you will be at Mrs. Collonel Blaggs about five of ye clock on Tuesday night next, where I will not faile to meet you. Proceed, I most humbly beseech you, in this matter (which shall be ye only caution I shall give) without any regarde to me, whose felicity consists in your content-ment, so as if that be secured, I have not a wish beyond it. Oh! how incessantly am I (sleeping & waking) tormented with ye apprehension of making you miserable. But my comfort is ye wages of such a sinn must be death. Or God may yet avert this heavy judgement however if you, my dearest, be not involved, come what will come.

3.   My dearest life

For yet I hope I may so call you; how I love you and what I have of late suffered for you can only be made demonstrable be-twixt us; but I, to what degree I have done either, for my peace (a strange request you will say) do you no more think on : let ye trouble for ye love of God be wholly mine. For if anything can alleviate the pressures of my life, it must be ye assurance that yours is undisturbd. Live you happily, and I cannot die miserable. I have now no hope beyond the quiet of a grave, nor a fear beside ye passage to it, which I foresee with horrour must inevitably be through innumerable disquiets. There will be rest, here is none. Therefore if you lament me when I am once laid down in ye dust, know you doe but wish me here againe to contend with an insuperable destiny, & cease to injure your dead friend.

4.   My dearest life   Nov. 18, 1651.

Now I perceive it is but vanity to hope a constant good fortune, it is but reasonable to provide against likely inconveniences ; and in this rank I place meeting with you in a thronge of people ; ye evil may be thus lessend if you please to return me a paper sometimes. How much of late I have wanted this comfort, shoud I tell you would trouble you, & for this reason I forbear : though my heart be very full, my trust is in ye tender mercys of God, who, I doubt not, coud I live worthy his favour (which by his grace I shall endeavour and by his blessing hope in some measure to attain) will, when my father and all earthly friends forsake me, take me into his protection. I say not this as having ye least distrust of your kindness, my dear dear Heart, which ye vehemence of ye expression may possibly make suspicious ; tis true you are concerned, but not in that sense, who are all joy, pleasure & delight to me. Such may you meet with, & I can wish no more for you.   Every Saturday let me have a little paper, that I may know how ye world goes at Babram, and this tho I see you, for ye want of intelligence is ye vexation I have complained of.

5.   My dearest life

You have with extraordinary dexterity carried on this business hitherto. I approve very well of ye design to let it be anything rather than your own act. That last remedy woud be yet most unseasonable, considering how many accidents may possibly intervene to interrupt it, and then ye wisest can but have their suspicions, and those fooles may have too. Still diligently pursue this point; with confidence tell your mother you have nothing to object against this match, especially since she is pleased to express her self so desirous of it, or to this purpose what you shall think fit; for I am fearless as ever that not ye powers of Hell shall be able to prevaile against our chaste affections. No certainty, if so many prayers & tears profit not, but after all you must be anothers, & I again my own. Heaven we may then safely conclude has done it, whose justice will not more eminently appear by this extraordinary way of punishing the wickedness of my life, than I trust it shall in ye rewarding ye innocency of yours with all temporal enjoyments. Peace and prosperity be ever to you, with me Gods will be done.   I sacrificed ye dear paper to your commands, & therefore cannot say that I am troubled that I did so; but grieved I had not an art to preserve ye ashes.

6.   My dearest life   Nov. 29, 1651.

So tempestuous a night as we last parted in I never see, yet we came well home; ye miserable take no harme; consider this is said when I am from you, & ye expression will appear significant enough. Woud you had seen ye change in ye whole company upon your departure. Indeed I thought I coud not have loved any assembly so well where you had not made one. I know not which I was ye most delighted with, their mirth while you were there, or their sadness when you were gone; both were so seasonable. The chiefe mourner, who he was you do more than guess I am sure, I dare tell you besides this more of him, that he never forgets you in his prayers, he it was who loved you as soon as he knew good from evil; by this time you cannot but think on me, & no other, who is yours & only yours.

7.   My dearest life   Dec. 13, 1651.

    These two days together have I with as great
confidence looked to see you as to give this into your hands when I am next
to be made so happy, and upon that score had made my self very fine; my
mind was all ye while so taken up with what I missed, as I can give but a
very imperfect account of that I saw. Nor needs it that I say anything of
that, since others will more at large inform you than this peice of paper
can. But on better consideration I conclude you restrained at this time
rather by devotion than discretion, tho that too were very likely to work ye
same effects. Our company, to speak with freedom, have been most ridi-
culously mad, & such as you must have been ashamed of had you been a
witness to them, such have been ye follys we are joyfully guilty of. There
was somebody besides my self who I believe was no better pleased than I
was; and yet I say wou'd you had been amongst us; which at ye worst
signifys but ye passion I have to your company. Wonder not one that
has done so extravagantly should speake so wildly. Farewell my dearest
Heart.

8.   My dearest life   Jan. 12, 1651.

    Till we part never to meet again, all I can suffer
will come short, sure, of ye trouble of our last parting. But I must not enlarge my self on this theame, ye only way to add to ye fullness of ye
measure of my own griefe, by making you a sharer in my sorrows. Peace
be to your soul, the God of all mercies bless you with a prosperous life in
this world, & ye joys of Heaven hereafter. His holy angels pitch their tents
round about you. Amen.

9.   My dearest life   Jan. 28, 1651.

    I know not whether I shall have an opportunity
of making my excuse in another place; therefore give me leave to do it here.

I was resolved to have come to Bury yesterday, had ye pleasure of thinking to see you all ye morning ; but just before dinner Sir Thomas Barker came in. He was wellcomer I hope to ye rest of ye family then to me. By this time I know I have said enough of this. And now, my dear heart, to that which must be thought on, when and where, for meet we must sometimes ; else why do I live ? Write now & then if you woud save a soul. You cannot imagine how impatient I am grown; you cannot nor will I take pains to let you know; you are good & would be troubled at it, & God knows, woud that relieve me, I had yet rather be devoured of my greifs then be eased at that rate. If your kindness interesses you in my evil fortune, I am as unhappy that way too as may be.

10.   My dearest life   Jan. 30. 1651.

I heard by some of our family who came from Bury that you were yesterday a visiting. I thank you, my dear, that you will seek out any divertion. To endeavour the pleasing of your self is the greatest kindness you can shew to him who is for ever yours.

11.   My dearest life   Feb. 7, 1651.

I have now taken order not to be surprisd as I was writing my last ; and I may speake with a confidence great as you ought to have in what I say ; which is that I love you more than I can tell, doing less than you deserve. But, my dearest heart, you cannot be so unjust either to your self or me as not to look on this rather to your own glory then my shame. Think on me and pray for me ; as I spend my own time I woud that you do yours; tho you may excell me in fervency of devotion, you shall not yet in constancy of affection ; for till death I am unalterably yours.

12.   My dearest life   Feb. 10, 1651.

It never till this minute enterd into my heart to deceive you in ye least; but now (let not ye confession injure me) I acknowlege my self about to dissemble to you my griefe, coud I by any art have conceald it. Truly my impatience grows strong upon me, & I have the quicker sense of my trouble, because you cannot be unconcerned. Would you know how the time passes with me? At night I lye down to heavyness & in ye morning rise again to sorrow. But God, I trust, in his good time will turn all this into joy. My leisure woud give me leave to say more, but my spirits are so depressed I can only bid you farewell.

13.   My dearest life   Feb. 20, 1651.

          The company did yesterday use such violent solicitations as without great suspicion I coud not have stayd behind; & I am not yet so perfectly recoverd of my fears but that I am jealous of everything said or done, least there may be some design to make some discovery. But by too long a practice in this unhappy art, I have learnd to secure my self against ye subtleties of ye most crafty inquisitor. To this add and reflect upon ye continuall care & watchfullness of Heaven over ye innocent, and I need say no more to remove from you all apprehensions of danger.

          If you can possibly get out on Saturday about 4 or 5 of clock, let it be to your sisters.

14.   My dearest life   Feb. 25, 1651.

          I can never sufficiently thank you for your last kindness; by ye favour of that I am restored to such peace of mind as makes me already think I may live to be merry again. You may this way use all ye freedom in the world with great safety, since I commit every dear paper (after innumerable kisses & reluctancys) but to my memory, not daring any where else to trust such a huge treasure in so malicious an age. Be assured no torture shall wrest from me what you entrust me with as a secret.   Saturday in ye afternoon about 3 or 4, if you can conveniently be at your sisters, I shall meet you if I be alive.

15.   My dearest life   Feb. 28, 1651.

Here has been a grave consultation held, whether my Lady Duncombe or no should amongst ye rest be invited. After a long debate it remains yet doubtfull, but I hope it will be carried for her coming (which is much labourd), and that you will not be so long resolving to bear her company. It woud be time vainly spent to tell you with how great impatience I bear your absence, & then necessarily to as little purpose to persuade you not to decline a handsome opportunity of giving me that pleasure & satisfaction of seeing you; therefore I shall not enlarge myself on that subject.

16.   My dearest life   March 2, 1651.

You seemd to me so much troubled as I suspected my self either in words or actions to have contributed towards it; such mellancholly impressions did that unusuall sight make in me. But after a strict scrutiny I am in some measure easd, yet cannot be perfectly satisfyd, since possibly to compleat my misery you may have misinterpreted somewhat said or done by me, tho I am so little conscious as I can not but hope too that I have misunderstood you, which woud be an offence you cannot in justice reproach me with, since you your self made me commit it. Wonder not, my dearest Heart, that I have changed my opinion; to do that is incident to ye distracted, & such I am now in ye highest degree, as you may well judge by ye perplexities of this paper. Be chearfull, at least dissemble better your grief, if you love me.

17.   My dearest life   March 3, 1651.

All ye signs of mirth & jollity in ye world have been amongst us. Why you made not one, I shall desire to know. If you stayd for any other reason then because it was writing day with you, I am ye more curious, because I thought you woud have been at Hengrave, having so earnestly by all hands been invited, had not somewhat very extra-ordinary fallen out. Tis most unspeakable ye vexation I endure from such accidents as these, & I suffer so much, perticularly from ye present, as I can scarce put my words together to make sense of what I woud say; & that which adds to my trouble is ye impossibility of preventing ye like incon-veniencies for ye future. But in ye greatest pressures I have ye assurance of your affection, a joy which triumphs over all misery.

18. My dearest life   March 4, 1651.

I long most extreamely to have what your last promisd to informe me of. If you have not written this morning, or cannot find a time to give me your paper, let me desire you it may be ready against night, and tell me (for it was done in such hast as I am allmost afraid) whether you took not my paper yester-night in your mothers chamber; but if I be not much deceived, I saw you when you came down take it out of your pocket, & put it where your master languishes to be. I cannot say positively that I shall meet you at your sisters to day, having passd my word to your brother, nor that I shall returne by way of your house, being at his dispose. My dear, ye God of peace be with you.

19. My dearest life   March 6, 1651.

Since I can make no better return to your kind-ness than words, give me leave to thank you for your last very full demon-stration of it. Continue to love me, & I shall not complain of my fortune; for all other wants will most abundantly be recompenced in that satisfying fruition. God make me worthy of it. But how think you, my dear, I shall be able to live this week, being to morrow to go to Ickworth to lye there for so long, when I cannot promise my self in all that time ye felicity of seeing you; & yet I am taken in for one to make a merry journey. I like well this ignorance, & shall cherish it wherere I find it. By this it is plain ye witt you are so offended at is (as I ever told you) but harmless mirth, & as such you will hereafter pardon it, being so clearly convinced of its innocence. I

Vol. I.   B

most extremely thirst after your intelligence, not only in matters nearly
concerning us, (for these I know tis needless for me to desire you not to
omit,) but even in lesser things, such as may serve for diversion when I am
by my self alone, which is now very much, having no kind of ghuest (taste)
or ever can have in any conversation till God shall see it fit to restore me to
ye enjoyment of yours, to whose protection I commend you, you joy of my
life, delight of my soule.

20.   My dearest life   March 16, 1651.

Sure there is something more than ordinary in
this Newmarket journey, it runs so in my head. I shall not be so merry at
home as ye company will be goes thither. If it may be for your good, God
prosper them, as I doubt not but he will. The success shall convince me of
my unworthyness, if it be such as my fears suggest ; & leave no compassion
in you towards me, but what is common to all men, miserable & afflicted.
At their return tell me for Gods sake tell me all.

21.   My dearest life   March 20, 1651.

I have much to say & ask; for neither of these
will this poor paper suffice. Pray God, when I shall come to speak with
you, I be able to express my self; trust me I am not without some fear for
that, were a convenience now offerd of doing it. In such confusion was never
poor creature, and for you all this.

22.   My dearest life   March 24, 1651.

The greatest business I had at Bury ye last time
I saw you was to satisfy my self whether at my going out of your chamber
door on Saturday night you offered not to put a paper into my hands. This
ran so in my head that I slep'd not that nor ye next night for fear it might
be dropped & somebody find it. I woud have given my right hand to have
spoken but one word to you. To prevent ye like danger for ye future I am

content to want that pleasure. I expect not that you write any more, but let this be ye rule hereafter, & be sure, my dearest heart, you mistake it not. I will ask you whether ten, twenty or thirty : if ten then it shall be a sign things go very well ; if twenty indifferently ; if thirty (which God forbid) that they are at ye worst. Now if you require of me ye continuance of this way of entertainment on my parte, let me know your pleasure, & I am ready in this, as in all other your commands, to obey you. I shall find time I hope before I die (& should then leave ye world in peace) to let you know how much I love you. But actions will speak this plainer than words. It must therefore be ye business of my life, not of this paper. Blessings, such as my wishes for you in their greatest extasys can not reach, fall on you, my dear dear love. Yours unalterably, & for ever so is.

23. My dearest life   March 13, 1652.

My letters from London give me this day some business, so as I am not certain whether I shall see you ; or at best be forced (if I do) to part with you sooner or come later then I woud. No man, sure, was made for bussiness more than my self, if I can make any reasonable despatch but in matters which must some way concern you (as this present affair in no wise does), since I think that thought but ill imployd that is not particularly directed to your service. That you trouble not your self to think what ye matter may be, be pleasd to know tis only to take order for the releasing a friend of my brothers who is in prison for debt. You may give a guess at ye man, & therefore let me beseech you not to say a sillable of it, for it will be thought you had ye story from me, which is to be a secret, and so let me once again begg of you it may be. The discoverie of any such little intelligence between us is (may prove) a step to ye great revelation.

24. My dearest life   March 27, 1652.

I was in Town on Thursday, but had not ye least hopes of seeing you, you having told me ye night before you shoud be all

that day busy in removing. I had, I will assure you, otherways disposd of
my self, had I thought you would have been abroade. My letters this week
from London will I believe make us lay aside our so much talkd of journey
to ye Bath. For my brother tells me the small pox have not been so much
in London these twenty years as they are at present. God preserve my
dearest heart from all infection.

25.   My dearest life   April 20, 1652.

When I shall next be with you alone (for to ye
happiness of that hour I reserve my stock of mirth) look for a very pleasant
story which is too long for this paper, & least I may forget to tell it be sure
you call for it. I know, my dearest, you wish to see me on a better score,
(by my own I measure your desires,) & woud to God I had my liberty in
this, what restraint soever were put upon me as to all other things. This
my soul longs for; in this her peace would be established. Let me know
sometime where I may meet you abroad, & I'l fail not in that no more then
in being yours unchangeably.

26.   My dearest life   April 24, 1652.

I was much rejoyced at my last unexpected good
fortune of meeting with you, taking that as an happy presage of better, at
least an earnest of more of that kind. But as some alloy to this I was not
a little troubled that I could not prudently resist the importunities of my
brother Gage, who urged me with that earnestness to go with him as if he
had been set on worke to try me whether or no any sollicitation coud force
me to leave my dear. God knows he had in vain tempted me with any
allurements of pleasure, if I might have been allowed to follow my own
inclinations; but I am too much yours to intend my own delights to your
prejudice. I woud not, I protest, not so much as think on this, though it be
my only sollace in your much lamented absence, had you not so freely

declared your self pleased with this way of entertaining you. My dearest
heart, by all that's good I love you with a most intire affection, & may you
for ever hate me when I do less then at this minute, in which I solemnly
profess I would chearfully lay down my life for your good. Peace be ever
to you, my dear dear; as to my soul I wish it you. I cannot otherwise
contribute towards it then by my prayers; & those (by ye faith I have so
often vowd to you) shall not be wanting.

27.   My dearest life   April 30, 1652,

              The danger of carrying about me such a paper as
this being great, as is my uncertainty of seeing you, I must here tell you
that, unless you enjoyne me to do it, I shall not hereafter but upon very great
occasions write any more. Thus much let .me add : I have 'been hugely
pleased with ye quiet of this place since ye company left it ; & now I dread
nothing more than their return. Much of this time has been rightly
employed in praying for you, or thinking of you, which I never do but with
extasys of joy. May you, my dearest joy, be happy as you have made me.
Less I woud not have you, & more I cannot wish you.

28.   My dearest life   May 7, 1652.

              Having of late been so often deceived in my hopes
of a free & unmolested communication with you, I resolved again upon this
way of holding intelligence when all other means of address are denyd me.
I shall not trouble you with every petty misfortune. The complaints I shall
make I wish for your sake, no less then my own, were not so well worthy
your consideration. God knows ye small delight I have in any thing I hear
or see ; my thoughts are only pleasant to me, and those so ordinarily
interrupted by ungratefull company as I allmost hate ye society of men.
What pitty tis I dare not say, I love you. How full of peace woud my life
be might I avow it. Here I may do it most securely. Think then, my

dearest, how much you excell all other women, and by that do you judge of my passion, who am yours (my sweetest dear) intirely yours, dearest heart, eternally.

29.   My dearest life   May 15, 1652.

        I never thought time so mispent as ye other day we went not out of Town till past twelve at night, yet coud I not at this time make a handsome escape, being from ye hour I parted with you employd by my Lady Penn : till it was too late for me to return to you. This, my dearest, was such mortification on my fasting night as I assure you a more rigorous pennance coud not have been injoyned me. Had you come home with us, I believe we had been very merry, which for my part without you I can never be ; this a long and woefull experience has too well manifested. I swear, my heart, I am so tender of your quiet, as did I think your sufferance equalld mine, it woud make me allmost wish a diminution of your love, that so your trouble might be lessened too. When I next see you in private, I have that to tell you will be no unpleasant entertainment. Till then farewell, my dear dear. Yours for ever.

30.   My dearest life   May 22, 1652.

        I have been these two days engaged in a match at bowles. Your brothers being concerned made me imagine you might have been in the green. But now I begin to think you might be disuaded by our subtle adversarys, that I might not have ye advantage of so good an humour as a sight only of you woud have put me into. It was not ill thought on, for ye hope of this made me victor ye first day ; nor coud they gain anything uppon us ye second till it was so late in ye evening as I dispaird & coud not attend to those little successes, having faild of my greater expectation. On Tuesday next soon after dinner, if you please so to order it as to be ready, my sister Kez & I have agreed to waite on you to Rushbrooke. I tell you of this here to make sure, for I woud not but have this journey go forward for anything. Tis impossible you should live in health & never stirr out of that strait hot house. Let me beseech you go abroad sometime & divert your self. God Almighty be with you wherever you are, & keep you from all evil and mischeif.

31. My dearest life   May 30, 1652.

   I confess I was yesterday in no excellent humour, & be you judge whether there were any reason I shoud when I saw my fears so perfectly fullfilld. Soberly, my dearest, I am allmost a weary of this discreet part, tho I consider for whose sake it is I endure all this, which woud else be intolerable. I coud sustain more yet, nay perhaps submit to the seeing of you but seldom, did that appear absolutely necessary to ye advancement of any of your purposes: but so long as I continue thus divided betwixt what is fit (as my mellancholly often urgeth that to be) & what is to me most delightfull & as my better temper tells me to you not unsecure, pitty my condition. Never, oh never, my dear heart, can I be fully at peace till ye happy hour in which without injury to you I may lay by my disguise; & even this I woud not wish if you may any other way be happier. So much I love you above my self, who am yet ye dearer to my self for being so intirely yours.

32. My dearest life   June 4, 1652.

   I wrote not yesterday because my intentions were to have spent ye whole day with you. How I was diverted give me leave to tell you. My Lady Pen: sent all over ye Town in search of me being in great want of a bowler. At last I most unluckily fell into ye danger where I sought for refuge; at your sister Duncombs I met with her, where she asked me her self to go into ye green, & told me we shoud leave off time enough for me to go to my Lady Pooleys. Indeed I think I had better have

refused her in order to my design ; for though I stayd, every word and action
might easily betray ye constraint I did it with.   If this be wisdom to be
thus continually tormenting one self, I envy ye fool his folly, and ye mad-
man his humour. Tomorrow my sister Hanmer sets againe.   I dare not say
I will be there ; but I wish that she woud, for I think not to stirr from thence
all ye afternoon, nor from ye faith & affection I have vowed to you all ye
days of my life.

33.   My dearest life   June 6, 1652.

       It is some comfort to me in my trouble that I have
not been wanting to my uttermost endeavour of seeing you ; and I may say
you woud take pleasure in my pain did you know with what griefe I
sustain every disappointment. God's will be done, my dearest. I am happy
that you love me in spight of all that fortune can do to me besides. Tomorrow
I shall be at Bury about a little bussiness, and this shall excuse me from any
other.   If my design of spending a good parte of ye day shoud miscarry,
I hope yet it shall not through your fault, but that you will hasten ye
dispatch of your letters. To morrow my sister Hanmer sets again.

34.   My dearest life   June 11, 1652.

       Indeed I had not courage enough to bring me to
Bury since your brother James his coming was talked of; for with him
another coach they told me came along ; my heart failed me, thinking
verily ye youth was then come to make an end of all his woeing.   Had I
known certainly he had come to Town on horseback, it would not have troubled
me near so much as that terrible apprehension of his equipage.   From
hence I concluded he comes not without his father's consent. And now I may
truly say it is good for me that I have been in trouble ; for in that I am
undeceived I account my care and anxiety abundantly recompenced.   Who
is there breathing woud not for such dear treasure be hugely thoughtfull !

In any other loss my reason might be of some use to me, which in this woud serve but to torment me. When I have desired you, if you can conveniently, about 4 or 5 of ye clock be to morrow at your sisters lodging, I have only to bid my dear heart farewell.

35. My dearest life June 28, 1652.

I had layd my plott on Fryday to come to Bury had ye company, as it was resolved ye night before, (gone) to Mr. Calthrope. But they all staying here (nor woud that alone have done it) and having given out that you were gone to Horringer, spoiled my design. Though I say it, I think I was then ye merriest companion with so sad a heart that ever was seen. So dextrous am I grown through long use that I can be drunk & not reveal ye great secret. I am then indeed most transported when ye vulgar believe me soberest. I dare not trust to my reason in point of happyness, & less to my passion. To you then, my dearest, give I my self up to be ruld, governed, orderd, guided and directed; & if I knew a word more expressive of submission or perfect conformity to your judgment, that, my dearest, as ye aptest to my purpose had been made use of by your most unalterably intire.

36. My dearest life July 6, 1652.

How do you? For I have of late been so unhappy as not to be with you time enough out of a throng to ask ye question & receive a deliberate answer. This inquiry looks as well to your humour as health. Woud to God, my dear, but one hour in ye four & twenty were allowd us freely to converse. But since this is denied us, God in his mercy hear me when I beg for patience.

37. My dearest life July 28, 1652.

I have spent ye time so very ill since I saw you that I am ashamed almost to confess. We were till presently after dinner yesterday to so near supper time at ye Squires as, had he not been a Justice of peace too, he woud have had ye manners to have invited us. To morrow, my dear heart, we shall have a great deal (you know of what kind) of company. How wearysome will all this be to me, judge you, when besides the trouble of entertaining those I so little care for, I cannot have so much pleasure as to hope to see you all ye day. The tempest was not so terrible to you as will ye noise of this assembly be to yours for ever.

38.   My dearest life   Aug. 30, 1652,

I will now no longer defer ye account you expect of my health, having passed this last night without any ye least distemper; which since I was first ill I coud not say before; for every each night at a constant hour nere eleven a clock I was taken with a chillness; out of this I fell into a sweat which held me five or six hours. On my ill nights I slep'd very little. Thanks be to God this fell to my lott, when for ye punishment of my sins he might have suffered it to have been your portion, the chastisement in ye world I shoud have ye quickest sense of. How, my dearest, is it possible for us to contrive a meeting but for half an hour? You cannot imagine how I long to see you. I live not but then, till when, my heart, farewell.

39.   My dearest life   Sept. 14, 1652.

Tis not to be expected that I shoud this day have other convenience then here I have of telling you I love you above, & that so far above, all other things of this world, as ye whole Creation besides without you could be nothing to me. But in you I am so perfectly happy as I have only to wish you equall contentment. This is ye centre of all my desires; and if to ye injoyment of such tranquility my prayers may contribute, you shoud this instant enter into an earthly paradice, and so continue whilst translated to an heavenly one, whither God of his most infinite

mercy bring us both. Amen.   If you go to Boxstead be merry and
be sure love him.

40.   My dearest life   Sept. 20, 1652.

I so little thought of this senseless journey as
when they were taking coach I was ready to come to Bury, & was met with
by my sister Gage, who, after I had twenty times already denied her, assaults
me afresh & with incessant importunitys prevails.   I have paid dear enough
for my folly already, though you be not offended at me.   Had I been allowed
but so much time as to have let you known of it, I had eat better, slep'd
more, & have laughd sometimes.   I wish you, my dearest, merryer tomorrow.   As you love me, let it be your study to please yourself.   It shall
not be my fault if I see you not before your return ; but to come alone would
sett ye small witts to work.   My brother Gage I hope will remove that im-
pediment which is ye only one betwixt me & much contentment, more then
you with all your goodness can believe, though told you by ye person you
woud give most credit to.   The God of peace be with my dear heart, my
sweet life.

41.   My dearest life   Sept. 25, 1652.

It has run most strangely in my head that this
Bansfield journey had other ends then appeard either to you or me.   Who
you met with there, if your kindness or discretion shall conceal from me, I
am not to make farther inquiry ;   & if there be any such thing as foreknow-
ledge in matters of this nature to persons interested, it needeth not.   But
heaven has given you vertue proportion'd to ye temptations it hath assignd
you ; there is my comfort, & I may say, who but my self was ever blessed
with such a treasure as in your love that had not a thousand feares of being
dispossessd !

42.   My dearest life   Sept. 27, 1652.

But in great extremity I woud not put you to any trouble. You know while there was any tollerable freedom of any other means of converse, I never urged this. Now in your closer imprisonment I most humbly beg of you that by such faithfull messengers as these your condition may sometime be reported, to which I am otherwise like to be a most unhappy stranger. God keep you in health, & me in my right witts, for I was about to say I must & will see you. First let me advise with you, & then I dare, (if it be your pleasure) I fear nothing, or what is more, for your sake can be afraid of anything.

43.   My dearest life   Sept. 30, 1652.

You know what I did yesterday ; but how I spent ye day before you must not, for my greifs & fears excepted I communicate all other things ; but here I challenge a sole propriety, & you sin if you covet ye least of them from me, they being my birth right. Without them I coud not have had you, who are to my mind as is health to ye body.

44.   My dearest life   Oct. 2, 1652.

I was most extreamly troubled that I coud not take my leave of you last night ; and though I have been trained up to these kind of contradictions, yet I do still suffer as much by ye last as ye first disappointment gave me of vexation. So unchangeable has been ye affection I have had for you ; which having continued thus long without ye least alteration, I see not why it may not reasonably be thought to remaine perfectly the same to our lives end. I protest to God you never were, nor ever can be, dearer to me than you are at this minute. You are ye life and joy of my youth, and I trust you are reserved to be ye comfort of my age, and a means to bring me to eternall happiness. * On Tuesday,

---

* Here Sir Thomas has written in pencil, This prophecy I liv'd to see throughly fulfilled.

if you can come abroad, I shoud be very glad to meet you at your sisters about 4 in ye afternoon.

45. My dearest life   Oct. 7, 1652.

I made an appointment with your brother Bap to have gone a setting; but having other business I wrote to him to excuse me. This I hope came to your knowledge, for so it was I cheifly intended. With whosoever I break my word, to you I shall to a tittle make good all promises, or when I fail in ye least circumstance only, it shall so evidently appear not to be my fault, as, were all your love jealousy, you shoud not entertain a distrustfull thought. You may have occasion to pitty me as unfortunate, but never to despise me as unfaithfull. When I give you any reason to think that, think no more on me, a curse, malice it self can not invent another like it. On Saturday I am to fetch Jud from Rushbrook in our way home. I know she will visit at your house. I hope you will not be abroad: write for God sake any thing; above all be sure, my dear soul, be sure you love your most intirely.

46. My dearest life   Oct. 15, 1652.

When I have tryed all ye pleasures of this world, ye rest are empty in respect of your conversation. That is indeed a jewell of price; and if I can compass it, though but toward ye latter end of my life, I shall think ye time past most happily employd. This it is which to think on only ravisheth me beyond a possibility of being troubled for present mischances. How many thousand times a day do I meditate upon my dearest, & bless God my lott is fallen in so fair a land. The Lord of heaven & earth have you always in his holy protection, my dear dear heart.   I came to Town yesterday, was as far as Dr. Buckenham's onward the way to you, where I met with my Lady Duncombe who told me you were not at home. This was about 4 in ye afternoon, which made me choose a new day to see you in that I might have ye more time, for alas ! how little is it we two are like to be together in : & ye rest of my life how nothing is it to me; you are all in all.

47.   My dearest life   Oct. 16, 1652.

Besides ye continuance of your kindness I have nothing more to ask of you then that you woud be merry, the greatest expression of that you can possibly make me. Be assured, my dear heart, I had rather see ye face of death then any discontent in yours : this is literally true, as that I am my dears & only hers.   I have changed my chamber for that next Jude where my sister Hanmer lay, & take no—none indeed.

48.   My dearest life   Oct. 20, 1652.

I have stollen from our jolly company to see you for an hour or two ; and, but that your interest persuade me, woud not take so short a time, unless my life it self were of no longer continuance ; & that woud seem tedious too, were it not for ye hope of that reward to my travail which my soul longeth after.

49.   My dearest life   Oct. 23, 1652.

Tho' it be long since you have made one in such an assembly as have of late been at Hengrave, yet you cannot have forgot that eating, drinking & dancing is all that is there done. The only extraordinary accident in this late one was such as I am loath to tell you ; & yet you cannot in justice reproach me ye folly of being drunk, since you were ye occasion of it by your not coming ; & here I coud explain, but that were to grieve my dearest, and when I avoide not that with all possible industry, may ye trouble, sorrow and vexation of my present sad condition never have end. I love you with all my soul, and expect a better fortune upon ye score of being, my dear heart, yours.

50. My dearest life   Oct. 27, 1652.

Since I cannot with freedom have your company,
I am resolved to be as little interrupted in thoughts of you as may be; & in
order to this spend much of my time by myself, & find it so pleasant as I
begin to grudge almost my best friends an hour or two in ye whole day; &
truly they shoud excuse me for this too, but that you know who tis
commands me to do otherwise. I that obey you here coud lay scepters &
crowns at your feet, which I want not but for this use. If you have humbler
wishes, you are then richer then these coud make you, being mistress of a
heart perfectly despising them. There is no treasure like your love to
yours intirely.

51. My dearest life   Nov. 3, 1652.

To morrow we must part for a little while, and
when in this case I can say so, you may be confident a fortnight or three
weeks will be ye longest I shall be from my dearest. If you be not merry
in my absence, (which I begg you woud be,) you not only take away ye
pleasure of my journey, but of my life too: for you cannot love me and deny
me this. I think enough has been said to persuade you to seek out
divertisment. Remember me in your prayers, & you may be as confident
of my safety as you have reason to be assured of the intireness of my affection.

52. My dearest life   Nov. 5, 1652.

I kept my visit till this day that I might rejoyce
my self with you at ye return of it. God almighty prolong your days upon
earth, that he woud with them give unto you health & prosperity, and my
heart is at rest in this world, where my greatest business is to contrive your
happyness, or rather, when I have experimented ye vanity of that, to pray
for it. If I were with you, my dear heart, I woud tell you how continually
I think upon my dearest; I never loose a thought of any other object; in

body and in minde both I am intirely yours.   If Tuesday be a fair
day, about 4 I hope to see you at your sisters.

53.   My dearest life   Dec. 5, 1652.

Never did man return from banishment with a
heart so filled with joy as I am come to you. Why you have not my picture,
I am so well furnished with excuse as I will not (when my sisters are by
while I write) trouble my self to give you in this place an account.   Your
kindness to me I am confident of, which will direct to this good opinion of
me that I can never be other then, my dearest heart, most intirely.   Brave
London storys I have to tell you.   God send me opportunity.

54.   My dearest life   Dec. 14, 1652.

My father has commanded me to wait on him to
Ickworth, whether he goes this day ; & to morrow I think to follow him
that this time of pennance may ye sooner be over.   I account such because I
shall not have it in my power to see you while we stay there.   This will
spoil my being company to him, ye end for which he carrys me.   I shoud be
ashamd of being less fond of so sweet a creature.   Your worth & excellency
makes that in me vertue which in another would be weakness.   I love my
dearest, by her self I swear I love her passionately, & with such undivided
affection as I am hers alone.

55.   My dearest life   Dec. 22, 1652.

I have sufferd too much by ye unhappyness of
my being thus long kept from you, although this be not added to my
misfortune, to have you think that any power less than a fathers could have
prevaild with me.   Indeed, my dearest, since I saw you he has (excepting
one day which was spent in setting for my picture) employd me ten hours in
ye four and twenty.   On Saturday, when I thought you might have lookd for
me, I sent to let you know I coud not come, for so I hope my sending was

understood. To have said so in express terms had been death ; & not to have done that which to you might signify ye same thing had been ye worst of tortures (measuring your impatience by my own) to, my dearest, your most constant.

56. My dearest life   Dec. 30, 1652.

I will not here complain of my misfortune in missing you. I shall never willingly interess you in my ills : when any good arrives to me, I shall in that hastily concern you. But I know you are in this perticular so abundantly satisfyd, as to enlarge myself were time thrown away. Therefore to new matter. This day I visit Mr. Jermyn. If I return not by Bury, yet I wish me with you : for, trust me, I am in pain when I am not. I hope to see you at night when I come back ; if I do not, be confident tis not Leanders fault but fate. Farewell, my dear dear heart, farewell.

57. My dearest life   Jan. 3, 1652.

It fell out ye other day (& as all my life indeed almost has done) as I feard. In time, I hope, my fortune may so change as what I wish may come to pass. But I cannot but accuse my self of great unreasonableness that I have thoughts beyond ye happyness my present condition gives me of being yours.

58. My dearest life   Jan. 18, 1652.

I had yesterday come to town had I not been hindred by no small indisposition of body & mind both, which, thanks be to God, is now well passed over, and I am again as well as ever in all my life I was. When I rose in ye morning, my head was as light for want of sleep as is common after great fitts of sickness ; in earnest to that degree it was giddy as I was glad to throw my self upon ye bed, not being able to keep my leggs. You know from whence all this proceeds, the spleen, which

Vol. I.   D

those that have but little talk much of as a fine thing ; while those that are
indeed troubled with it can scarce breathe out so many words as to signify
they have it.   But this naturall infirmity can never prevail so far against my
understanding as not to leave me reason enough to let me see I am ye
happiest of men in being my dearest hearts her own most intirely.

59.   My dearest life   Feb. 9, 1652.

I know you have heard ye report of our dancing
with all the aggravations a little witt and much malice coud set it forth.
Whatever my folly was, I am sure my chastisement has equalld it ; for I
left you when I might have been half an hour longer with you.   I have
these two whole days since been in persuite of you, and could never see you.
I was at least seaven times at Mr. Sharps yesterday, confident to ye last
minute you woud come ; yet I question not ye reason of your failing, nor
complain not but of my ill fortune.   On Tuesday next I hope to see you here,
though I have not so good assurance for this as ye other ; for I believe you
think not anything more decent then keeping your word, especially to ye
person in ye world who woud for no consideration receed in ye least from
ye promise he has made to you for ever to be, my dear dear life, your
intirely.

60.   My dearest life   Feb. 16, 1652.

If I did consider as much of what I speak as of
that you say to me, I might pass for very wise.   But in this I glory more,
preferring infinitely ye rendring my self worthy your kindness above ye
esteem of all ye world besides ; which truly to me in respect of this is lighter
than vanity it self ; & when I have said all I can, my heart will be yet full,
so inexpressibly am I, my dearest dear life, yours.

61.   My dearest life   Feb. 25, 1652.

That which has kept me from you these three or
four very tedious days will again part us this night sooner then usually, or

then willingly (I am sure) I woud leave you. My father has been so strangely ill as I coud not but in duty and good nature be near him. To morrow will be his sick day & Monday; so that till Tuesday I cannot hope to see you again, my dearest. Till then farewell, my joy, my life, farewell.

62. My dearest life   March 5, 1652.

I shall not fail as often as conveniently may be done to give both an account of my actions and notice of my purposes, which here I thus begin. Yesterday I dined at Saxham; how to morrow will be spent you may imagine. On Munday I am by appointment to meet some company, but Tuesday I long for to put down into my Almanack. I can now no longer refrain from boasting, & say that, if I had not managed ye matter well, my Lady Bacon had carried it against my Lady Pooley, & ye day too had been changed; then how shoud ye 3d of March have been celebrated. Thanks be to God for ye greater & lesser blessings of that most fortunate day, which, while I have a day to live, shall with much zeal be performed by my dearest her own most intirely.

63. My dearest life   March 7, 1652.

I shoud this day have been amongst ye merry youths, but my father is pleased otherwise to employ me. I am turned solicitor, & if our case miscarry not, of which there is but little hope unless that falls out in law cases which commonly is seen amongst men, that ye best have ye worst fortune, I am afraid I am in at this trade for my time, at least my fathers, for he growing infirme will be unfit for business, & so ye trouble fall wholly upon me. I shall be almost every day this week in Town, & yet God knows whether I shall see you; thus will it be too often with me by reason of my affairs. But why do I call them mine? I renounce all business, when I may chuse my self, but that which brings me to your conversation.

64.   My dearest life   March 15, 1652.

On Saturday last presently after dinner I receivd a letter from my father commanding me that afternoon to come to Ickworth about some business of his; and this I told to so many as I hoped it might come to your knowledge. This day I shoud have dind at Saxham with my brother, but I have not ye patience to be longer from you, tho' I have of late been often told of my friends who are so kind to pity my condition that I must give place to Mr. North; that you are to marry him all agree; yet am I still as confident without great reason you will not consent to ye making me so miserably unhappy as I am that such can never be given you by your most obedient.

65.   My dearest life   April 4, 1653.

I have not for this day set my heart on more then is likely to come to my share; to give this to you is all I hope, whose business it is to beg a meeting to morrow about 4 in ye afternoon at your sister Duncombes. Somethings I have to tell you and some I woud advise with you in; of both more then this paper is capable. I was at Bury on Saturday (not knowing ye least of your Millnall Journey), and stayd in Town till nere eight at night to see you; but all ye satisfaction I received was to think I had done my duty. I was on horseback to have come on Thursday, when I heard ye Rushbrook company was with you; & then I coud not expect an opportunity of half an hours private discourse. God almighty keep you, my dearest, to all eternity.

66.   My dearest life   April 25, 1653.

I have since ye last which I gave into your hands written two or three other papers, but still wanted courage to present them, because they too boldly spoke my desires. This shall only beseech you to consider so throughly of ye matter, as what you shall do may be ye least to your own trouble without any respect to my suffering; and with that my wishes are compleated. Yet think not that I had not rather a thousand times die, nay almost (forgive me, my dearest heart, if I say) hope you may, then so part with you.

67. My dearest life   May 1, 1653.

       I put you in mind of my journey into Wales thus long before, that you may have time to deliberate whether you can for a month or 6 weeks give me your free consent; without that I resolve not to stirr; and I most earnestly begg of you not to believe that in staying of me you debarr me of any so great pleasure as I shall find in conforming to your will. We heard from our Welch friends this weeke. My sister Hanmer in this as in all her letters she does commend her to you in particular. I love her more for being kind to you than that she is my sister. Shoud you buz me ten times a day, I must yet love you at this rate; and if he lives that loves you better, I will lay down all pretensions to your favour, and never after call my self yours.

68. My dearest life   May 13, 1653.

       I doubt not but that I have allready satisfyd you as to ye ordering of your self in extraordinary occasions, if any such (which God defend) shoud in my absence fall out. All I have to do here is to take my leave of you not to leave me out of your prayers; for from them rather than my own I expect happyness in this & blessedness in ye world to come. Farewell, my heart, my joy, my life, farewell.

69. My dearest life   July 12, 1653.

       You are so taken up with your present employments as I very very difficultly get access to you. Wherefore let this speak, & I trust it may without danger to my dearest, & tell you I love you so passionately that to suspect your kindness to me, or but to imagine you distrustfull in ye least of mine, woud prove equally destructive of my quiet; & all ye other benefits of this life without this great addition coud not secure one moments contentment to me; believe me, dearest heart, they coud not. I bless God I am as perfectly satisfyd in this point hitherto as my heart can wish, and by all those happy houres we two have spent together, I am as intirely your own, my dear dear Soule.

70.   My dearest life   July 18, 1653.

            This is ye 3d (God send it better luck than ye two former) that I coud not find a fit time to give into your hands.   These m s-chances might in comon affections produce dangerous effects; but our, I hope, are of another nature, over which time or fortune shall never triumph. Not all ye malice in ye world coud make me waver in my opinion of your kindness to me, having for ye foundations of it ye word & honour of (without all question) ye worthyest person this day alive.   It woud be too long a story for this place to let you know what pains I took on Saturday to get a sight of you, & how surprised I was at your unexpected parting.   I had so much reason only left me as to perceive I spoke not one word of sense all the night after.   Sure we are too scrupulous, my dear, and we may as soon this way betray our selves.   Yet I know not what to advise.   God almighty direct you, that you may do what will be least displeasing to your self; then you need not take any thought for me, who know not how to wish till I be first assured what are your desires; so much am I, my dearest heart, yours.

71.   My dearest life   Aug. 10, 1653.

            I have been ye stronglyest terrified with reports from several people of your being sad, as when you know this, my excuse is made I have not of late come into company.   I am not yet so melancholly as to think I have in ought contributed towards it.   But God knows how that humour may encrease with these rumours.   You can not, my dearest harte, forget what I have so often urged upon you.   A thousand times have

I conjured you not to conceal from me your discontents. This lookes like unkindness; and death with torments woud not than that be more dreadfull to yours for ever most intirely.

72.   My dearest life   Aug, 22, 1653.

   I had great temptations to have come to Bansfield; but I am not so given up to my pleasures as to make you blush for them, as I am sure you woud have done to have seen me there. I dreamed two nights together (see how melancholy I was in your absence) that your mother had opened ye little trunck uppon your table, & discovered all. The second time I coud not be satisfyd till I went into your chamber & saw all things there in good order, but my self very much discomposed (tho' first secured of ye danger I so much apprehended) that I had not all I coud wish for, which was ye happyness of your company, beyond all other earthly blessings incomparably deare to me, believe your faithfullest.

73.   My dearest life   Aug. 31, 1653.

   You have so lately plowed with my heifer, as I can tell you nothing new but what concernes my self. I was yesterday at Mr. Calthropes, which is all I will say of that too, for fear you reproach me shoud I tell you either in what manner or with what company I spent ye day. To morrow comes old Mr. Tyrell to conclude ye match; and tis well it so falls out before ye Act of Parliament for marriages be in force*; else

---

*The dreadful Act of Parliament which young Tyrell and Kezia Hervey were just in time to escape, was passed on Aug. 24, 1653. It enacted that whoever should agree to be married after Sept. 29, 1653, should deliver to the Registrar for the parish where they lived their names etc., and that he should publish them on the three following Lord's days at the close of the morning exercize in the public meeting place commonly called the Church or Chapel, or (if the parties desired it) in the nearest market place on 3 market days in 3 successive weeks between the hours of 11 and 2; and that they should then come before a Justice of the Peace, who, after each had taken the other by the hand and made the prescribed promise, should declare them man and wife. [Burn's Hist: of Parish Registers, p. 26.]

scrupulous Kez upon my conscience woud hardly be drawn into ye bonds. Friday or Saturday I hope to see you, Love me my dearest, & for ye rest let time do her worst.

---

*To these chaste loves & pious parents pray'rs
Are to be' ascrib'd ye blessings on their heirs.

[Between the above love-letters and the following anniversary lines lie 28 years of wedded life, of which this letter-book has nothing to tell us. The letter-book contains lines written on six anniversaries of Isabella Hervey's death, all of them copied by one hand, which was not that of Sir Thomas. But in Lord Arthur Hervey's account of the Hervey family (1858) there are given a few lines as specimens of these anniversary poems, which include some written on the seventh anniversary. And in a note to the lines on the sixth anniversary in which Sir Thomas calls upon the palsy to shake the glass and make the few remaining sands of his life pass more quickly, Lord Arthur says, "The tremulous handwriting, quite changed since the last anniversary, explains this allusion to the palsy." It is therefore clear that at that time (1858) the lines existed not only as copied in this letter-book but also in their original form as written by Sir Thomas. I suppose they are still at Ickworth, though I cannot hear of them. Having only the letter-book before me, I can only give so much of the seventh anniversary poem as has been printed by my father. Why that poem never got copied into the letter-book I cannot say ; perhaps death intervened too quickly. S.H.A.H.]

---

*These two lines are in the writing of John, 1st Earl of Bristol.

The first anniversary on ye death of ye excellent Issabella Lady Hervey, my dear wife, who dyed ye fifth day of June, anno domini 1686, att five of ye clock in the morning being Saterday, (the day of her birth also.)

O decus atque dolor.

Mysterious Union, Thou,
Lord, at ye first did make us two,
 And then we two anon
 Thou madst to be but one;
 And now that she is gone,
 Lord, am I two or one?
For as I count, I'm neither one or two,
But nothing, if not less then nothing, now,
Since thou in taking her from me hast tane
Me from my selfe; and then what can remain.
She my fair figure being from me gone ⎞
I'm but an empty cypher left alone; ⎬
She gave ye value, I alass have none. ⎠
 Then what to doe have I
 But to desire to dye:
 Lord, bring me to that bliss,
 In which I hope she is.
And there together lett us ever shine, ⎞
Where I nor hers shall be, nor she be mine, ⎬
But may again be joyn'd in being thine. ⎠

The Second Anniversary.

The rowling year once more hath gone its rounds,
Coelestial bodies all within their bounds
By God appointed have in motion been;

Vol. I. E

The sea hath ebb'd & flow'd & ebb'd agen,
Man to his labour, beasts goe forth to prey,
Thus these ye nights, thus those do spend ye day;
Nothing in nature but my grief stands still.
O restive grief, thou stuborn child of ill,
Thou first begotten of that monster sin,
Without which grief or death had never been.
My sin was the bold ravisher alone
Coud tear thee from my side; cause Legion!
No single arme could have prevail'd 'gainst love,
Which would as sure have overcome as strove;
In case of any other violence
I might at least have dy'd with thee in thy defence.
Then had we two together been till now,
And lov'd each other as we did below,
And hand in hand have wandered through ye aire,
Till we had reach'd ye seat of perfect rest,
Which now thou doest enjoy among ye blest.
But thou who govern'st all, since tis thy will
The shadow of my life be stretch'd out still,
Grant while I live that this may be my song,
Blest be thy name, who lent her me so long.

The Third Anniversary.

Just at ye hour that she was wont to pay
Her morning sacrifice each springing day,
God tooke her to himself and answer'd all
Her past petitions with ye gracious call,
Come faithfull servant. This I am sure was said
By her sweet smiling after she was dead.

Methought I saw her soul taking its flight
Towards ye regions of eternall light,
And in a moment grew so wonderous bright
It dazel'd as it went my mortall sight.
Twixt flesh & spirit hence arose a strife ;
One cal'd her saint, ye other cry'd my wife.
Jacob and Esau like, twin'd greife & joy
Struggl'd within me; but the hairy boy
Rough Esau, griefe, rush't out ye first o' th two,
And did (in spight of all that joys could doe)
With horror & amazement fill my mind,
Till Jacob, joy, who was not farr behind,
Rescued my soul out of ye hunters hand ;
The younger this ye elder did command,
As thou, O Jacob's God, said it should be ;
Let Grace o're nature then prevaile in me.

The Fourth Anniversary.

Thousands of tedious days and nights are gone
Since thou, my dear, didst leave me here alone,
My days darker then other nights have been,
My nights all black, as black as was ye sin
That caus'd our separacion, dearest dust.
Heaven which did joyne us once, that Heaven is just,
And will again unite us in ye grave,
(For I'le no other second marriage have,)
Where once arrived ye tyrant Death no more
Can then divorce our marriage as before.
Our mingled ashes quiet shall remain,
Till the last trump shall raise them up againe.

But here I must unto ye world present
That vast & ne're before enjoy'd extent
Of happiness by man which I enjoy'd
With her, was always full & never cloy'd.
To her my joys & griefs I did impart,
Into her bosome pour'd out all my heart.
She tooke upon her all domestick care,
By love she taught her children how to fear ;
Her bounty did engage her servants so
As ye Centurions could not faster goe.
Her charity diffusive did extend
Not to relations only, or a friend,
But all without exception did pertake
Of that for her own God & conscience sake.
She suffer'd not ye needy eyes to waite,
But watch'd for them, & did despatch them strait
And greater pleasures she did take to give
Then they could have in what they did receive.
In exercises such as these she past
Her life, & was thus doing found at last.
To summ up all, take this epitomy   ⎫
Of what is due to her dear memory,   ⎬
And on her tomb lett it engraven be: ⎭
Though nought but dust doth to ye eye appear,
Beauty, Witt, Bounty, Vertue, all lye here.

The Fifth Anniversary.

I blush to see my selfe thus long survive
Thee, without whom I thought I could not live

So many dayes as now I have done years.
Say for your selves, my sighs, & you, my tears,
Have you been feign'd ? Have you been counterfeit,
That you have done no execucion yet
Upon me, broke my heart or made me blind ?
Can you be false & I my selfe not find
It out ? But when I turne my eyes to thee,
My God, how legible's ye mystery.
Thou heap'dst upon me blessings in a wife,
O rare example of a spotless life !
A maiden matron, and a matron maid,
Nice in her age, and in her youth was staid ;
A sensuall love she never understood,
Or what was ill but by ye contra good.
She was so oft upon her knees in prayer,
She made a constant perfume in ye air.
All this I did observe in her and more,
And yet was not ye richer for her store.
Still I went on i'th beaten path of sin ;
I joy'd in her indeed, but what was 't in?
Her angell face, more then angellick mind,)
The quickness of her witt, or some refin'd }
Exterior good or beauty, me inclin'd.   )
No wonder then, since I did render vaine
This blessing, itt should be resum'd againe,
And I condemn'd to many years of woe,
And what I would not learne be made to know.
Thus malefactors on ye wheele are broke,
Thus, not with one blow but many a stroke.

The Sixth (and I hope last) Anniversary on ye death of ye excellent Issabella Lady
Hervey, my dear wife.

Since our last sad farewell, I doe believe
I've done all that you'd have me doe but grieve,
And faine in that would I observe you too,
Instruct me, my dear angell, what to doe ;
I spend my time in counting up ye joys
Of my past life with you.   Farr from ye noise
Of company I seeke you every where,
And say the same things as when you was there.
Then (for all other objects I despise)   ⎫
I sett your lovely image 'fore mine eyes, ⎬
And give attencion to your sweet replyes ; ⎭
For soul with soul intelligence doe keep,
As mine with yours, whether I wake or sleep.
When preexisting they acquainted were
They made agreement sure when to be here,
And where to lodg themselves.   Yours whispering said
To my soul, Goe & be not then afraid,
I'le follow ye, & find ye where thou art ; ⎫
So we did meet, and when we were to part, ⎬
I well remember, for I ha't by hart,   ⎭
Thou saidst to me, Pray goe to heaven, my dear,
As much as is to say, Pray meet me there.
But my soul of a grosser composition
Then yours sticks to 'ts earth, now yours is flowr
Unclos'd up to a purer region.
My thred of life, I hope, is well near spunn,
And my last lazy sands ready to run ;
Else, kindly palsey, help to shake ye glass,

That they may mend their pace & quicker pass :
For what remaine lye heavy on my hands,
Not like to graines, but like to shoales ot sands.

The Seventh Anniversary.*

This tribute to your memory is due,
And I'll not fail in being just to you
Who wert to me inimitably true.
Twas not in this or that that you were so,
It was in all you e'er did think or do.
All your contrivances center'd in this,
My present happiness and future bliss.

.   .   .   .

Twas by your prudence that a small estate
Afforded all convenience of a great ;
Plenty flow'd in upon us with full tide,
Which you by comely order beautified.
How can I live now you my guide are gone,
Or move who wert my staff to lean upon.

[Here ends Sir Thomas Hervey's portion in this letter-book.
Henceforth the letters copied into it are those of his son John, first Earl of
Bristol. S.H.A.H.]

---

* As I have said already, the lines for this anniversary are not in the letter-book, so I can only give
the extract from them which was printed by my father in 1858,

74.   To Sir Richard Rothwell at Stapleford near Newark on this side
              Trent.   [of cheif rents.]

Aswarby, Aug. 9, 1692.

By the dates of the inclosed arrear may easily be discerned how great an unwillingness those interested have all along shewn to proceed in the recovery of them by any other methods than what were amicable & neighbourly; but seeing hitherto no likelier fruit of so long a forbearance than the utter loss of them forces me give you this trouble to know your positive determination concerning them, that I may know what to trust to. Mr. Burslem, who made the extract, tells me he hath often demanded them (as at Sleeford about 2 years since), & that you never denyed them, but always told him you woud take care about them. I suppose you need not to be told that things of their nature admit not of long discontinuance without danger of exstinction, a consequence, I dare assure my self, you woud not aime at taking the advantage of. Wherefore, Sir, I once more desire you would let me have your peremptory resolutions herein by this bearer.   I am, Sir, your humble servant.

75.   To ye Reverend Dr. Gardener, Subdean of Lincoln.

Sir,   Aswarby, Aug. 11, 1692.

Yours of the 8th instant I received yesterday by Mr. Parnell, and (so far as I am able) do intend to fullfill the contents of it. As for the £600, I hope ye whole estate late Sir Robert Carrs will in a short time be sold for the payment of his debts (pursuant to a Decree of the Court of Chancery in that behalfe obtained) ; but if such sale shoud not fall out time enough for your purposes, I will then endeavour to provide so much of my fathers money as may pay off the mortgage upon an assignment from those legally authorized. But for the commutation you speak of, (it being for us to take houses for land,) I believe it will not be found proper for us to deal

in it, having already so many (and those very much out of repair) in ye
same town. However, Sir, I will not be positive against one, till the lands
& houses in proposall have been surveyed, and in case upon the whole
matter it be not found very inconvenient for us, I shall not oppose it, being,
Sir,   Your humble servant,

76.   To Martin Folkes Esq. at Grays Inn.

Sir   Aswarby, Aug. 23, 1692.
              Having throughly experienced your great suffi-
ciency and sound judgment in all matters of this nature, & being no less
sensible of your particular kindness in the constant direction & effectual applycation of them to the advancement & safety of my interests,
makes me now have recourse to your opinion as to the arrears of rent
accrued upon the estate before ye date of the order of the House of Peers.
My reason for renewing the quere proceeds from the readiness I find in the
tennants to pay them to me, in case they might have my security to indemnify them against Lord Holles ; & also that because, suppose ye Lords
shoud be prevailed with to make an explanation of this order & thereupon
shoud adjudge them due to the present Lord Holles, I can at last but refund,
& in ye mean time the use of such a considerable sum (being to ye value of
2 or 3000 £) will not be very disagreeable to the posture of young peoples
affairs, whose fruits in expectation (altho' most of them at the end of their
Autumn) are not yet fallen.   But ye whole I referr and submit to your much
better understanding of it, & shall trouble you no farther at present but to let
you know that a timely word or two of advice from you herein (as to my proceeding or final desisting) woud be very welcome to me, as also how Coll :
Cornwalls affair standeth.   I am sure my Lord Dovers with my fathers lyeth
at a strange pass, not knowing this day what we are yet to depend on.   I
hope Mr. Smith hath been to wait on you with ye note for £750 promised
upon Lord Dorsetts account.   But I forget how little time you have to spare.

Vol. I.   F

That therefore you may afford me ye rest in writing, which otherwise I might have kept you in reading, I will conclude, assuring you of my being with all sincerity,   Your most faithfull friend & servant.

77.   To the Right Hon. ye Lord Dover at Cheveley.

My Lord   Aswarby, Sept. 3, 1692.

Seeing treaty by way of letter, instead of advancing ye business so long depending between your Lordship & my father to the ordinary and usuall conclusion in such dealings, hath only hitherto multiply'd misunderstandings, where I dare be bold to say and hope the friendlyest correspondence is mutually intended, I once resolved to make no farther attempts of this nature. But Michaelmas approaching, against which time you were pleased to promise (in one of yours to him) that, in case none of your then proposed conditions were liked by him, you woud pay of the whole debt both principall & interest; & neither of us having yet received any later notice to that effect; & ye having a security beyond exception now offered him for about such a summe to be taken up next terme by a clyent of Mr. Pooleys; enforces me to beg ye favour of your Lordship that he may not then fail of it. Tis now a year (come November) since I deliverd in ye stated account to your Lordship, wherein that arrear of interest will plainly evince how great the losses must have been by its growth & continuance; & I can best tell the inconveniencies he hath before and since been put unto by reason of its not being paid. And here I must not forget to rectify a great mistaking either of Mr. Poley by your Lordship or of me by him; for that I shoud send your Lordship word by him that I was willing to turne the interest of ye £8000 mortgage into principall & woud take your bond for it at £4 per cent, was a thing so wide both of common practice & ye little understanding I have now acquired in managements of their nature, that on ye contrary I had more then once taken occasion to say before him, sure we need not take £4 at a time when very near £10 per cent was to be made of ready money; & therefore I only refused your Lordships proposal by Mr. Molins, not in ye least receding from any of my own. Neither can our not accepting your Lordships single bond for so considerable a summe (tho doubtless safe enough) be deemed so; for according to Sir G. Elwes report of your conference at Cheveley, he not only insisted upon Lord Jermyns being jointly bound, but that your Lordship also agreed it should be so since required. And for its being so, ye general practice doth so universally warrant it, that ye most sufficient particular men cannot take ye caution amiss. But were the common rules and forms to be dispenced with, I am sure my late Uncle Herveys character (who was none of the worst judges) & recommendation of your Lordship to my father, confirmed by his own experience of your honour, woud first induce him to do it towards your Lordship. I shall trouble your Lordship no farther at present but only to desire that, as Mr. Pooley by his to me of ye 28th past said his clyent required a speedy resolution whether ye money could be furnishd then or not, so that you woud please to enable me to send him an answer one way or t'other. However, shoud the principal be uncompassable by that time, I question not but your Lordships justice will order payment of the whole arrear of interest, ye disappointment of which hath been of unspeakable prejudice to my fathers concerns. I am, my Lord, Your Lordships most obedient servant.

78. Lord Dover to me.

Cheveley, Sept. 13, 1692.

If you woud be pleased to be steady in any of your proposalls, I shoud be in some hopes to satisfy you. But truly as tis I find very little liklyhood of my being so happy. In ye first place, I am much persuaded Mr. Poley will not deny that you were satisfyd to take my bond with interest for the money owing above the principall secured upon Lidgate and Cropley, tho' since you have not approved of it. But as to that, you shall hear no more of it, nor truly shoud you then, had I not thought my bond for such a summ (either living or dying) as good security as any in England; for I shoud be full out as sorry to be be holding to any body upon such an occasion as you can one shoud.   In the next place I do believe Sir Gervaise Elwes will not say otherwise but that we concluded in this very house, that you woud take Midsummer last past ye £4000 due upon ye Market house, and my Lord Jermyn and my bond for ye interest of what is owing by mortgage upon Lidgate and Cropley. This you fell from too, and a fine letter with it from Sir Thomas Hervey, naming a long term before he woud receive his money, and till then and not till then woud he have it, & altogether to, otherwise none. And about a month after this delicate pened letter another is wrote to me with an inclosed I know not what that I must sign, & have it witnessed, otherwise you woud not look upon anything I sayd as an advertisment for ye receiving money. Thank God, I never borrowed of Sir Thomas. And after this then, and not till then, in yours of the 3d instant you fall from all this again, and ask nothing less then that I will pay you £15000 about a month hence. I have told you a plain & true story, and I think, if you please to consider it, you will find the proceedings something extraordinary. Midsumer last past I coud have paid you what was agreed. Now tis more then I can do. I have met with people a little easier then Sir Thomas Hervey, and they have taken their money, which I am always ready to pay when I have it. However, when my Lord Jermyn comes over, if you think his bond and mine good security enough for ye interest owing you, you may command it. I believe it is sufficient enough to please the hardest man in nature, lett him be hard enough to refuse a little warter upon ones own ground, if such a man were to be found; & so remaine, Sir, Your most humble servant D.   Sir Robert Davers is gone to London; he says that of his money & a friend of his there will soon be about £12000 that I shall have to pay you. You shall have timely notice of it.

79. To my dear father after he went from Aswarby.

Sir, Aswarby, Sept. 19, 1692.

The above written reply being as quaint & notable as the proceedings on his part (which occasiond it) were generous & reasonable, hath made me not only take the pains to transcribe, but also to garble & anatomize it, that you may see the author is every jott as ingenuous in treating as he hath shown himself fair in dealing. For instance, at first he positively affirmed in a former * letter that I sent him word by Mr. Poley you will take his single bond for the arrear of interest upon Lidgate at £4 per cent. In disproof of which I sent him such convincing testimony that now his particular assertion is put generally—with interest. And after his manner of acting I begin to think his security real or personall (according to his own darling parenthesis (living or dying) to be equally safe & eligible. What you may loose by this I know not ; but surely never was such a summ so long lent with so little profitt received. After this follows the so-often-urged argument concluded between him & Sir G. E., the substance of which (O wonder!) he varies little from, with this difference only (like as in ye other), that his latter relation of it comes much nearer matter of fact than the former. † How any man can be said to fall from a thing he neither

---

* Here John Hervey makes the following note in the margin, "July 18, 1692, wherein his words were these : Let us return to the affair of my bond, which you say you dare not;accept for a year or two. Pray, how dus your mind come to be so much chang'd? If you have forgot what you sent me word by Mr. Poley, ask him about it ; I dare say he has not ; which was that you were willing to turn ye interest due upon ye £8000 mortgage to principal money, & would take my bond for it at £4 per cent. Tho new I offer to do it by Mr. Mollins, your answer is, You dare not do it."

† Another marginal note. " As to what was concluded here with Sir G. E., I dare say he remembers it, and I am not sure but he has it in writing, that you were to take my bond for ye interest above mentiond at Michaelmas next, & I to pay ye £8000 at the same time. [Thus far tis peremptory as to ye challenged acceptance of his single bond for above £2800 ; but then his conscience misgiving that written words would not accomodate themselves to his purposes thought good to add :] Tis true he desird, if you should insist upon it, that my Lord Jermyn shoud be bound with me, & this of my Lord Jermyn is so good a proof of what I tell you that perhaps it may have credit enough with you to incline you to believe it before you hear from him, tho' I have not to take my bond, which [here comes in that poor hackney prostitute parenthesis again] (living or dying) I take to be as good security as any you have."

offered or accepted, (neither of which were done by your self or me, it being impracticable to get Lord Jermyn jointly bound (who was then at Jersey) within so short a time as between that treaty & midsummer,) passeth all understandings but his Lordships.   As for fine delicate penned letters, which title is given to mine as well as yours, (and to write but as well as you is the utmost of my wishes, (I am sensible far beyond my present ability) by that conjunctive (another), I know few people (especially considering what might naturally be expected from one once thought fitt to to be so deeply employed in matters of Church as well as State) worse qualifyed to gloss or comment upon either order of matter, elegancy of stile, or true orthography. Witness his beginning a letter with a little i, his stedy, likelyhood, approved, believe, Lord Jermyn, (which wants an s with a syncopal mark in that place,) and my bond with a little b, morgage, to instead of too, then his I know not what-ship. I wonder not at all he shoud terme ye warning I inclos'd for him to sign—the inclos'd I know not what—for I must needs say he hath discoverd himself to be sufficiently ignorant in transactions of this nature. The reprise he makes—of the till then and not till then—is very shrewd, & I believe most pickquantly meant. Ten to one had he had the ordering of these words at first, instead of a blundering tautology which he is guilty of but in the recitall of them, (for your words were only—then & not till then,) he would have put them thus, viz. then till not & then till. Tis also certain that—living or dying—and—fall from this again—are corrival expressions in his—ships—affection ; otherwise he could never hale them in by head and shoulders so upon all occasions without reason or to no purpose. For I have most intentively perus'd the whole paragraph, and could not find since the former—this you fell from too—there was any thing in proposal urged to ,ground the charge upon ; unless he would insinuate that because he neither signd or returnd the warning, ergo I fell from accepting it according to my desire ; a fit conclusion for his—ships logick.   Were it not that I have heard Truth may be followed so close till she beats out ones teeth, your case but truly & plainly stated woud show whose proceedings have been not only ye most extraordinary but exorbitant & unwarrantable. I cannot help remarking that ye word —story—was a very unhappy chos'd epithet in that place, because I have read that, Conveniunt rebus nomina sæpe suis. Without dispute those people who have taken his Lordships money off his hands had no very great arrear of interest due; or, if so, were such to whom his Lordship had more grace then to propose ye discharge of their principal, only & as it were to put off payment of ye interest sine die; or, knowing how he had served you, were glad to take eggs for their money; or else I will so far consent with him as to esteem them easy, very easy people indeed. That he is always very ready to pay when he hath it, no body can more sufficiently refute then my self; for to my knowledge Mr. Mollins had once this summer more money of his than would have cleared the arrear of interest, which was all that was required.   As the end crowns the work, so Martial like he closes his epistolary epigram with that viperous deadly sting in ye taile of it—Let him be hard enough to refuse a little warter (pray observe his spelling again) upon ones own ground, if such a man were to be found—I suppose you know whereto it would allude, tho' need not be at all conscious of its being justly apply'd; for the mans fetching water out of ye parke was never deny'd him, only that the great gate should not be open being advertized; he would have made use of that to other purposes, as putting in his cattle to greaze by night, stealing ye wood, etc. I remember very well Sir Robert Davers was a very warm solicitor on ye mans behalf till I cooled him with ye reasons already alledg'd, who by a true representation of the matter might have help'd his uncle to avoid the reproach due to so frivolous, immorall a reflection.   Notwithstanding ye postcript, I fear Mr. Poley should be told his clyent ought not to rely on you for ye money I once thought you might have furnishd; for unless Sir R. Davers's (friend) be such an one as Hen: Killigrew's, (who us'd to boast that Sir (Francis) Josiah Childe and himself could borrow £10000 upon their bare note,) I doubt (what between pyracy and architecture) he'l hardly be able to command £12000 between this & next terme. This trouble which I have given you & taken my self is only to show what little shifts great men take up with when foul practices require specious colours to be la d upon them, & that as never man was more in the wrong, so consequently hath he throughly verifyed what I remember Ovid saith : viz. that Causa Patrocinio non bona, pejor erit; & so I'l leave him to your better thoughts what course ought next to be taken with a man whom no reasons can bring to reason; an effect that if it be not speedyly wrought by some cause or other, I am sure Lady Hervey will never leave till she baits me out of all mine, when 'ere I get to London, towards which place our whole family sets out on Wednesday the 28th instant.   Saturday last was Carrs birth-day, which was celebrated with great solemnity; a feast at dinner, ringing of bells, fiddles and dancing, & in Joane Saunderson made one himself, saluting the whole company.   I am, Sir, your ever dutifull son & servant.

80.   To ye Earle of Montague.   Oct. 5, 1692.

My Lord

I would not have given your Lordship this unseasonable trouble had not a very unreasonable unexpected one been given me. But remembering your Lordships civility to me heretofore when I apply'd my self to you in a matter of the same nature puts me now again upon desiring your Lordships mediation between my Lady Hervey & father. For because I could not come to Town from my country house (above 100 miles distant) just when ye £400 became due, and that too but since the latter end of July, & altho' I sent her word from thence by Mr. Hoy the sollicitor that I should be in Town by the close of September, & woud then be sure to pay it ye day after my arrival; yet in the interim her Ladyship gives order for a motion before ye Master of ye Rolls for leave and an order thereupon to put our Recognizance in suit; so that when I came to tender the money according to promise, her Ladyship refuses it unless her costs (which with how much reason & upon what provocation they were expended, I appeal to your Lordship) might be paid also. That therefore your Lordship would so far interpose as to signify to her by me or otherwise, as you shall think fitt, that you would not have her to insist upon so very rigorous and (as the present case standeth) so unpractic'd a demand is the desire of, my Lord, Your Lordships humble servant.

81. For John Crompe Esq. at Rochester in Kent.

Sir London, Oct. 6, 1692.

I made severall attempts to find Mr. Durrant at home (and twas a kind of little journey from my house to his) before I succeeded, otherwise the money had been sooner paid then to day, which was done according to direction, being £120 for the renewall of ye lease, & £5 for the fees of its inregistring, ingrossing, etc., in all £125, together with a surrender of the old lease into his hands, of all which I desir'd him to give you advice by this nights post, that you might expedite the execution & dispatch of ye new one, which will find me if directed to Mr. John Hervey at his house in King Street near St. James's Square. I must not forget to observe to you that considering how ill rents are paid, how low they are, and how high ye taxes, my father thinks the fine something hard. I am Your servant unknown.

82. For ye Reverend Dr. Gardiner, Subdean of Lincoln.

Sir London, Oct. 6, 1692.

To let you see I'm one of those who do not only promise but perform, I've since my arrival prepard the money pursuant to your desires & occasions. I have likewise by this nights post sent direction to Mr. Burslem that he shoud accomodate you with what summ he is able ; as also to Mr. Shore that he would expedite & contract the severall assign-

Vol. I. G

ments into as narrow a compass as he can ; and I hope since I have been so ready in providing, you'l not be long in receiving it. If you have present use for any of it, to be paid here in Town, let me have an order signd by the Excrs : together with their joint receipt for ye summe, specifying upon what account etc., and it shall certainly be answerd upon sight. In the mean time I hope no interest will be expected after this notice, having called in the money on purpose, and tis not square that my fathers interest (whose money it is) ceasing on the one hand shoud not be accrewing on the other. The money attends your order, and I am, Sir.   Your humble servant.

Shoud you by this time have ordered your affairs so as not to have imediate use for this money, let me know it; for I can quickly turn it to better advantage for ye intended assignee.

83.   Oct. 12, 1692.
Mr. Jodrell

Your advice being grounded upon Sergeant Philipps opinion as to an arrest or a sci : fa :, I have followed it, & dismissed Lady Herveys teazers with a very coy answer, telling him if she woud not take ye money, I was councelld not to allow any costs. But what the consequences may or are likely to be, I desire to know from you, as also ye speediest notice of any motion which they shall, or we ought to, make.   Your friend & servant.

84.   To my most dear and pious father on ye death I need not say of whom.

From my sad and memorable Epoch ye 47th day.

O Sir !   23rd April, 1693.

My having seen you so happy, and you me, in ye more rare and pretious sort of Heavens chief earthly blessings, a wise & vertuous, kind & pious wife ; and my rackt heart having oft suggested to

Isabella, Wife of John Hervey.
1670 - 1693.

me that, if its pains are capable of any relaxation or remission, it coud only be procured by giving of its grief some vent, (having learnt that Strangulat inclusus dolor, atque cor æstuat intus ; that Sua vulnera nutrit qui tegit ; that Quo magis tegitur, tanto magis æstuat ignis ;) where it might promise it self ye meeting with a kind reception from a sympathizing compassion ; had sometimes almost determind me (even without your command (my now only law after God Almightys) to make choice of your well furnishd breast as ye fittest prepard receptacle for the overflowings of a sorrow, that derives its origin from the like fatal source of misery & woe which first created yours. In ye bitterness then of my present soul, suffer me, Sir, with wretched Job (who surely was but the type umbratick of my accomplishd misfortune, ye loss of my most dear delightfull Cousen Don, (O memorable name) comprising all in it, (even what remaind to him the living man,) for I may truly say,

> The fatal day in which she died
> My death as well as hers contrivd ;)

first to breath out (as all undone and ruind men are apt to do) a few fruitless wishes ; then a complaint or two, (not foolishly taxing the divine dispensations toward me, for in its severest inflictions I must still say, Righteous is ye Lord, & upright are his judgments); and when I have done thus, (as you once upon occasion told me,) I hope to find my self the better for it. O then ! that I were as in times past, as in the days that God blessed me ; when his candle shined upon my head ; when the Almighty was yet with me, and together with his gracious favour the (next of blessings) most deservedly lov'd fellowship of my unwearying, most entertaining charming wife ; a wife who, like the fruitfull vine upon the wall of my house, bore unto me the sweetest prettyest children, setting like olive branches (and well indeed may they be calld so, springing from ye stem of Peace it self) round about my table. For then my glory was fresh in me ; then I us'd to lift up my hands and eyes & heart to heaven, acknowledging my lott was

fallen in a fair ground, yea that I had a goodly heritage; then said I, Blessed
be ye Lord who hath dealt so graciously with his servant; Thou, O Lord,
hast brought him to great honour, and comforted him on every side; then I
confessd the Lord hath done great things for me; and then it was my heart
was glad & my glory rejoiced; then my mouth was filled with mirth and
my tongue with joy; then all things wrought together for good to set my
mind at ease and make me throughly happy; and then it was I said unto
my self, I shall never be removed, ye great and mercifull God of his
goodness hath made my hill so strong. But alas! in ye full possession
and at the zenith of all this my prosperity, it pleas'd him in the secret
council of his unscrutable providence (whether as a punishment for my
former sins, (which with shame & horror I have strictly scannn'd even from
my first remembrances, & upon the severest disquisition have been able to
satisfy even the most jealous scruples in all my conscience that twas not
either any abuse of, or unthankfullness for, the now withdrawn blessing,) or
as a touchstone of my faith, or for ye worlds unworthyness of her, or her
ripe worthyness for Heaven,) to turn his face from me & I was troubled.
The thing which I so greatly feared came upon me, and my joy was suddenly
turned into sorrow, my felicity into adversity. I was at perfect ease, but he
hath broken me asunder. He in a moment destroyed me on every side, and
I was gone; my hope and my only comfort did he remove far from me,
leaving me utterly destitute, even like a poor disconsolate sparrow sitting
alone upon the house-top, making me most sensibly to feel that when he is
angry all our days are gone, bringing our years to an end as it were a tale
that is told. He with one breath over-threw all my fences, and in an instant
broke down my strongest hold. He with one blast exstinguishd all my glory,
and the days of my (now worthless) youth hath be shortend. He hath
thought fitt to vex me with one of his sharpest storms, and with his rebukes
hath broke my heart, filling it with bitterness, making it drunk with wormwood, even to ye forgetting of prosperity, and refusing comfort; so that

henceforth my (once delighted) eyes are now no more to see good in this life, being reducd instead of happy days to possess months of vanity, and in lieu of peacefull rest, restless and dismal nights are appointed me. Wherefore by the waters of Babylon let me set down and weep when I remember thee (dear cousin Donn). Henceforth let me hang aside my harp upon the willows ; or if I 'ere shoud touch thee more, thou must stand ready tun'd to those sad notes which are expressive of the deepest sorrow, and for our future Hymn let this be set unto her plaintive farewell.

(1)

Farewell for ever to that happy life
I us'd to lead, when blest with her chaste love,
Who of all vertues wishd for in a wife
Did the great pattern & example prove :
Faithfull as Sarah, as Rebecca wise,
Devout as Hester, which all else implies.

(2)

Yet this and more had bounteous Heaven bestowed
On her, whose loss I ever must deplore ;
And for a proof how much her worth I lovd
Can never relish this worlds pleasures more ;
Her absence changd it so, that since she went
Prosperity would seem but punishment.

(3)

But sure she cant be dead and only sleeps ;
Impossible that so much worth and truth,
(If our vile Israel ye great Shepherd keeps,)
Shoud be snatchd hence i'th prime of all her youth,
Where her bright actions would have done more good
Than all the rest she left behind her could.

(4)

Yet dead she is.   But thou forgetst, my heart,
That God this righteous one away did take,
Not only for thy punishment & smart,
But for her goodness & her vertues sake ;
And with her's gone my heart, my joy, and all
That we poor mortals pleasure us'd to call.

(5)

What then have we now more to do, my lyre,
Than thou in silence and unstrung to lye,
And I thy wretched master to expire.
Hush then, O good my lyre, and let him dye !
But if just Heaven my pennance will prolong,
Let her due praises be our constant song.

O tell it not in Gath ! neither publish it in the streets of Askelon, that ye
beauteous glory of all our Israel is departed. She, even she, who was (O
dismal tense in happyness) so lovely and pleasant, usefull and innocent in
her life and conversation is now no more! O daughters of Israel, lament and
weep over her, who was your polar star guiding and directing you into the
paths & practice of all those virtues, which, if but imitated to the least resemblance with that fair copy she set you, will surely bring you to that blest
estate where now she weeps no more.   O what have ye all lost, young and
old, rich and poor ?   And if ye general loss be thus considerable, what must
my particular one then be ?   O behold and see if there be any sorrow like
my sorrow wherewith the Lord hath afflicted me in the day of his fierce
anger, which forceth me to my cry out a fresh with the royal prophet, My
God, my God, look upon me. *. . . What ? shall we receive good at ye hand of

---

* Here follow a number of verses from the Psalms & elsewhere strung together, with a quotation or two
from Tertullian and Augustine, and reflections of his own, which fill more than a large closely written folk
page in the letter-book, and which I omit. S.H.A.H.

God, & shall we not likewise receive evil? Ney, so far am I from thinking that a bare resignation is only required of me, that in my thanksgiving I never omitt blessing his goodness, which assignd me the possession of that rare treasure (before all mankind) which he thought fitt to lend our world but for so short a space. 1587 days I enjoyed her, and had she been continued to me as many years would nere have bred satiety. She was my first, last love, my ever new delight. But Est quoddam prodire tenus si non datur ultra. And therefore now thus must thou say, my soul; that while God gave thee good days he loved thee, and that now he sendeth thee evill ones loveth thee also; and hope that he would not have sent this evill but to be a cause unto thee of greater good; that being call'd home thereby thou mightest be at peace with him; and I pray thee learn and know that afflictions come not forth of the dust, but are directed by an infinite eternal wisdom, that those who mourn may be exalted to safety; and that notwithstanding thou art so full of present heaviness and so disquieted within me, yet do thou still put thy trust in God, who can easily bring good out of evill, and will not utterly forsake them who place their only hope in him. Tarry then the Lords leisure; be strong and he shall comfort thine heart; cast thy burthen upon him, and he will refresh thee. Do thus my soul, and then, altho' he sent this in his wrath, yet will he remember mercy; yea altho' he killeth thee, yet be thou sure to trust still in him, and say, O Lord, in thee have I trusted, let me not be utterly put to confusion.   Glory be to God.

85.   I need not superscribe ye sad occasion.

O Mr. Cullum   April 30, 1693.

Heaven and perdition cant be states more different than those in which I wrote my last to you and that wherein your last but one found me; the first in a most tranquile fruition of all that happiness my prayers ere asked or heart coud think to wish for, blest with ye sweet company, true love and friendship of such a faithfull peerless soul, whose ever new endearments created to me such a Paradice on earth as Heaven (you see) grew quickly jealous of, bereaving me of that which might in time have proved (altho' it had not yet, for he himself can tell I n'ere forgatt from whence the blessing came, or sending up my daily thanks & praises for't,) to have been esteem'd a good so full and so sufficient by these my earthly organized conceptions, as to have renderd me supine and careless in the pursuit of that rich future Canaan which his omnisciency well knew to be much more compleat & permanent. And therefore as preventive physic I have strove to take it ; but certainly a draught more bitter or more nauseous (may'nt I say) to weak recoyling nature could not have been pourd out of ffates Probation-cupp, tho' all its medicinal druggs had been infusd together ; for what can more befall a man (humanly speaking, and so I woud be understood throughout) than to be at once deprivd of all that was delightfull, good or valuable in his eyes, of all that truth & piety, worth and virtue, wit and honour, (pardon me these plain expressions, as she's now mine no more,) which affording ye (by much) most agreable of conversations insensibly beguild (and twas the sole deccipt I ere knew her guilty of) this life of all its (otherwise) inseperable attendants, cares and un-easynesses, and which alone was able to make it seem to me worth staying in. Pity then, my friend, this most deplorable inversion of ye most happy fortune ; and believe me, Mr. Cullum, tis (with ye miserable (such as me at least) an almost decided question that twere much better never to have been in bliss than live to feel its sad privation. Nulla sors longa est ; dolor et voluptas invicem cedunt, brevior voluptas.—Brevis est magni fortuna favoris. And this my own experience hath already verified ; for even the time since our late fatal seperation hath seemd much longer to me than all that other during our pleasd and blessed union. For

> This with a silent, speedy foot passd on,
> That with a pace as if twould 'nere be gone.

But could inexorable time yet clap more weight upon its leaden wings, and out of that dead lifeless lump, which to compleat the measure of my punishment is yet assignd me here, could wire-draw each moment out into a year, I shoud be so far from finding myself beholden to its length for any cure, as twould only turn that misery into a lingering disease, which woud much better have been let run to an acute one. Time is a remedy so base and vulgar, that he who once proposeth to himself an ease by 't ought never to survive such wishd effects. And he who unawares shoud find it wrought in him unlookd for, ye very thought of having once forgot (oblivion being the main ingredient of this ingratefull medicine) an object so worthy of continual reverential memory as that dear saint I now condole, would quickly kill him with surprise and shame. Remember her, then, I not only always must but would, how dear so 'ere my grievd heart pays for 't. And

> each day I shall
> For her make hours canonical.
> Since then no way can give me help or ease,
> I seek with verse my greifs t' appease ;
> Just as a bird that flies about,
> And beats it self against the cage,
> Finding at last no passage out,
> It sets and sings, and so o'recomes its rage.

But I forget (altho' I cannot her) that some relief there is in store, and that ye best and most effectual, even faith & resignation. Let this be then thy creed and cure, my soul; that God is all wise, most mercyfull, & omnipotent; wise through his prescience, mercifull in all his dispensations, & so infinitely powerfull as to bring the most unexpected goods out of ye greatest seeming evills. And for thy song take this: God's will be done in earth as tis in Heaven; for he only is excellent, his grace extendeth over all his works, who woud not have brought this sore calamity upon thee & thine, but to have been a cause unto us all of some much greater good. In this safe acquiescence then tarry thou ye Lords leisure, O my soul, without a murmur, and be content to dye dayly here for some short time, knowing the recompense of ye reward to be fulness of joy and life eternal with God & her I loved next him.

86.   .   May 4, 1693.

O Mr. Le Roy !

> Non est in medico semper relevetur ut æger ;
> Interdum doctâ plus valet arte malum.

Otherwise your good and apposite advice might well have wrought some sort of cure in me. But, Levis est iste dolor qui capere consilium potest, et clepere sese, saith Seneca. And mine alas ! is not of that complexion, my grief proceeding from such a radicated, invincible disease, as is incurable by any other medicament than that specifick soverain Catholicon, which gives poor mortals their quietus from all those numberless, intollerable evills humane life is subject to.

> Mors optima tunc est
> Cum petitur, vitæque piget, cum funus amatur.

And can it be more welcome than to those who, having been transcendantly supremely happy, are thence precipitated by one sad accident into its antipodal condition ? Oh no ! Wherefore (with ye Preacher) I praise the dead which are already dead more than ye living which are yet alive ; yea, am now come to think that better is he than both they who hath not yet been. For then (since you have quoted Job) shoud I have lain still and been quiet ; then shoud I have slept and been at rest, who now can take none ; then had I remaid innocent from those great and vile offences, which have provokd ye Almighty to afflict me with this sore calamity I labour under ; nor then shoud I have thus abhord my self and life, calling to mind the mispent years of my youth in the bitterness of my soul. But of all the ignorance, sin & follies of it I now repent in dust and ashes, and henceforth shall endeavour so to redeem ye past by a diligent improvement of my future days, that I may the sooner grow prepard and fit to be dissolvd and be with Christ, which is now the fervent prayer and only purpose of your unhappy friend and servant.

87.   May 6, 1693.

My dearest Sister Widdow

I must confess, as thoughtless as I am of every thing but what I've lost, my letter to my father was very, very (and yet I cant say too) long : its subject being so divine and copious as either not a little or nothing at all ought to have been said.

> For my dear Saints perfections were such
> I could not say enough, he hear too much.

Besides when once the vein was breathd, methought the more it ran ye more it easd, and therefore had not loosd ye ligament so soon but that I recollected it was pouring where twas full before, which made me reason thus with my afflicted heart :

> No ! to ye grave thy sorrows bear,
> As silent as they will be there,
> Rather than cost a fathers tear,
> Which by thee should be held so dear.

And so I brought it to that abrupt conclusion ; not that the matter faild ; for as her goodness was an unexhausted fountain, so it woud have furnishd endless eulogies. And therefore since the kindness of your letter gives me fresh occasion, let me here resume ye thread of that discourse, and try to tell you (what's ineffable) how irreparable, inestimable a loss ye Almighty hath been pleasd to bring upon me, a loss so repletely fraught with all those circumstances which constitute a finisht misery, that I'm not only what's called miserable, but ye large paraphrase and mapp of misery it self. O my dear sister! know then (for I can tell you news it may be, since I am now at liberty to speak out,) that I have lost ye very best of wives, the faithfullest of friends, and most delightfull of companions.   First in the wife all this. Tis said whoso findeth a good wife findeth a treasure, & is a sign unto him that he hath found favour with the Lord; for tho' houses and riches are the inheritances of fathers, yet a prudent wife is from ye Lord : that a good wife is a good portion, which shall be given in the lott of them that fear the Lord : that a silent & loving woman is a gift of ye Lord, and that there is nothing so much worth as a mind well instructed ; that well is he and happy shall he be that dwelleth with a wife of understanding ; that blessed is the man that hath a vertuous wife, for ye number of his days shall be double, (which if so, then indeed I may be said to have livd 8 years, 8 months & 12 days between the first of November, 1688 and ye 7th of March, 1692, O fatal day! let a cloud dwell on thee, let it not come into the number of ye months, let it not be joynd unto ye days of the year,): that a vertuous woman rejoyceth her husband, making him to fullfill the years of his life in peace : that the grace of a wife delighteth her husband, and her discretion will fatten his bones : that a faithfull modest woman is a double grace, and her continent mind cannot be valued : that as ye sun when he ariseth in ye high heaven, so is ye beauty of a good wife in ordering her house : that a faithfull wife is as a pillar of rest to her confiding husband : that when meekness and kindness are seated both in heart and tongue, then is her husband not like other men ; that tho' children and building of a city continue a mans name, yet a blameless wife is counted above them both ; the heart of her husband safely trusteth in her ; she'l do him good and no evill all her days ; her children shall arise up and call her blessed, her husband also, (I praised her). Thus much then and more have I lost in her as a wife. And as a friend and sweet companion, what not ? Her honourable breast was a repository as safe and secret as the grave she lies in ; whose conscience and fidelity I stood in much less fear of than my own. Her soul was so close knitt to mine that as her own she lovd me, even with a love (like mine for her, as God can witness,) passing the love of women. She had ye clearest understanding, ye readyest apprehension, exactest prudence and most vertuous will that ever soul was blest with. Many daughters had done vertuously, but she excelld them all. Her counsell, as it was founded upon the stable basis of a solid judgment, guided by the impulse of a happy genius, and meditated with a strong affection, did ever prove so rightly given, and by her prayers renderd so succcessfull, that in all deliberations of any moment she was my constant, only oracle. Her discourse was always reasonable and so well chosen, that it was a most effectual lenitive to ye heaviest pressures on my mind. Her chearfullness and gayety was so well timd and entertaining as did soon dissipate the cloudiest spleen.

> Her mirth was the pure spiritts of various witt,
> Yet never did her God or friends forget.

In fine her conversation through out was so usefull, easy, innocent & pleasing, and her mind so richly adornd with all those nice and necessary essentials which capacitate for ye great & noblest offices of friendship, that never was a pilgrimage on earth refresd with such a blest society ; and well, I find, might Syrach's son conclude that ye pipe & psalt'ry made sweet melody, but that a pleasant, joyfull tongue was much above them both ; as also that a friend and his companion never meet amiss ; but above them both too was such a wife as mine to me, her then happy husband. Yet this and more, much more, am I now quite bereft of. But language, alas ! thou art much too poor and scant, even in thy (for other themes) most hyperbolical expressions, justly to set forth either her great & various worthinesses or my forlorn undone condition caus'd by her final absence. However I find it is not possible amidst these killing thoughts, (as that she's dead and I still living; that she is no more for whom I only car'd to live, for ever gone who only was

> That cordial drop Heaven in my cupp had thrown,
> To make the nauseous draught of life go down ;

my joy, my life, my all,) longer to refrain from exclamations like those of David for his Absolom. O how my soul's distressed for thee, my dearest, faithfull, only, everlasting love; very pleasant, yea passing pleasant, hast thou been unto me in thy life time, O my dear wife Isabella, my wife, my friend Isabella ; would God I had died for thee; life and this world will henceforth only trouble me. O Isabella, my wife, my friend ; for thee my griefs blow fresh and new each morning that I wake; for thee I mourn as frequent and incessantly as the poor moaning turtle his lost, lov'd mate. Thy pretious memory I dayly celebrate with fruitless wishes, prayer, and weeping, respect & reverence.   But rouze thy self, my soul, and cast off nature for a while ; and then thou 'lt hear the saving voice of grace thus questioning thee: Why dost thou mourn? or why is it that thou grievest thus? Hath not the wise, the good, ye mercyfull and just great God done this? (who, as Ezekiel saith, doth nothing without a good and gracious cause.) Yes certainly. Let this then strike thee (as a sheep before his shearer) mute and dumb. Cease thy complaints; wipe away thy tears, and lament not any more, as those without all hope, as if thou discernedst not the promis'd great reward for blameless souls, not considering that the righteous are taken away from ye evill to come, that she whom thou bemoanest so is enterd into Peace, sleeping with Jesus, in company with the blest society of ye spirits of just men made perfect, that her righteous soul is in the hands of God, he having provd her and found her worthy for himself. And tho' the righteous are sometimes prevented with an early death, yet tis because they'r thereby calld to endless rest and bliss; for having pleasd God, and being belovd of him (living among sinners), she was translated. Neither is honourable age that which standeth

in length of time, or measured by a number of yeares : but wisdom is the
grey hair, and an unspotted life is old age. She being made perfect in a
short time fulfilld a long time. Thus the righteous which are dead shall
condemn the ungodly which are living; and youth that is soon perfected ye
many years and oldest age of the unrighteous; for they see the end of the
wise, but understand not what God in his counsel hath decreed of her, and
to what end the Lord hath set her in safety, how she's numbred among the
children of God, and her lott among the saints, enjoying a glorious kingdom.
and receiving a beautyfull crown of glory from her Lords hand.
Now after such a view and contemplation as this, what can I farther say
than that naked came I into this world and naked shall I return thence.
The Lord gave and the Lord hath taken away ; blessed be the name of the
Lord. O Lord have mercy upon me. Glory be to thee, O Lord !

88.   To my dear father, (ye very best of men.)   May 13, 1693.
      O Sir !

            The power and efficacy of so great and good
examples as I have had the advantage of in parents and a wife do far
transcend the most voluminous collections of all the wisest phylosophical
instructions : and yet too weak too have I found them all to help me in my
present sad necessity ; especially when my inquisitive, suspicious thoughts
fall on that fearfull consideration, viz. that those vile sins, which I through
ignorance & folly had comitted before the knowledge of her winning vertues
had converted me, may have provd the cause efficient of her being taken
from me, who was so good a wife, so tender a mother, so dutyfull a daughter,
so true a friend, and (in fine) so universal an instrunent of God Almightys
glory in her generation. O dire reflection ! But as one souls salvation is
of greater price in Gods wise mercifull esteem than the temporal satisfaction
of so numerous relations involved together, so hath he withdrawn their
common and my particular delight (withall inspiring that anxious thought)

on purpose to beget in me so great a hatred and abhorrence of all sin as may effectually produce a lasting firm repentance not to be repented of, thereby securing to himself my new recoverd soul, which otherwise, it may be, might have relapsed to its wallowing in the mire. And were it not for this interpretation, which his grace and mercy hath led my understanding to pick out of his late seeming wrathfull message, I'm sure the thought without it would long ere this have quite distracted me. But this is now become ye anchor of my floating soul, (which was adrift till this construction took the helm). This makes me ride securely between the Scylla and Charybdis of negligent presumption and a black despair. This makes me rather bless than deprecate the salutiferous antidote, knowing she's calld to endless happyness, and hoping it was sent to qualify me for that blest society she now enjoys. And this it is that renders me submissively resigned to his unerring providence, enabling me to say with (then forsaken) David (as to temporals), that tho all this be come upon me, yet have I not fallen off from thy commandments, or behav'd my self frowardly under thy corrections ; for which Gods holy name be bless'd and praisd. And thus, Sir, stands my heart as to the divine and spiritual part. Wherefore let me intreat you, Sir, rather to joy than grieve yourself because of me,; tho' as to humane considerations, I must confess, I have nevertheless such dismal feelings as I woud for the future make no mention of, were they recountable, my heart being ever most intensely busy on its loss, and, instead of valuing what she hath gaind with that it can but for a time endure, will fix upon comparing its days past of happyness with those which are to come of misery. And how tolerable, how comfortable, a scene that needs must represent, I can appeal to no such judicature as your own experience, our cases being (if you can pardon ye comparison) parallels throughout, distinguishd only on my side by this undeniable aggravation, that as God did mercifully ordain you two shoud live together enjoying many tranquile years in love and friendship, our hopefull growth was most untimely killed before the blossoms of our loves were yet well set. And after this must nature be enjoynd a senseless apathy? Must she in the season of her keenest sensibility feel her essential vital part torn from her without being sufferd to express some struggle or reluctancy? Must she neither grieve, nor pine, nor languish, tho' backed with the authority of our great Exemplar? For doth not the disciple whom our Saviour loved testify that Jesus Christ himself did groan in spirit, and was troubled, ney wept, for his friend Lazarus, whom he, however, knew he could (and after four days lying in the grave did) raise to life again? Will my ungovernable sighs and tears offend him then for the death of quite as righteous a soul, whom I can n'ere resuscitate from that irremiable (sic) estate? If they that sow in tears shall reap in joy, if blessed are all they who mourn for they shall be comforted, and if one deep calleth another, why may I not hope ye deep of my misery shoud rather move the deep of his mercy than farther chastisement? And as all the sorrow my poor heart conceives is but the satisfying a debt most justly due to the deserving memory of her who had made me so very happy in her life time, can gratitude offend the highest justice so long as tis not paid by my forgetting what I owe to him? Ney, the very remembrance of her doth continually exhibitt fresh matter for thanks and praise and glory to ye Lord of Heaven; my thankfullest acknowledgments and heartiest praises to his stupendious, providential goodness, which singled me from out the race of humane kind to bless with the rich (tho' short) loan of so inestimable a treasure; and glory to his omnipotence, which fully shewd it self in making such perfection and keeping it so spotlessly untainted from all the frailties incident to humane nature; for was it not miraculous to be so supernaturally good as she was? Thus in death, as well as life, was she appointed my tutelary angell; who living had converted me from vice, and won me to the love of vertue; and after death had left such deep, indeleble impressions of her matchless worthyness in my heart as will most safely guard it from all seducing, vain temptations for the time to come. May I

Vol. I.   I

not then for so beneficient a Saint keep Holy-days of weeping, prayer and thanksgiving? And if ere we are to meet again (which God alone can tell), how much ashamd should I appear to have been wanting in ye least punctillio towards her, who, I am quite assurd as much as if I could have seen it, would have o'repaid me in all observances of gratitude and kindness, had God thought fit to have put her in my wretched place. Can I lament or half enough regret the loss of her whose presence was my pride, whose conversation was my Paradice, and whose breast I found the harbourer of such an heart as ravished mine when a blest inmate there, and wanting now that sweet retreat wanders most restlessly from place to place, just like a helpless fawn which late hath lost the hind. O Sir! my pen could dwell for ever (as its dictator must) on this sweet, sad, tormenting, pleasing subject, (for tis not quite without its rays of some complacency, tho' grief and sadness are throughout predominant). But recollecting how very much I misbehavd my self when last I took this liberty forces me to a conclusion. Only let me subjoin this just request, that you woud not count me a discontented Belial under those shews of resignation I profess. No sir, be assurd that were there no searcher of all hearts, I love and honour, reverence and respect you much too much, not only as my father, but as that noblest of relations you were pleasd to allow me in one of yours to Mr. Porter, to deal with any unsincerity or dissimulation towards you. Therefore, pray believe me, Sir, that from the bottom of my soul (in my sedater thoughts) I with submission acquiesce in and rest intirely satisfyd with his wise dispensations towards me in all events. But mutinous, rebellious nature will be obtruding her (sometimes) irresistable complaints; and therefore, whenever I lett fall the least expression interfering with, or any ways repugnant to, the tenor of my avowed faith, look upon it as proceeding from a man of sorrow, who out of the abundance of his pain and grief hath spoken hitherto, but who in the height of all hath ever said, God is wise, God is mercifull, Gods will be therefore done on earth as tis in Heaven.   I am no more I.

Postscript. Sir, having made Cross the limner take a copy in miniature from the picture Brook drew at Bury for my dear wife, and being very desirous to have something engraved on the backside of it which might be some epitomy of her beautifull soul, I have sent you this inclosed (being well acquainted with your happy genius to poetry) not for an approbation but your correction. I have hewn it rough out ot the rock, you are desird to adorn and pollish it. The size of the paper being that of the picture will confine you to a dozen lines to represent infinite vertues in. Ah Sir! Si propius stes, te capiet magis. Or, Si propius steteris, te ceperit magis. The words were these.

> O mihi fida comes, merito nunc sancta beata !
> Felix morte tuâ, neque in hunc servata dolorem,
> Fato (quod volui luctu) Deus obstitit æquo,
> Mors aliter jucunda foret nec vivere vellem.

Mrs. Isabella Hervey.
> None but Apelles shoud have drawn thy face ;
> Thy mind Lukes pencil coud not too well grace ;
> Rachel nor Judith were not half so fair ;
> Hester such love in all did never share ;
> Thou wise and prudent as Rebecca wert ;
> More faith and truth nere dwelt in Sarah's heart ;
> So many vertues thy rich soul possest,
> Thy husband's heart in thine did safely rest ;
> Thou didst him good (no evill) all thy days ;
> Envy her self thy worth was forced to praise.
> O virtue ! all thy daughters have done well,
> But this, even thee, her mother did excell.

O decus atque dolor ! in te interii.

Domina Isabella Hervey, conjux facilimis, jucundissimis, suavissimis moribus ; summa integritatis, humanitatis, fidei ; liberalissima, sanctissima, prudentissima ; omni genere virtutum ornatissima.

*Siccine fida cadis conjux ? nec nostra tenent te
  Vota, dolor, gemitus, immaculatus amor.
Sancta morare anima ; en propero (charrissima) tecum
  Vivere cum nequeam, te moriente, mori.

89.   To my father.

Alas Sir !

      There's not a day but as it comes does more and more acquaint me that my wound is mortal, and therefore 'tis all one what methods I pursue in dressing of it; or if a difference there be, neglecting it would work ye speedyest cure ; for if my grief were suffered to lye bound up within my heart and never opend, ye sore would quickly rankle, and so effect a lasting ease. But why am I again beginning on a subject which may do you some harm and can do me no good, an argument sufficient (were I capable of reason) to persuade an everlasting silence. Here then let me begin to end it. The enclosed is designed for the backside of a lockett of a yet less size than the paper. Pray, sir, afford it the same sincere opinion you gave as to ye verses for the reverse of her picture ; for not a word shall be engravd untill it first obtains your Imprimatur. I thought one or two Laconick sentences woud be proper for the lockett. But on ye backside of ye picture I was desirous some fuller memorandum might be made of all those various graces God and nature had adornd her with, to remain in our family as an incentive for the future daughters of it to emulate in ye imitation of. Something of that sort I must beg your assistance in. They are both for my private wearing, and shall be shown to none without your leave, being still if anything, sir, etc.

---

   * These four lines are added in John Hervey's writing, and do not appear to be part of the intended inscription for the miniature. S.II.A.II.

The words to be engravd on ye lockett were as followeth :—

Domina Isabella Hervey. O decus! O dolor! Una tecum tota domûs nostræ gloria occidit. Multæ fœminæ egerunt probe, tu vero omnes superästi, dilecta Deo, chara mortalibus. Ob. 7 March, 1692.

90. To the Bishop of Norwich, Dr. John Moore, on a visit he made, and two books he gave me, on the death of my matchless wife.

My Lord

The kind and charitable civility your Lordship shewed me before your leaving of this place, met with so sensible a reception that I cannot satisfy my self without giving you ye trouble of my acknowledgments for it, and withall to assure your Lordship that neither were ye arguments your books containd without their answerable effects ; which, considering they were perusd by a mind so prepossessed by grief as (till then) refusd all councell or consolation, is no slight instance of their force and energy, they having at last obligd my reason as well as faith to subscribe to that safe and peace-giving conclusion, viz. that as God is the source and fountain of all wisdom and mercy, so he disposeth all events, whether of good or seeming evill unto men, according as the circumstances of their present condition require ; and that how bitter soever it hath pleasd him in his unerring providence to mingle the cupp of my chastisement, (even to ye making me drunk with wormwood, so that I staggerd at the unintelligible surprizing evill which befell me,) yet I trust in his infinite mercies twas sent with the gracious design of working for me in the end that good we cannot purchase at too dear a price. This I am sure was the highest I could pay, for better was my faithfull friend and faultless wife to me than ten sons, father or mother, riches, health, or honours.

I am, etc.

91.   To Mrs. Fox.

Madam   July 22, 1693.

If you can but suppose a possibility of forgetfulness where, even through natural instinct, ye benefits you've done ye parents (one of them at least) must be for ever sensibly rememberd by ye conscious offspring of a match your self with so much kindness and success first laid ye corner stone of; what then shoud others apprehend who have nothing that can justly recommend them to your memory, so as but to make oblivion ye least failure in you which in those who only ever knew Mrs. Fox would prove a fault (like that of sin) inseparable from its own punishment; and therefore to prevent that which might so pardonably happen (tho' not innocently, for I shoud receive much hurt by it) from you toward me in this kind, I have taken ye liberty you gave me to remind you there is still such a one in ye world (and that's all) whom once you thought not altogether unworthy of ye noblest and most valuable possession that yet ere came within ye gift of Providence; a good so perfect and compleately qualifyd to consummate my earthly happyness, as from its presence and privation ye rise and period of all my joy bears date. But tho' ye sun of my prosperity went down so soon, yet am I not ye less indebted to your goodness, which helpd to turn ye ballance of my destiny when at its nicest crisis, an obligation which hath ingraved it self with indelible characters in ye heart of, Madam, yours etc.   Give me leave to beg my humble service to Mr. Fox.   My daughter woud send you so many and so great thanks for ye honour of your letter that she dares not undertake it till riper thoughts can dictate them.   Your godson presents his duty.

92.   To Mr. Fox.

Sir   Sept. 9. 1693.

This is to return you thanks for ye trouble you gave yourself in sending me an account of what you had done in Lincolnshire; to ye particulars of which I need say no more than that what repairs you thought necessary I hope are ordered; and for a steward, Mr. Wayet, I find by a letter from Mr. Shore of ye 2d of August last, is willing to accept ye management of the estate; but hearing no house was kept at Aswarby, expects an allowance for his board over & above ye £50 per annum salary; which being a new proposal I referd him to your self when you shoud be on ye place; in ye mean time I have sent Mr. Thomas Burslem no other answer to his desire of knowing whether he was to be continued any longer than Michaelmass, but that timely notice should be given him whenever it shoud be thought fit to make an alteration. As to ye letter concerning ye tolls, I think ye proposal of those officious gentlemen who woud procure a tennant that will free the inhabitants from that custom and yet take a lease of them at ye present rent for 7 years ought by no means to be closd with; for ye grantees privity to such an exemption (upon condicions too) may in futurity be construed to amount unto a concession of what they aim to divest us of; the abolition of which custom they would be in ye right to compass only by taking ye trouble to collect the proffits for ye term proposd. That tis a just due ye constant payment will evince; and that ye tennants of Quarrington and Holdingham are priviledged prove nothing for them. Therefore since the duty hath been questioned, tis my opinion ye best way will be to have it settled by a tryal. Ranceby, if corn keeps the price, will be one of ye greatest pennyworths in all that country, there being a vast extent of land for a very small rent; but, as improveable as that and many other parts of that estate are, my father can never with convenience compass the whole, nor have I now any inclination he shoud do so were he able, the foundation of all my purposes on that side being taken away.

I am etc.

93.   Dear Mr. Duncombe

Sept. 9, 1693.

The sence of what I've lost hath so benumnd & stupified ye faculties of my soul, rendered me so lifeless and inactive, so tepid and indifferent to all ye future accidents of my life, that I am sometimes tempted to believe the metamorphosis of Niobe and Philomel were not fictitious, but realities; for those things (whether of joy or grief, good or ill success,) which would have made deep impression heretofore do not so much as superficially affect me now, the kindness of your friendship only excepted, of which you lately gave me such gratefull, acceptable proofs as have for ever won and bound me to be yours, even to ye creating some sort of solicitude in me for ye interests of my country, since yours are more immediately involved in and blended with them. And this I can most faithfully assure you is no mean expression for a heart in my condition to make you, it not having conceivd a wish since ye fatal privation of its cheifest glory and only treasure but to follow where that is gone before; and tis but natural, methinks, when ye main root which nourishd all ones happiness is cut away, for the branches of it (delight and love of life) to wither and decay: indeed when my condition was a thorough refutation of Horace's aphorism—Nihil est ab omni parte beatum—twas worth my care to study its duration; but now that's totally reversed my prayers are turned into good Simeons Nunc dimittis. Till that good time shall come, the whole expence of mine will be bestowd in begging God Almighty's grace to qualify me for the blest communion of his saints, where (at my safe arrival) her joy as well as mine may be augmented (if capable of any) by contemplating ye wonderfull effects of her religious virtuous example, when on earth, by whose prolifick influence my crude and dormant seeds of grace came first to germinate, and which, through the kindly warmth of that zealous affection I bear her sacred memory, I hope are daily ripening for ye harvest of salvation, her sweet, sad remembrance being a sovereign antidote against ye subtlest poysond sins ; for the whole world is not able to exhibit a temptation which can deserve the name of vertue to resist, unless it be my invincible, immoderate regret and grief, which proves the Hydra's head, and, like Sisiphon's stone, rolls back again upon me after my utmost endeavours to keep it at some allowable distance; to remove it quite, I cannot say I would, it being to me ye best companion I can supply her absence by ; nay, such a complacency do I find in the representation of her bright, spotless image to my thoughts that at once I'm grievd and pleasd ; and so much the latter (altho ye first predominates) that I shoud think it a second loss if I had not her dear idea to entertain and cheat my tedious hours withall. That you may never be reduced to this my sad necessity my heartyest wishes are made you ; and if ye intercessional requests of a forlorn wretch, whose vileness hath left no room to hope for any reward from works of supererogation, can be aright available, you'l not only escape the loss of your fellow-traveller, (to whom I'm not less a faithfull servant than I am also indebted to* for her great kindness in the beginning of my sorrows,) but also pass your pilgrimage in such mutual, durable tranquility, love and friendship as was once ye portion of etc.

94.   Speech to Bury Corporation at my being first chosen Burgess, 31 March, 1694.

Mr. Alderman and you Gentlemen of ye Corporation,

     The general custom of my predecessors in ye station ye have placed me hath left it as a kind of duty on me (altho their most unable successor) to say something to ye upon this occasion. Since then it must be so, give me leave to observe to ye that (for ought I know) it might have made me near as proud as I am wrongly thought to be, could I with justice have appropriated this honour ye have done me to any merit of

---

* Mrs. Duncombe's name seems to be accidentally omitted here. —S.H.A.H.

my own. But I am yet too rightly conscious of my wants to think I hold
your confidence by such a title, knowing how equally so groundless a presumption would taste of ignorance and vanity. I'm therefore full as well
content (for all our sakes) to owe this great expression of your kindness to
ye gratefull sense ye still retain of your good friend and my dear father's
past services; who in ye retrospection of his life (I can assure yee) meets
with few passages that present themselves with greater comfort to his
thoughts than those wherein he labourd with the utmost diligence, affection
and fidelity to advance the interests of this Town and Corporation ; whose
good example in all things, but more especially in this, I feel such powerfull motions of zeal and emulation successfully to imitate him in, that their
effects (I hope) may grow in time to yield such fruits as may in some degree
both vindicate your choice and help my insufficiency; a choice concurrd
in with such unlooked for unanimity, that ye very manner wherewith ye
have reposed this most important trust in me is no less acceptable to me
than the matter of it ; because it gives so promising and pleasing an
earnest of that future good intelligence I shall endeavour to restore among
ye. [Note—There were great heats about ye choice of their Town Clarke.]
For which or any other office I may hereafter be found usefull to ye in, your
love and approbation will most abundantly requite me. And such returns
alone I ought to wish might pass for current payment in exchange of
favours done, since I have nought at present but my naked thanks to offer
ye ; but they are tenderd with such sincerity and hearty gratitude as you'd
do well to afford a satisfy'd reception to. I'le only add (to do both you and
me some right) this firm assurance, that ye have cast ye lott on such a
man, who always thought and may most safely say, Curst may he be who
for any by-end or self consideration shall 'ere assist in or be consenting to
ye removal of those sacred land marks, which ye unwearied care &
admirable wisdom of our ancestours have so judiciously & critically laid
between the just and necessary prerogatives of ye Crown and ye inestimable

happy priviledges of ye People ; a sort of Geography which hath of late
employd my strictest search and closest study, being fixdly purposd according to ye best of my perception and ability impartially to endeavour ye
maintenance and preservation of both in their allowd extents or limitations ;
ye golden mean appointed being ye only recipe to keep this nations
constitution in a lasting health and happyness, both which ye have bound
me to wish ye all with all my heart.

95.   Mr. Hopes   Jan. 9, 1693.
Having receivd a letter from Mr. Smith whom I
appointed Chaplain to the Hospital, wherein he discovers some apprehension that his name sake intends to supplant him in that employment by
endeavouring to gain votes enough among the clergy concernd to disseise
him, this is to let them know that I am something surprizd to find any
thing of such a nature shoud be transacted without my privity, expecting to
have that deference (at least) paid me to be acquainted with and consulted
upon all alterations ; which I desire you would inform ye rest of, in the
meantime declaring all proceedings void wherein my concurrence hath not
first been asked.

96.   On ye death of ye very best of men & fathers.

Dear Mr. Duncombe   Aug. 1694.
Your pious precepts and ye affectionate kindness
with which they were urged might justly have expected an earlier acknowledgment ; but promising my self your discernment could not wrong my
gratitude so much as to place ye omission to any neglect or forgetfulness,
(from both which my heart so throughly justifys me as I shall make no excuse for either,) and having once before so misbehavd my self when passion
dictated, I thought it not adviseable to trust my self again when ye fire
was freshly kindled, being made to perceive the ignorance and folly of so

offensive a conclusion to God's omnipotence as my amazed and wounded heart seduced me to, when in his wisdom he saw fit to extinguish all my glory, and with one stroak of providence to deprive me of that only treasure I valued as my all; for at that sad privation (you, I fear, can witness for me as well as my own remembrance) I blindly us'd to say, Fate had not in reserve an earthly accident could touch me sensibly again, (that being fraught with such accumulative misery as I supposd woud drown all sence of future ills.) But tho' I justly lookd upon

Ille dies primus Lethi primusque malorum,

yet—Hic labor extremus—& as Cardan said, Fatigatum magnis adversis oppressit me hæc extrema infelicitas. After having lost such a wife, and in that wife such a friend,

Heu ! genitorem, omnis curæ casusque levamen
Amitto Anchisen—

and as at every turn I want his counsel, blessing & direction, I cannot help expostulating thus with his memory:

Hic me, pater optime, fessum
Deseris heu !

For he knew how unable my first loss had renderd me to discharge those duties are now more imediately incumbent on me; and had the world askd him, who knew every corner of my heart, whether £30,000 could have shown itself a Catholicon for my distemper, he would have told them they spoke without book. However I have had a great honour done me in ye very rumour and supposition of ye thing, which would have over atton'd with any man that had not placed his greatest in being rightly understood; but I find ye sole reward I am to expect from that necessary virtue I exercise on that subject must result from my own conscience, which, whenever I look into, yields me ye pleasantest prospect I have ever seen since I beheld the cause. If I depend on any forreign comfort, tis in the reflection of your being left my friend, which sufficiently barrs my having to say, All is lost; and that you shoud make ye exception was always ye predominant wish of, Sir, etc.

97. To Sir John Playters.

Sir   Oct. 18, 1694.

I cannot but own tis some surprise to me that you shoud never answer any of those letters which brought you notice of my desire that you woud provide both ye principall and interest money due upon your security against ye next Michaelmas term, which I acquainted you with in June last. My occasions for it are indispenseable, I being to make up the purchase money of an estate I have articled for lying in Lincolnshire, by which Articles I have obligd my self to pay ye money this next term, otherwise to loose ye benefit of them, which will prove greatly to my damage, and that will center whence soever ye disappointment proceeds. I have all along depended on your money, as silence is (constructively) consent, and therefore hope you have taken effectuall care in it. This messenger comes on purpose to bring your answer what time in the term it will be ready, and to show you how ye account betwixt us standeth. Sir, if there be any omissions made by my father of any entries of payments in his book, I shall most willingly allow for any receipt you have of his not therein accounted for, those being all the payments within ye knowledge of, Sir, etc.

98. To Sir Roger Potts.

I am concernd to find that anything which came from me shoud give occasion to variety of thoughts, for all my meanings are direct & simple. Therefore give me leave to say, Sir, if any suggestions resulting from them supposd any sinister design in me to wrong you of a

scruple, or lay any difficulties upon you but such as ye nature of old unstated
accounts necessitate, (where former transactors are dead and no other
guides remaining but (as it seems) imperfect books,) they both deceivd you
and misrepresented my intentions, which are just towards all men, and not
only so but would be friendly to Sir Roger Potts.   If you receivd but something of an accompt from me, it was because nothing more appeard where-
out twas drawn, and therefore, unless the spirit of divination had been upon
me, could ne'er have known of that payment for which (by Mr. Batt) you
produced a receipt dated ye 4th Oct. 1689 ; an allowance whereof you will
find in ye last paper I sent you by him ; and should have done ye same for
that you mention, (supposd to have been made in 1688,) had ye same evidence
been brought by you, or my book afforded any testimony concerning it,
which Mr. Batt can assure you it doth not.   If there be any such thing as
a farther mistake in ye account betwixt us, or any receipt lost or mislaid,
I should be as glad it were rectified as your self, most stedfastly beleiving all
unjust gain (like moths in cloath) consumes that which harbours it ; shall
therefore make diligent search among all my dear fathers letters to see if
any of them can give better light into this affair.   In ye mean time I hope
you will order ye discharge of your security out of hand, having
covenanted for ye payment of a considerable sum of money this terme, of
which this must make a part.   But of this I hope no more need be said than
of my assuring you I am still   Yours etc.

99.

Dear Mr. Gage   (My cousin Germyn)   London, Dec. 18, 1694.
                You hold me by a tenure paramount to all ye
brittle tyes of casual relation ; and that is by your own merit, which (alone)
without ye alliance of our familys would have given you a just title to my
best wishes for you, and a most affectionate inclination towards you.   There
is a friend that sticketh closer than a brother ; and under that character I

am pleased we may reciprocally consider each other, a blessing I could never have found vanity enough to have made ye supposition of, had not your kindness & professions authorizd so agreeable a faith in me, which never staggers but when I look into ye object of your friendship, which opens so jealous a scene of disproportion between it & and that of mine as tempts me to infidelity, which nothing but my knowledge of your goodness could reassure me from, and give me hopes of a lasting correspondence, notwithstanding ye invitations to one & ye mutuall (which should be) benefits to be expected from it are so unequally promising ; but ye greater will be your vertue, ye less satisfaction you can pay your self with from our commerce. I am very sensible of ye kind part you take in my recovery* ; and since it hath pleased God to spare my (hitherto) worthless life, I hope ye repreive was granted out of his prescience, that I might live to find favour enough in his sight to obtain grace sufficient to consecrate ye remainder of my days to his service and that of my friends ; whereby if any good may accrue to you or yours, twill make health ye welcomer to etc.

100. To the Earl of Sunderland.

My Lord   Jan. 21, 1694.

Having lately recoverd several of ye deeds and writings out of those peoples hands who so illegally rifled my uncle Mr. John Herveys house after his decease, among ye rest I found a bond, wherein he stood joyntly bound with your Lordships mother, ye late Countess of Sunderland, for ye payment of £300 & interest to one Mr. John Hodgkins, bearing date ye 25th April, 1667 ; and to indemnify him against this obligation her Ladyship gave him counter security. However in April, 1674, my uncle was compelld to discharge the same by paying ye said £300 to one Josiah Key & Joan his (then) wife, ye relict and adminis-

---

* A marginal note in John Hervey's handwriting says, small pox.

tratrix of ye same Hodgkins, as by ye release thereof to my uncle appeareth. And cases of this nature deserving ye justest consideration, I take ye liberty of giving your Lordship this trouble to acquaint you with it; submitting its merits intirely to whatever determination your Lordships wisdom and justice shall think fit to make concerning it; as I also do in relation to another debt of £103, due from your Lordships sonn, ye late Lord Spencer, to, my Lord,   Yours etc.

101.   To the Marquiss of Hallifax.

My Lord   Jan. 26, 1694.

         Having retrievd several of ye evidences relating to ye estate of my late uncle Mr. John Hervey, which in a lawless manner were taken out of ye house he livd in soon after his decease; and finding ye inclosed papers amongst them; I take this liberty humbly to move your Lordship for your direction & advice, both as to ye person properly to be applyd to, and ye fittest method to be observd in procuring ye repayment of ye sum still due upon them; which as it was lent out of friendship deserves ye justest consideration; and that I am so sure of from your Lordship that I need add no more than begg pardon for this trouble.

102.   To Doctor Felton.   (My dear father having living & dying desird me to marry again, there being but one son by my first ever-dear wife.)

Sir   London April 9, 1695.

         This is to thank you for ye kind overture you made me (by yours of ye 31st past) of a correspondence so much my interest both for profit and pleasure's sake industriously to cultivate. In order whereunto, (remembring Dr. Taylor sets down usefullness as a prime ingredient in ye composition of friendship,) I have made my self so far serviceable to you as to give Mrs. Baron ye oculer (tis your part to acquaint her with ye actual) satisfaction of your feelings for her. I have also put in your claim to a right of carving for your self; but shoud you be advised to sue ye promise and ever come to cast her in an action upon ye case, let me caution you to refresh your notices in anatomy, conjecturing you may meet with difficult dissections. Beware likewise in ye interim how farr you indulge to silent admiration; for it may be, I can experimentally tell you, that nothing can be more uneasy than — tacitum nutrire sub pectore vulnus. Tis an inhuman violence we offer to our hearts in stiffling that which, if disclosed, might vent a part of its oppression; for—quo magis tegitur, tanto magis æstuat ignis. Admiration is a dangerous guest; as subtle an intruder as sin its self, and (like it) when once entertaind (whatere restrictions we prescribed it in its approaches) usurps a power we dreamd not of allowing, and makes us slaves to what distroys our quiet. But it seems you (I was going to say we) are past taking ye advantage of resisting its beginnings. Wherefore there's now no other choice but Cowleys councel. Tell her as boldly that tis she as I can you sincerely that I am yours etc.

103. To Mrs. Edon. May 20, 1695.

There's nothing comes from Mrs. Edon but carrys with it such an intrinsick value of its own as needs no forreign help to recomend it. However, I must confess, ye favour this is to thank you for did so far supererrogate as (by its application) to create an accidental merit, equivalent even to ye substantial part of most others. When this is said, I need not use many arguments to convince you of my exactness in ye execution of that agreeable clause in my comission, as to ye delivery of your inclosed by my own hand; ye circumstance proves ye fact; and twould be little less impertinent to tell you I could not comply with ye other part of your command, as to ye making any amendment in it, without being guilty of as vain and injudicious an undertaking as his was who would attempt a

Vol. I. L

correction of ye Magnificat; or to illustrate ye perfection of it in its kind
by an apter simile, I thought it faultless as ye correspondent twas addressd
to; no product of your mind or pen can err on ye defective side; and if
ought should prove superfluous, it must be ye fruitless (but thats not your
but my fault) repetition of a name I am sure she overlookd, if ye destructive Brillants treated them with ye same regardless usage their bearer
thinks he meets with; but her indifference (they say) is an universal griev-
ance, and as such is borne with alleviating, pleasing hopes by yours etc.

> Cease to defend an amorous heart
>   Against a second flame ;
> Where two may claim an equal part
>   Without reproach or shame.

104.   Mrs. Felton to Mrs. Edon.
Madam   Boxted, May 24, 1695.
            I hope you are so just to me as to believe I would
not loose so pleasing a correspondence by any neglect. Tho' I was so forget-
full as not to send a direction when I came out of town, it was not long
before I orderd one, from which I propose a great deal of happyness, if,
according to your promise, you will make use of it often. I cant complain
for want of news, since I hope ye dulness of ye town will make you think
of leaving it ye sooner, that we may be happy with your company in the
country, which I believe you have not been often enough in to know how
welcome letters are; none can be so truly sensible of it as those you oblige
with yours, which favour I hope, Madam, you will not refuse to continue to,
Madam, your etc.

105.   To Dr. Felton.   June 1, 1695.
            Knowing twoud not be reasonable for a debtor
to expect you shoud give further credit to him, (who, whenso'ere he pays,

must for ye standard milld you lend return you an alloyd clipt coyn,) untill he has repaid in tale (at least) what he cannot in weight, makes me to send this to ballance ye accompt between us as to number; but for ye intrinsick value, (unless your goodness will accept of will for deed, or satisfy your self by ye pleasure of pleasing,) that's a due I know not how to cancell; which makes me fear when you are casting up your costs, (tho' they're not great, for the more valuable things come easy from you,) & profitt in our correspondence, you'l find it so like ye Indians traffick with ye Europeans, that you'l grow quickly weary of bartering gems and ingotts for glass and tinsell. That this may carry with it some tincture (I term it, not supposing your passion of ye deepest dye) of a merritt, Mrs. Baron's name shall here adorn it, which is more than her looks have done their wearer since you left this place. She calls her ail a faint, uneasy sickness at her heart, which by ye description I have christend love or admiration (very near relations). But how come I to name ye last again? That common breaker of ye peace of hearts! So irresistible and so notorious an offender against some of his Majesties good subjects, that even ye power and authority of one whom he hath made a Justice in 3 counties has been baffled by it, whenever he endeavourd to bind it over to its good behaviour.

> Nil admirari prope res est una Numici,
> Solaque quœ possit facere et servare beatum,

is a Gospell-truth of Horace's; and I (am) so well convinced of it, that dispairing of a second Phœnix (in ye same age) to be my lott and consequently ye object of my happyness as well as admiration, I stedfastly determined (in order to secure all ye future quiett a state of universal indifference could afford) to commence misogynist from ye fatal day which rob'd me of that meritorious mediatrix, whose winning virtues had power alone to reconcile me to her sex. I was an atheist to their goodness till she converted me, and being a libertine, I judgd accordingly.

> The loose wild paths of pleasure I persued,
> Till Isabella taught me to be good.

But I'm not only cured of so injurious an incredulity, but can give faith even to ye supposd fiction of ye Phœnix herself from what I have seen of late.

> Some angell copied (when she dy'd) each grace,
> And moulded every feature from her face ;
> Her soul too like hers by all that I could see,
> If Heaven coud make throughout an other she.

Yes! She's her very counterpart, ye wonderfull resultancy of her sacred ashes, sure !

> Sweetness, truth and every grace
> Which time and use are wont to teach,
> The eye may in a moment reach,
> And read distinctly in her face.

> Quidquid agit, quoquo vertigia movit,
> Componit furtim, subsequiturque decor.

But why do I begin a theame which would employ eternity to finish (without any hyperbole); but were it one twere here no fault, for Tum hyperbole virtus cum res ipsa de qua loquendum est naturalem modum excessit. These last words, which would have been a full excuse for such a fault, (coud one committ any unless on ye hand of a defective extremity in treating such infinity of decencies & fitnesses,) admonish me of one I'm sure you must find me guilty of, and that is exceeding both ye bounds of a letter & your kind patience, which ought to be modestly & tenderly managd by, Sir, etc.

106. To Mr. Cullum, after a visitt he made Mrs. F. at Boxted. Causa patet.

Dear Brother Nobbs (at least)   June 4, 1695.

         That our correspondence may livelily represent two colts a nabling one another, ye widdow* shall be my theam as ye maid* was yours; and because I would not bite where I should only tickle, [(remembering how much ye worst on't Tom had with Jack (in Sir John Suckling) concerning ye eligibility of whole or chew'd meat, foul or fresh water to wash in, a nutt uncrackd or one where ye squirrel has been, or (if in prison) whether ye common side is to be chosen before a private room,)] intend to wave comparisons of preference as you discreetly shun'd metaphors in treating of a subject illustrable by nothing but its self.

> Your tropes might blazon common beauties, she
> Makes pearls and planetts humble heraldry.

No, brother Nobbs, since you so pleasingly clawd my itching by ye ingenuous confession of her humours surpassing the dress, (tho that was very agreeable,) I shant scratch you by chalking out differences in running of parallels; ney, had you but brib'd me with ye repetition (for tho I know all she says must rather loose than gett by one) of any one apothegm or bon-mot which she feasted you with in that delicious tete-a-tete conversation you mention, for ought I know it might have byassed me to allow that, as my maid hath no equal, your widow (quasi vidua) hath no superiour; and this being her greatest character, would you, Tom, who pretend to love her so well, destroy it by giving her a head over her. But were yee half an hour together, did you say? a happy rogue indeed! Alass, I have asked more questions upon ye various conjectures of my fancy than you are aware of, ... , this being her picture,

---

* Here is a marginal note by John Hervey, "Sister Elwes. Mrs. Felton."

> Seu quicquid fecit, sive est quodcunque locuta,
> Maxima de nihilo nascitur historia.

For could your sight be dead to such a quick
And well tun'd face, such moving rhetorick,
Did not each look a flash of lightning feel,
Which tho' it spares ye body's sheath yet melts ye steel,
Thy soul must this confess, or grant thy sense
Corrupted with its objects excellence ;
Strange magick which can make five senses lye
Conjurd within ye circle of an eye.

Where ye temptation to idolatry works so strongly upon our reason,
apostacy looses both its name and nature.

> She attacks ye heart so irresistable a way,
> As without guilt does constancy betray.

And if thou becamest not this laudable heretick upon reading her but half
an hour, a worse character is your due, and that is (you must give me leave
to tell you as a friend) a dull atheist.

> Whene're those wounding eyes so full
> Of sweetness you did see,
> Had you not been profoundly dull,
> You'd have run mad like me.

Perhaps you think all ye attributes of virtue, witt & beauty false, if they
appear not just as they are represented in your mirrour of vidual perfection :
but you must know

> All hearts alike all beauties do not move,
> There is a secret simpathy in love ;
> The powerfull load-stone cannot move a straw,
> No more than jett ye trembling needle draw ;
> Her graces only on my heart can act,
> All other women it in vain attack.

You'l say, Every one as he likes. But remember, Tom, ye man spoke it upon kissing a cow; and tis a question whether he made her ye compliment after ye fourth calving or not. When I considerd your judgment in its native state of health & liberty, I feard ye soundness of it might have created me a rival; but upon recollection of ye prepossessions tis diseasd with, I began to change that fear for an other. Methinks I see you (instead of devouring every look & word) with your eyes fix'd Bury-ward (tho' she both lookd on and talkd to you) counting how many tedious lazy hours must pass before your day of permission would come again, ruminating upon some chance hitt she made when you last saw her, and privately applauding it by a silent sigh, and crying Gods-ooks (to your self); her vein of good sense is like her sister widdows inexhaustible cruse; and all this time greater rarities lost upon you by ye company you were in, which you know no more of than how often you shake your foot or bite your thumb nail. But I'le be even with you next time I get into ye little room, and be as much at Boxted there as you were at Bury when at Boxted. What woud some people have given for that you valu'd not.

> So have I seen ye lost clouds pour
> Into ye sea a fruitless shower;
> And sailors careless of that rain,
> For which poor shepperds pray in vain.

The application (brother Nobbs) may serve both you and your faithfull kinsman in love.

107. To Doctor Felton.

Ah Doctor! June 18, 1695.

       Twas a prophetick calculation you made in fixing ye period of our mutual gayeties, when you said, By this time I presume tis time for you and I to be serious. For you'd no sooner beat ye measure, but that nice pegg which tun'd my humour to those chearfull straines I

lately playd to you in was lowered by a hand (justly indifferent to ye
meaness of ye performer) which turn'd my harmony to discord and confusion.
The pleasing scheme my fancy drew from ye imaginary possession of my
new discoverd Canaan began t' enliven and refresh my drooping, weary
pilgrimage, and seemd to bid me hope a life of golden days again.   Whereupon

> Tandem lætus ait, Dii nostra incepta secundent.

But fate (it seems) designd to show me ye tantalizing prospect from ye top
of Pisgah only, which, had my heedless heart suspected, it would have made
much stricter covenants with my eyes when I ascended Nebo; for I must
own they ne're surveyd ye charming country but made such frequent, just
reports of its inviting beauties to my attentive heart, as made it wish (it ere
it must transplant itself, the sun being sett which cheard ye kindly soil
wherein its first sown love took root & grew so prosperously) to have its
tent pitchd there, where it might fix its rest for ever; and as my faithfull
worthy Isabella was its Alpha-choice, to have adopted your (only qualified)
adorable Armida for its Omega-inclination.

> Cynthia prima fuit, Lesbia finis erit.

It hath already seald this secret promise to her meritt.

> Ultima talis erit, quæ mea prima fides.

And woud have made her heiress to that inheritance which, tho' a poor
estate, yet, thro' ye humble goodness and prudent management of ye last
proprietrix, had made her rich in all contentment.

> To greatness she so little did incline,
> Her heart ask'd never any thing butmine.

And this was part of ye intended settlement I had assigned her.   But your
(amiss when once you calld her mine) Armida is doubtlessly reservd for
fairer fortunes than my low, vulgar recommendations can pretend to build.

I always feard Heavens justice would adjudg her virtues and ye indear-
ments she is mistress of to be too great and absolute to be bestowd, where
they coud meet (at best) but with ye partial payment of limitted returns,
seeing I must have set apart some share of love to have commemorated ye
ever fresh-springing sweets of her remembrance, whose memory can never
dye with me.

> Twas my own want I grievd, who had no more,
> That she must borrow of a bankrupt store.

Tho' this I coud have told her with a safe conscience:

> Tu mihi sola places, nec jam te præter in orbe
> Formosa est oculis ulla puella meis.

And have so far confirmd it (as I thought at least) by a proposal I sent her
father, (whose qualities made me desirous of a more intimate conversation
with him too ever since I coud distinguish men,) that since he thought not
fit to comply with it, call me no honest man whene're tis elsewhere made ;
and believe me, Doctor, when I tell you she is ye only woman I know, to
whom I would have offerd my self, of any portion, age or quality. Well!
seeing ye necessitys opposing her being mine are reciprocall, (and knowing
those on my side are insuperable I can ye easylier suppose his so too,) I must
succumb to destiny, and try to linger out the insipid remnant of my now
endless life as that by this late disappointment seems to chalk out for me.
To hope by farther search to find ye rarity that can please me carries despair both in ye task & thought.   No, Doctor !

> Nunc licet e cœlo mittatur amica Johanni,
> Mittetur frustra, deficietque Venus.

Unless it were my lovd Eurydice again ; by whose most sacred ashes, (ye
deities of my love), by my misfortunes, and as you hope for happyness, I
conjure you to do that right to my sincerity & truth as to assure and convince
those concerned that nothing but ye necessity of parting with what must

Vol. I.   M

have destroyd my credit (when rightly understood) where I had aim'd
at being entirely confided in, coud have had force enough to make me use
ye last of violences I am thereby prevaild with to exercise on mind and
body. My justice, gratitude, love, honour & conscience are all concern'd
in what I'm now transacting ; and shoud she 'ere perceive I had wrong'd
or wounded either, (altho' ye gaining her were ye temptation,) could ne're
think on me by ye character of such a man as he must be who can deserve
her just esteem; and that's ye treasure I'd not only get but keep. Could I
without forfeiting some or all of these (as my affairs at present stand
circumstantiated) recede from what I've ask'd, I would not sleep before I
had sent him carte-blanche to write down his own terms upon ; and think
ye mighty purchase cheap at any rate coud I preserve her good opinion,
and ye delightfull conscience of having done no wrong to ye dear offsprings
of our innocent first loves.

> But shoud I do what sure I never can,
> How coud she love so infamous a man ?

This being ye case, pity my condition ; and tho' I'm not designd by
Heaven to be your nephew in law, yet, as you ought to be my friend in
equity, let me find so much favour with you as to represent it so that ye
weighty addition of her misconstruing any part of my well-meant intentions towards her in this important vaste concern may not consummate ye
infelicities of   Yours etc.

> Nec memorare pudet tali me vulnere victum ;
> Subditus his flammis Jupiter ipse fuit.

103.   To Mrs. R.*   June 27, 1695.

Whenever I woud borrow half an hour from my
indulgd companion, melancholly, and am endeavouring to please my self,

---

* A later hand has added "amsey?"   S.H.A.H.

my usual recourse is to ye agreeable recollection of what I've heard you say concerning me. But in that search and contemplation my conscious reason never fails to start this mortifying question; viz., whether I'm beholden to ye (impossible) deception of your discernment for it, or that your penetration pick'd me out as ye fittest subject for you to show the world that by ye God-like agency of an omnipotent invention a specious something might be made of nothing. Your supposition, that telling me what Lady Ess: Griffin said woud more then compensate for ye loss of what Mrs. R. had written, has throughly resolved my doubts; for you mistake my taste if you believe even your prose will make a full attonement for ye disappointment of your verses; as in ye one you only speak, (tho' that's a feast when one expects no more,) whereas in t'other you both do that and sing together. I own they seperately deserve ye name of musick; but having fancy'd such heavenly harmony in consort, nothing less will now content ye thirsty, longing eyes and ears of your attentive auditor.

109. To Mrs. R. June 29, 1695.

      I am glad to find my care for you so vigilantly active as to prevent even your own apprehensions, (a remark you may apply more generally than ye particular instance of ye verses extend to); for I'd no sooner left you but (from their own beauty) fell into a distrust a coppy might be coveted, not for ye resemblance they bore to ye unlike subject, but as they wore ye noted livery your genius gives to every part of its retinue; and knowing hurtfull uses have been made of innocence misunderstood, I charg'd ye fact upon her in so peremptory a way as guilt surpriz'd coud not conceal. When ye confession was once extorted (and of a treason against you), I hope you need not be told I never discontinued prosecution till she had made ye restitution you required by

           Yours etc.

110.   To Doctor Felton.

Dear Doctor   June 29, 1695.

   I cant but own Alexanders wish of two worlds was a moderate desire compard with my expectation of finding a second wife (mistakenly) kind enough to love me as ye first. However, your matchless niece being ye only woman I could ever give my self leave to think of as a fit successour to so pearless a predecessor; and my reason having all along represented her (in the frequent consultations judgment hath held with observation) as ye sole production of humane nature whom most excusably, ney laudably, I might make so; after various conflicts, (for I dare acknowledge

> Be witness, Heaven, how piously I strove
> To ridd my mind of this inchanting love.

Non est gloriosa victoria nisi ubi fuerint laboriosa certamina.   *St. Amb :*

But finding

> My self I could not to my self restore,
> Resolving still and yet still loving more ;
> The swift contagion glides along my veins,
> And in my breast ye pleasing poyson reigns.)

the result was this. Yesterday I waited upon your brother and my father-in-law elect with a resolution (founded upon ye confidence of God Almighty's blessing and direction attending it after so many zealous & earnest suplications as I have put up to him for both in this immense concern) to accept of what he had last offerd, in case I had his word (which is & shall be his bond with me) he coud now give no more; averring which beyond a doubt, I told him if he coud find in his heart to bestow his daughter where there was but a slender revenue in possession, and seeing he could not farther increase it, she shoud be most welcome to all it coud afford, and I'd be thankfull. We are so far agreed that he has consented to

my going down with him to Boxted Saturday next, if I can stay so long ;
or rather I shoud have said, if my indispensable affairs here can admitt of
my going sooner.

> Moments to th' absent lover tedious grow ;
> Tis not how time, but how ye mind does goe.

Ah ! Doctor ; I am quite an other man than when I wrote last ; sure never
any mortal was under a greater distraction of mind ; but for my justification
ye cause deservd it.   It touchd me to ye quick when I had so just fears the
valuable originall of that agreeable picture you (Hoskins like) had drawn
of her in miniature woud not be mine at last : of whom I may truly say,

> Cujus amor tantum mihi crescit in horas,
> Quantum vere novo viridis se subjicit alnus.

And who I hope will prove

> That cordial drop Heaven in my cupp has thrown,
> To make ye nauseous draught of life go down.

If my being intirely hers will make hers drink as her taste woud wish it, I
can assure her when my heart is once gaind tis an unalienable property.

> Nec cito desisto, nec temere incipio,

being the temper of her admirer, and   Yours etc.

111.   To Mrs. R—y.   July 1, 1695.

Could I reasonably have expected a milder fate
than shipwrack for my unballasted vessel in ye nice and dangerous voyage
it is making, (setting sail without ye compass of that kind character your
friendlily indulgent fancy hath made of (or rather for) me to lye as land
marks for my morality to steer by), this had borne date from Boxted.   But
wanting ye infallible direction of that touchd needle, which woud have
shown me what I ought to be by letting me see what I was not, I dare not
venture out to sea for fear of foundering in sight of that blest haven I woud

arrive at. Who knows but that your tastes (she being indifferent too) may be ye same; & if so, her penetration would certainly have hitt ye same blots your goodness may have aim'd at ye amendment of, by giving such comendations as might have wrought th' effects of formall exhortations ; and this was a view so worthy of your friendship & generosity, of such absolute necessity to my desird success in becoming her Philocles, that unless you will yet afford me ye charitable assistance of it, you will consequently hear she has determind to keep her title of ye maiden Queen of hearts, rather than forego it for such a medley of mistakes and awkwardnesses as she will (otherwise) discover in (that only thing he can promise himself he is in ye right in being)   Yours etc.

112.   To Mrs. R—y.   July 17, 1695.

Where indifference resides, all our purposes become precarious, subject to every divertion, even to ye common avocations of Park and Play. To tell me ye company you went with was agreeable ought to abate ye pretensions and silence ye complaints of those who are not so, and make them not only suffer but approve your preference in ye competition between them & me. But when I consider you as ye salt & form which animates & gives ye relish to all ye conversation you find your self a part (I might say ye whole) of, and that ye satisfaction you feel must necessarily either result from or center in yourself, I then conclude those who are capable of ye greatest meritt towards you are such as can taste and understand you best ; and if that inference be rightly drawn, all your relations nor acquaintance deserve not more than I. If want of time was a good reason why yours (which this is to thank you for, tho' not accompanied with ye character,) was so short, ye same woud sufficiently excuse ye abscence (it cant be calld, because it woud not have been found a want) of this, it being written at a time when every letter shoud be taken as a volume, and every moment alienated from ye contemplation of what she is,

and how to make my self blest in her being happy with me, is reckond a
kind of eternity lost (were it bestowd on any but Mrs. Ramsey) by

Yours etc.

113.   Mr. Hervey to Mrs. Felton.*

My ever-new Delight   July 20, 1695.

The gratefull goodness you have shown in bring-
ing so much nicety of taste and natural indifferency as you are owner of to
sett some little value upon a man whose greatest meritt is loving and
thinking of you as he does, abates of the vanity might otherwise have been
justly charg'd upon me in supposing you should interess your self enough
in what concerns me to care how I passd my journey; but the kind permission you allow'd me to take the pleasing liberty of writing to you being a
farther warrant and excuse for the trouble I am giving you, I will employ
the happy priviledg to better purpose than acquainting you with my being
well come to this place. Lett me bestow it in venting and doing justice to
a heart full of love & faithfulness towards you. To tell you it is everything
you coud wish it in your regard is not yet expressing rightly what it means
and feels for you; no, saying it pays you by anticipation all that you can
invent or expect or require from it, (were your demands unreasonable
enough to be proportion'd to the virtues which lay claim to it,) would not
come up to that degree of love and admiration Armida's charming pretty-
nesses and touching decencies have created in it.

> Thou'rt now become my thoughts perpetual theme,
> Their daily longing and their nightly dream.

To please and make thee happy shall be the sole drift & constant meditation
of my soul; and whenever I steal a moment's consideration that doth not
tend directly and immediately to that end, tis how to make my self so in

---

* The difficulties alluded to in some of the foregoing letters being overcome, they were married
at Boxted by Dr. Felton, July 25, 1695. S.H.A.II.

thee ; in order whereunto I have been this night with Mr. ffolkes, who hath promisd to give the most expeditious turn to my affair that his witt can contrive ; but saies it is not practicable by Tuesday ; had it been so, my impatience to see thee again is such that even that day, as early as he may count it, would have been and is look'd upon as distant as doomsday to an expectation like mine.   And now I have said this, lett me ask pardon for the rest I broke you of the night before I died ; (for is it not a death when soul and body seperates ?) but now I think on't, if that be a fault, no body is so criminal as your self towards me ; lett us then cry Quitts as to that matter ; but I must observe, you coud sleep when I was there present, which is more than he can do absent, who is, sleeping or waking, dead or living, worthy Armida's unworthy lover, friend & servant.   J. H.

114.   My ever-new Delight   London, Sat. 11 at night.   July 20.

Remembering you sometimes gave the News-papers a reading, I send you the inclosd.   Since my first I've heard Papa* is well.   I was to have seen him about 9 this evening, but he was not at home.   I hear by Lady Carr (who is your servant or else not my relation) he was to make a visitt here this afternoon.   Tomorrow I shall make him another.   When I shall make mine to thee, God knows ; (may he in the mean time protect and bless thee ;) only this I know, it shall be the soonest minute possible within the power of him who is absolutely and totally in yours.   J.H.

115.   From half-way Hedg between Aswarby and Kirkby.
My dearest Treasure   Sept. 2, 1695.

Could'st thou conceive th' uneasyness
Absence (tho' short) in me creates,

---

* Her father, Sir Thomas Felton.   S.II.A.H.

It wou'd augment thy happyness,
Tho' mine the torment much abates.
It the world's poverty betrays,
When that wou'd please & thou'rt not by ;
But thy dear presence all repays,
Forgetting past adversity.

116.   To Mr. Hervey at Newmarket the same night he went.

My dear dearest life   Fryday night, Oct. 18, 1695.

I woud not give you this trouble, but, having so good an excuse for it as the sending the news, I coud not loose so favourable an opportunity to repeat the old sentence, Dear dear, how I do love you ; to tell you how often I have said it in thought to day would be more than I could do (being without number), and to say how much it is is as hard to be expressd. As my head used to hang sometimes, it is now the constant posture of it, and nothing but the sight of you can lift it up, being like a lilly (as you have often calld it), and your dear dear self the only sun that can revive it. I am sure you woud not grudge the time in reading this bitt of paper, if you coud guess but half the pain your absence causes me, and know the ease I find in doing this, hoping it will put you in mind of the last words you said to me, which was that you woud come home to morrow. Now I must tell you I have been very exact to all your commands, eating and drinking as much as I could, and will do so as to sleeping as farr as I am able. But when I think [of your absence], I cant help shedding some tears, which I hope you will excuse as proceeding from a most sincere and hearty affection of your dutifull & obedient wife, E. H.   P.S.—I must beg once more, if you love me, not to forget to morrow.

117.   To Mr. Hervey at London.

My dear dearest life   Jan. 29, 1695.

I find such true pleasure & sattisfaction when I

Vol. I.   N

am any way conversing with you, that even in this (which is but a shadow
of it) I take more delight then in all things els this world can give. Theirfore, my dear Angell, when ever I am without the substancial good, give
me leave this way to pleas my self by repeating how much I love & how
intirely I am with my whole heart and soul your most duttyful & affectionet
wife,   E. H.

119.   To Mr. Hervey.   To the Parliament Hous, Feb. 3, 1695.

        I beg you woud come home & dine before you go
into the citty, for fear you shoud be sick with fasting so long. I have sent
you some cheescakes, which I hope you will eat for her sake who is with
the greatest heigth of affection, my dear dear,   Yours for ever.

119.   To Sir Charles Holt.
Sir   March 24, 1695/6.

        The reason of my giving you this trouble is that
(by ye means of Mr. Sergeant Le Hunt) my late uncle, Mr. John Hervey,
having lent your late father, Sir Robert Holt, £700, which was secured to
be repaid with interest by a judgment, but never was repaid ; and being
informed that you have a plentifull estate, subject either in law or equity to
discharge ye said debt ; I thought fitt first to acquaint you therewith, that
I may understand from you whether you conceive yourself obligd, and are
willing to make satisfaction for this debt, before I attempt any legal proceedings in order to ye recovery thereof. My title is that my late uncle
made my late father, Sir Thomas Hervey, and my aunt (his wife) executors
of his will, and my said father residuary legatee, (my said aunt being
limitted in ye bequests to her,) and my father left me his sole executor. I
shoud have addressed you sooner, but there having happened great controversies between my said aunt & father touching my said uncle's estate,
and several transactions between her & me since my father's death, we have

had our hands and heads too full of that suite to mind other matters, altho'
in themselves considerable. I pray favour me with an answer, and you
will oblige Your etc.

120.   Mr. Sergeant Le Hunt to Sir Charles Holt.

Sir

Some occasion calling me to London, I have been
apply'd to by Mr. Hervey (whose uncle & father were my very good friends)
to discourse me touching a sum of £700 was lent to Sir Robert Holt your
father by Mr. John Hervey ; whereupon to ye best of my remembrance
there was such a sum lent, & afterwards a judgment was given by Sir
Robert for securing ye repayment thereof. Sir, I do at ye instance of Mr.
Hervey give you the trouble of these lines, that you may be informed of ye
reality of ye debt, and to avoid expence in law or equity, and do think it
proper that you apply your self to Mr. Hervey to accomodate ye matter,
since I'm sensible that ye loan of this money was very serviceable to your
father, & is incumbent on you to satisfy ye same, for that I am, Sir, yours
etc,

121.   My ever-new Delight   Newmarket, April 24, 1696.

As weary as I find my self with the fatigue of our
journey hither, (which is not a little,) I can assure thee 'tis nothing when
compar'd with that I feel for the world and every thing I have mett with in
it, since I parted with the only cause and reason I have to care for being in
it. The sole entertainment of my thoughts since I left thee have been thy
self, *. . . . . thy loving, faithful   J. H.

---

* I omit nearly a page filled with this sort of stuff. This letter was written at "almost two
o'clock in the morning." S.H.A.II.

122. My ever-new Delight   Newmarkett, April 25, 1696.

Didst thou not bid me write by the post too? This is to show that thy requests shall alwaies meet with a most religious observance from me, especially when kind and reasonable; but thine can be no other, unless when you ask me to love you more, and that's a forfeiture of the last qualification, it being impossible, both as to its own superlative degree, and from the circumscribd finiteness of humane nature, having already carried that to its utmost extension; and altho' vaste consider'd with respect to mortality, yet too limitted and narrow for its object (thy perfections), they being infinite, I must confess.   I hope the letter I sent this morning by the coach will have reach'd thee before this, because it will tell thee we all came well (tho' weary) hither. I long (you know how uneasy tis to do so) for to morrow's post, which (I hope in God) will bring me the good news of your and the young black-eyed gentleman's welfare. . . . . And now I am speaking of him, lett me remember those in being. God of his infinite mercy, who hath blessd me with yee all, keep and protect yee together in health & happiness, that yee may live for his glory, and for the pleasure and comfort of their thankfull father, and of, my dearest life, thy entirely faithfull and loving husband,   J. H.

P.S.—Make my compliments to all our friends. I drank to our friends in Jermyn Street privately last night at Lord Godolphin's to Papa, whose company the more I have of it the better I like it and him, because I see he loves thee most affectionately.

123.   Mrs. Hervey to John Hervey, to Newmarkett.

My dear dear life   London, April 25, 1696.

If I shoud begin to tel you all the uneasynes & pain I have been in ever since you left me, and how much I long to see you again, it woud take more time to read then I hope you disine to stay; for endeed, my dear, tis more then I can bear to breath without you: (I cant call it liveing, for thats not posable for ye body to do when the soul is absent.) I think the nearest to my present affliction is Lady Essex ; 'but as none can give such true pleasure and sattisfaction as your self, so I cannot alow any body to feel the same trouble in the want of another as I do for you ;) her condision is endeed very sad, her Lord being to go so soon into fflanders, & she is not yet certain wether she shall go or not. I went to see her yesterday in ye evening, and we shut our selves up in her closett to cry, which we did for some time. She and Mrs. Howard came to sup hear after, & we did ye same thing again ; they staid tel 12 a clock ; but tho' it was so late before I went to bed, I coud not go to sleep tel I had spent some time in washing your pillow with my tears, & kissing every part of it, for fear of missing that where your dear head had lain. I ris this morning by 8 a clock, thinking bed was the uneasyest place I coud meet with ; but I find every one so that I come into. O dear, dear life, the pain I feel is not to be expressd ; I want more sand to dry my tears then ink upon this papar ; this is ye only time I ever wish'd my dearest life to love me less then I do him ; but even that I can bear with more eas then to have you suffer what I do now. But I forgitt Newmarkett is not a place for my complaints, tho' I hope they will in pitty send you home the first moment you can, which I hope will not exceed Wensday. I beg to meet you as farr as the Green man at least, (I woud be glad to do it farther,) that I may have the pleasure that day of thinking every step I go is nearer to my dearest.   Lady Manchester being a great news monger, I went their last night to see what I coud pick up for to day ; she told me their came in a ship yesterday which seconded the news they had the day before of Admirall Rook, that he was come out of Cails very safe, this ship setting sail with him from thence, but being of so much lighter carage got hear before him, but they think he cannot be farr off. They say the Parlement will be up on Monday or Tuesday, & that the King will go the latter end of ye week, but others say nether can be so soon. My Lord Durrantwatter, they say, is dead, & so is my Lord Powes, in France. I sent Charls this morning to hear news; he went to the Admiralty offise to a frind their, which told him their has come too expresses from Admiral Rook, one last night at ten a clock which brought the account I have sent you in print, and another this morning which ses he is arriv'd at Spithead with ye richest fleet that has been seen this many years. I was not willing to trust to Charless intelegence, but sent to Lady Man — r to know if it weir true, but she was not at home, but I hope to give a just account before I seal my letter. They talk about ye town that the King will besiege Dunkirk & Calaiss both by sea & land, and that he will go aboard ye fleet before he goes to Flanders. He has orderd the noblest entertainment that can be made to be at Portland hous on Tuesday for the Venetian embassatore, which is ye day they make their entree. And now, my dear, I have told you all I know of ye publick, I must give you some account of home, that all our young frinds are well, only your daughter was a littel out of order yesterday, but is pritty well again to day. I count every muinett an hour tel the Coach comes in in hopes of a letter. Pray present my servis to Mrs. Elwes; I hope you will prevail with her to come to London, & that she may be in such hast for it as not to let you stay longer then the time sett, tho' I hope their neads no other perswasion then the ernest request of your ever faithfull & obedeiant wife E. Hervey.   All ye news I told you of Admirall Rook is certain; they are about 190 sail in all. They say Lord Litchfeild & Lord Gerate of Bromly are sent to ye Tower, & my Lord Petterborough confind to his house. I am glad to hear you are got well to Hockerell, but I stil wait with impatience for Bury Coach.

124.   Mrs. Hervey to John Hervey.

My dear dear Angell   London, April 26, 1696.

I give you a thousand and a thousand thanks for

your kind letter; but I wish I coud have been sattisfy'd of your being safe & well at Newmarkett any other way rather then by giveing you so much trouble when you weir so weary with your jurney. I have often heard their is no great pleasure but is mixt with some pain. I am sure I found it so last night, haveing sufferd a great deal before I receivd your letter; for just as I had sent mine to ye post, (which was ye laitest muinett I coud, in hopes to send you word I had receivd yours,) Charles came from Bishops-gate, and told me he had askd the coachman and every passenger their, but they had no letter for me, and he heard by one of them that their had been a great fire at Newmarkett just by Mr. Nelsons, which had burnt 3 or 4 houses. Think, my dear, what a condision I was in at that time; but it did not last very long, for a porter brought the wellcome letter before I got to bed, a place which I have very little reason to go to, for I am sure I have not slept 6 hours sence I saw you. Dont think, my dear, (for fear you be deceivd) to find me alive if you stay much longer; for endeed tis more, much more, then I can bear to be without you, thou life, heart & soul of ye body you have left behind. I cared your letter to bed with me, and waked this morning at 6 a clock, (according to my usiall custome sence you left me,) and read & kisd it over & over a hundred times, & fancy'd every place your dear hand had lain upon in ye writing of it, and that was doubly kis'd. Pray, my dear, dont forgitt to writ a Tuesday by ye coach what time & where I shall meet you on Wensday, for I hope that is ye longest day. I am sure if it is not so of your comeing, it will be so for my life. It is in vain for me to pretend to discribe what I suffer; tis imposable; theirfore I will say no more, but hope you will not think me at all behind you in reckoning ye time, for if I devide a muinett into 50 parts, I shoud count every part an age tel we meet, which that it may not be long will be ye constant prayers of, dear dear life, your most faithfull & obediant wife, E. H.

Your children present their dutty to you: our young unknown frind is as well as can be, considering his uneasy habitasion.

125.   My ever-new delight

Newmarket April 27, 1696.

This is to thank thee for thy two kind, pretty, sweet, dear letters, which gave me the only pleasure I have tasted since I saw thee. The best return and answer I can make them is to tell thee that I can nor will not stay any longer from thee; but, if God bless me, will be with thee Wednesday evening, notwithstanding there will (I believe) be a match that day; a poor expression I confess it is, but were the denial much more difficult, I shoud rejoyce to make thee a sacrifice of it. Indeed tis hard (properly speaking) to make thee any of this sort, for inclination must be of thy side; and then who is thankworthy. But, my dear, I must make this bargain with thee, that you would not venture your self backward & forward so farr upon the stones as you must necessarily do to meet us (Papa & I) at the Green Man. I'll send my scouts before, and, if I hear you offer to come, will (if I can) goe back again; but I must own that's impossible to be done without thee; for, from what I've lately felt in thy absence, this resolution has been created, that I will never suffer the like if I can help it; for as to little sleep and many tears I can vye with thee in those particulars, as well as in any other effects of love; and I'll be bold to say that the dear letter you said catch'd so many of thy precious tears in the writing receivd as many in the reading. My heart was full before, and that pouring in so much more passion made it soon over flow. My dearest love, I'm called away, but will stay to send my blessing to all my children, not forgetting the sweet black-eyed boy, altho' ten to one (that's a Newmarkett wagering phrase) he little thinks of us. May God Almighty farther his growth and perfection, and make him but like his mother, and then he must be a blessing and comfort to the darling, pleasure and pride of her faithfull, loving & affectionate husband, J. H.

P.S. Wednesday, dear Wednesday, how I long for Wednesday!

126. To the Directors of ye Royal Bank.

June 12, 1696.

Gentlemen

Having given my self ye trouble of coming thrice ye last week to no better purpose than ye receiving of £46..05..00, I thereupon resolvd to do so no more my self; but being then told by Sir William Hodges, Mr. Rayworth and Mr. Denn who were in waiting, that if money came in I might expect £200 on Saturday last and £300 more this week, £700 being ye sum I was at that time obligd and am still very much pressd to pay, makes me now send my servant to know if ye yet think fit to comply with a request so reasonable, and whether upon second thoughts you will not contrive and order me such a sum as may accomodate ye necessities of a friend which are purely of your own creating, and much ye worse born because happening to a man totally unacquainted with ye burden of creditors complaints. Having told you my case, I leave it in your judgments whether I deserve not some distinction, and unless I find my self so treated you will necessarily oblige me to take such measures as ye exigency of my private affairs will enforce me to pursue, which other wise woud never have come within ye imagination nor intention of, Gentlemen, Yours etc.

127. To ye Earle of Dorsett & Middlesex.

June 26, 1696.

My Lord

The circumstance of so great an arrear of Interest money as £2500, and ye necessitous condition my affairs are reducd to by its growing such a sum, (having considerable rent charges issuing out of my estate, which I have borrowd money to keep touch with,) will, I hope, both acquit me from ye charge of importunity and excuse ye liberty I now

Vol. I.   o

take of giving your Lordship this trouble, to remind your Lordship of ye
favourable answer you were pleasd (by letter) to send me in November last;
viz. that you woud within a month at farthest discharge ye interest (at
least); in expectation whereof I have attended ever since. But ye want of
this money being sensibly felt in my little concerns, and ye supplying of it
by my credit being very chargeable, forceth me to beg ye favour of your
Lordship that you woud either please to order the payment of this arrear of
interest, or otherwise convert it into principal; that what this then will
yield may satisfy ye use of that I have been obligd to borrow in its room to
answer ye occasions of, My Lord, Yours etc.

128.   To ye Corporation of Bury St. Edmunds.

Nov. 24, 1696,

Gentlemen

The bill for farther regulating ye ill state of our
coyn being this day read ye 3d time, I think my self obligd to acquaint you
with ye passage of it in our house; and also to inform you with ye particular
heads and clauses of it, which for your satisfaction and ye benefitt of trading
men I have abstracted from ye bill it self, and are as follows : viz. that all
clipt or unclipt silver money brought into ye mints between ye 4th of
November last & ye 1st of July next shall be receivd at ye rate of five
shillings & four pence per ounce; that all collectors, receivers etc. shall
take ye said hamerd money from Nov. 14 instant till 1 Feb. next at five
shillings & eight pence per ounce for all loans and arrears of taxes and
revenues due to that time, and shall receive ye said hamerd money for all
future aids and taxes till June 1 next after ye same rate of 5s.8d. per ounce ;
that after Dec. 1 next no hamerd silver money shall pass in any payment
(except as aforesaid) but by weight at 5s. 2d. per ounce. Then follows a
clause to impower receivers etc. to account by taile in ye Exchequer for all

such moneys as they shall have receivd (pursuant to ye Act of Parliament) having ye major part of the letters remaining, or for sixpences not clipt within ye inner rimm, before Nov. 18 instant (of which ye said receivers are to make oath) to Dec. 18 next, and have time given them to pay ye said sum of money into ye Exchequer untill Jan. 10 following. Then follows another clause, whereby all receivers are obliged to carry ye taxes etc., which they shall receive in this kind of hamerd money, to ye next adjacent mints in ye several countries, that ye same may be more expeditiously recoynd to be returnd up to ye Exchequer. And so closes with a clause relating to ye receipt of moneys collected for ye making ye rivers Wye & Lugg navigable, which, being forreign to your concerns, I will not trouble you with. Thus you see what is determind concerning this nice and important affair, which, when all things are considerd and come to be experiencd, will (I hope) prove to every man's satisfaction; for now all doubts & uncertaintys (none of ye least grievances which have attended this misfortune of our coyn) will be dissipated, every one knowing what he works or sells for; now ye will infallibly see new money appear, which you coud not reasonably expect to find in trade so long as 10 or 11 pence (and so pro rato) would discharge a contract for one shilling; now ye poor day labourer who hath been a weekly looser by ye old money, (the shop-keeper not affording him above 9 or 10 penny worth of victualls or commodities for ye piece of money which was paid to him for a shilling,) will know what he works for, and what provisions it will purchase for his family. And lastly, 'tis by this method alone we can arrive at that necessary and much desird point of having but one species of money current, which is the only thing can quicken and augment our trade at home, and settle it upon a right bottom in respect of our neighbours abroad; and these considerations (being for ye good of England & of every particular member of it) were ye motives which induced ye consent of, Gentlemen, yours, etc.

129.   Mrs. Hervey to John Hervey.   London, Dec. 24, 1696.

My dear dear life,

It is imposable for me to tel you ye pain & uneasynes I have felt those few but tedious hours you have been gon ; I cant call it absent, for you have never been one moment so in thought when awake, or in my dreams in ye little sleep I took after you went, which was not gaind without a great many tears. Mrs. Ramsey dind with me, & was so angry with you that she did not think you worth reproaching. She & I and Jack went as soon as we had dind to Papas, where Jack was in very good humour, & Papa so with seeing him ; so that I was ye only perticuler body in ye company ; which was so visable that Papa disird Mrs. Ramsey to cary me home to write, & see if that woud put me in better humour ; but I find that only an eas to what nothing but your presence can cure ; theirfore, dear, dear Angell, (but I hope I nead not disire you,) make as great dispatch of your bisness as you can. Hear is no news but that ye Lords past ye bill by seven votes. The Duchess of Norfolke was before them and ownd the receiving of a papar from my Lord Mon—h, and giving it to Lady M. Fenick, but that she did not know what was in the papar ; but they deferd any farther examination, & orderd her to appear this day fortnight ; tel which time they ajournd. Her grace behavd very well in all her answeirs, which was aprovd by everybody. Charls was at ye bank, but coud gitt no mony. The children are all well. I will take up as little of your time as I can, so will say no more but that I am, dearest of all creatures, your duttyfull & obedient wife, E. Hervey.

My servis where you pleas ; my Papa presents his to you ; hear is a letter from Mr. Gage, but I oppend it, & found their was no bisnes, so did not send it.

130.   My ever-new Delight   Newmarket, Dec. 25, 1696.

Had the Bury coach gone for London to-day, you

woud have heard from Bishop-Stafford how unable I there found myself to bear thy absence (not only long but at all); how much wearier of the world without thee than of my journey, (tho' a tedious one, but how coud it seem otherwise wanting my dear fellow traveller); how impatient to see thee again, and how many resolutions I then took never to part with thee more; and if this was my state of mind there, I may leave you to judg (by your own I hope, ney know,) how farr that condition of my soul has been improved by being farther and longer from thee; describe it I cant, neither woud I if I coud, for thy sweet sake; but sympathy will do it whether I will or not, and therefore will give my heart the ease of saying, 'tis as miserable (mayn't I say more) as thine can think or even an enemy wish it; but I have one resource, and that's the post, which I expect with an impatiency that tells me is allyed to that with which I long to see the author of those lines I hope to read within an hour, ney sooner now, for he's this minute gone by, and I'll send after him for the precious charge of love I'm sure he bears. Should I tell you the chief reason of my staying here to-night was that I might have an earlier sight of thy dear letter, I know you would be unjust enough to conclude Elephant had a share in the determining ascendant; but I can forgive any suspicion of yours, knowing the nice principle it proceeds from; only give me leave to acquaint you (for I don't know whether you think so or not) that you may be equally jealous of him with any one of my sett of beauties, which is saying no small thing either for yours or my virtue, (or rather my justice, taste, and temper). And now lett me thank thee for thy agreeable letter, which serves as an opiate to all my pains, and yet letts loose and heightens my sence of love and pleasure; for who can reflect on the tears you mention without a mixture of both, yet the latter most predominant, from knowing there is a sweet feeling both in the source and all its pleasing streams. Thanks to my dearest for the news; more for that of your being all well; but most of all (tho' that was none) for telling

me in such welcome words how much thou lovest him who is to thee that
and more (for thou deservedst it) than thou canst think or wish, being with
all the powers of my soul thy faithful lover, J. Hervey.

P.S.   My duty to Papa : as much to Mrs. Ramsey as she sent me.   Remember me most kindly to all our dear children, for whom, God be praised
for evermore.

131.   Mrs. Hervey to John Hervey.   London, Dec. 26, 1696.
My dear dearest life and soul,

I woud not miss a post, though I am forced to write
this in my bed ; for the pain I had for want of you and that I had with the
tooth-ach would not let me sleep all last night ; and remembring what you
said to me when you went away, If you love me, (which is and ever will be
a sacred tye to me,) pull it out, I did to-day with a great deal of difficulty
do it ; but the pain (which was very great, being forced to be pulld twice,)
and the fright together has put me very much out of order ; but Mr. Draner
gives me a sleeping draught to-night, and I hope I shall be better tomorrow, and able to meet you at the Green Man very quickly ; for indeed
after all the complaints I have made, those of my mind for want of you out
weighs them all.   Though I was not able to go to Papa, I sent to him, and
he says there is not a word of news ; therefore I send you this lampoon,
hopeing that will give you some entertainment.   There is another made of
the men of the same nature, as you may see by the beginning of this.   I
am promised that too ; though they are neither of them very new, I believe
you have not seen them.   Mrs. Berkeley is the body that furnishes me, of
who I enquird after private news, since I could meet with no publick, she
sitting with me yesterday in the afternoon, I desired her to pick up all she
could, but I can hear nothing.   Therefore my dear dear, I will trouble you
no longer, though I could write all night, for then, methinks, I am in some

sort conversing with my dearest life, which is the greatest pleasure this world can give me, and the best relief I find now to my pain. But I will enter no more upon that subject, but live in hopes of hearing by Wednesday post of a happy meeting at the Green Man on Saturday, till which time, my dear dear, farewell, and believe me to be your ever constant and unchangeable E. Hervey.

P.S. Mrs. Manley does not set out till Thursday, no coach going sooner.

132. My ever-new Delight,   Bury, Dec. 28, 1696.

I am much concerned to hear you are under any disorders from heart or tooth-ach, and that the pains of both sorts should be created and increasd by my absence and advice. The first cause (I hope) carries its own excuse along with it, which is necessity; (for nothing less shoud or could seperate my body from its soul;) and for the last, I doubt not but ere this time you are come to think the future ease you may now expect was not too dearly purchasd at the momentary price of pain it cost you. My ignorance of your intentions to undergoe so formidable an operation, (not suspecting your courage capable of an effectual resolution,) spard me the incessant pain of knowing you were to suffer any, especially that of so exquisite a nature which you felt; which, tho' 'tis over with you, I cant but in some measure be yet sensible of for you. Some relief you have given me (by one symptom) that you are not very bad, when you think of being at the Green Man on Saturday, ney though you had omitted the addition of come sevenight, for sure even that would be too early for your venturing so farr into a sharper air than that you live in under ye circumstances; but be they better than you describe, I'll make ye utmost haste to thee my business here will possibly admitt of, (which assurance I hope is needless,) and shoud they be worse (the least worse) than you have told me, (which I conjure you by my love to impart to me, by the first opportunity, with the same truth

and unreservedness with which that has made me so entirely yours,) no
consideration shall detain me one minute here after the sad news arrives.
In the mean time I commend thee (with the most zealous devotion) to the
care of that good God and his providence, (who first made thee so excellent
a creature as I have found thee, and then thought me worthy the possession
of thee,) that he would protect and bless thee and thine till my return,
which, I must again repeat, shall be the earliest day within the power or
contrivance of him who (already) longs more to see thee again than the
blind light, or (to use a better simile) the miserable the resurrection and
revivification of those whose loss they long had mournd, being with all the
faculties and by all the endearments of a charmd and gratefull heart, my
dearest life, your most affectionate and ever faithfull, J. H.

P.S. My duty and kind remembrances as before. You did not say one
word of my dear bratts. Tell Mrs. Ramsey I am Purdy; yet I (you wont
give me leave to say love her) will be her friend : for I love none but one.

133.   Mrs. Hervey to John Hervey.   London, Dec. 29, 1696.

My dearest life

I give you a million of thanks for your dear letter,
& for your charettable intentions to me (tho' disapointed by the coach not
coming) of sending a letter, which woud mightyly have relievd me from ye
great pain I sufferd, not knowing how you passd your jurney, which I
feard would be so tedious to you. I cant tel you how often I have wishd I
had taken it with you upon any terms, tho' I am glad you have not seen
(because I am sure it woud have troubled you) what I have sufferd ; nor I
hope had any sympathy of it, tho' you so kindly & so justly judgd of mine.
Indeed, my dear dear, I am loth to tel you how ill I have been, and how
unable I am now to write, if it weir not to my dear love : but sure it cant be
pain to convers with you. But I must give you an account of my ilnes
sence I writ last, when I told you I had my tooth drawn, and hoped to be

better, but instead of that have grown wors & wors   I tooke my sleeping draught that night, but to very little purpose, for my pain was so extreem that I never layd my eyes together tel 4 a clock, but was forcd to use fomentations to my jaw all night, & by the morning it had swelld up the inside of my mouth of that side & of ye out side quite up to my ear.   I kept my bed most part of Sunday, and by Papas advise sent for Mr. Levech ; he found my jaw not broke, only some splinter of it, & a verilent humour fallen upon ye part ; he has laid my jaw oppen again to day, which has given me some pain, els I hope I am something better, but cant yet rest without sleeping draughts every night ; but I believe ye recept I had when I lay inn woud do better, which I hope I shall not be long without.   I am sure I have not eat ye quantety of a chicken sence you left me, nor any thing without great pain.   Now after this dismale account I am sory I have no news ; but I sent to my Papa, & he tels me their is not a word.   I see as little of Mrs. Ramsey as you hear from her, so can say nothing about her.   The children (thank God) are all well.   And now, my dear & everlasting charmer, I must take my leave, and hope this is the last letter I shall have occassion to write.   But I beg to know by Thursdays post if you will be so good to come onn Satherday, which is most ernestly wishd and disird by, my dear dearest, your most faithfull and obediant wife, E. Hervey.

I have sent ye things by ye carier.

134.   Mrs. Hervey to John Hervey.   London, Dec. 30, 1696.

I can't let any body come empty handed near my dear dearest treasure, though 'tis not many hours since I wrote before, which I do most heartily repent of, since I find by your dear letter it will both disorder your mind and business ; but I beg (and I never sue to you in vain) you woud do neither, for by all those things you conjured me (which is very sacred) I hope I am better, nay so much that the ladys were here at pam to-day ; and now I've told you this I must again entreat you not to give your-

Vol. I.   P

self the least disturbance, for, should you do that, it will quite cast back that health I hope now recovering. They tell me I only keep my chamber to bring you home again, finding how much I wish and long for it; but to gain even that I woud not deceive you, which you may see by my writing you such perticulars last night, that were so large I think I had hardly room (not enough, I am sure,) to thank you for your dear kind letter; but now I am so full of both, I can't tell where to begin, nor (if I did) where to end, for it must be all love, and that to you is quite unbounded, and will, I believe, at last carry me to the place I have so long talkd of (Bedlam), for absence (which I hope (and heartily thank you for the resolution at Bishop-Stafford) never to try again) has, if possible, increased it, which makes it, sure, at ye full growth; but I find it like the meritt of the object, tho' ever great, is still improving. Your first dear letter (as I design to do this) I carried to bed with me as a sleeping-cordial, but it had a quite contrary effect, for I coud think of nothing but that and the dear author of it all night. To say how much I long to see you is needless, finding (with joy) how much you equal it, and therefore must be sensible of mine; so will say no more, but assure you (if I coud) how much and dearly I love, and am your sincerely faithful wife, E. Hervey.

P.S. The children are all well. I beg your pardon for forgetting them last time; but you'll forgive it when I tell you the thoughts of you would leave no room for anything else. I told Mrs. Ramsey what you said, but she says she has nothing to say to you, but wishes you health and happyness.

135.   My ever-new Delight   Bury, Dec. 31, 1696.   3 aclock.

After the unwelcome (but how can any thing be properly so call'd which comes from you) relation (which I have sett up for till this hour) you sent me concerning your indisposition and the ill accidents which have attended my well-meant advice, how can you think I will stay one moment from thee, my dearest life. Altho' none of the business I came hither about be yet settled, I am resolved to take places in to-morrows coach, if any goes for London this week (which I much fear); and shoud they not, I will hire one on purpose if they can possibly get through as the weather and roads have been; and shoud not that way of conveyance prove faisible, I will try to come on horseback; and shoud that be found impracticable, I'll come on foot, ney on my head, rather than be longer absent from thee now thou art ill, finding it but just possible to subsist without thee when ne'er so well. Therefore till Saturday good-night, or rather good-morrow, to my dearest life. Farewell! till then all ease and peace for thy affectionate J. Hervey.

136. Mrs. Hervey to John Hervey. London, Dec. 31, 1696.
My dear dear delight & pleasure

I cant help writing tho' I hope to no purpus; for ye cheif thing I live upon is ye thoughts of Satherday. O my dear, shoud I be disapointed, what will become of me. How could I soport that weighty addision to what I already feel. But I will say no more upon that subject. I shoud be glad to tel you some news, but I find their is no such thing; theirfore you must content your self with the prints. My dear dear, come away, and dont make me wish il to all my neigbours that are blesd with your much lovd societty, while I am missarable for want of it : but if I begin with complaints, my papar will not hold out; so will conclude with teling you a most neadles thing, which is how much and dearly I love and am most faithfully and intirely yours, E. Hervey.

I saw Lady Essex to-day; she wants you, tho' not so much as I do; hers is bisnes, mine is love. Ye children are all well, & your daughter very entertaining with her songs by my bedside.

137. My ever-new Delight, Newmarkett, April 7, 1697.
When you laid your kind injunction on me to write by post & coach, you did not believe my first letter coud begin with a

reproof; but endeed I cant help chiding you for disiring (if I lovd you) that I would leave you for this place, a change so much to my loss that I can hardly believe you coud be ye occasion of it to me. O the many sighs of repentance and regrett that I have fetchd (which I thought imposable too) for taking your advice or complying with your request, for fear your recovery might not be perfected, or at least that you might feel some degree of those disquiets & uneasynesses which absence never fails to cost me; both which considerations serve to augment my pain; all my comfort is ye days will be but few (tho' the time very very long) before I shall have all repaid with seeing thee again, and better, I hope, than thy disease found thee, which will be an unspeakable satisfaction to thy most faithfull constant lover, J. Hervey.

Remember me kindly to our dear children.

138.   My ever-new Delight   Newmarket, April 8, 1697.

Last night I sent you word by the coach that the days of my stay here woud be but few, meaning on Sunday to have been with thee. But this morning I find the mare which is to run against Dunn is brought to town, and Lord Carlisle here to back her; so that I fear my banishment will be prolongd to Tuesday; but that shall be the latest day, being under the last impatience to see thee again, tasting no pleasure where thou art not, ney, and a partaker too with me, or else the sweetest delights are but imperfect in their charms. To fall from these abstracted contemplations, to tell thee Elephant is just leading out to run for the plate, and time forces me to end, will be no better a reason for leaving off a conversation with thee, than sinners can give why they barter away Heaven for empty nothings, the disparity being near as great between the first as all allow the last. Yet before I conclude, lett me beg of you in the first place that you would take such care of your self as that I may find you in perfect health, and in the next that you woud not lett pretty Jack forgett his affectionate papa, and your entirely faithfull friend and lover, J. Hervey.

P.S.—Remember me kindly to my other two dear babes.

139. Mrs. Hervey to John Hervey. London, April 8, 1697.

My dear dearest life

It is impossible for me to consent to your hearing of me by any hand but my own, since that is able to tell you that I am as you left me very much mending; but that is very little to my purpose, since it cant express how much I love you, which is indeed, dearest treasure, inexpressible, and can never be known but by the window I have desired you to make into my heart, and wish you had at this minute a perspective glass into it, and there you woud find what is beyond any tongue to utter. Dear dear, how I do love you; but when I am upon this subject, I find my spirits carry me beyond my strength, which is indeed very small, and I am afraid like to continue so, for I have quite lost my stomach with my dear nurse, whose return must make every thing as it shoud be with me, and I hope that will not be longer than Sunday, though by no means I woud not desire it, if it be the least hurry or inconvenience to you. Two of your children are well; I cant say poor Jack is so; he crys night and day with his teeth, and sleeps very little, and will eat nothing but his buby, his cough is very much increasd and is indeed very bad. Dr. Raitcliffe would have him by all means go to Kensington for a little while till we go out of town, but he woud not have him go farther out of his or my reach. Mrs. Rickeson was here to-day, and is of the same opinion; but I'll leave all to the wise thought of my dear angel to determine. I sent to my Lady Manchester to-day to know what news, but she said there was not a word. I cant tell how to say I can write no more to my dearest life, but indeed my head is so bad it is impossible; so farewell to my dear dear everlasting love, who am your most dutyfull & obedient wife, E. Hervey.

140.   My ever-new Delight   Newmarket, April 10, 1697.

I can hardly tell which was greatest, my joy to see a letter from you, or the pain it cost me to think you shoud give your self so great a trouble when your head was so ill, and your spiritts exceeded your strength. But I hope by this time the latter is recovered proportionable to the former, if Mr. Barnavelt sent me but as faithful as he did a full account (which I thank him for) of the state of your health, whereon all my peace and all my happyness depends ; for, O my pretty excellence, what rest for thy poor Cousin Donn in this life, if pain or diseases should but threaten thy removal to a better, or only destroy thy ease in this ; that therefore thou mayst enjoy an uninterrupted series of that chief of blessings for both our sakes, thou hast my daily prayers. I am sorry to hear your several complaints of dear Jack ; I hope they are only the common attendants and incidents to the breeding of teeth ; however, by all means let him be immediately removed out of town, according as you have been advised, without staying for my coming to town, which cannot be till Tuesday night, Lord Carlisle being resolvd to run the mare against Dun. And now I am digressing upon these matters, (for my letters woud naturally be nothing but love,) I must tell you the news of this place, which is that yesterday Capt. Walpoole (Lady Ann Cookes husband) won the plate, Elephant pretending no farther than to save his distance ; and that to-day Lord Godolphin's horse beat Lord Devonshire's, whereby you won something ; but to-morrow I fear part of it must be parted with again, poor Cripple being lame for want of moister weather and softer ground ; however, we have resolvd to run him, though without much hope of beating Mr. fframpton's. Lett what will come of to morrows or Mundays success, the days will be welcome to me, as they bring me nearer to my chief concern, which is thy self, and as long as thou art well and lovest thy cousin Don, lett the rest of the world go which way it will, it cannot much affect the heart or add to the felicity of thy faithful friend and constant lover, J. Hervey.

P.S.—Dont lett the sweet babes forgett papa : yours is very well, and glad to hear you mend so fast.

141.　My ever-new Delight　　　　Newmarkett, Aprill 10, 1697.

This is to lett thee see I never can forgitt and so will alwaise keep my word, having sent a letter this morning by ye coach, which will supply till this arrives, & next day you will have ye author, who longs so much to be with thee as never to have an easy moment till that be accomplishd, and the longer tis protracted ye less I can forgive ye obligation you laid upon me to leave thee for this place, which I find (as I must do all others) intolerable without thee ; but I am sure you advisd it for my health, and so I pardon the kind mistake ; for how can the body thrive when the mind suffers, as mine must do when ever absent from its better part, thy self. Pray, my dear, never say (if you love me,) if I love you, again upon ye like request ; for tis a thing I cannot grant, and would never refuse thee any thing. I am this moment sent for to Lord Godolphin's to settle Cripples match, which is within an hour of being lost, as all my time hath been & will be till I am with thee again, thou dearest charmer of his soul who is thy faith- full friend and constant lover, J. H.

142.　Mrs. Hervey to John Hervey.　　　London, May 1, 1697.

My dear dearest Treasure

Tis now ten a'clock, till which time I have waited (and do so still) with great impatience for a letter by the coach, which I hope will bring me the welcome news of your safe arrival at Newmarket. I have sent one to wait for its coming in, but have not yet any answer ; now I hear the voice of the welcome messenger ; but I find he is quite contrary so to me, coming empty handed, and tells me Bury coach does not come in to night. I did not need that weighty addition of affliction to what I felt before ; but I have been this hour in your dear closett, where my tears have been some relief to me. And now, my dear dear love, I must beg that nothing but death may ever part us again if I can out live this, which is a triall of my utmost strength. It is impossible for me, my dear, ever to express my heart and soul, which is beyond all expression full of love to you, my dear dearest life ; the only thing I live upon is the Green Man a Wednesday ; and, sure, the sickest stomach need not a greater cordial to revive them than (I hope) I shall meet there. The cruel post will give me leave to say no more but that the children, thank God, are all well, but my self farr from it both in body and mind. I need not tell you the disease of the last : the first is what you left me with, which I fear is rather worse than better ; our young unknown friend is as well as it can be in so ill a habitation. I have been at my Lady Manchesters to day in hopes of some news, but can meet with none. Mr. Morris's letter gives you an account (though a very ill one) of your own affairs ; so my only business is to tell you (if I could) how much I love you and am your dutyful and obedient wife, E. Hervey.

P.S.—This minute the dear letter (which I heartily thank you for and the kind promise of another on Monday) is come, which brings me the welcome news of your being got safe to Newmarket, which I hope will give me a better nights rest than I had last night. My duty to Papa.

143.   My ever-new Delight   Newmarket, May 1, 1697.

Notwithstanding tis 3 a clock in the morning, that I can get no paper (unworthy to be endorsed by thy dear hand and lodgd among the other records of my love,) and that my pen is for its part yet worse than that ; yet I cannot goe to bed (and much less rest when I am there) till I have first done what thou desiredst and satisfied thee of our getting well hither ; well, did I say? a very false and improper expression for my being or doing any thing without thee ; for it is impossible I can be or do well where thou art not. To morrow, please God, I'll write to thee again (I shoud have said to day) by the post, this way of conveyance by the coaches being uncertain ; but besides twas your request, and there needs no other motive to make me do any thing, unless (which is not supposeable) you'd have me love you less, and that, I confess, is out of my power to comply with, being unalterably, without remission or division, my dearest life, thy faithful friend & constant lover, J. Hervey.

144. My ever-new Delight   Newmarkett, May 1, 1697.

Going to bed so late this morning, I am gott up just time enough before ye post goes away to tel thee I shall be happy again in [seeing thee] on Wensday. However I woud by no means have you come to meet me any part of ye way in heat & dust, not knowing whether I shall not return with ye Duchess of Devonshire, whose ways are uncertain of comeing into town ; & it woud give me a double uneasynes to miss thee & to have thee disappointed too, which I would be glad thou couldst have to say thou never wert on my account in any thing or upon any occasion, it being my cheif pleasure to think how perfect in heart I feel myself towards thee, & ye completion of my happyness is in reflecting how much (and more than that if humanity did allow it) thou deservedst it from, my dearest life, thy faithfull friend & constant lover, J. Hervey.

145. My ever-new Delight   Newmarket. May 3, 1697.

Knowing how kind a welcome all my scribbles meet with where they are addressed, neither heart nor hand can forbear, when any opportunity offers, to tell thee (tho' but by faint images of the former) how much I long to be in the place of this my harbinger, tho' perhaps thou mayst not see it but few hours before my arrival, which by the grace of God shall not be deferred one moment beyond Wednesday night ; for all time is worse than lost that's spent where thou art not, thou only relish to all other pleasures. Tis you alone that sweetens life, and make one wish the wings of time were clipt, which not only seems but really flies away too fast, much too

Vol. I.   Q

fast, for those that love (shall I be vain and say) like us; for that instead of breeding a satiety in either, (you see I answer for you boldly,) the common fate of vulgar friendships, does but heighten the vehemence of our desires for a more intimate (if that be possible) and lasting enjoyment of each others conversation and love. Ah! my dear, how I could expatiate on this fruitful theme, were it not day-light already, which if thou knewest, I am sure, Pray, my dear, goe to bed, would be your request to, my dearest life, your faithful friend and constant lover, J. Hervey.

146.   Mrs. Hervey to John Hervey.   Bury, October 25, 1697.
     My dear dear love,

                     Ye hundred things I had to say when you left me, (& shoud endeed have so if you weir to be with me as many years,) must now be only to repeat how much and dearly I love you & have wanted you these few but tedious hours you have been absent. . . . . . Though I coud dwell for ever on this subject, yet I am sure you woud be angry with me if I did not tel ye wants those bills you left me to pay has put me in more then I thought for; but £20 will effectuially do my bisnes, which sum, if it is not easy for you to send, a note for Mr. Cook to receive it at London will do as well; for he can let me have that or any other sum I want; but I shall nead no more. Sence I have lost so much time & papar from my cheif bisness (love), I will add a little more to it by teling you ye four sisters have been hear this afternoon, & (as they never come unattended) brought with them Mr. Ga——, Mr. Down——, & Mr. Bo——. Part of them staid & playd at whish tel this moment, which is past eleven a'clock, tho' they are to hunt to morow morning. I had like to have forgot my Lady Russell, which I wonder I shoud, sens she never dus you; nor, to give ye rest their due, they did not nether, finding that ye only subject coud entertain me. But I forgitt Newmarkett is not a place to receive, nor (I am afraid) to write long letters in, tho' I shoud be very glad to have one; in ye hopes of that I will let you loos no more time in reading this; so, my dear dearest, good night to you.

Their is a bundell of writings in your closett which I am afraid you forgot; let me know if you woud have that or any thing else brought you.

147.   To Mr. Ling, Alderman of Bury.   November, 23, 1697.
      Mr. Alderman,

                     The addresses which come dayly up from all places makes me take ye liberty of reminding you and ye rest of my loyal townsmen that Bury woud seem singular to be silent at a time when even those congratulate who neither wishd well to our Prince or peace; & our Corporation being (to my knowledge) as eminently zealous for ye prosperity of ye one and ye continuation of ye other as any other body politick in England, I would by no means leave them liable (by any omission) to be misconstrued on this occasion, as (to my great dissatisfaction) they have been mis-represented by former appearances; and therefore to prevent future ones I hope ye proposition will be approvd of by them; and in case you & they from my past behaviour in ye trusts you honourd me with shoud esteem mine ye properest hand to present it by, I believe twould be as graciously received as any of ye rest from their and your, etc.

148.   Mrs. Hervey to Mr. Hervey at Lord Fevershams.

                     London, January 4, 1697.
                     I have been in such a fright that till this moment I coud not think of sending you word of it, haveing no body left in the house, but all gon to Papa (by his disire) to help him to remove his goods, part of which are hear already, & himselve a coming as soon as he has removd ye rest, I believe. I nead not tel you how very great the fire is. Ye last messenger brought word the Chapell was just going to be blown up; my Papa fears their is no stoping it, so God knows how farr it may go. You

cant have your coach, for it is gon to fetch things from Papa's lodgings. My dear dear, farwell. For God's sake dont attemt going to Whitehall, for their is such a crowd that their must be a world of mischeif don, & my Papa will be hear before you can possible gitt their.

149.   My ever-new Delight,   Newmarket, March 2, 1698.

Because I knew you woud in the first place be satisfied that I am come well hither, this is to assure you of it ; and in ye next to tell you how unable I find myself to perform any of the businesses I proposd to my self when I left you, since they will necessarily (if executed) keep me from you longer than I feel it possible for me to live without you already. My house (as little as it is) appears to me with a melancholy emptiness . . . thy most faithfull friend and constant lover, J. Hervey.

P.S.—Kiss and bless all the dear little and great children for me, as I have kissd mama's picture and blessd God for the original. Lord Godolphin saies Sunday ; and now I desire it may be Saturday, which made him laugh. No Green Man expedition in the cold and over the stones, I enjoyn.

150.   Mrs. Hervey to John Hervey.   London, Aprill 4, 1698.

My dear dearest life,

Tel this moment I knew nothing of the pleasing releif I am like to have in my afflictions by the post going (and I hope to find the same from its coming) every day. I am now at the Duchess of Graftons, where I sup, & she finding the nead I had of this pleasur, which conversing with you (in any kind) allways gives me, has lockd me up in her closett with a pen & ink, ye welcomest entertainment she coud give me, weir I but able with it to express to my dearest dear what my heart feals. O my dear life, coud you but tell (but that for your own sake I woud not have you) the pain I have indurd sence we parted, & how often I have repented ye not going with you upon any terms, tho' it had been never to come nearer to you then Bury, nay and to say more, I woud be content to be lockt up all day with Mr. R—— and F—— so I coud see you but one moment in that time. Theirfore dont trust me with but saying, you have mist me, for fear you shoud not do it many hours after; but next to that I have the best & kindest offer by my sister widow, ye Duchess of St. Albains, who has been with me all day, & begd of me to go with her to Windsor, where we might talk & cry together tel you both come back to us. I have changd my room sence you left me to ly in the nursery with Jack, who, as if he studed to entertain me, calls all day upon Papa. Thank God, they are all well, as I hope their dear orrigenall is, & that you got as well to Newmarkett as I heard you did to Hockerell. Super is upon ye table, so I must bid my dear goodnight, a better then I fear I am like to have by what I felt last night. Once more, my dearest, farewell, E. Hervey.

All hear are your servants, & wish you good luck.

151. Mrs. Hervey to John Hervey. London, Aprill 5, 1698.

My dear dear love

The being abroad last night when I wrote to you made me forced to break off, though I was ready to burst, and am so full now I dont know where to begin; but if it shoud be of love, I am sure I shoud never end without more time than I hope I shall need a pen and paper to express it. This, I believe, will find you at Bury, where I design to direct it; but I have sent you a box by the coach, which I orderd to be left at Newmarket. I dare not tell you how near I was bringing it my self the same way, for fear you shoud chide me. You will find some biskets at the bottom of the box, which I desire you woud eat with some sack before you go on to the Heath, and not forget chocolate with my Papa: for my sake I beg you woud do this: I have sent you the only things I coud think of that you like. My poor melancholly dutchess was with me this morning to drink yours and the Duke of St. Albans health in chocolate. We are all day a fancying what you are doing in every minute. The town is so empty it affords no news ; nor no body talks of any thing but Newmarket. I suppose I need not tell you of the pistol that was found in the Chapel, for you must have heard of it, and it is too long to hear twice at Newmarket, as I am afraid my letter will be, since the post comes every day. Therefore, my dear dear everlasting love, I woud only tell you (if I coud) how much and dearly I love you, and am your most faithful wife, E. Hervey.

P.S.—The children are all well, but Jack did not sleep very well, which was a double trouble to me, the fear of his being ill besides the being waked so often, for my lodging is still with him.

152.   My ever-new Delight   Newmarkett, Aprill 5, 1698.

If you coud hate all that came with me (and your Papa of ye company) because they seemd to take me from you, how well do you think it possible for me to love poor Jack, who I look upon as a sort of rivall that hinderd me of ye greatest pleasure I have on earth, I need not say thy being with me hear, a place I am as weary of without thee (and love it yet less than thou dost) as I shoud be of ye whole world, wert thou not in it; and long already (already is a wrong expression, & injures much my heart, having felt ye strong desire of being with thee again from ye moment I left thee,) for ye day of my return. I can yet send you no news from this place only that ye King came well, tho' late, hither last night. I went to waite on him at his arrival, and was most graciously receivd, as I was likewise by Mrs. Ramseys pretty fellow, ending the night at bassett in his lodgings, after having suppd with Lord Essex & Lord Scarburr (the officers in waiting) by invitation. I promisd you a diary, and this is to perform it, as I ever have, & will do even of ye minutest consequence every one that ever I made thee, being fast bound in justice & gratitude to a strict return of love & truth by thy dear & good example to thy constant faithfull lover, J. Hervey.

Commend me kindly to our sweet children.

153. Mrs. Hervey to John Hervey. London, April 6, 1698.
I cant help thanking my dearest dear for his letter, tho' this is the third I have wrote within these 48 hours. I confess my impatience to hear how you got to Newmarket (and never being disappointed in any thing by you before) made me expect a letter by the coach on Tuesday so much that I sent Corbet to wait for its coming in, that I might not loose a minute in hearing the welcome news of your being got well thither. I wish that were no more my rival than Jack is yours; but for all the hatred I have to it, I cant help wishing my self there every minute in the day; I dont say in the night too, because I am always with you in my sleep, and am very angry with poor Jack when he wakes me from that pleasing dream. The gentleman I am talking of is just come in calling upon dear Papa; he cryd and would not be qniet in the morning till they carried him into your dressing-room, and then he went directly to your closet door, knocking and calling upon you to let him in. He and all the rest are well. You did not send me word what luck you had at Bassett. I shall be glad to hear both of that and your matches. Oh my dear dear love, could you want to see me but half so much as I do you, or as you told me (I fear only as you knew how well it woud please me) in your letter, you woud have bid me follow you, and then you woud have seen how long Jack coud have kept me from you. I only wish that Elephant and his companions may keep you no longer, and then I shall soon be happy with the sight of my dear dear & everlasting pleasure; in the mean time I shoud be glad if you woud any way employ me, that, next seeing you, being the greatest pleasure that can be to, my dear life, your faithful & obedient wife, E. Hervey.

P.S.—I have heard nothing of Mr. Panceford.

154. Mrs. Hervey to John Hervey. London, April 7, 1698.
My dear dearest love
I believe it very unnecessary (yet I cant help doing it) to tell any body at Newmarket that four to one is great odds; but I

hope you will find more benefit by taking of it in betts than you have done in my letters; for coud you have had (which if it had been possible I am sure you woud) as many score of them, it woud have been a cheap purchase to me for that one dear kind letter from you which I must again thank you for. I cant help being so unreasonable as to beg I may not loose the advantage of the post coming every day, but that when you have not time your self, you woud make that monster Welch Tom get Charles to write for him to me. I hate him now more than ever for being so happy while I am so miserable; but pray dont let him have the pleasure to know my misfortunes. I can have no hope against him now but that the great coach horse may have made him so sore in his journey, that he will not be able to see a match, and that woud please me as well as any thing can do now. For God-sake, my dear, if there be any thought of your staying a day after Saturday come sen'night, send me word that I may come to you, if ever you design to see me alive again, which you woud believe there was some danger of, even in that time, if you coud but know what I feel; and to add to my spleen I have had twenty impertinent visits since I began this small, but greatest, ease I have now to my poor heavy heart. My Lady Robinson is here and presents her service to you. She says she dare not say any kind thing to you for fear I shoud not write it, and any thing otherwise would be contrary to her inclination: but now I've told you this I think she need not mistrust me for any thing else. I hear no news, but I will keep my letter open for some as long as I can, though I durst not put off writing for fear I shoud be hindred, my Lady Hartington (who has been here already) and my Lady Ross promising to come in the evening to play at picket, which puts me in mind of a debt I owe Sir James Forbes of 4 guineas and a half; I forgot to pay him before he went out of town; therefore I desire you would do it for me. My Lady Robinson says I have wrote enough for six letters, and will not let me say any more; but the old sentence I am so full of I must repeat; dear dear, how I do love you, and how much I am with all sincerity entirely yours, E. Hervey.   P.S.—The children are all well.

155.　My ever-new Delight　　　Newmarkett, April 7, 1698.

Having read no Gazette, or seen any other advertisments sence I came hither, kept me a stranger to ye good news you send me of ye posts going every day between us ; whereby I can assure you faithfully I shall feel an equal reliefe (at least) by venting a heart full of you at all times, & hope a greater benefitt (than can accrue to you) by a frequent converse this way. But hitherto I've gained nothing by it more than I should have done without it, having received your dear kind letter of ye 4th but last night a little after ye box, for which I thank thee heartily. Notwithstanding ye honest caution you gave me, that I ought not to trust you with ye knowledg of my missing & wanting you ever since I saw you, I must again repeat (what I've already told you in my last) that my condition is so imperfect, life such a nothing without thee, that farr from being what's called living it ought not to be termed a bare existence, when under such sensible privations as absence from ye only thing we love. Yesterday I was at Bury, but so maloncholly at ye sight of every place where we had been together, by comparing my circomstances then and how I found myself at that time, that I could hardly bear it, & so returnd ye same night hither for the refreshment of thy letter, which gave some ease to thy distressed lover, J. Hervey.

156.　Mrs. Hervey to John Hervey.　　London, Aprill 8, 1698.

My dear dear life & soul

To tel how much I love and long to see you is equally imposable, which makes me a little more sencable of my frinds misfortunes, whose love is, I think, as near to my own as the object can bear, meaning the Duchess of St. Albains. She has not heard yet from her lord ; theirfore I disire you would put him in mind of it, tho' I am sorry he neads it. I am very compassionett to my sister widows, & theirfore hope Lord Ross received ye letter my Lady writ hear last night, for she was in great care to know how to direct it safe. I am afraid by your not staying at Bury on Wensday night you did not receive ye letter I directed thether, for I have writt so many I cant tel by yours which you have received, but I have not miss'd one day sence you left this poor dismall place, yet I did not find ye post by any print, my love being always inquisetive to know how it may be oftenest exprest. The town is visably empty ; one may go all day abroad and not meet ten coaches ; the men being all with you the ladys stir very little ; theirfore I nead not tel you their is no news. Lady Harttinton & Lady Jersey supt hear last night ; to morow we dine with the latter, which will be ye first time I have eat from ye poor bratts sence you left us, they being now all ye comfort I have. They are all well. Jack & Betty lay in bed of each side of me, & ye other two by ye bed side, while I was drinking your health in joccolate, which that it may continue as long as I am sure my love will last is the constant prayers of, my dear dear angell, your ever faithfull wife and servant, E. Hervey. Mr. Pancford has brought me £ 17.

157.   My ever-new Delight   Newmarkett, Aprill 9, 1698.

      In your last you told me you were afraid twould be to long, & ye reason you gave for't (but could their be any I'm sure not a good one unless it were to ease you) was becaus ye post came every day, which has been so farr from making me ye happyer by it hitherto that I did not (only) receive any Thursdays, but also miss'd of one by ye ordinary post last night ; which I so little creditted that I went my self to see (tho' late,) and tumbled over all ye letters twice, one by one, but all ended in ye sad disappointment of finding none from thee ; wherein I've no resource but hoping you'l be hear to night, or els that I may meet with one at Bury, whither I am this minute going with Papa, but shall return big with ye expectation of seeing my present want effectually compensated by thy dear presence here, without which I can no longer subsist ; but should this find you before ye resolution be putt in execution, considering your ease and safety rather than my quiet or satisfaction, I begg you woud not think of coming after Monday, because (if possible) I'll see you in Town on or before Sunday. I'm sorry to hear my rivall slept no better, & more so because it disturbed our pretty mistress, who I woud have never know any uneasyness but that which absence causes in a more supreme degree within ye heart of her most faithfull constant lover, J. Hervey.

Hoboy was beaten yesterday, & we are half undone, £556.

158. My ever-new Delight   Newmarkett, April 9, 1698.

Since I sent my letter to the post, I've been agreeably surprisd with two of thy dear letters at once, for which this is to thank thee with all my heart, & will reduce ye odds from 4 to one to 5 to 4, ye match between us being so kind a sort of strife (and others may we be alwaies strangers to) as who shall please each other most, it makes this riddle good, that those who are outdone winn most; & tho' in all things else your pleasure is more studied than my own, yet I must own I woud be still orecome where I'm so great a gainer & you can loose so little. You know not how improperly, ney worse, how most injuriously you speak, when'ere you do but call (for think so, I'm sattisfied, you cannot) Newmarkett, or indeed any thing else, your rivall, there being neither pleasure to be tasted or person to be seen in this world that ever did or can stand in any competition with thee for ye least morsell of my heart, which is so individuably thine as wants a simile to express it by, & woud be best defind by saying (only) tis what it is, to thee. Welch Tom was ye very spectacle you describd & wishd him after riding ye coach horse ; & for a farther mortification to him (that I may indulge your spleen towards him) have this moment sent him to Bury on no better a padd than Bullet head to make your Papa's excuse, (who sends me word he felt some touches of ye goute last night,) that we coud not meet our Lord Lievtenants there as we had promisd. I must conclude with a reproof for one passage in your letter of ye 6th, which contains a double injury to my love; first to soppose I do not want you half so much as you do me, (but that I can forgive as a resultance from ye intensness of your own feeling;) but ye parenthesis is inexcusable, that you fear I only told you how much I was at a loss & undone without thee, becaus I knew how well it would please, which is a suggestion that wrongs my love, & not only so but questions my truth, which shall alwaies be most inviolably observd by me (as a thing most peculiarly your due) in every action of my life, which I desire may last no longer than till I deviate from any one profession of love or truth I ever made thee; and were my lease of life to have continuance till such forfeiture, I shoud survive even ye term of years thy kind wishes in discourse have often seemd to compound with providence for. May God allmighty love us both so as to preserve our loves & frindship here; which coming so near ye joys of heaven, & giving us such antepasts of ye pleasures there, may make us more carefull to deserve meeting with one another hearafter, to live with him for ever, is ye prayer of thy undeserving frind & lover, J. Hervey.

159.   Mrs. Hervey to John Hervey.   London, Aprill 9, 1698.

My dear dearest life

        I have deferd writing all day in hopes of a letter, and am now come to Lady Orkneys, where my Lady Jersey is, & they will not lett me leave omber any longer then just to keep to my old custum of writing every post, and to lett you know I sent you a present yesterday by Mr. Smith, which I hope came safe to your hands. I had sent you word of it by the letter I wrote last night, but that I was not sure it woud be done time enough, for Mr. Chambers did not send the butten home till 12 a clock, & spoyled it at last, which I fretted heartyly about. I satt up tel between one & two to fitt ye riben, which I hope succeeded well, for I measurd it by ye lockett you usd to wear. The picture, I believe, has some falts, but he has promist to alter any thing you dislike, (it is Sir Godfrey Knellers brother that drew it ;) but be it as it will I hope you will ware it tel you have ye orrigenale, & take it as it was ment by her, who is, my dearest life, your most faithfull & affectionett wife, E. Hervey.

Your children are all well, but Jack did not let me sleep 2 hours; he cryd all night.

160.   My ever-new Delight   Newmarkett, Aprill 11, 1698.

The kind (I cant call it pretty, at least not half so much so as its dear inimitable origenal) present you sent me by Mr. Smith was so agreeable an apparition to me upon unfolding ye woole wherein it lay, that I coud scarce conceal ye surprise it wrought from all ye company before whom twas opend.   Lord Carlisle (especially) discoverd my condicion, & thence grew curious to understand ye cause, which least he should mistake (from musing as he uses) and think it came from any hand but thine, I just gave him a cursory view of it, and kissing of it calld it my only inclinations representative; who so much deservd the glance I lett him have of it as to say, he knew by what I said & did whose it must be, had he not seen ye face at all. My dearest love, with what affection I received it, considering thy kind part in it, can no more be told than you describe (I'll please you with a comparison) your love to me ; and this comes by ye first oppertunitty to thank thee for't with all ye kindness it deserves, and to lett tbee know I put it on my arm ye moment I beheld it, & there have kissd it ore & ore till I have almost spoild ye crystall. My sleep was better for its company last night, & (tho' it wrongs thee very much) am grown fond already, because it bears some marks of a resemblance to my matchless mistress. You needed not have sent a quickener to make me more impatient than I was before to see thee; however, this last expression of thy kindness has gaind a day, being determind to be with thee on Satherday, whatever happens. I dont know whether this will find you sooner than that which shall succeed it to morrow; for tho' you send & I write by ye extrodinary postes, yet I have never received any but on ye ordinary daies; & then they bring them two by two. I am summond in hast to look after ye boys weight that is to ride Stiff dick this day, wherein you being interested, (I having a great deal of mony on ye match,) I will force my self to conclude here; otherwise I shoud have left no more room in this than ye last paper, having a heart as inexhaustable of love as its dear object is of charms, being all things in perfection that coud make or can continue ye happiness of, my dearest mistress, your faithfull constant lover, J. Hervey.

I have paid Sir James as you disird. Lord Sherrard has paid ye forfeit of ye match I made with him; & now ye tide seems to turn as to W: & L:.

161. My ever-new Delight   Newmarkett, Aprill 11, 1698.

Notwithstanding I writt to thee not above 5 hours since, yet (hearing ye poste is not gone) I cant deferr letting you know any good luck of mine one moment, because you joy or grieve in all things with me, being my an other self. I am therfore retird (in hast) from all ye company to tell you Stiff dick has beat Careless, and that we have wonn above six hundred pounds upon him, which will near bring you off both hear & for ye winter. Tis impossible any thing shoud conclude amiss where so much goodness is consernd as dwells within that heart, whose owner is ye treasure of J. H.   I have just now kissd ye picture, & hope to serve ye original so on Satherday.

162. Mrs. Hervey to John Hervey.   London, Aprill 12, 1698.

I this morning received ye welcome news of my dear dearest life having won his match yesterday by three several hands, Lord Conesby, Mr. Montague, & Mr. Smith; the two first sent as soon as they came to town; & the last came himself with Mrs. Smith, not only to tel this news, but that of much greater consern to me, your being well, & that the remembrance I sent you of me (tho' by what I have ever found I am sure you did not nead it) came safe to your hands. I hope you ware it, and that it was the image of her, whose heart is always with you, brought you so much good luck, & will still continue to do so. I supt last night with the Duchess ot Grafton at Mrs. Smiths, where I was invited to day to dinner, but I told her it was imposable to bear the sight of seeing her so happy as to have Mr. Smith again, while I sufferd so much by your absence. Pray, my dear, dont forgitt to tel me the happy day when and where I shall meet you, which is so impatiently longd for by, my dear dearest life & soul, your ever constant & truly affecttionet wife, E. Hervey.

I sent for Dr. Hobbs to Miss, but he is gon out of town, & left directions with his servant. The other 3 are all well, & Jack slept well, which was more then I did, being very il with my old complaint.

163.   My ever-new Delight   Newmarkett, Aprill 12, 1698.

This, with ye two I sent yesterday, will turn ye odds on my side; which, considering all ye possible leisure I can have hear, will best convince you how much better I love your converse than any thing this place or ye rest of ye world affords; ney, I have hitherto outdone thy self, shoud I this morning receive ye letter (I have again sent to see for) which ought to have come last night. The Duke of St. Albans is about buying your dun mare for his Dutches, & being in discourse about her price I took occasion to lett him know I woud not sell her at all, were it not that her grace (I knew) was more in your books than any body; to which he answerd he coud assurr me no love was lost between our wives. I also grafted upon this conversation the hint you disird I woud give him about her not having heard from him at his first coming down. My dearest love, I coud never have digressd thus long from talking of our own loves, but that I must show you I can never forgitt ye least thing you desire of me, which

putts me in mind to tell you how punctual I have been in an other injunction you laid on me at parting ; & that is, never to go out fasting ; which I
have observd so well as to grow fatt upon my exercise; for very often I
have eat more than I naturally shoud have done with thinking, had you
been by, you woud have said, My dear, you have eat nothing ; you'l be
starved ; pray think of some thing else, or I wont eat a bitt these three daies.
Thus you see how ever present you are to me when you little think on't ;
but what meritt is there in contriving to give ones self the pleasure of
making what one loves as much with us as absence can admitt of; the
satisfaction is mine ; but still I know twill be no small contentment to thy
heart to know how much I live (in some maner) and converse with thee
at this distance; and how often ye resolution has been taken of never
suffering an other absence by, my only joy, your faithfull friend & constant
lover, J. Hervey.

> **164.**   Mrs. Hervey to John Hervey.   London, Aprill, 13, 1698.
>   My dear dearest life
>   I received this afternoon 3 of your dear letters, 2
> of which (I find by ye date) shoud have come yesterday, a loss too great for
> me ever to forgive ye post, both as to there own value & ye bringing me ye
> welcome news so many hours sooner of my seeing you a Satherday. I hope
> to know the place where I am to meet you by Frydays post, for to morow I
> cant expect it, having never received a letter but by ye generale post, tho'
> you (who are my oracle) tell me you have writt of ye other days. I am
> glad my picture found its wishd success in pleasing you so well, which has
> doubly paid all ye pains I took to gitt it done so soon ; yet I cant help
> envying the dear kind kisses you say you have so often bestowd upon it.   O
> my dear dear love, how I long for ye happy hour of our meeting again, for
> I think it is an age sence I saw you last ; a tedious time indeed, and longer
> then I hope I shall ever live withcut you again. Jack is all this while

calling upon Papa, & dus so every day, which is ye only thing I can find him like his mother in. May he & all that I have or ever shall have second me (equale I am sure they cannot) in love to you, is and shall be ye constant prayers of my dear dear angells ever faithfull & affectionet wife, E. Hervey.

The children are all well. I shall write no more, sence you may come part of ye way on Fryday.

165.   My ever-new Delight   Newmarkett, Aprill 13, 1698.

This I hope will be ye last you are to have, intend-ing (God permitting) to be with thee on Saturday; but at what time or which way I shall come cannot (indeed will not for fear of accidents) tell you; & in this I mightily deny my self for thy ease and safetys sake, being more impatient (than you (I will say,) can or ought to be) to see thee than ever hitherto I was. Mr. Gage is just come in, & ye post going out, so I must conclude with again assuring thee Saturday shall make me as happy with thee as I have been uneasy without thee. J. Hervey.

I must tell you I shall come by ye Green Man.

166.   My ever-new Delight   Aprill 14, 1698.

Whether twas thy dear picture, or the postscript which told me how strong your good wishes were for my better fortune, have turnd ye tide of my ill luck, I cannot tell; but one or both together have at last prevaild; for yesterday Turk did not only win ye 100 guineas I backd him for, but honest Lobcock by ye most supernatural invincible goodness that ever was shown in any creature at last betterd Looby, tho' he run much too fast for him, & had beat him ye first 7 mile of ye 8 they run; but upon Lobcocks being whipt & spurrd from shoulder to flank, he at last conquerd his adversary & wonn us 325 guineys; ye odd 25 was a bett ye king made with me against Lobcock, who was more pleasd with this match than all he ever saw before. I have been ye more perticular in this relation, becaus I am sure twill be some sattisfaction to thee to know how much this victory must have pleasd me; which endeed it did more than ever any match did before, because it succeeded almost to a yard according to ye presumption on which I made it. But why have I been thus long from telling thee how very strangely I love thee, more than ever; how insupportably impatient to be with thee; which no accident (God willing none) shall be able to divert from by Saturday, having this morning bespoke a sett of horses to bring me as farr as Hockerhill towards thee. . . . . . J. Hervey.

167.   Mrs. Hervey to John Hervey.   Bury, May 7, 1698.

It has been some pleasure to me in my afflictions to see so fine a day for my dear dearest life in his jurney, & I hope we shall have the same good luck Monday & Tuesday tell 2 or 3 a clock, (& then, lett it rain or shine, my heart & eyes will be so full with ye object of my everlasting happynes it will leave no room for any other thought,) by which time I hope to dine with you in Jermyn Street. In the mean time I wish any thing in that place coud give you the same thoughts ye papar you left did hear, in ye absence of her who is and ever will be to ye last moment of my life my dear dear angells faithfull constant & obedient wife, E. Hervey.

Mrs. Berkeley presents her servis to you; we have had ye musick hear, & I have heard ye old muincutt (by my own desire) with tears for this hour (which you left me brim full of).

168.   From ye parlement house. June 29, 1698.

My ever-new Delight

I spoke this morning to Lord Feversham about a place for you at Somersett house to hear (if you care for it) ye musick; who hath promisd me to order them that they shoud lett you through ye Queens lodgings. What I shall be able to do, I know not; but if I can I'le meet you there, shoud you resolve to go. I am without division or remission your faithfull lover, J. Hervey.

169. Mrs. Hervey to John Hervey. To ye parlement house.

June 29, 1698,

My dearest life

Sence you went out, I find I have given you very wrong intelegence conserning ye musick to night, having told you it was to be upon ye watter; & Lady Burlinton sent to me just now to know if I woud go with her to Somersett house garden to hear it. I am not certain of ye hour; but I believe you will be at liberty time enough, if you care for it. Pray send me word how you are inclind, & accordingly I will order my affaire, being under no ingagement, but shall be ready ether to meett you there, or at home, or to take ye air, all places being equally pleasing with you, & none so without you, to your most affectionet wife, E. Hervey.

170. To Mr. Ling, Alderman of Bury. London, July 7, 1698.

Sir

This being the last paper I shall send you of this session or Parliament, I cannot let it come to you without my thanks to your self and ye rest of my friends in your body for ye particular honour they have twice done me in so unanimous a choice to ye placing me in a station of so great a trust, wherein I must do my self ye justice to assure them and you that I have acted with all ye faithfullness and zeal for theirs and ye nations true interests that an honest heart coud dictate; that I ever have and by ye grace of God ever will keep a conscience void of ye offence of any partial, prejudicial leaning towards ye Kings prerogatives or peoples priviledges, but endeavour to preserve ye Monarchy and Hierarchy in their just and legal rights; that ye people may be protected in their liberty and property, which, I hope, peace and plenty will make them masters of. I shall add no more at present but by you to make a tender of my service to them; &, whether they think fit to continue me their imediate servant or not, to assure them I shall nevertheless remain their faithfull friend, to promote everything that shall or may tend to ye prosperity of Bury and its inhabitants, as long as I have power, life or interest left me. I never did nor will prescribe any thing to influence them in their Elections, not doubting but men of their substance, understanding and integrity will never think of conferring so great a trust on any man but such as they are sure are friends in the first place to our present happy settlement, and consequently no less lovers of all that is or shoud be dear to all mankind, viz. the Protestant religion, liberty, property and ye preservation of our ancient, wise and happy constitution. Next week (God willing) I intend to be amongst ye, and shoud be glad to do any service for you or them before I leave this place, being their & your etc.

171.   To my Lord Chancellor Somers.   Bury, Sept. 17, 1698.

May it please your Lordship,

The occasion of my presuming to give your Lordship this trouble is to acquaint your Lordship with a vacancy that has happend in ye Vicaridge of Cavenham in Suffolk within your Lordships gift, and humbly beg ye favour that you woud please to confer ye same on this bearer, Mr. James Davies, who, I know, is so good a schollar, and a man of so sober and charitable a life and conversation, that I intend to present him to ye adjacent Rectory of Tuddenham, now likewise void by ye death of ye last incumbent, Mr. Le Roy, who held them both by union, as his predecessors have done by reason of their insufficiency (when seperate) to yield a comfortable maintenance to their ministers ; & if your Lordship in your wisdom shall think fit to continue them in their former method, (which I know to be necessary for their affording a competent subsistence,) your Lordship will do an acceptable act to both ye parishes, and therein also further oblige one who is already with most sincere respect and veneration, my Lord, etc.

172. To Mrs. Auchmouty. Nov. 30, 1698.

Dear Cousen

Yours of ye 16 July I receivd not from Mr. Ridley till we met at Newmarket; from whence you woud have had as imediate an answer as ye nature & circumstance of ye affair it treated of seemed to require, coud I have discoursd Mr. Pooley sooner in it than at my arrival here; which I have now done, and finding in him ye same disposition to comply with your desires as I carried along with me, which is most willingly to accomodate you with ye money in case I be securd by ye same decree which is to indemnify him, and that you will suffer it to be settled to ye same uses in France (wherever disposed of) that your friends insisted on (and your husband so kindly consented to) for your sake, and which it now stands subject to here. These conditions being fulfilld both principal and interest shall be ready whenever calld for by Mr. Pooley or your assigns. You have made me ye more happy by telling me you are perfectly so, were it not for ye allay your losses here have mixt it with; which you may remember enough of me and mine to conclude could never happen without giving a deep tincture of black dispair to all hopes of future worldly felicitys in me. But as it has pleasd God to shew not only his infinite mercy but power towards me, in making good again in one friend (as far as humane nature is capable of) what I had sufferd by ye many he took from me; so I hope Mr. Auchmouty supplys ye same deffects in your fortunes that my present wife has wonderfully retrievd in mine; who I cannot commend more then in thinking & calling her ye counterpart in all virtues and perfections of her (but by this) inimitable predecessor. I had a father whose memory I more and more revere, as my mind becomes capable of comprehending ye excellencys that dwelt in his; a mother whose virtues and good deeds I look upon to have been a yet greater inheritance than was left me by my wise and kind uncle; a brother and sisters that I loved without a jealousy, either with regard to interest or my parents affections ; and, as a crown to all these, you knew ye wife I had, whose virtues (were it necessary to tell them you) were so boundless as to make them unspeakable; and yet (I wont wonder if you shoud be incredulous and think it most impossible) such a Phœnix has arisen out of those sacred ashes, as shoud any one put Elkanahs question to me, (such is ye fullness of my present happyness and satisfaction in that dear friend I'm blessd with,) it coud not very easily be resolvd by, dear Mrs. Auchmouty, yours etc.

173.   Letters in London upon several occasions. 1698.*

My dearest dear

I think it may be of use to you now you are at Westminster to know Mr. Chamberlin has just been hear from my Lord Mont— & Lady Hervey, who have both seen your papar, & reffer it to Mr. Jenings to dispute ye matter with Mr. Pooly, when you have given him your instructions, and appointed a time most convenient to them, and what they agree on to be referrd to my Lord Chancellour or any third person ; or (if you like it) my Lord Mont— hopes they will agree it, so that you may deside the differance your selves, without giving my Lord Chancellour (he having so much bisnes) or any body els the trouble. I fear I have given you an imperfect account, but I hope to mend it when we meet ; tell that long time farwell to my dear dear.   I forgott to tell you, Lord Mont— thinks you both being upon honer may determin it your selves.

174.   My dear Angell

I have sent your letters, but was forcd to oppen them for ye Duchess of Grafton, she being very disirous to know something

---

*This heading refers to Nos. 173, 174, 175, 176, all from Mrs. Hervey to her husband. S.H.A.H.

of ye Duke, having not heard from him this 3 posts, & is very uneasy about it; if you can tel her any thing, pray do, & come home soon to, my dearest life, yours for ever.

175. My dearest life   Monday.

This comes to tell you I shall not stay at home (as I told you I shoud); my Lady Orkney not being well has disird Lady Burlinton & I to meet there. I not being very well my self shall not see you at ye Princes's, but beg you woud call me (or send ye coach) as soon as ye drawing room is over, for it woud add much to my ilnes shoud I be without your dear company again; and I shall be glad to come home as soon as you please, for I cant possibly sup abroad, being almost dead, and nothing but your dear company to my self can revive me; therfore I depend upon you : tell when, my dearest dear, farwell.

176.   Thursday.

I am sory to find my dearest life can bear so long an absence, when you know I am come home, & may easyly guess with what impatience I wate for a sight of you after above 12 hours parting, which I count an age, & is indeed so in pain such as I feel when seperated from my dear & better part; but if I weir to say all I could upon this subject, ye reading woud keep you longer from me than you have been already; therfore I will say no more to my dear dear life & soul, but if you love me, see me quickly.

177. From London to Newmarkett.   March 2, 1698.

I hope this will find my dear dearest life safe at Newmarkett, & that you have not increasd your cold by changing your bed or finding it unaird, which I have great pain about, knowing Charls to be a very il orderer, and Roger as il a performer. I shoud be much conserned to

see such bad wether, but that I hope it will bring you back ye sooner, & that
to morows post will give me ye relief you denyd me at your going away by
bringing ye wellcome news of your coming home sooner then you intended ;
(I think I nead not have explaind my self upon this, your denyals being so
few to me of any sort you woud easyly have known what I ment by this.)
I stood yesterday at ye window as long as I coud hear ye coach, (seeing I
coud not pretend to, my eyes weir so full ot tears,) and then I went to bed
again ; but seeing your poor pillow ly bare for want of your dear head upon
it was as sure an andidote for me against sleep as oppium is for it. The
Duchess of St. Albains came to day to comfort me, & staid diner ; & I am
now come to sup with her upon condisions she woud tell me all ye news she
coud, & lett me make an end of my letter with her ; but I can meet with
nothing but that Mr. Newport has carryd his election by 12 votes. Mrs.
Ramsey (who is hear with us) bids me tell you it is ye first point ye Whiggs
have gaind this sessions. My Lord Dover has found very il effects by his
gout medcin, for his head & face is extreemly swelld, and he is in some
danger. Sense I have nothing more of ye publick, I will tell you some
thing of home, (which I believe will pleas you as well ;) the children are all
in health, & Miss has been very good, & had her teeth drawn with very little
pain, & is very well after it. I dare say no more for fear ye post shoud be
gon ; therefore, my dear dear, farwell ; love me but half so well as I do you,
tis all that's askd by your faithfull wife, E. Hervey.

178.   Letters in London on several occasions.   1699.*

Monday 6 a clock.

I have been much disapointed to day in missing
of my dearest life. I went first to Westminster, but found it imposable to
see you ; therefore made some visetts in hopes to find you after at Mr. Rowes ;

---

*This heading refers to Nos. 178, to 186 inclusive, all (except 183) from Mrs. Hervey to John Hervey.
S.II.A.II.

but missing you there, I must sitt down in dispair tell the wellcome hour of your coming home, which I hope will not be late, if your jurney holds for to morow. By an unlucky mistake, ether of my Lady Orkneys servant or mine, I must be forcd to play at omber there, so cannot go with you to Mr. Folks's; I tryd to put it off; but their having been so many blunders I found it imposable; therefore desire you woud call, or send the coach for me, when you come home, (tho' I fear I shall be there before you ;) I am sure I will not be a moment after I know you are, for I long more to see you then can be expressd, being with all my heart & soul, my dear dear, your ever faithfull wife, E. Hervey.

179. To Sir John Germains.

My dear dearest life

Tho' I have mett with one disapointment in ye not bringing you home, I hope it will not be seconded by another in your staying long after me. I woud not have given you this trouble, (tho' I find it so imposable to live without you,) weir it not for a life much dearer to me than my own, for I know your health will be much indangerd if you sitt up; I beg therefore you woud remember this is ye first day of your being abroad, so I hope I nead say no more, but bid my dear dear love farwell. I am just going to bed with a fitt of ye cholick; but that you shoud have known nothing off, did I not feel much greater pain by your absence.

180. My dear

I was mightyly disapointed when I came home & found you weir gon to Ossendays, for I pleasd my self with ye hopes of suping with you; for, if you recollect, you will find I have not eat with you this 6 meals, which is an age to her that loves like me & is intirely yours with all heart & soul. I hope you will not think me unreasonable to disire you woud come home by 12 to super.

Vol. I. T

181.   To ye Duke of Devonshires.

I cant help giving my dear this trouble. Your neces* being gon abroad, I am left to my own thoughts, which have been contemplating upon your perfections so long tell I think I may say (if that be posable) I love you better than ever I did in my life, & coud not help venting my self this way, tho' I had much rather have done it by word of mouth; but if you have a mind to stay longer, dont lett this bring you a muinett sooner to her that impatiently longs to see you, my dear dear.

182.   My dear dear Angell

Super will be ready in a quarter of an hour; & if in that time you have not dispatchd your bisness, it will kill me quite, I long so much to see you. I am now so sick I can say no more, but that I love you with all my heart & soul; how much no toung can express, nor thought conceive, but your E. Hervey.

183.   Your faithfull frind & constant lover stays for your company to Hide Parke. J. Hervey.

184.   To ye Parliment hous.

My Lady Marlborough has been hear just now to call me to go with her & her Lord to see Lady Albermale, & to tel me she had forgot the musick when she made ye appointment with you for Saterday; therefore Mr. Row must come to morow at 6 aclock, that she may have an hour before ye drawing room & the coming after in her own power. Pray lett my Lord Kingston & Mr. Dunch know this, for I sent them word yesterday ye partty was put off tell Saterday. My company will be gon early to night; theirfore I hope you will come home to supper, for I have not eate a

---

*Isabella and Amy Elwes. S.II.A.II.

meal with you this three days; so if you have a mind to be rid of me, tis but to stay away, & I shall be starvd to death. I fear you will think this long episell very unseasonable at this time; so, my dear dear, farwell.

185. To ye Duke of Devonshires.

If my dearest life has no use for the horses, I woud be glad to have the six to cary my Lady Suffolke to High park; she has sent to me to call her; but if you have any occasion for them, a pair will do as well. I hope your going to Kinsinton wont make you stay out ye latter; tor if you are not at home by ten a clock, I shall break my heart, tis so long sence we have supt together alone. Remember the pain of your sholder, & be asurd I feal double the pain for fear of its increas, which I am almost sure of if you sitt up, which I must again beg you woud not; theirfore will take up no more of your time now, but to bid my dear dear love farwell.

186.

I fear my dear dearest life will dread the sight of my fist, it proved so unlucky last time; but I hope Lady Marl—— bisnes may be more successfull than mine; (which is always to gitt you to my self.) She sent to speak with me to day, & this weighty consern was to disire we might take leave of bassett to morow, & begin at 5 a clock, at which hour she will certainly be with me. I thought this a proper time to settle this affair, the company being together, els I woud not have troubled you, tho' I am always glad of any oppertunetty to repeat how much & dearly I love you, & am intirely yours, E. H.

I will only add, remember your cough, and if there be any hopes of seeing you soon, let me know ye welcome news by this messenger; els he stays to come home with you.

187.   To Mr. John Hervey of Thurleigh Hall, near Bedford.

Sir   Bury, August 16, 1699.

What'ere becomes of our proposd agreement, I am sure to be the gainer by its consequencies, since it afforded me ye satisfaction of your acquaintance& ye pleasure of your correspondence, which I desire may be continued, altho' ye happy occasion of both shoud prove abortive.   But as I find ye same inclination in you to leave ye inheritance of Thurleigh Hall to a known descendant from that ancient stem, (having no issue of your own,) that I can have to secure ye possession of it to a name it for some ages past has had for its constant owners ; so I doubt not of your accepting ye same terms (at least) from me that you thought fit to offer it at to Mr. Stephen Hervey [of Surrey] ; and if ye speedy performance of them on my part will work any ease or convenience on your side, ye consideration money menciond in the draught Mr. Brace sent me shall be forthwith prepard to discharge your several debts therein enumerated against such time as my council (Mr. Martin Folks of Greys Inn) can have perusd your family and marriage settlements, and approvd of proper conveyances to answer both our purposes. If this be what you think well of, you need give your self no farther trouble then to send your title deeds to Mr. Folks, who shall have direction to make all ye dispatch possible from, Sir, your etc.

188.   To Mr. Macroe.   London, Jan., 4, 1699|1700.

Sir

The good intelligence between us is (I hope) too firmly fixt for you to believe my silence has proceeded from any neglect or forgetfullness of you or your affairs, and therefore shall wave all apology for it as unnecessary, having made it my business to find all opportunities of discoursing the Bishop of Norwich, (in ye unhappy misunderstanding between you my friend and my old Master Leeds,) with whom I have had two long conferrences (one at his Lordships house & the other at mine) upon that subject, & have made him master of ye whole matter; whereupon he has desird I woud leave ye statutes with him (which I have done) in order to consider maturely what is fit and necessary to be done, that ye like accidents may be prevented for the future, being of opinion that any new law absolutely enforcing ye Master to receive all (or prohibiting his reception of any) Schollars after their admission to Cambridge may prove of equal ill consequence to our School; both extreames then being in their nature prejudicial, and that you have experimentally found leaving a discretionary power in ye Master to readmitt or reject arbitrarily may be injuriously made use towards particulars, I think his Lordship hath done in this (as he always does in other) business very prudently to require longer time to find out ye golden mean to be pursued for ye future. You woud have receivd an account of this matter sooner, had I not attended some time out of decency, seeing ye Governours were pleasd as ye Town has done to joyn ye same gentleman with me in this service, in expectation of being askd by him to wait upon his Lordship in it; but hearing nothing from him to that purpose, and finding his Lordship well enough inclind to terminate this matter with me alone, I enterd into this negotiation with him my self, ye result whereof was as hath been already shewn you (and I hope to your satisfaction) by your etc.

If there be any thing more in this or any other concern wherein I can serve you, pray never spare me.

189.　To Mr. Edward Leeds, Schoolmaster of Bury.
　　　Sir　　　　　　　　　　　　　　　　　　　　Jan 4, 1699.
　　　　　　　I attended (till very lately) in expectation of receiving some notice from Sir Robert Davers (who was jointly comissiond with me by ye Governours order) when he intended to wait on ye Bishop of Norwich in order to accomodate ye accidental misunderstanding between

your self and Mr. Macro; but hearing nothing from Sir Robert, and having some time since receivd a coppy of ye School statutes, with an intimation at ye same time that twas desird I woud lay ye same before ye Bishop for his perusal, I thought my self obligd to move his Lordship in it, which I accordingly have done, and stated ye whole case as impartially to him as if my two brothers (equally belovd) had been plaintiff and defendant; whereupon (after two long conferences, ye one at his house, t'other at my own,) his Lordship was of opinion that ye making any new law, absolutely compelling ye reception of all scholars after their admission to ye Universities, or entirely prohibiting ye readmission to School, might prove equally pernicious in its consequences; & therefore has wisely desird I woud leave ye said statutes with him, & farther time more maturely to consider of such a mean as may not only satisfy those concernd in ye present dispute, but likewise obviate all inconveniencys that shoud arise hereupon for ye future; wherein I doubt not but his Lordship will determine with all ye tender regard to you and to ye interest of ye School that can be wished to either by one who, tho' by his own fault he provd an unproffitable scholar in your hands, (which rarely happend,) yet hopes always to approve himself a gratefull friend for your former care and pains and good intentions towards, Sir, your etc.

I desire a copy of your reasons which you read to ye Governors at their Board.

190.   Honest Will Covell   London, Jan., 10, 1699/1700.

I am (in all sincerity) concernd to find so much disquiet shoud arise to you in ye management of my affairs from ye unreasonableness and injustice of those with whom we have to deal, especially at your time of day, subject to be ruffled by every adverse accident that happens, in a matter too ye success whereof you have all along set your heart so much upon to see justly and amicably ended. But since ye like dispositions are not to be found in others, who (in good conscience) ought as little to be without them towards me and the interest of my family in ye present controversy, I shall take your will in as good part as I resent ye deeds of others. But no more of that. As to Mr. Cooks quaint letter concerning ye stable wall and window, yourself and others on ye place can best judge whether there be any thing in either inconvenient to or unfit for me to impose on Mrs. Crofts; for if there be, I desire it may be alterd to her satisfaction, my principles and purposes being to live kindly and like a Christian with all my neighbours, more particularly with a widdow, ye relict of so honest a man and so good a friend of my good fathers. But, I must remark, their taking away ye old materials, and suffering ye building to go on so far without controul, seems to me as if somebody, who were a friend to neither of us, had put her upon this but just now, when it woud occasion so great a disorder in ye building, and reflect ye fault upon your self; but if there be nothing injurious or a nusance to her, I hope Mr. Cooke will be twice advised before he sets workmen of his own on to destroy that which mine have reard, he not understanding Littleton quite so well as his namesake did, & therefore not ye consequences of such an undertaking, for as ye Quaker says, I dont love to be provokd neither. I had written thus far when yours of ye 8th instant came to my hand, which necessitates me to ye resumption of my first discourse, which shall in ye first place be imployd to give ye lye to all Chamberlanes impudent assertions of my reading an affadavit of yours deposing £1500 to be ye damage of ye Mansion house alone, which according to his ancient and laudable custom in conversation is false in every part of it, there never having been any deposition of that nature (as yet), neither did your letter which mentiond that sum restrain it to ye dilapidations at Ickworth hall, but comprehended ye value of waste sufferd on ye joynture estate, and it was never otherwise understood by ye referee, from whom I thought Chamberlains insolences had receivd reprimands enough to have in some measure abated them for a while; but it seems he soon forgat reproof, and impertinence is ye nature of ye beast. I'm sorry your brothers mention must follow so soon after ye other, and that what he avers admits of equal contradiction; for Sir Gervase Elwes was so far from making you ye incendiary or agravator of my damages in Ickworth, that he has often told me of severall remarks of his own on that account as he passed between Denston and Bury, and rather feard you might represent ye reall mountains as molehills of mischeif only, by what he saw go unpunishd for 20 years past; and in a late letter dated but ye 23rd ult., speaking of our reference, he calls it ye great wast in ye wood, timber etc., which in a parenthesis he says is but too true; and how far these passages agree with ye discourse he pretends to have had with Sir Gervaise, & ye matters of fact upon which it is grounded, I leave even himself (or Mr. Chamberlain once again) to judge of. I have said ye more in disproof of these two points, perceiving you thought your self sensibly touchd by them, and hope I've made it sufficiently appear who ought to be most ashamd. If Loud be as adroit at managing of evidence for his clyents purposes as father Betts, I doubt not but ye result of ye Redhouse meeting will be as much to my disadvantage as your brothers partialities, (to give it no harsher term,) Chamberlaines prejudices, & Louds procurd perjuries can in conjunction contrive it. But I woud wish ye tennants to take better council than to act in concert with ye rest; for, if they do, I can yet lash em with ye rod has hung so long over them unfelt hitherto thro' my abusd clemency; and, if I once begin, it shall be usd to purpose; whereas on ye contrary my friends shall meet with more indulgence, amongst whom (for ye truth and zeal you've shown on this occasion) you shall ever be esteemd and rememberd by yours, etc.

191.   Dear Cousin Duncomb   July 13, 1700.

I have executed ye deed of assignment (as you will see), and signd ye receipt indorsd for ye £1667..04..04 due upon ye account of Lady Bonds rent charge, whereof it seems Mr. Thomas Bond and his sister are to have £590..01..06 in ye first place paid to them according to ye Act of Parliament, (which by ye way I have not yet had a copy of,) and ye residue I hope you will not only take care to see lodgd in a safe hand upon a note made payable to us two joyntly, but also consider how to dispose well of it as soon as may be for ye advantage of those for whom we are intrusted; and at ye same time you transact this affair with Sir H. Bond, to see ye security finished which he is farther to give for ye remainder of ye monies due upon bond. I am etc.

192. To Colonel Whichcot. Bury, Sept. 21, 1700.
        Sir
                This is to acknowledge ye favour of yours dated ye 10th instant, and withall to thank you for ye good opinion you therein express to have of me, so kindly backd too with ye offer of your interest, which I think so well employd where tis already lodgd that what I can command shall be directed to augment your own; wherein I shall most effectually discover my judgment upon ye discriminating point you'l appeal to me in, it being very naturall for every honest man to approve him best whose actions tally nearest with his own, which according to my observation yours have all along done in ye H. more than any other of our County Candidates with those of your most humble servant, etc.

193. To ye Lord Castleton. Bury, Sept. 23, 1700.
        My Lord
                I receivd ye honour of your Lordships dated ye 14th instant, which this comes to acknowledge, ye contents whereof my early care to serve you had in a great measure prevented, having (upon ye rumour of a new P.) felt ye pulse of all people in every place I went to with relation to your Lordships interest, which I coud wish were as universall as

Vol. I.   v

I think your Lordshipps meritt towards our county may justly challenge from ye long experience they have had of your Lordships great integrity & constant strict adherence to ye true interest of this nation. But I must beg leave to own I met with great disappointments wherever I could not pretend imediately to direct & influence, which (being a stranger in ye country) lyes in ye narrow compass of my neighbourhood ; but that your Lordship shall be sure of according to ye promise of, my Lord, yours etc.

194.   To ye Bishop of Lincoln.   Nov. 7, 1700.
My Lord
                       I receivd not ye honour of your Lordships letter till my coming hither, and am not a little concernd to find therby that ye Churches rights have been so far from being proportionably improvd (at least) with the rest of ye estates at both ye Hales upon ye late inclosures there, that on ye contrary they are rather impaird by them ; whereto I can at present only answer for my self, that I am sure ye injunctions I laid upon my cousin Cawdron with relation to this particular (amongst other preliminary requisites agreed between us) have not been so punctually pursud as I expected they woud have been, when I reposd the trust in him. But I will write to him concerning it, and recomend both to him & all others interessd therein, that such farther advantages may be allowd the Vicar as he in reason can insist upon ; or shoud it happen that he and Mr. Cawdron cannot hit ye terms, I shall propose ye leaving of them to your Lordships arbitration, (if you will please to take ye trouble upon you,) and whatever your Lordship shall think fit to award therein shall (as to what respects my estate) be cheerfully complyd with by, my Lord, your etc.

I beg leave to remind your Lordship of writing to Dr. Cawley, desiring him to bring back his Visitations to Sleeford, your Lordships & his objections to that place being (I hope) now all removd.

195. To ye Corporation of Bury. London, Dec. 31, 1700.

I deferrd this trouble, which I am obligd at last to give ye, in hope I might have been at liberty ere now to have dischargd to ye by word of mouth ye necessary errand it comes upon; which is to acknowledge all ye former favours I have from time to time receivd from ye with that just sense of gratitude they deserve; & more especially for having not only so often, but so unanimously, chosen me to ye honour of representing ye in Parliament ever since your good friend & my dear father (who grew old in your service) was no more in a condition to perform it; to whose past merit I am content, ney pleasd, to stand indebted for your first kind thoughts, which deemd me worthy of so great a trust; wherein, if I have all along acted with such integrity and those tender regards to ye true interests of England in general, and those of my second mother (if I may so call) Bury in particular, as ye expected from me when ye reposd it in me, I may with less imputation of arrogance once more presume to offer my best services to yee in that important charge; which, if ye shall be pleasd to confer anew upon me, nobody shall be found who will acquit themselves of it with more exact fidelity (that being all ye present law of ye land & ye perpetual one of modesty allows me to promise) than, Gentlemen, your etc.

196. To the Bishop of Norwich. London. Jan. 7, 1700/01.

My Lord

I hope, ney beg, your Lordship will not insist upon a greater fine than my ancestours have ever paid, or than ye present rents will really warrant, according to ye known accustomd rates held by these sort of tenures, which I need not tell your Lordship is ye bare value of one years cleare profitts; & that £250 is rather more than remaines, the following particulars will demonstrate.

Imp. For Dersingham Tythe	....	, .. 60..00..00
For Langham Tythe (which was but £50)	..	60..00..00

The land at Hobbes	....	....	.... 20..00..00
The farm at Scotto	....	....	.... 40..00..00
The estates at Thirne, Ashby & Owby			
(once let by Watty for £80)	....	....	168..08..08
The Tythe at Hoxton (which was but £45)	....	....	50..00..00
			————————
			398..08..08
Whereout deducting ye reservd rents & pay-			
ments of	...	....,	.... 137..13..04
And there remains but	....	....	.... 260..15..04

without allowing anything for repairs, which are and must be very chargeable, ye joyntress having left every thing in no better a condicion than they
usually do when reversioners are out of favour; and besides I woud desire
your Lordship to consider that my father & self will (when this is paid)
have expended near £1000 in fines without having yet touchd one penny of
ye rents; and that over and above ye £250 to your Lordship there is near
£50 more to be answerd to ye Dean & Chapter their Clerke the Secretary
and your Stewards fees; moreover, as ye price of all grain is falling, and
that ye rents intirely depend on corn, they must consequently abate, and
some trouble and charge twill cost me to recover severall lands which otherwise will be lost by ye Church; and as taxes have been and are like to continue, I dont doubt (ye premises considerd) but your Lordship will think
£250 such a fine as leaves me no great gainer in the main. As to that point
which your Lordship seems chiefly to dwell upon, your Lordship may please
to remember we were ready to treat for ye renewal of these leases at ye time
when ye first 7 years therein were elapsed; but your Lordship then being
newly come to ye see, and unacquainted with ye state of its affairs relating
to these matters, desird time to inform your self concerning them, which
ought not to turn to our prejudice (especially now had it then been our fault)
who had prepard ye usual fine (as I have at this time likewise done) for

your Lordship. I might here add what my good father once urgd to your Lordship, that if he woud have filld up ye 21 years with your Lordships predecessor, (who, when he felt how twas like to go with him, offerd to do so,) he might have done it on very easy terms ; but that was not thought so much upon ye square as your Lordship shall always find from, my Lord, yoursetc.

197.   To ye Corporation of Bury.   Jan. 13, 17 oo/o1.
                    Mr. Town Clerk having acquainted me (by your order) with ye honour you have done me, I cannot satisfy my self without giving you the farther trouble of my thanks for it ; and withall ye full assurance of my being as faithfull in ye execution of ye trust as I am sensible of ye particular kindness and civility wherewith you've placed it in me ; for coud any of your favours have receivd an additional value towards me, ye circumstance attending this last of its being so unanimously conferd upon me in absence woud have effectually augmented its indearments to me. But as nothing can make me more your servant than I justly was before, so I can only renew the promise of employing most of my time & thoughts for ye advancement of your interests ; wherein that small credit I have in ye world shall be intirely made use of; and shall always esteem those passages of my life most fortunate that afford me ye opportunity of doing Bury any good ; which is most ardently wishd, & shall in all things be most zealously pursued by, Gentlemen, yours etc.

I intend to wait on you before ye Parliament sitts, to receive your commands and instructions.

198.   Newmarkett, May 2, 1702.
        My ever-new Delight
                    After having so often told thee that the constant happy converse I have held with thee for seven years past hath totally

unfitted me (& I wont soppose any thing I ever said of that kind faild of
faith with you,) to bear thy absence with any tolerable peace to my mind;
how could you suffer me (being so much in your power as you know too I
particularly am in this point) to putt my self upon any consideration into
ye uneasy condition I now feel by it, for I am very sure ye builders & brick-
burners coud never have cheated me out of any thing half so valuable as
this jurney hath. Lett me never then for ye future pay so dear for ye prevention of any il as this hath cost me; and if you'l promise me not to
consent to our parting an other time, I'll make ye best of my present resource,
dear Jack, your faint resemblance, by kissing him a 1000 times in remembrance of his dear mother, ye only treasure of her J. Hervey.

199.   Mrs. Hervey to John Hervey.   London, May 2, 1702.

It is impossible for me to express, my dear dearest
life, what I've sufferd in these two days absence. I am sure, (by the tenderness I have always mett with from you,) if I coud represent the state of
my heart and soul towards you, the coach woud not come empty home on
Tuesday; but as that is impossible, so I fear is the hope of the other. In
the mean time my chief and only pleasure is to get you what entertainment
I can. Yesterday I spent in visits, (as the most disagreeable thing I coud
think of, and therefore best suited my humour at that time,) where I did
not hear any thing but chit chat; therefore I sent this morning to my Papa
to dine here (in hopes to be better informd), but he coud not come;
therefore I went to him, but he coud tell me nothing then, but said he woud
send you a letter from the Secretarys Office, which will, to be sure, inform
you of the foreign news, which indeed I shoud not care to be the messenger of,
it being represented to me as very ill. The Kings will is opend, and he has
left all to the Prince of Nassaw, which will occasion a quarrel between him
and the King of Prussia. He has not left a legacy to any body, only twenty

thousand pound to my Lord Albermale, and a joynter to my lady if she outlives him, which was settled upon marriage. There has been a counsel to day, and the two Secretarys are out, and the Queen intends to let the Parliament know that she thinks fit to declare a warr. There has been a report to day, but I dont know the truth of it, that the Dukes of Somerset and Devonshire and Lord Carlisle have laid down, and that Charles Churchill is Lieutenant of the Tower, and Colonel Godfrey in Sir H. Goodrick's place, and Mr. Vernon is to be a Teller in the room of Mr. Palms. As for private news I know none but that my Lord Mounthermon is dead of a fever beyond sea. I hope I have disposd of your musick tickets to your likeing; my Lady Spencer being in distress, I gave her one and went with her, and Nethes the other; every body liked it and the womans dancing extremely; it will not be fare to give my opinion, my heart and soul being at Ickworth, where I wish were all the remains of, my dear dear angel, your for ever & ever faithful wife, E. Hervey.

P.S.—I stayd till the musick was done for more news, but this is all I hear. The bratts are well, as I hope you and those with you are.

200.   My ever-new Delight   Ickworth, May 3. 1702.

If any place could have alleviated the weight which hangs continually on my soul when it feels thee seperated from ye body it informs, this might do it. But alass: as I have been so much longer from thee than I had been when I last wrote to thee, so it is become less in ye power of it to please, ney, to be tolerable to me. But as motion is naturally supposd to divert pain, so to morow I intend to ride to Thetford ffair, & have been this day twice at Church with my four children on foot (ye coach being to bring you this part of its way to morrow); & finding in my self so strong a temptation to come with it my self makes me (vainly some woud say) think it necessary to enjoyn you, by all ye injunctions of love & conjugal authority, not to make part of ye cargoe which is to return with it, for all the good I hope from this fortnights absence is to find Dr. Radcliffe hath made you fitter than I left you. . . . .I was afraid ye post woud have come in to late for me to have seen thy dear letter to night ; but Will hath just now brought it me, & with it ye very picture of a heart, whereof mine (I will say) is the truest orriginal, & ye superiority you must alwaies yield me, when you consider ye objects excellence which gives life to it & all its feelings for thee. I thank thee kindly for thy laborious collection of news, altho' I like none of it but that concerning my Lord President & his followers ; tis a noble example, & I hope they wont want disciples. Tis now past one a clock, & I must be up by six ; yet cant conclude without thanking Sir Thomas for his pacquet, & disiring you & him to use Mr. Arch Deacon Clegat (who will be at London Tuesday next) with all courtesy & assistance in ye business he goes about. Once more I conjure you not so much as to dream of coming hither with ye children ; for when I consider your state of health, & ye consequences that may attend your jurney, it may produce ye unwelcome miracle of your not being welcome to your J. Hervey.

201.   My ever-new Delight   Ickworth, May 4, 1702.

Altho' I wrote to thee last night by ye coach which went towards London this morning, and notwithstanding I am just now come from Thetford fair more fatigued than I ever felt my self; yet I can take no rest that will refresh me, till I have securd you against meeting with any disappointment by not hearing from me this post; and I hear again repeat my former injunction, that you woud not think of loosing ye opportunity you now have (from ye season of ye year & my absence) to gett your health better established by some course where you are, & not sacrifice so essential a good to both our happineses by an untimely jurney hither. I nead not tell you I'll come ye soonest moment I am able ; for I'm no sooner from thee but uneasy to ye last degree till I am with thee again, there being no pleasure or peace but with thee for your faithfull J. Hervey.

202.   Mrs. Hervey to John Hervey.   London, May 5, 1702.

My dear dearest life

I yesterday receivd the welcome news of your being safe got to Newmarket, with the pleasing addition of having it under your own dear hand, which I thank you as many times for as there are letters in it, for every one that is there gives some spirits to a heart that is so entirely yours, that absence woud quite sink it without that relief, which I hope you will let me have as often as you can, though I hope there will not be many oppertunitys for it before you come; since you tell me my power was great enough to have kept you, I hope it may be so to bring you back, which I beg (by the love you have always shewd me) may be ye first minute you can with ease to your self, which I must always first consider, let my sufferings be what they will. I do most heartily agree to the promise of never parting again upon any terms, though I shoud go in a litter, which I believe woud be the only way I coud compass a journey at this time, else I had once some thoughts of coming with the children; but I am so farr from being mended of any of my distempers, that the cough I had when you left me has increased so much ever since, that I cant lye down in my bed, it gives me such an oppression upon my stomach : I can hardly breath, and I quite loose my voice twenty times a day. I have sent for Dr. Raitcliffe; I believe he will order me to be let blood, which makes me write this morning. My papa has promisd me to send you a letter from the Secretarys, (I suppose I need not tell you the new ones; they are Lord Nottingham and Sir Charles Hedges,) with the printed news. They talk mightily of Ja. H. to be Post Master; but the Merchants declare openly, if he is, they will have some other way to send there letters, that they shall not come through his hands; and all the Foreign Ministers will send theirs by curriers. All things seem in a mighty bustle, and every body disatisfied; Sir Cr : Mus : is namd for a Teller. I was yesterday with my Lady Albermale, (she goes

Vol. I.   w

no more abroad till she is brought to bed,) and my Lord sent for the inclosd letter for me to send you, to give an account of what they did yesterday, they design to print them, they had also a debate about the Glos: and Norwich address, and a book which had something in it to the same effect, I cant remember the full title of it, but I hope you will know it enough by the second part of Whig and double; they have orderd the printers of it to come before their House to morrow. I have not seen my Lady Marl-borough since you went; my Lord has been so ill; he was mending, but they send me word to day that he is worse. Dr. Raitcliff has been with me while I was writing, and orderd me to be let blood presently, which I fear has hinderd me writing so as you can read; he has orderd me a drink to take twice a day, and a draught at night, which I hope will make me sleep and dream of my dear and invaluable treasure, which will make some amends for the tedious day. The doctor says my pulse is very low, which answers what I feel in spirits, and I must tell you (though it may seem a riddle) much more since I receivd your dear letter, for there you namd a fortnights absence, which indeed, my dear, is more than I can bear, and what I woud take care to prevent by coming with the children, if I were able, notwith-standing your commands, (which nothing else coud make me swerve in the least little from). I have sent you this lampoon; though it is not quite new, I believe tis so to you; there is another coming out, they say, of the same sort, and there was another with this which I have not seen yet. I did not conclude my letter till night in hopes of a visitt that woud tell me some news; but I have not seen any body but Mrs. May (who tells me of the death of the poor squire) and my papa; he says Lord Godolphin is declard Lord Treasurer to day; the Queen told my Lord Carlisle last night she intended to take it out of Commission. The House of Commons have voted an address of thanks for the praying for the Princess Sophia. Pray, my dear, take more care of your self, and dont sitt up till one a clock when you are to rise by six, for you will certainly be disorderd with it, which will add too great a weight to the already sunk spirits of your poor E. Hervey.

P.S.—I breath much better since my bleeding, and hope to be well enough to take the air with Papa to morrow. I dont hear how you like your bed-fellow Jack.

203. Mrs. Hervey to John Hervey. London, May 6, 1702.

I cant lett any body come to my dear dearest life without repeating what my heart is so full of, how much & dearly I love you, tho' I fear ye tedious (I cant call it letter) vollem I sent you last night by ye post will make you repent ye makeing me your news monger; and much more when I tell you the only part you likd a Saterday was not true, tho' they talk still that it will be. Ye Queen has been at ye hous to pass bills. I have inclosd sent you the same in print you had before in writing, with ye addission only of her answeir. I hope to pick up some thing more by to morows post, which I believe you will have in a few hours after this. I chous to send ye children in 2 days, becaus they may take ye coole of ye morning, ye wether is so extreemly hott; but ye more weighty reason is that you may have ye coach sooner to bring you back to her that most impatiently longs to see you, & is & ever will be to ye last moment of her life yours intirely, E. Hervey.

P.S.—I nead not say I have deliverd your message to Papa, when I tell you how often he visetts me, last night, this morning, & at diner; he staid tell I went to take ye air, which I think has done me good; tho' I much fear a relaps to morow, when I find ye children gon without me to my dearest dear.

204. My ever-new Delight Bury, May 6, 1702. 11 at night.

Had not the postcript of your letter (which I've but just now receivd) relievd me from the fears the body of it had raisd in me, you had seen me to morrow at night by the flying coach, altho' by sending I had found no other place woud be vacant for my passage to thee than the coach-box, and that I must have left all affairs on foot at Ickworth* in the last confusion; for the head brick-burner is run away indebted to all his under workmen, who are above twenty; and Will Covell having paid no body, nor executed one article of the instructions we last left with him, and have told him plainly he shall meddle with no more of my rents for the future; and I am now forced to pay my self for all the cows that are bought, (which are already seventeen, and more are buying in daily,) and for all the stone that come up to Worlington, but even the workmen their wages; and without I can find a new steward to take this burden off me, the business which calld me down will prove the hydras head, and multiply upon me faster than I can possibly dispatch them; but lett things here run into a yet more inextricable Chaos than they are, yet, shoud not your next letter bring me a more comfortable account of your more precious health, I am determind to venture post to you the next minute, as unfitt as I find my self for such an expedition, being throughly tired at night even with the common fatigue each day brings; for I am sure, when you can be brought to be blouded without my intreatys to back the Doctor's advice, tis not a lame-leg tyed up to beg my return with, knowing too no artifice is needfull, since all things naturally are restless till they arrive at their center, and thou art only such to thy impatient J. Hervey.

P.S.—I thank my pretty industrious bee for all the (I wish I coud follow on my metaphor by calling it honey) news she gathers for me. Major Norton, Mr. Macro, Grove and Batteley were the better for't to night, having stayd with me till now at the post-house; where, and at all other places, I've religiously observd the promise I made you about wine. Jack lay with me

---

* The farm-house at Ickworth, now Ickworth Lodge, had just been converted into a Mansion house. S.II.A.H.

the first night, but was so unquiet I coud not rest an hour together tor fear of his being smotherd in the cloaths, where he woud throw himself the moment after I had raisd him again upon the pillow; but we are never the worse friends, he bearing thy image much to his advantage. He and the rest are all very well.

205.   Mrs. Hervey to John Hervey.   London, May 7, 1702.
   My dear dear eternal unalterable inclination
                        How much and how dearly I love you, no tongue can express; much less then can my poor pen pretend to describe it : yet still (short as it is of the heart it woud express) I must always begin and end with that subject ; and I fear (though I coud dwell for ever on it) it will be the only one I shall have to write upon at this time, having seen no body to day but Papa, who can tell me nothing. He has made an appointment with the Arch-deacon to dine here to-morrow, who is sure to be welcome, being recommended by your dear hands. Mr. Manley was with me to day about a Kings-waiters place, which is by Patent and in the Queens gift ; I have been with my Lady Marlborough about it, but did not find her ; I have desird an appointment which I hope will prove successful, being what I am sure will please you ; my Papa and I considerd of the best means we coud to effect it. I dont know if I told you in my last that my Lord Pembroke does not goe to sea, but Sir G. Rooke goes in his stead. I know no private news, but they talk of three weddings ; the Duke of Gra : and Lord Char : is to marry my Lady Normanbys two daughters, and Lady M. Egerton is to have my Lord Byren ; but I dont know whether any of them be true ; but the last I believe is. I have been mightily askd to go to May-Fair to day, which everybody now runs mad after ; I dont know a body that is not gone to day ; I have promisd my Lady Spencer before it ends ; but I hope you will be here first to be our gallant. My Papa desird me to ask your

leave to carry your nieces ; but he said he believd he might venture before
he had an answer. I am now going to my Lady Albermale, where I hope
to meet with some news before I conclude this. I am much disappointed
having mett with no news here as I expected. If there is any from abroad,
you will have it by the Secretarys letter, which my Papa has promisd me
to send you with the Gazette and votes ; therefore all I can tell you more is
of my self, which is that I am much better of my cough and hoarseness,
but my shortness of breath and want of spirits is still bad ; but you know
the sight of you will be the best receipt, and that makes me not despair of
a speedy relief, because it is so much in the power of my dear dearest life
for his ever faithful E. Hervey.

P.S.—From my Lady Albermales closett (where she has shutt me up to
conclude this). Lord Marlborough goes to morrow, they say, if he is well
enough.

206.   My ever-new Delight   Ickworth, May 8, 1702.
                    The dear children of the second cargoe are all
come safe & sound hither, and were the more welcome as they brought me
an other of your letters, (which I coud wish were all volumes, but that they
woud give you so much the more trouble to write,) and it self was so, as it
gives me the pleasing expectation of another by this night's post, which
I've sett up for beyond my usual hour in hopes of receiving, my converse
with thee this way being all ye entertainment I have to unweary my spirits
with after the tedious employment they are at present so deeply engagd in
by my having taken Will Covell's province entirely upon me, from his
having faild to acquitt himself of late with even less regard to my interest
as a landlord or reputation as a paymaster than (you know) he usd to take
care of both formerly, which shewd it self then in so slender a degree as to
make me wish for so good an oppertunity as he hath now afforded me, by

letting out work at 30s. which I coud get performd for ten ; and tho' he hath
executed few or none of the instructions, yet the poor workmen follow me
about in shoales crying, We are ready to starve, and can gett no money of
the noble Captain ; so that I've been forced to pay off all their bills myself,
and write all their acquittances for them etc. But why do I trouble thee
with this narrative, which will vex thee as much in the reading as the
occasion hath me in the remedy ; and with this aggravation (tho' it needs
none) that I cannot possibly settle this new scheme of œconomy sooner
than to be with thee the latter end of the next week, being to fix the purchase of the little Common Field next Monday at Mr. Underwoods, and
have appointed twenty people to meet me about several businesses at Bury
on Wednesday next ; but these and everything else had never been thought
of had not you been well again, having sent to secure places in to morrows
flying-coach, in case this nights account of thy inestimable health had not
answerd my best prayers, which are ever put up to Heaven with the same
zeal, where thy invaluable life's concernd, as I can do to prevent the endless
death of my own soul : and such devotion for thy dear sake is but a piece of
justice in me, since as poor Cousin Donn was the author, thou hast been the
finisher of that virtue, (if I may so call it, for)

> Thy unexhausted charms have fixd my love,
> Nor can a change my happyness improve ;

whereby it must hope for salvation. Thy dear letter is just come in, and
(blessd be God for His goodness) brings me the joyful news of those prayers
being heard ; but were mine less, thou hast such an abundant store of vertue
as to make them efficacious where thy good's concernd. I have yet one
more to make him, that he woud by his merciful Providence continue to me,
not only the blessing of thy precious life, but love, that being the chief, ney,
only one, which makes him reckon his own so, who is, and ever must be,
without division or remission thine even beyond the grave, J. Hervey.

207.   Mrs. Hervey to John Hervey.   London, May 9, 1702.

My dear dearest life

Your last letter has put me in a greater disorder than your affairs can be. To think that I shoud be such a fool to miss the opportunity of coming with the children (upon any consideration) at a time when I might have hopd to have been some help to you in the many troubles you are surrounded with, and also to have had the addition of the greatest happyness this world can give; sure, I need not say that is being with my dear everlasting love, without whom I can tast no other pleasure but this way of conversing, which I have shewd so much since you went away that I believe I have established the title of a prude. I have given your musick tickets to your two nieces and Mrs. Hopes; they are gone in my Papa's chariot and my chair. I hope they will bring some news home with them before I finish my letter, for I have not seen the face of a creature to day to tell me any, not even my Papa. He dind here yesterday with the Arch-deacon, and we mett last night at Court, which was full of nothing but Sey——s; it was the saddest drawing-room that ever was seen. I was yesterday morning with my Lady Marlborough about Mr. Manleys business, (which I gave you an account of in my last;) she told me the Queen had been spoke to already about it, and that she made answer it was in my Lord Treasurer's disposal, and that she woud not meddle with it, upon which I went immediately to Lady Herriett Godolphin, but did not meet with my Lord, nor he was not to dine at home, but I left the certificate with Lady Herriett, and told her the business, and she readily promisd me to do me all the service she coud in it, and if this shoud fail, (which I have some reason to fear is promisd,) to get something else. I have stayd till ten a clock in hopes of some news, but the musick ladys are not come, and I am willing to goe to bed, being to rise early to go to St. James's Chapel, where you are sure to have a large share in my devotions. Pray God they may be answerd in setting you at ease from all your troubles quickly, and bring you back in safety to ye longing arms of your ever faithful wife, E. Hervey.

P.S.—Pray, my dear, send me word when I may expect you, though I hope for it before I can have an answer. In the mean time I beg you for my sake dont give your self so much trouble and uneasyness, for nothing in this world can come in competition with your precious health. I am much better of my cough ; I wish I coud say so of my other complaints.

208.   Mrs. Hervey to John Hervey.   London, May 12, 1702.

My dear dearest life

Though every word you write (to an afflicted soul without its dear and better part) is more welcome than opium to a rackd body, yet your letter yesterday gave so great an alay to the pleasing expectation I had of its bringing me the welcome news of your coming home to day or to morrow at farthest, which with the addition of the dismal part of Veranes and Athenais in Theodosious, (which I never saw till yesterday with Lady Hartington and Lady Herriett Godolphin,) made my heart and eyes so full, that I coud not hinder my self from being ridiculous to every body near me. I dind with Lady Herriett, and love her better than ever ; when I tell you my reasons for it, I fear I may have cause to be jealous on your part ; of hers I am already. I go with her and four more of the ladys of the Bedchamber and the Dutchess of St. Albans to May-Fair ; we are to meet at Burlington House at 6 a clock, but am not certain when we shall come home ; therefore dare not trust the finishing of my letter to give you an account of it. I give my dear angel ten thousand thanks for his kind prayers, which coud not miss of a good effect from so divine a soul, but particularly in my love, which is increased to a heigth beyond expression, and must remain so (to use your own words) beyond the grave with your unchangeable E. Hervey.

Vol. I.   x

P.S.—I am now with Papa, who is laid up with the gout. He can tell me no news, though there is a great deal talkd of in town; but I believe there is so little ground for it, I wont tell it you, having given you so many wrong informations already. What is true Papa will send you with the News-letter. Pray thank your son for his letter; I am glad to see that he improves in his writing.

> **209.**   *To Sir Thomas ffelton, concerning Sir R. Gipps information against me.
>
> Sir   Ickworth, June 26, 1702.
>
> Altho' I had been told here by several poeple what your letter mentions concerning Sir R. Gipps, yet, considering ye complication of villany that must concurr to produce so monstrous an information against me, I own tis still incredible to me. But since you desire an explanation of ye meaning of it, I must relate ye whole story of it as it happend. There having been two timber-trees of mine cutt down & carried away by night out of Oxwel wood in Bradfield about ye 22th of April last, which were drawn out of ye wood into a close of Sir R. Gipps's next adjoyning, & there one of his waggons brought to convey them from thence to a place between Sir R. G.'s house & his parish Church, where they were wrought into a May-pole & sett up accordingly on ye next day. This happening to me in a corner of ye country where I have a great deal of wood & timber, & wherein Sir R. G. hath formerly told my agents how grossly my ffather & self had been abusd, & how much we had sufferd by such practises there, and (as I hear since) hath frequently ridiculd our management & care of that estate for suffering such wrongs to be so often repeated upon us with impunity; & being informd by Morris who lives in my ffarm

---

* This letter and the next have not been copied into the letter-book, but lie loose in it in John Hervey's writing. S.II.A.H.

there that Sir R. G.'s own coachman & footboy, together with one Willingham, a carpenter that works constantly at his house, were all employd about this May-pole; and being resolvd to proscecute this notorious piece of thievery for ye sake of my own & ye rest of ye wood remaining in that neighbour-hood; I went to Sir R. Gipps's house out of pure good manners to acquaint him with it, & to do me justice in it himself if he thought fitt, & so to have had no further noise in ye country about it; but he seeming to decline medling in it, I then only desird his leave to send for ye aforesaid persons to some other Justice of ye Peace to be examind. Whereat he broke out into such a violent lunatick passion (which runs very high in his bloud) as I yet never saw, nor Mr. Pitches who by great good luck was there, the Minister of Haustead, who can & will be a substantial witness both of ye dutifulness of ye expression wherein her Majesty was named, & of my temper & civility towards Sir R., who spoke such provoking & opprobrious things to me that nothing (I am afraid) but knowing ye misfortune of his brain coud have kept me from resenting it, as such treatment woud have forced upon any other man. Among many other expressions he told me that he valued me no more than ye dirt under his shoes; that his ffamily was better than mine, and that he had had a much better education than I coud pretend to; that I must not think to domineer it in this, as I had done in ye last, Government, affronting all ye Gentlemen of Suffolke as my wife had affronted all ye Ladies; that no body but I would have taken notice of such a trifle upon such an occasion; at which I interrupted him only by saying, (for he said ye Queen should know of it,) Ye Queen is so well satisfied of my duty and affection to her & her Government, & so great a lover of justice, that I'm persuaded had timber been necessary to have made her crown or any part of it for that days solemnity, & her Majesty had known ye person had so stolen ye wood twas made with, she would not have taken it amiss in me or any one else to have proscecuted him for it; & this, upon ye faith of that good Christian &

ye word of that honest man I hope you know me to be, is verbatim what I said to him thereupon ; and this Will Covell too (who was also present) is ready to testify was ye very thing I said to him upon it.   But I am told he never would have dreamd of sending any information up, but that he heard I was resolvd to challenge him ; & to divert that purpose, & to gratify Sir R. D. (who, I am informd, advisd him to comunicate this treasonable sounding speech of mine to ye Council for fear of misprisicn in him, but others are of opinion more out of design to make a noise in ye Court & Country, to blast my reputation, and so collaterally to blacken yours in these parts, & so to frustrate our Election at Bury, which they find is in too fair a way of success,) up, it seems, it went.   If you find it necessary for me to follow it, pray send express for me; but whatever his wild & latitudinarian fancy may have made of it, I hope Sir Edward Seymour, who is one of ye Council, will commemorate ye piece of evidence against Sir R. G. in ye Comittee upon his election at Totness ; viz. that ye first thing he did in that town towards gaining an interest was to single out ye parson of ye parish, to prove to him that there was no God.   And when they know my worthy, honourable deponent can be capable of such propositions, & of undertaking to make them out by demonstrative argument, they will doubtless give that creditt to his information which it deserves.   It seems I am not ye only gentleman (by 3 or 4) of this County that he hath used thus or worse, if possible, in these frantick fitts ; who have all pardond him upon ye terms I should willingly have granted him, which is of saying he was sorry for what he had either said or done; but this last delirium hath putt it past his power to make me satisfaction that way.   What I am farther to do in this affair, which I look upon to be a great misfortune, as his base & villanous heart may have cookd it for me before ye Council, tho' there's none can be ignorant of my zeal & steadyness to this Government, (for you can answer for me, I have alwaies esteemed ye last & this ye same, & so resolvd to support it,

as I did ye last, to ye best of my power,} I hope you'll lett me know, as soon
as you can throughly inform your self, how it really is, & what is fitt farther
to be done in it by your obedient humble servant, J. Hervey.

I'ray keep this, for I have no copy of it, it being past 1 in ye morning.

210.   To Sir Thomas ffelton concerning Sir R. Gipps's affidavit, etc.
   Sir   Aswarby, Aug. 17, 1702.
            Having already given you so much trouble in this
unlucky adventure of mine with Sir Iago Bessus, it woud have been unpar-
donable to send this additional one after you but by your own command ;
and as your kind concern for me putt you upon desiring a copy of those articles
of so very high a nature (as Buxton their learned Council in open sessions
declard) which were exhibited above against me, so you'l exuse me if I
lengthen this epistle by making some remarks upon them.   And first I must
observe that he hath rather composd a plausible tale (by adding or omitting
any circumstance in ye conversation that passd between us which might
make for or against him) than a strict affidavit, wherein ye whole truth &
nothing but ye truth should have been sett forth ; for Mr. Covell, as well as
my self, will depose that he was so farr from offering to turn his servants
away, that he rather justified than blamd ye fact, telling me, if he were they,
& once under prosecution for 't, he would do ten times more mischief in my
wood.   Then, as to ye treasonable words, sure I was not in so poetick a
mood as to answer him in rhime ; but his licentious brain in often revolving
how to give ye worst turn of interpretation to them, & having heard that
chimeing terminations heightens ye sence, was resolvd to lett it run in verse,
tho' in ye body of so solemn a piece of prose as a deposition ; & tho' ye
malicious bratt is born with less frightful ffeatures than might have been
feard from ye parents keen lust of revenge which begatt it, yet I must do my
self ye right to repeat them verbatim, as I doubt not but Mr. Pitches & Will
Covell must and will agree them to have been deliverd ; viz. the Queen is

so well satisfied of my duty & affection to her and her Government, & so great a lover of justice, that I dare say had timber been necessary to have made her crown it self or any part of it for that days solemnity, & her Majesty had known ye person had so stolen ye wood twas made with, she would not have taken it ill of me or any one else to have prosecuted him for it. And for his nameing you or your place in ye reprimand he speaks of, Mr. Covell will also swear he never made ye least mention of either. And I will leave any one to judg how likely it was for him to say in ye same company & at ye same conferrence that if they had cutt down all his trees on that occasion, he should not have prosecuted them for it; when not a quarter of an hour before, speaking of his being (among others) turnd out of ye Commission of ye Peace, he was pleasd to express himself in these words; viz. If things are likely to go on at this rate, for my part I care not how soon there is occasion for an other Coronation. And this Will Covell is also ready to testify upon oath. That I in no wise excusd ye rudeness of my expression, or made not ye least apology for ye same, was owing to ye consciousness of my own integrity, meaning nothing in what I said but a compliment to illustrate her Majestys love to justice by. And that I've been animated to ye unwarrantable action of enquiring after him, or going where he usd to be, from knowing he labourd under any such indisposition of body as renderd him uncapable of defending himself, is as false (to use ye aptest comparison) as his own affidavit. I have also sent you a copy of Kiplings letter, to shew you ye malice of those Justices, who were concernd in ye conspiracy against. me & my reputation just at ye nick of time before Bury Election was to come on; for tho' they well knew ye writt was not directed to them as a Bench, and that they could neither execute or make a return thereof as a Court of Sessions; yet to bring me under ye mortification (as they thought at least) of appearing before them & my Towns & Country-men as a criminal, they contrivd this summons by their Clerk, which when I had complyd with they found themselves obligd to sign ye return of it by 3 Justices, as in their seperate capacities. Whether ye writt it self were legally granted, (I not being first heard to ye articles exhibitted,) and if so, whether issued according to ye statute of 21 Jac: 1, C. 8., which avoids all such when ye motion & declaration are not mentiond to be made on ye back of ye said writt etc., must be my business to enquire after between this & ye next term; wherein our great & good ffriend could advise better than all ye world beside, would he think me, & the cause for which I've sufferd thus, worthy of his thoughts. As long as this letter is already, I cannot conclude it without letting you know that I very much hope you have not proceeded towards fixing your self in any other place than my house; which is a request I most heartily & sincerely joyn with my wife in; & we doubt not of your granting it, (notwithstanding the many inevitable inconveniences your own apprehensions may justly suggest to you from it,) could we but make you rightly sensible how great a satisfaction & happiness would necessarily result from it to her & your most obedient humble servant, J. Hervey.

Mr. Battely desires you would direct your venison to Mr. Craske, ye Town-Clerke.

211. *Wm. Covelli affidavit, fyled ffeb. 4, 1702.

Gipps, Miles, v. Hervey, Armiger. Ex parte Hervey.

William Covell of Horninger in the County of Suffolk, Gen, maketh oath that on Munday about the eight day of June last this deponent went with John Hervey Esq. to the house of Sir Richard Gipps of Whelnetham Magna in the sayd County Knt, where the sayd Sir Richard and Mr. Hervey fell into discourse aboute electing Knights of the Shire for

* I picked up the original copy of this deposition out of a London bookseller's catalogue about 25 years ago. It is not in the Letter-bock, but I print it here as bearing upon the squabble which is the subject of the two previous letters, 209 and 210. S.H.A.H.

the sayd County. Sir Richard Gipps falling into passion abused Sir Robert Davers at an high rate (who was one of the Candidates at the sayd election), and pulled out a letter which Sir Robert Davers had written to a third person desireing his voice and assistance; and Sir Richard Gipps sayd by that letter he woud expose him for a greate lyar; for that Sir Robert had declared he never thought of setting upp untill the gentlemen of the Countrey had put it on him; when by that letter he had made interest for it long before; and Sir Richard Gipps sayd it was hard for the County of Suffolk to choose a gentleman for their representative in Parliament who could neither write sence or true English, and redeculed the letter, & sayd that if he had a boy of six or seaven yeares of age could write noe better, that he would whipp him, or words to that effect. And after some discourse upon that subject, Mr. Hervey sayd to Sir Richard Gipps that he was come to him for justice, for haveing two oaking tymber trees cutt down in his grounds, and sett upp for a Maypole, and would gladly find out the authors thereof. Sir Richard Gipps in very greate passion replyed that he was turned out of Commission. Mr. Hervey answered that he had seen the list of those that were to be turned out and of those to be put in, and he was none of them. Sir Richard Gipps made answer in that morning he had received a letter from London which gave him notice that his friend Seymor (meaning, as this deponent believed, the honble Sir Edward Seymor, Bartt.) out of an old grudge had moved the Queene, and that he was turned out by her command; and in a most angry manner further sayd that, if matters went or were like to goe so, he cared not how soone there should be another Coronation; which words this deponent tooke especiall notice thereof; for in a short time he went to Mr. Hervey, and asked him whether he tooke notice of those words. Mr. Hervey sayd he did, and was sorry that this deponent did; but sayd the gentleman spooke that in his passion which he hoped was not in his heart, or words to that effect. Sir Richard Gipps continuing his anger, and disputing the lawfullness of cutting trees on that occasion, giveing to Mr. Hervey very bad language, Mr. Hervey sayd that if the Queene were to be crowned with a wooden crowne, and any one should steale trees from him to make the crowne, he would endeavour to find out the thiefe. Sir Richard Gipps in very great fury replyed and sayd the Queene should know it; to whom Mr. Hervey made answer, (with as much duty and respect to her Majesty as could be spoken,) the sooner the better; for he knew her Majesty so greate a lover of justice that she would not deny it to the meanest subject she had. And this deponent further sayth that the Reverend Mr. Pitches, Rector of Hawsted, was present at parte of the discourse, and, as this deponent believe, not being pleased therewith some time after went out of the roome. And further sayth that he was in the roome or within hearing the discourse from the ffirst to the last; and sayth that he believe that the letter which gave him notice of being out of Commission was the cause of all the disturbance. And also further sayth that it amazed this deponent to heare that processe of good behaviour was granted against Mr. Hervey, when there was not the least word spoken nor action done by Mr. Hervey that deserved the obtayning thereof to the best of this deponents understanding. Will Covell.

Jurat apud Buriam Sancti Edmundi in Com: Suffolk, 23 die Decembris, An: Dom: 1702, coram me Edmo: Colman, mro: extraordinar: in Cur: Cancell:

212. Mrs. Hervey to John Hervey. London, March 2, 1702/3.

My dear dear life and soul,

A very apt expression at this time, for I have had no sign of either since you left me; indeed, my dear, it is impossible for me to express what I feel; it is so much beyond what I ever felt before as is above description. Nothing shoud have hinderd me seeing you to night but the uneasyness it might give you from your kind fears of me; as for my self, labour is such a trifle to what I suffer now that I woud have come,

Vol. I. Y.

though I had been sure to be brought to bed at Hockerel, to have been 25 miles nearer you. But Mrs. Carell (who I consulted about it) was so much against it, I durst not venture. My heart and eyes are so full I am not able to bear this subject, though indeed I can think of no other. For God's sake, my dear, come the first minute you can, but not till your business is done. All I beg is that Bury may not hinder you by making them happy while I am so miserable. I hope you have had good luck to day ; I think I had worse yesterday than usual, because it made me loose some bets for you. To day I dont stir out, but hope to recover them at home, or else I will not venture any more till you come your self. I'll keep my letter open in hopes of news ; at present I know nothing but misfortunes. Lady Diana Howard has lost her only son, a mighty fine youth ; pray God keep us from the like, and send us to meet soon again in safety, shall be the constant prayers of, my dear dear, your ever faithful E. Hervey.

P.S.—Pray send me word the very day and hour when you think you shall be here, that I may live upon that till I see you.

213.   My ever-new Delight   Newmarket, March 3, 1702|3.

Altho' this be but the second, yet I hope twill prove the last letter of this already long and tedious seperation. My being still here made me loose the pleasure of seeing your dear letter by this nights post, which I intend to send to Bury for very early, that it may meet me as a cordial to morrow at Ickworth, where my craving impatience to see the dearer author of it will be so justly importunate, as to suffer me to make but a very cursory superficial dispatch of all those various affairs you know require a better regulation and settlement than I shall find them in ; and a better you ought not to expect, where the ambassadour carries with him but half the powers requisite to conclude them as they ought to be, my mind being as unsettled for want of you as my business is for want of whole me, which it can never have when I've not you with me. I have no news to tell you from hence but that we won 210 G. of Vane against Hobler, and that Sir Richard Gipps hath lost his lady, who, could I think he lovd but with a spark of that flame my heart burns with for thee, I could not (as little as he deserves common humanity from me, whom he hath falsly traducd & misrepresented to our good Queen,) but pity with all my heart. What then do you think I felt for poor Lady Marleburghs loss, who deserves the reverse of that worthy Sir Iago Bessus from, my dearest life, your most affectionate friend & lover, J. Hervey.

214. To ye Duke of Marlborough. March 12, 1702/3.
 My Lord
 I shoud be altogether inexcusable in offering to give your Grace a trouble of this sort at a time when I but too well know you have so many other, (especially that* wherein I can most sincerely assure your Grace no friend you have bears a juster and consequently a deeper share than my self,) did not my heart necessarily urge me to it; which is so full of ye sense I have of my great obligations to your Grace in ye kind part I'm satisfyd you took in ye great honour her Majestie has been so graciously pleasd to confer on me and my family, that I can feel no ease till I have made your Grace my acknowledgments for it ; tho' to do that as I ought will, I fear, prove as difficult as throughly to deserve ye occasion of them ; only thus farr (I may safely say) it found me quallified to receive it, that even this signal mark of distinction which her Majesty hath shown me cannot possibly engage me farther than it found me (for otherwise I shoud n'ere have thought of asking such a favour) in all things that concerns ye interest and support of her Majesties Government, which I had before resolvd shoud never fail of (tho' at ye same time I hopd & wishd neither

---

* John Hervey's marginal note says "son's death." S.II.A.II.

might ever want) all ye service and assistance that could come within ye
narrow compass of his poor power, who is with all duty and gratitude her
Majesties most obedient faithfull subject, &, my Lord Duke, your etc.

215.   My wife to ye Dutchess of Marlborough.

Madam

Mr. Hervey and my self have both so long &
justly sacrificed ye satisfaction of our own to ye ease and quiet of your
Graces mind, that, could you know what incessant importunitys we have
resisted from ye one, you woud ye easilier forgive the unseasonable interruption we fear this must at last prove to ye other ; but ye sense of our
obligations to your Grace calls too importunately upon us to be any farther
withstood ; and therefore we rather venture this intrusion upon your solitude
than to be longer silent upon a subject which requires ye earlyest endeavours
after all returns that can be made your Grace by us for it. I know nothing
we have so much at heart (unless it be ye due sympathy we feel of your
Graces present condition*) as how we may in some sort deserve ye great
honour her Majestie hath been so graciously pleas'd to bestow on us & our
family by your Graces kind mediation ; & how we may ever worthily acquit
our selves of so generous a piece of friendship towards your Grace, which I
am sure we both think ye future study of our lives can never enough compensate, unless your Graces usual goodness will accept of ye most zealous
and gratefull will for payment ; and then we conclude ye chief of those very
many who are bound to be your Graces well wishers must remain as much,
if not more, indebted to you than I know Mr. Hervey (so qualified) to be, as
well as, Madam, etc.

---

* A marginal note says, The death of her son. S.II.A.H.

216.   *The Duke of Marlborough to Lord Hervey.

My Lord   Hague, March 23, 1702/3.

I am very much obligd to your Lordship for the honour of your letter of the 11th instant, and your kind acknowledgment of the small share I had in the honour her Majesty has been pleasd to conferr on you, to which your Lordships merits had so just a claim that there was scarce need of any other interest or argument to induce her Majesty to gratify your Lordship with this distinguishing mark of her favour. What ever credit my services may gain with her Majesty shall be chearfully employd in the behalfe of such as are most zealous for the interest and support of her government, and I shall be glad on all occasions to give your Lordship assurance of the truth and respect wherewith I am, my Lord, your Lordships most humble servant, Marlborough.

217.   To ye Corporation of Bury.   London, March 23, 1702/3.

Gentlemen

The great honour her Majestie hath been pleasd to do me in my removal to ye House of Peers is ye occasion of my giving you this trouble, to pay you my most gratefull acknowledgments for having so long & so unanimously intrusted me with your particular & ye Nations general interests in ye House of Commons ; and more especially for ye pleasing token you have repeatedly given me of your kind acceptance and approbation of my small services there, by having reposd ye same important trust in one† who (I hope) you find discharges it as worthily as twas by you most generously conferrd upon him. Could any thing have created in me a more lively sense of all those marks of esteem you have been so good to

---

* Eight letters, including this one, headed "Copies ofthe Duke of Marlborough's letters to me when I was Lord Hervey," will be found together in the folio letter-book, immediately after Sir Thomas Hervey's Anniversary poems. They are of different dates from the date of this to Dec. 1713. I have printed them in their chronological place. S.II.A.II.

† John Hervey's marginal note says, Sir Thomas Felton. S.II.A.II.

shew towards me and my family than I was full of before, this additional favour woud have perfected ye measure of my respect and affection for you, which were too compleat to admit of much increase, even to that degree as to make me place one of my cheifest pleasures in ye expectation of living to do some good for a Town and Corporacion, who have so just a title to ye best services of my life ; which, whenever Providence will bless me with ye happy occasion of exerting them, shall be as indefatigably pursued, and as faithfully performd, as if I had still ye honour of being more imediately, Gentlemen, your servant.

218.   To Sir Richard Cocks.   March 25, 1703.
Dear Sir

Tis none of ye least sensible satisfactions which results from ye honour her Majestie hath done me to find my friends as well pleased with it as my enemies have already shewn themselves otherwise ; whose villanous plotts to represent me as no well wisher to ye present government, (which we can answer for one another we always intended to support and maintain with ye same zeal and assistance that we ever did ye last,) are by this signal mark of ye Queen's favour so intirely disappointed, that shoud they happen to be as throughly defeated in ye rest of their expectations from this Government, twould go near to make them really own themselves what they maliciously endeavourd to have me only thought to be. The advantage which will attend ye change of company you mention lyes too aparently on ye side you place it ; but when Gloucestershire shall again do right to them selves and your meritt, then probably times may be so alterd as to make me wish my self once more in yours, which always made me value St. Stephens Chappel ye better for it ; and that this new accident may not tempt you to have ye less friendly esteem of mine, pray doe me ye justice to believe that I've not only taken but will strictly live up to this motto : Honores non mutabunt mores of, Sir, your etc.

219.   Mrs. Hervey to John Hervey.   London, March 30, 1703.

I think my dear angel told me he loved a letter from me, and I am sure that is what I ought to study as well from justice as inclination, and this is a trial of it, for it is a rack to me to think of being at such a distance to need this way of conversing; but I will not enter upon that subject (indeed I am very unfitt for it) for fear my kind indulgent partner may have his share of it, which I woud not wish to the worst enemy I have; the hopes of Fryday is all I have to live upon. Jack is up and well, but Will is very bad with his cough and a fever very high upon him; the best to be hoped for is the measells; Mr. Maltes thinks to let him blood if nothing appears to morrow. I have sent you inclosd Edwards's letter, for fear you may have forgott the many things which were to be settled with Mr. Covell, who I hope you will find time to speak with on Thursday morning, else it will be a great hindrance to the Dairy. I cant think the killing a calf for our family proper; tis impossible to be eat while it is good; but I'll leave that, with the rest, to you and Mr. Covell; but I believe it will be necessary to be settled soon. Dr. Raitcliff is better. Pray God to keep you well, and bring you safe back to her that loves you with all her heart and soul, and will be to the last moment of her life, my dear dear angel, your ever faithful wife, E. Hervey.

220.   Newmarket, March 30, 1703.

My ever-new Delight

I remember you have often told me you coud not help envying those who had my company in your absence; but did you know how very much less desirable it is by my being without you, even envy it self would alter into pity, especially for your poor Papa, who hath had no manner of good by it or me, but only the benefit of being thrown the less about in the rough waies, which the frost had made joggy enough to make me not repent of not leaving you behind, altho' you are now become so absolute a part of me that I can strictly say, I'm really not my self whenever or wherever I miss you from me. I have seen but one passage of mirth, (tho' Welch-Tom makes one at every thing,) and that was occasiond by my asking him what could make him so thoughtful, (as at that time he seemd to be,) unless my humour had infected him. To which, with his usual airs of head and heel, he was pleasd to reply, Why, I was thinking that my Proh (God help her) was thinking of me as well (look there) as your Bess is wishing again for you. But this you had not been troubled with, had not your self brought up the rear of his comparison, after old Proh, and by that familiar name. However, he made you amends to day, making you a proverb for beauty and for chastity and loving your husband. For my being that blessd man of all this whole creation, God's most great good name be praised, and may I find favour enough in his sight to deserve but the continuance of what he hath vouchsafed to bestow, and then thy safety will be best secured; for which my daily prayers are sent up to Heaven with the most intense devotion of a heart entirely thine as farr (I wish he knows it not to be farther) as is allowd by Him from one creature to another; and sure some allowances are made where vertues nearest approach his perfections, and then my love hath been less criminally placed than it coud have been elsewhere. Farewell. J. Hervey.

221.   To Mr. Recorder Welds.   London, April 10, 1703.
  Sir

    The favour of yours of the 31st ult. (which came not to my hands till ye 5th instant) had not been thus long without my acknowledgments for it but for ye accident of my wife her being brought to bed since ye receipt of it, which, when you've been as happy in one as I have been in two, you will easily admit of as a very just excuse. I am almost sorry ye Gentleman you desire to make one of my chaplains shoud happen to be so agreeable to me in all respects upon his own score as to leave no room for me to shew you how readily I would otherwise have done it on your own ; and therefore you may tell h im (with my service) he may depend on't I cant conclude without taking notice of ye wise designation I hear ye Corporation hath voluntarily agreed in as to my successor in their service ; which is a choice all must approve as unanimously as they made it ; among whom I own my self one of those who entirely like of it, both for their and ye nations interest ; being with much sincerity and esteem, Sir, your etc.

222.   Lady *Hervey to John Hervey.   London, Aprill 22, 1703.

My dear dear Angell

Sure it is neadles to repeat how much I love you, & more than that I am not able to do at present.   I felt more at parting with you than I was willing to show ; but ye effects of it fell very severely upon me in the night, and I was forcd to send for Mr. Maltas ; I thought I coud not have livd an hour; the perteculers I leave him to tell you, not being able my self ; something he gives me every 4 hours has done me more good then any thing else ; which is all I can say.   Farwell.

223.   My ever-new Delight   Newmarkett, April 23, 1703.

I have just time before ye coach goes (it being now 4 in ye morning) to tell my dearest life we gatt well hither ; & that if I dont hear by ye next opportunity that thy most precious health mends apace, I am fully determind to sacrifise all my business to the ease of my mind, wherein I am vain enough to think yours also consists in some measure, & that is to meet again sooner than I had your consent ; but when'ere that welcome accident happens, I hope you'l be more resolute in keeping ye

---

* I presume I am right in thus styling her.   In his diary John Hervey tells us that the Patent for creating him a Baron bears date March 23, 1702/3.   No. 223 is the first letter in which he signs himself "Hervey." S.H.A.H.

injunction I lately laid on you than you were in that of not giving your leave for our ever parting again ; but as tis a result of thy goodness & prudence, tis equally love, tho' it pains thy (at present) uneasy friend and lover, Hervey.

224.   To his Grace ye Duke of Ormond.   London, May 25, 1703.
My Lord

Nothing (but ye accident of my wife lying so dangerously ill, as she had been for some time before your Grace left this place,) coud have prevented me from paying my duty to your Grace (as I intended) to have wishd you a good journey, (which I hope this will find your Grace well at ye end of,) and to have assurd your Grace that, as no friend you have was better pleasd than my self with your being placed in ye administration of ye Government, (Ireland,) so no body more passionately desires ye continuance of that great reputation your Graces merit hath so justly intitled you to through other services by as happy success in this. And since I have taken ye liberty of giving your Grace this trouble, I know you will have goodness enough to pardon me if I only lengthen it to beg your Graces countenance & protection towards my brother Porter & nephew Elwes, (both of them Captains in Lord Windsors Regiment,) who, I can answer, are so farr quallified to deserve any favour your Grace may please to shew them, (or otherwise I should never have appeard their advocate,) as to have had ye same due satisfaction at your Graces being appointed their Governor with, my Lord Duke, your etc.

225.   To Colonel Porter.   May 25, 1703.
Dear Nobbs

I'm sorry to find you so warm in mentioning ye Colonels & Captain Tyrels parts with relation to ye Majors post in your Regiment ; for through ye best observation I could make in treating with them upon that subject, I really found them both much more inclind to have you succeed in it than Sir Thomas Travel; & particularly my Lord Wharton told me that he shoud be very glad ye knight woud not comply with ye time limited for payment of ye £300, for then he shoud have a much better officer (in you) by it for that important station; and for this reason I am thus early in my answer to yours of ye 11th instant, to prevent any farther expressions of your discontent in their regard. As to your title, I'm not well read enough in ye military law to judge of it; but if it be retrievable, I dare say upon your delivering the inclosd to ye Duke of Ormond, (which if you approve I desire you woud do when seald,) his Grace will be very ready to give you all ye encouragement and to show you all ye favour in your pretensions that shall fairly lye in his way. I thought it better in my recomendation not particularly to mention your claims to ye majorship, because I would have you consult your best friends, and be throughly well advisd as to ye validity of it before you publickly move in it; for these things when once stirrd naturally beget uneasiness, and may bring on reflections, or at least difficulties, where you design em not; and, at last, perhaps, be so far from compassing ye present drift as to make it rather an obstacle to your preferment hereafter. But these are rather meand as hints than any thing else, of which you may make your own or no use at all, as you shall see occasion. My wife hath been very ill ever since ye 5th ult, when she was brought to bed of her twins; but is now (God be praised) on ye mending hand. I have more than once told you that if I can be of any use to you in Lord Powes's or any other of your affairs here, that you may freely command your etc.

226. To Mr. Gage. London, May 25, 1703.
Sir

Having receivd an intimation from a very authentick hand (who hath lately heard Mr. Gipps voluntarily enter into ye discourse of ye exchange depending between him & me) that he is both ready & willing to perfect it, if I woud renew my solicitations therein, makes me repeat the trouble I have already given you in this affair, to desire you woud once more apply to him as my Plenipotentiary to make an end of it, and tho' there should be something finally insisted on which may be (even by his own friends) deemd unreasonable, yet I woud beg of you rather to concede them on my part than to leave him room to recede any more from ye profession he makes (to other people) of his inclination to oblige me in ye particulars concernd.   This is a request which necessarily entails a second, which is that you woud excuse this friendly liberty taken by your, etc.

227.   To Sir Thomas Hanmer.   June 15, 1703.

Sir

IIad any farther persuasion been necessary than that which naturally resulted from ye consideration of Mrs. Manleys relation to my family and ye helpless streight condition of her own, she could not have pitchd upon a more powerfull advocate with me than your self, The particular place I had in view for Frank was to have succeeded one Burdett, a land-waiter in this Port ; but upon strict inquiry found my self under a necessity of entring into a concurrence against my Lord Sunderland for it, had I pursued my solicitations with my Lord Treasurer ; but seeing his name to ye petition which recomended Franks corival to ye same vacancy, I thought it more adviseable to make such a merrit by our present desisting as might create a stronger title to both their favours, whenever an other opportunity shoud put me upon renewing my suite on his behalfe ; which, you may assure both mother and son from me, shall not be neglected, notwithstanding ye father did not use me very well in letting me suffer as a surety for one of his daughters, in a matter which, tho' of very small value in it self, yet thro ye manner of it might have provd distastfull enough to any other body to have been of much more consequence to his children than my piety (if I may so call it) to my ancestors will give me leave to make of it. My wife and I are extreamly obligd to ye Dutchess of Grafton, (to whom we desire you woud return our most humble services,) Mrs. Ramsey & your self for ye kind inquiry you made after her recovery; which I thank God is now well enough establishd to think of going into Suffolk this day sevenight, where we shall no sooner be arrivd, but ye want of so essential a part of ye pleasure of it as Wales hath occasiond will proportionably improve ye just envy, which hath been for some time conceivd against it by Mrs. Ramseys constant admirer & your etc.

228.   To Mr. Vanbrook.   July 26, 1703.
     Sir
               I'm sorry my journey into Lincolnshire was so un-
luckily fixd as next Saturday, since otherwise it seems you would have been so just to your promise as to have given me ye satisfaction of seeing you here; which now must be adjournd till my return from ye Bath, to which place I shall be hastening after a cursory settlement of my affairs at Aswarby; but in ye mean time I desire you may have ye ease of knowing that Risbrook rather declines than improves in its unequall competition with Ickworth; for I find ye latter such a sort of beauty as—si propius stes, te capiet magis; & from thence feel so strong propensions to make it so much a more noble seat than ye other is capable of that less persuasive reasons woud have secured my choice than were by you employd to, Sir, yours etc.

229.   Lady Hervey to John Hervey.   Newport, Aug. 7, 1703.
                                                      11 a clock.

     My dear dear Angel
               I am this minute come hither weary to death, and
yet cannot help writing to beg you woud not go over the Wash, which has

given me more pain than I can express, since I rememberd you did not promise me you woud not; which I beg you woud by a letter next post, for indeed, my dear, I dont need that addition to the pain I already feel in the want of you.   I am a little lame, and my leg, I think, is more swelld than ever, for which reason I am going to bed as fast as I can.   Your disconsolate wife, E. Hervey.

P.S.—I wish, if it were not to much in your hurry of business, that you would leave a line to come by Tuesdays coach (to relieve my fears of the Wash,) for fear I shoud be gone before the post comes on Wednesday.   The children are both well.   I open my letter again to tell you my fears of the Wash are not without reason, for the waters we passd came pretty high into the coach.   Coulledge begins to be lame again.

230.   Lady Hervey to John Hervey.   London, Aug. 10, 1703.
         My dear dearest life

I have been all this evening in hopes of a letter by the coach, but finding none makes me fear you have not receivd my long epistle from Newport, to beg you woud not go over the Wash.   I have waited so long for the coming of the coach that I fear the post is so near going I shall not have half time enough to tell you how much and dearly I love you; but indeed I coud not do that if I had employd all my time since I left you, which has been a continual hurry, which I am very unfit for, having abundance of complaints, though the tooth-ach (which is one) is enough alone; I hardly rested all night; tis a swelling between my cheek and my gum, which they tell me will break, but tis now very painfull.   Sir Richard Blackmore was here, but says he is afraid his advice nor the waters will be but of little use without you, which I agreed with him in.   I intend to send the horses away on Sunday (after a days rest) if I hear nothing to the contrary before from you, though my Papa fancyd stocks being risen so much would tempt you to come by London.   The children are well; Miss was yesterday at Chis-

Isabella Carr Hervey.
1689 - 1711.

wick with Mrs. Baron, and maid our compliments to my Lady Fox. The Du: of Monmouths wedding (which is certain) has quite silencd the talk of that. My Lady Jeffreys is married to my Lord Windsor. These weddings are the only news stirring. The Court goes into mourning for the Prince of Hanover on Sunday. I have got your suit according to your directions, which shall always be punctually observd by, my dear dear Angel, your faithful wife, E. Hervey.

P.S.—There is a box of tea sent by mistake to Aswerby, which I beg you woud bring with you.

231. My ever-new Delight Aswarby, Aug. 11, 1703.

According to my usual observance of all thy dear desires, I left Ickworth by day-break on Monday morning, (altho' my affairs there remain in a very unfinishd condition,) and was forced to ride above fivety miles that day (having seen and settled my running horses and their summer quarters by the way to Wisbich) to get here last night; where instead of being refreshd by thy dear company, which never fails to drown and dissipate the sense of inconvenience or uneasyness from outward accidents, my mind was so struck with the solitude and desolation which necessarily presents its self where thou art not, (and more especially where I've been made so often happy by thy enlivening presence,) that it hath scarce recovered strength enough to endite its own feeling, having ye additional oppression of a wearied body too; and that so farr from being relievd by last nights rest, that an innumerable army of my old enemies the knatts kept me waking most part of the night to wage warr offensive and defensive with them; and tho' many were slain on their side, yet I am wounded in several places. But my wearied and wounded body are petty ills compared to the sufferings my heart endures from thy absence, which is intolerable, and throughly verifies the observation, that as absence impairs and diminishes vulgar & mediocrital passions, so it augments and strengthens great ones, like the winds which extinguish

lesser flames, but increase such fires as thy love and goodness have kindled
in the soul of thy most faithful lover, Hervey.   P.S.   Have you
thankd Sir Thomas Felton for his letter and news? and will you let him
know how well I love him? Kiss the children for me.

231.   Lady Hervey to John Hervey.   Reading, Aug. 12, 1703.

    I cant say I am well come to this place, for I
have a mighty sore throat added to my other complaints, I am extremely
weary already, so that I believe I shall be quite dead when I get to the
Bath.   But all this is but little to what I feel in my mind for want of my
dear dear Angel; but I am resolvd it shall be the last journey I will take
without you till it be in a coffin; I am sure if I shoud make many of them,
that woud soon end them; but I will say no more upon this subject, since
we are so many miles asunder that it is past remedy.   If there is a calash
in Bath, you shall have it at Northampton (which I find is the road) by
Monday night.   I send you this notice in hopes your business may be done
to meet it part of the way, for every hour is an age (till we meet) to, my
dear dearest life, your faithful wife, E. Hervey.   I am very impatient
till I hear you are safe at Aswarby.   The children and Papa are well.

233.   My ever-new Delight   Aswarby, Aug. 14, 1703.

    Measuring the degree of your desire to hear often
from me by the longing impatience of my own for your dear letters, (which are
the only cordialls to support my drooping spirits in this worse than ever
separation,) and feeling so sensible a disappointment in missing one from
you by this mornings post, makes me resolve to omitt no opportunity of
writing to you, that you may be securd from experiencing the same concern
it gave me.   But I comfort my self partly by thinking you left London at a
time that made it impossible for me to receive one by this return.   Corbett
was pleasd to write to me about coales, but never mentiond when you went

away, or how you did; which shews how great a tenderness his wife hath created in him by the care he took to tell me what was become of mine. I labour incessantly at my accompts, and hope to compass them by this day sevenight, so as to sett out for Bath the Monday following, but whether by London or cross the country I am not yet determind. Be it one or t'other, if you have no manner of use for the horses, I shoud be glad of four of them, if you coud borrow a calesh to send with them; for Nutting is fallen ill of the small pox since he came hither, and besides one of my saddle horses is also disabled by the great expedition I usd in getting hither; but still I can make shift by the stage-coaches if you find you have the least occasion for your own; and in this, (as in all other things I think, ney know you are,) pray be most sincere with one by whom tis nicely repaid you, even to the most minute matters, being most faithfully & entirely yours, Hervey.

P.S. I hope the tooth-ach is abated. What woud you have done with the linnen which came down with the tea boxes, etc? and would you have me bring both the tea boxes with me? My service to Papa. Remember me to the dear children.

234. Lady Hervey to John Hervey. Bath, Aug. 14th, 1703.

My dear dearest life

I receivd a letter this morning from Ickworth of your being safe and well set out from thence; but it woud have added much to the welcomeness of it, if it had been under your own hand, which I was in such hopes of that I sent to the Post by seven a clock this morning. Indeed, my dear, my mind is as uneasy as my body (till I hear from you), which Dr. Raitcliff says is much out of order. He has been here an hour, & read over all the bills in my sickness, which I brought on purpose for him, and to morrow I begin his prescriptions. He makes every body drink the waters at the Pump, and has orderd me to do so as soon as I am well

Vol. I.   A A

enough to go out. My throat is something better, but my pulse is so bad, he has orderd me to eat no meat at night, nor but little at noon : that advice he might have spared, for I have hardly eat or slept enough to keep me alive since I saw you, and despair of doing it till we meet again, thou dear and only comfort of my life. The town is extreamly full already, and people coming every day, (but what is all that to Maxemus and me ;) I fear you will not like our lodgings ; but by what I hear of other people they are very good. I suppose the News papers tell you of the two Knights of the Garter, Lord Treasurer & Duke Shomberg, and the first of these is to be Earl of Bristol. For fear my letter may have miscarried, I must beg you again to bring the tea that went to Aswerby with the linnen by mistake. If the peaches prove good and you coud bring any safe, I woud be glad to give the Queen some. But tho' I say all this, I am in hopes you will meet the coach before it reaches Aswerby ; for till I have my dear dear nurse, I am sure all I do will signify nothing. I made the landlady at Marlborough drink to our good meeting, and burst out a crying to think we were asunder. I believe the woman thought me mad, as indeed I am in love, though I cant seem so to any body that knows the meritts of the object to his faithful E. Hervey.

    235.   My ever-new Delight   Aswerby, Aug. 16, 1703.

             Your letter which was to have given me the kind caution of not passing the Wash in my way hither, did not reach me till I had been some time here, the post master at Bury not sending it with the rest of my letters, which came the night before I left Ickworth. But you (I rant but own) deservd some punishment, if you coud do me so great an injustice as to be in any pain, least I might do a thing which you but once desird I woud not. Were it but God-Almighty's pleasure to give me grace enough to be as religiously punctual in all my dutys towards him as I am in every tittle, ney every trifle, (if any thing can bear that name which relates to the love between us,) which concerns your ease or happyness, and then I could not fail of being as blessed hereafter in his reward of my unprofitable services as thou hast made me here in the grateful retribution and welcome reception thou hast afforded to my honest well-meant endeavours to make thee as farr so as this imperfect life can possibly admitt of. Imperfect I may now justly call it in thy absence, having no ray of comfort but in the hope of seeing thee again quickly, and in the mean time

> Each day think on me, and each day I shall
> For thee make hours Canonical.
> By every wind that comes this way
> Send me at least a sigh or two ;
> Such and so many I'll repay,
> As shall themselves make winds to get to you.

Ney, I wish they raise not tempests, if I miss a third time hearing from thee, this morning proving as starving a post as Saturdays to your poor disappointed lover, Hervey.   P.S.   Never forget me to dear Papa and the children. Mrs. Burslem ever remembers you so much, as to think of nothing but how to provide cramming stuff enough for me.

236.   My ever-new Delight   Aswerby Aug. 18, 1703.

Tis this very morning but a week since I began to look into my affairs here, which so much want my inspection in every part of them that, unless a stricter government be maintaind, and my expences here be contracted into a narrower compass, (as well as at Ickworth and elsewhere,) I'm sure any building whether great or small must ruine me ; for out of all this estate, what between taxes, repairs, and the charges of this house and gardens etc., I have not actually receivd £3000 this year, notwithstanding my rental is upwards of £5250 per annum. Then the gardiners and his wifes civil warr against Burslem and his bride took me up one whole day to hear; and the former are found so much to blame, that it will take up two or three days more to examine the inventories of what they have in their custody to deliver up to their successours; but I have none at present for the gardiner, (who hath sold my trees out of the very walks, beside all the fruit,) altho' I wrote for one to Mr. Loudon or Wise, and Goodwife Doughty is the best I know of yet to substitute in Nans place, who even lett me find this house in as dirty and dusty a condition, as if there had been no body in it to prevent both. O my dear! could you tell the sufferings my mind hath endurd since I came, you would never let me feel so much again, for tis thy absence that aggravates every other cross or disappointment to an insupportable degree. I have not yet been once abroad, where no doubt things will hardly be found better usd by my tenants at a distance than the gardiner hath treated his charge which lyes so immediately under my eye. I am just now going to Hale; and as I have lost no one minute since I saw thee that could conduce to our sooner meeting again, so the same impatient diligence shall be incessantly employd, even to the robbing my sleep, to dispatch all my affairs here time enough to keep his Birth-day with thee, who was born to the very best fortune in life, as he was destind to be thy happy husband, Hervey.

P.S.—As I was going out, the coach came in which brought me thy kind, pretty letter. I cant say, however, twas as others have been, which brought me better accounts of thy invaluable health; and since you do but think your old nurse hath more virtue in him than your new doctor, I must e'en leave my business half undone, rather than both of us shoud be quite so by a longer separation, whose ill effects gather such strength upon me by continuance that I will venture all beside, and come as soon as ever the poor horses can bring me to thy dear arms, the only center of rest to thy now wearied, melancholy, pineing turtle.

237.   To my dear son Carr.   Sept. 17, 1703.

My dear son

I have hitherto kept ye anniversary of this day as one of ye most pleasing festivalls in all ye Kalender of time; & doubt not but you'l take care to make it fortunate also by becoming so pious, charitable, just and usefull a member in your generation, that not only you may be ye joy and support of my age & family, but one of the shineing ornaments of your country; to ye effecting whereof no care or cost on my part shall be omitted; & I make no question, since you know how essential your happyness is towards ye compleating of mine, but to see as ready a concurrence in you to prove as great a blessing as can be wished by your etc.

238.   To Mr. Manning.   Bath, Sept. 22, 1703.

Mr. Maning

I do agree to take one hundred and twenty tunn of stone of ye whitest bed, being sound and well scapled, at twenty shillings per tunn, deliverd at Wallington, between this and midsummer next, and will give order to Goodson that he receives and sees it landed where it ought to be for my use, and to give a bill of acknowledgment specifying ye quantities & qualities deliverd to him by ye watermen; and as for ye money, you may always assure your self of punctuall payment where you desire it to be made by your friend etc.

239.   To Mr. Charles Battely.   Bath, Sept. 23, 1703.

Mr. Battely

I have been very much suprised by a letter from Mr. Jodrell, wherein he tells me that there is a Sheriffs officer now in my house, to levy a tax chargd upon me by ye Commissioners in St, James's Parish in ye year 1697 amounting to £81..14..04, whereof £6..14..04 was for my capitation, and £75 for money at interest; for which said money and capitation too I was actually chargd and paid for ye same at Bury to Mr. Borrows, who will be ready to attest ye same by certificate whenever it shall be necessary to acquit me of this double demand; for which I doubt not of your advice to cure, though I cannot but think it might better have been prevented by a caution from you that my name was used amongst others in that process, as you know, being concerned in ye making of it out. Mr. Pooley advises me (to make ye best of a bad market) that I shoud desire Mr. Jodrell to undertake with ye Sherrifs officer or ye Sherrif himself, that he will be answerable for ye money for me in case I be not relieved upon my application in a proper place; and if ye Sherriff shoud want further security, I hope you woud be so kind to stand ingaged with him for it till that be done. I shoud take it very well if you woud give your self ye trouble to conferr with Mr. Jodrell how to extricate me out of this undeserved trouble, wherein I dare assure my self of my Lord Treasurer's favour, as far as in him may lye, to see justice done to one, who dreamd not of having so ugly a business come upon him, without having had some previous notice thereof. I am however your etc.

240.   To Mr. Jodrell.   Bath, Sept. 23, 1703.

I have advisd with Mr. Pooley concerning ye troublesome affair you gave me an account of, for which this is to thank you, and he tells me ye best thing I can do as matters stand, is to desire you woud undertake with ye Sheriff or his officers for ye payment of ye money demanded, in case I shoud not get reliefe when I apply for it in a proper place; wherein I am willing to give you any security you think fit for your indemnity, and shoud ye Sheriff require another surety, I doubt not but Mr. Charles Battely, who lives at Mr. Needhams in Deans Yard, Westminster, would willingly stand bound for ye performance of it with you, for indeed he is ye person to blame that ever this process came to affect me, for he being concernd in ye making out thereof, never gave me any notice that my name was used in it, although he is one of my particular friends, and one who, as a Bury man, could not but know I have ever since ye Revolution been charged and paid for all manner of taxes (except for my house in St. James Square) at Bury, that having been ye usual place of my residence in ye intervall of Parliament ; and did accordingly pay for this very sum of ready money, and ye Capitation duty also for ye same year 1697; and I make no doubt but to have justice done, by those in whose power it lies, to your friend and servant.

241. To Sir Richard Cocks.

Sir   London, May 27, 1704.

       I received not ye favour of yours of ye first instant till ye 9th, which found me in Suffolk, whereupon I made ye greater hast hither, that I might as soon as possible put my self in ye way of knowing ye truth of that report you desird to be satisfyed in ; which, as to my Lord Somers, I can assure you is altogether as maliciously & unjustly fatherd upon him as any other story you have ever known coynd by ye enemies of his merit and our settlement, to ye disadvantage of both ; for I find him strongly of my own opinion with respect to ye unhappy competition between your self and Sir John Guise, which is that, tho he'l act upon ye same honest bottom, yet we can neither of us come up to allow him near ye usefullness you'l be of in Parliament, who not only can but will speak those bold and timely truths we all want to hear again utterd there ; and we joyntly agree in this conclusion (without any prejudice to your concurrent), that there is no body we had rather have in ye H. of C. than Sir Richard Cocks. As to his Grace of Somerset, he hath done me the honour to call on me since I came, and I have been twice to wait on him, but allways missd of each other ; so cannot resolve your doubt concerning him : but if I can guess at him, he's as much wrongd in ye same point as ye other. I hope the broachers of this untruth will find themselves disappointed in their calculation as to ye timing of it, for I cannot perceive ye changes we have lately seen will produce a new Parliament this year ; so that you'l have time enough before you to remove any wrong impressions that may have been received from this groundless peice of Jesuitism ; and that at ye next election your county will retrieve its former faults by doing you justice, and thereby not only do them-selves but ye nation right, in endeavouring to return such to future Parlia-ments who may rectify ye mistakes & madness of others, that will hardly have time enough to finish ye laudable scheme they have so gloriously begun. Irony is ye safest figure in speech on these occasions ; but pray believe me in ye sincerest sense, when I tell you no man is your more faith-full friend & servant than etc.

242.   To Mr. Gage.   June 1, 1704.
    Dear Cousin

                    The former experience I've had of your kind readyness to do me all ye good offices in your power, never suffers any such injurious suspicions to arise in me (as you seem to intimate) of your being capable of forgetfullness or neglect where your friends (in which number I flatter my self with ye pleasure of being one) are concernd. As therefore that knowledge entirely acquits you of all blame in ye whole progress of that tedious & troublesome treaty you have had with Mr. Gipps on my account ; so it naturally leads me to ye laying of all delays and this last partial refusal at a door* I never expect any better influence from, where my interests are concernd, than proceeded from Pandora's box. And (had they not thought that usage too good) might with a much better grace have

---

* Here John Hervey has written in pencil in the margin, Sir R. D., meaning Sir Robert Davers.
S.II.A.II.

stiffld this nice nursling of ours in its birth by a flat denyal, than thus at last to murder it by piece-meal ; after Lord Dover's confession too, that ye £100 consented to by me for its preservation was more than he could have thought to ask. Since then nothing but trifling & ye spirit of disappointment seems to be predominant in those with whom we have to do, I'm of opinion ye best determination I can make, for your ease as well as my own, is to let them know peremptorily, (seeing they have thought fit now, when all things were lookd upon as adjusted, to except against an article so very insignificant in its utmost consequences to them, & so materially necessary to ye main drift of my design in ye exchange as that narrow slip of ground at Pestle peice end,) that I intend to sit down with ye phylosophical resolution of being contented with ye best my own will afford, in hope hereafter that Fata viam invenient. In ye mean time I must beg leave to say, (& I hope without breach of modesty, or being guilty of a wide miscalculation,) that in ye course of our lives something or other might have happend in my way to have made my neighbour Gipps (who I'm not ignorant may be swayd by collateral counsels to thwart my purposes herein, & so ye easylier excuse him) a full compensation for this favour, had it been granted as it was at first requested. I had last night an audience of Lord Treasurer, and among other things mentiond your expedient to him for getting over two horses to St. Victor as a thing wherein (were it faisible) he woud oblige me as well as your self; but he assures me yo're misinformd, and that he hath no authority of that kind, and believes twas never adventurd on in any instance since ye war began, ye penalty being very high both on ye master of ye ship, and all privy thereto. Sir H. Bond did me ye favour of a visit, but made no mention of Mrs. Gage's business. I shall make him one on purpose to bring that matter to a certainty, wherein Mr. Portington hath been inexcusably remiss. I shoud be very glad to do Mrs. Gage (to whom I beg my humble service) or your self any farther service in that or any other matter within ye narrow sphere of, dear Mr. Gage, your etc.

     Vol. I.   B B

243.   To my cousin John Hervey of Thurleigh.

Dear Cousin   London, June 27, 1704.

This comes to acknowledge ye favour of yours of ye 15th instant, together with ye particular inclosd, which rates ye estate at a much higher value than my present family circumstances will admitt of giving for it; and since I'm not in a condition to come up to ye terms proposd, I cant but hope my cousin Stephen & you may yet fall upon some expedient to keep Thurleigh (at least) in our name. He dind with me last Sunday, & I then acquainted him with its unsuitableness to ye scituation of my other affairs, having many children already to provide for, & ye prospect of more; which daily reminds me of converting what money I have to ye best advantage for them. But as taxes are very heavy on land, & may yet prove more so, & no ease in view from an happy conclusion of ye warr & them together, and that in ye mean time all trade (whereon ye rents of land chiefly depend) is likelyer to dye quite away rather than to revive from that languishing condition, which the unavoidable breach between us and Spain hath fatally occasiond, I dare not venture to part with so considerable a share of ye younger ones portions, to invest it in that which will yield so slow an increase as I find land estates afford; otherwise I shoud have been extreamly well pleasd to accomodate your matters, and at ye same time to have kept ye ancient stem of ours in ye Herveys. My cousin Stephen hath given me hopes that when you have disposd of matters to content in Bedfordshire, you intend to settle your self in the neighbourhood of this place, whereby a more intimate friendship may be cultivated between us, which (from my first knowledge of you) hath been sincerely wishd for by, Sir, yours etc.

244.   To dear Carr.   London, June 27, 1704.

My dear son

This is to thank you by way of encouragement

for your frequent epistles, and for ye accounts you send me of all my affairs at Ickworth; but particularly for that part of them which concerns your self and your studies; as whatever relates to your true happyꞧess and improvement much more affects me than any thing which imediately belongs to my self. Terence will make you master of purity in ye Latin stile (Cicero having considerd him as ye rule and standard of that language), and let you into ye characters of ye Menu peuple; but Salust is ye author who best sets forth those of ye great ones. Æsop and Phœdrus will teach you how to form your manners; Socrates & Epictetus will polish and perfect them. Tacitus inspires ye firmest politicks; and Thucidides instructs you how to speak well in either House of Parliament. The art of reasoning well must be learnd from Aristotle; that of writing from celebrated Tully. Plutarch will furnish various subjects for conversation; and Plato fill your mind with noble and sublime ideas. Homer livelily & naturally represents ye different conditions of humane life, setting forth mankind in all ye various scituations Providence can place him in. Enfin, ye older Pliny will open to you a vast diversity of learnd knowledge; and Xenophon and Quintilien give you that plan of education I intend for you; being throughly satisfyed with ye truth of that proposition, Qui educat pater magis quam qui genuit. I shall endeavour therefore to approve myself not only a good parent, but patriot too; since Diogenes and Pythagoras were of opinion that ye education of youth was ye best foundation and support of any state; ye proof whereof is best fetchd from ye famous Cornelia, mother of ye Gracchi, who being shewn a parcell of fine jewells by a Roman lady, calld for her children, and told her those were ye only treasure she set a value upon, whom she had bred up for ye service of their country. Aurelia, Cæsar's mother, and Accia, Augustus's, are bright instances of ye same wisdom, ye latter especially, whose comendable care succeeded so well (having neglected no opportunity that could contribute to ye greatness of her son's soul or to ye beauty of his body or mind) that he became capable at 12 years old (and alass! you're already passd that age) to make his grandmother Julia's funeral oration, & at 20 made a consul. Greece woud afford many examples of ye same kind; but I hope enough hath been said to excite your emulation so far to concur with my kind design of making you an accomplishd gentleman, that hereafter your performances may prevent my fondest wishes; & then I'm sure you'l prove as perfect as your own grace & my devoutest prayers can make you; being with all ye passion of a most indulgent parent, my most dear child, your etc.

245.   To Mr. Yorke.   London, July 8, 1704.

Being informd last post by Burslem that ye assessors for Sleeford & Haldingham intend to charge my estates in those two towns higher than ye last, or indeed any other year since ye late happy Revolution; and knowing how unequally other peoples lands are rated in ye severall districts, with respect to ye heavy burthens laid upon my own, occasiond orriginally by my necessary absence at that time in attending ye publick service; makes me address my self to you for justice on this occasion, and to beg ye favour of you that you woud employ your interest (with my humble service) to your brother Thompson & Mr. Gardiner in my behalf, to prevent their doing me such an injustice as will necessitate me to make some provision before ye land tax bill passes next year, by a clause to have a review & general reassessment made of all estates in ye several divisions where mine are chargeable, & then I'm sure great ease will particularly accrue thereby to, Sir, your etc.

246.   To Mrs. Fiske.   London, July 8, 1704.
          Madam

I have given order for all necessary tenentable repairs to be done at Duffon-hall, pursuant to my agreement with ye new tennant ; and thereupon expect and insist to have him enter and hold according to ye articles between us ; so that there is no room left for the present tennant to think of continuing longer than Michaelmas next. I do not know what reason he may have given you or other people to think well of his generosity or handsome dealing ; I can only say my wood can witness how ill a specimen he gave me of either since ye short acquaintance I've had with him ; beside ye jugling treaty I can plainly perceive hath been on foot, and is yet depending between his intended successor & him, with whom he us'd his artfullest endeavours to frighten from coming to live under me. However, I cant but thank you for ye trouble you have given your self in this affair, as being (I doubt not) well intended towards your etc.

247. To Sir R. Cocks. London, July 8, 1704.
    I hope ye accident of my wife her being brought to bed of a still-born boy will plead my excuse for not sooner sending you my thanks for ye Answer to faction displayd ; and your Vandyke-like picture of Westminster Hall. I observd your direction in transcribing them, & then shewd them to many friends, who were so pleasd with some passages in the former as to wish it had appeard early enough to have askd leave for printing it. Sempronia's* character in it is so much her due, that did you know her but half so well as I have ye happyness to do, you would find her merit as fruitful! as your fancy ; she would make you think of her as one said of ye sea ; that it infinitely surprisd him ye first time he saw it ; but that ye greater wonder was he admird it every time he lookd on't since ; & that ye last sight of it made always as wonderfull an impression as if he had never observd it before. She hath a most accute and elevated understanding, equally partaking of ye solid as well as ye shining faculty ; ingenious as necessity, & penetrating as time ; a mind so richly furnishd with

---

* A marginal note here says, Ds. M . . . h, meaning the Duchess of Marlborough. S.H.A.H.

all those amiable talents of prudence, justice, generosity, constancy, and love for her native country, that she ought to have been born in ye golden age; her virtues far transcending ye practice, & therefore (much to her prejudice) beyond ye credit of ye present age.

> Here bounteous nature all her strength combind
> To form ye finest body, noblest mind.
> No single virtue can we most commend,
> Whether ye wife, ye mother, or the friend ;
> For she is all in that supreame degree,
> That as no one prevails, so all is she ;
> The several parts lye ready in ye piece,
> Th' occasion but exerting that or this.

In short, one so every way worthy of ye favour she possesses, by her incessant vigilance and incorruptible fidelity in all ye Queen's interests, & (at ye same time) by so just and laudable an employment of it, wherever ye safety & prosperity of England is concernd, that ye people, as well as we her friends, ought to pray for ye continuance of it for their own sakes.   But as St. Jerom said on another occasion, Quædam abstraxero, ne incredibilia videantur ; and pass on to her lord, who by his late victory on ye Danube hath acquird to himself ye immortal honour of having secured ye liberties & peace of Europe from being in our days (at least) indangerd through ye voracious, restless spirit of that common disturber of ye quiet of mankind, Louis le monstre.   I hope ye warr of Portugal will also now proceed as prosperously, since they have at last thought fitt to send a man who hath Tam Martis quam Mercurii in him ; no less than a master in both qualifications being necessary for that post my Lord Galloway is going to execute ; who is not only like an Englishman in his person, but throughout one too in principle ; which shews how true ye saying is, Second thoughts are best. He did me the honour t'other day to dine with me, in company of Lords

Sunderland, Hallifax, and others of your & my good friends, who are all well pleasd with ye choice of him, & doubt not of good success in a righteous cause as ours is, when honest and able men are employd by ye Government ; & herein too is Sempronia cheifly praiseworthy, there being none she esteems so of, that are not recomended and patronizd by her. But I dwelt (I fear you'l think) too long on her character before to be allowd any enlargement of it here ; only thus much more I must add, (to take away all suspicion of flattery or partiality, which she neither needs, nor I am ever (intentionally) guilty of), that Si propius stes, te capiet magis ; and that she is one of those rare souls, who only want to be universally known, to be valued accordingly ; that definition of Heaven being in a moral sense applicable to her humane perfections, ubi totum est quod velis, nihil est quod nolis. But I beg pardon for entring again, and thus late in my letter, upon so inexhaustible a theme as her good qualities, which will at length shew themselves to much greater advantage than my injurious pen can pretend to. Shall therefore conclude your trouble in assuring you, nobody can be better pleasd with your corres-pondence than myself, and am proud to think you have pickd me out as one of those few to whom you care to impart your thoughts, which are always welcome to, Sir, your etc.

248. To Sir Thomas Hanmer. London, July, 1704.
   Sir

   Having observd your fund of good nature to be extensive enough to interess you with kindness in all things that concern even ye unworthyest of your well-wishers, in which class of friendship I hope you do me ye justice (at least) to place me, makes me venture ye troubling of you on this occasion, to let you know my wife was deliverd about six this morning of a still-born male child. Ye learnd, in reasoning upon't, impute ye loss of it to an over-throw in her coach, when last in Suffolk ; but

I'm apt to think it a most errronious conjecture, the infant appearing to be full grown & well nourishd enough to be perfectly come to its full maturity, and pretty even under ye levelling disadvantage of death. The afflicted mother is (all circumstances considerd) as well after it as can reasonably be hoped by your etc.

I am ye Duchess of Graftons most humble servant. May I beg leave to tell Mrs. Ramsey ye same.

249.   To ye Duke of Marlborough.   London, July 9, 1704.
My Lord

Remembring how great a trouble your Grace thought fit to give your self in honouring me with an answer, when I sent you my thanks for a most particular piece of service your goodness had done me with ye Queen, (which, as ye motto I've chosen says, Je n'oublieray jamais,) made me once resolve (tho' on this great occasion finding my self one of those whose consciousness of through good will & wishes towards your Grace coud easily have let me dare to dispense with forms) not to venture a second opportunity whereby your time, so precious to ye publick, might be diverted to less important uses than it is & ought to be employd in. But really, my Lord, as ye news of your Graces late noble action on ye Danube was too full of wonder to let one speak at all upon't at first hearing, so no sooner could our thoughts gett vent, but that they represent too many great and good consequences, too much glory to her Majesty and her arms, too many universal advantages to all her allies, too much security to ye future liberty & peace of Europe, and too much immortal fame to your self (from ye essential share your personal example and conduct had in gaining ye victory) to be possibly past over in admiring silence only by your zealous and faithfull friends, at a time too when even ye tepid ones of your prosperity, ney, ye very prejudiced themselves, are

forced to mention it with just applause. I have heard but of one fault these
Momus's can pick out to impute to your Grace in this whole affair ; which
is that you exposd your self much too much for a General, on whose preservation the success of ye warr so intirely depends; and herein I find your
friends do not differ much with them.   And seeing you are so prodigall of
life wherever her Majesties and your countrys service calls for it, may your
tutelary angel still protect you, and by thus contemning death, thus improve
& enjoy life. May her Majesty's reign, so successfully begun for her own
glory & ye happyness of her people, never want so usefull & so ornamental
a servant as your self, to carry on & compleat both those blessings, and to
consummate all my due desires ; may your credit always keep in its present
bright meridian, which, seeing how right an influence it casts around it,
shoud make Joshuas of every Englishman, to supplicate its solstice ; among
whom none shoud and doth put up that prayer with more sincere devotion
than, my lord, your etc.

250.   To ye Countess of Orkney.   Aug. 1, 1704.
        Madam
                Tis with a most welcome satisfaction I've received
so authentick a confession, from your nearer & more intimate observation,
of your having alterd that injurious opinion you'd once entertained of my
humility ; which was so throughly grounded upon ye conscious sense resulting from an impartial self-enquiry, that I never dreamed of suffering ye least
diminution in a companion so necessary to my other indifferent qualifications; but your native generosity, by thinking it self obligd to compensate
ye wrong it now feels your former judgment had done it, having put you upon
overvaluing my shaddow of merrit as much as you once thought my own
presumption might have done, (for otherwise you coud nere believe ye mean
talents I am owner of in any measure equal to ye task of publick business,)

        Vol. I.   c c

thro ye authority of so skilfull a judge & so sincere a friend as your self comended it almost to its own destruction, had not ye very thoughts and language wherewith you woud have persuaded me out of it, been too inimitably beautifull, for one of my taste, not to set me down again in ye same mortified station your letter found me. No, Madam, I'm still of Epictetus's mind :—

> He saw ye world was mean & low,
> Patrons a lye, friendship a show,
> Preferment trouble, greatness vain,
> Law a pretence, a bubble gain,
> Merit a flash, a blaze esteem,
> Promise a rush, & hope a dream,
> Faith a disguise, and truth deceipt,
> Wealth but a trap, & health a cheat.

You have often heard this distich :

> Men like our money come ye most in play
> For being base and of a coarse allay.

And another poet of mine sings thus :

> Many by servile arts and flattery rise,
> But none made great for being good or wise ;
> The honest oft grow useless, & are laid aside,
> But knaves of conduct always will abide.
> Integrity some lean employ may get,
> But he that sticks at nothing shall be great.

Therefore, Madam, upon ye whole, unless ye world were better, or I coud make it so, or my self fitter for it, I had much rather with our friend Cato (as to my being employd) that men shoud enquire (as they did upon seeing no statue erected for him at Rome) why I have not a place, than why I have one. So thanking your ladyships partiality for esteeming me capable, I'll end your trouble as soon as I can by closing this topick. As to ye wise and friendly cautions you've laid down in ye examination of a friend, I must do mine & my self ye justice to let you know I never admitted ye particular one your ladyship hints at into that sacred relation, till I had studied her most inquisitively, watchd every unguarded circumstance of her conduct, scrutinizd every principle in her essential to that noblest necessary office of life, and throughout approvd her, before her benefits to me and mine had set so strong a byass on me as you (I find) perceive. Whether I ought to own vanity enough to hope she's my friend in ye strict sense and notion of one with which you interrogated me last night, I cannot yet resolve you, being justly doubtfull of ye cause which shoud create her so ; and were any one to put ye same question to me concerning your self, I coud only answer for your ladyships most etc.

251. The Duke of Marlborough to Lord Hervey.

My lord   Camp at Seffelingen, Aug. 21, 1704.

           It was with great satisfaction that I received the favour of your lordships of the 7th past, having been always sensible of your friendship, and coud never doubt of your participating in whatever good fortune happend to me, or to the Publick, as I am sure your satisfaction will be much greater when you receive the good news of our victory obtaind over the enemy this day se'night ; their loss appears greater than any thing has been represented yet, & I hope they will not be able to recover the blow in many years ; for we reckon Monsieur Tollard's army in a manner intirely lost ; the Elector with the Mareshal Marcin have also sufferd & retiring towards the Black Forrest ; we are now come before Ulm, in which we find the enemy have left 4 French battalions & 5 Bavarians ; we shall block up the place till Prince Lewis comes with the heavy cannon, for we must not leave this city behind us ; when we are masters of it, I believe the French will hardly attempt coming again into this country. I do not intend to stay at this siege; but as soon as the necessary measures are taken for the carrying it on, I shall march to the Rhine, where it is thought the French will bring all the force they can. I need not tell you that our country-men have got immortal honour in these countries, and that I'm with much truth, my lord, your lordship's most obedient humble servant, Marlborough.

I beg you will make my compliments to Lady Hervey & Sir Thomas Felton.

252.   To Lord Orkney in Germany.   After ye battle of Blenheim.

My lord   Aug. 22, 1704.

Your kind remembrance of ye troublesome request my friendly concern put me upon making to you at parting, hath done my heart as much right as you've done your self justice in ye late glorious action near Donawert & Hochstet; wherein your Lordships share in both victories proves to be yet more considerable than even your best friends with all their due reliance on your known gallantry & experience could reasonably promise themselves. And if being truly pleasd for your own sake with ye noble part you personally had in those successes, and for my Lady Orkneys with your almost miraculous safety through it all, coud deserve ye honour your lordship hath done me, tis rightly enough bestowd; for I can faithfully assure you, those two considerations made ye news of ye whole much more welcome to me than it coud otherwise have been. We have but one alloy, which necessarily mixes it self with ye most prosperous events of warr, which is ye loss of so many brave men ; whose fates we at ye same time condole, can hardly keep our selves from secretly envying them, since born to so great and good an end, as to lay down their lives (which death woud have bereft them of some less desirable way) in ye defence of all that's worth living for ;

I need not say ye liberties & peace, not only of their own countries, but of all Europe, The sole retribution their countries in return can make them is to succour & relieve all their afflicted relations which they've left behind them, and to cherish & promote those who equally hazarded theirs, but yet remain alive ; and shoud I live to see my country but omissively ungratefull to either after ye seasonable service both have done it, (wherein I promise ye joynt assistance of my poor mite & vote or other interest to prevent its ever being so,) I shoud apprehend destruction due at last to't, instead of more such souls to engage again in its defence. In ye meantime, till we can shew our sense by effectual proofs, I desire your lordship and all our countrymen may know these are ye sentiments & purposes of, my lord, your etc.

253. To ye Duke of Marlborough. Aug. 22, 1704.
My Lord

I once hopd to have resisted this repetition of your Graces trouble, notwithstanding you have been pleasd to renew so tempting an occasion for it; partly for Pliny's reason to Trajan—Cum jampridem novitas omnis laude consumpta sit, non alius erga te novus honor superest quam si aliquando de te tacere audeamus. And more yet for Salust's concerning Carthage—Nam de Carthagine tacere satius puto quam parum dicere. For your Graces last unparaleld victory is one of those few themes on which, tho tis easy to say a great deal, yet tis impossible to say enough : an action, which by one masterly stroak hath changd ye ballance of affairs in Europe to that surprising degree, as to give even ye most aged desponders new hopes of living to see that dangerous power now reducd to safe bounds by her Majestys arms under your Graces wise & valiant conduct; which before ye youngest sanguine hearts in their most golden dreams could never promise themselves would prove a work of less time at least (if ever) than that which had producd it ; and it seems a just reverse of Fate that ye honest patriots (for so I esteemd your Grace one of them before you desird that only justice of ye House of Lords, to be thought so of) in an English reign shoud become ye happy instruments of retrieving those mercenary and almost irrecoverable false steps of a French one ; for one cant readily forget that twas to England's connivance, if not cultivation, that ye principal root and growth of France's threatning greatness is chiefly owing. But since steming ye inundation of that orewhelming torrent of intended misery hath been reservd for one of ye peculiar glories which are to adorn ye illustrious history of our good Queens Government, whose constant piety hath entitled her to ye blessings of Providence, as justly as your Graces faithfull and successfull services hath you, not only to her royal favour, but also to ye affections & prayers of her people ; so those who were accessary to ye cause have not only ye charitable forgiveness, but (considering consequences) it shall no more be imputed to them by, my Lord Duke, your etc.

254.   To Mr. Leeds, Master of Bury free-schoole.

Sir   Ickworth, Sept. 23, 1704.

Could I justly tell my self you had ever receivd a real benefit from any officious endeavours of mine to serve you, twould yeild me as pleasing a satisfaction (at least) as you could possibly have found by it ; there being few axioms which carry more sensible truth in them than— Qui digno dedit beneficium, dando recipit. The recomendation you were pleasd to honour me with concerning your son is embracd with all readyness, and shall be observd with all ye distinction due to his merit, and ye early obligations I owd his father, as my indulgent master. But ye various virtues of your well spent life have secured a much more certain provision towards his prosperity than all worldly friendships can pretend to effect ; since infallible authority teacheth us that a good man leaveth an inheritance (even) to his children's children, an entaile that reacheth a farther remainder than your own wishes extended to ; were mine to prevail, you woud still live to enjoy many years in a through indolence of body and mind, to ye advantage of our youth, & the entertainment of your friends; in which class I hope your justice allows me a higher forme than my fatal idleness intitled me to in your school, being with a most sincere respect your etc.

My son sends you his thanks for your kind present. I'll take care he shall profit more by your labours than his repenting father did.

255. Lady Hervey to Lord Hervey. London, Dec. 1704.

I am now at Papa's, where I hoped to have mett you. I sent John to keep a place for you in ye side box, but he came back again & sed he found a great many footmen there, but they weir forcd to go back to fetch ticketts, for no gentelman is to sitt their without; so you have put me to ye expence of a guiney for your company ; theirfore, if you dont come, you will extremly disoblidg me, & I shant forgitt it as long as I live ; you must ask for John of ye right side (that being ye side I sitt off), he has your tickett; I was saying to Papa how I shoud frett to see John sitt there for my guiney ; & he said it was but John for Jack ; but it woud prove a sad exchange for me. Pray make hast to diner, for fear I shoud be calld without it. I cant help makeing one remark, that many wifes woud give a guiney to have there husbands stay away, but few woud give it for there company but E.H.

256. To Sir Richard Cocks. London, Jan. 4, 1704.

Sir

I wish ye return of politicks for piety coud yeild you half ye pleasure or profit your last discourse of religion hath afforded me ; there being not only many irrefragable truths in it, but I have also ye satisfaction to discern my judgment jumps with yours in one as well as t'other; and from ye best observation I have made both of your desire to find truth, and to put its dictates into practice, I think I may safely wish my soul may accompany yours. But though I always took you to be an honest good man, I shoud never have believd you so able a divine, so skilfull a merchant, and so general a statesman as I find by your writings, there being a maxim in sciences, contradicted by my experience in you, which says, He thats an ubiquitary in knowledge, knows nothing well. Your remark concerning ye Duke of Marlboroughs modest behaviour, since such a success as would have turnd any worse ballasted brain than his own which contrivd ye occasion of it, is so just in it self and so due to him, that coud you guess without seeing as I have done with what a lovely decency and unaffected humility he wears it, twould charm you into as good an opinion of him as hath been long since paid you by, Sir, your etc.

I dare not set my name for fear of the 134; but hope by what I've said you'd know ye author, tho written in an other character than usual.

257.   To Mr. Battely.   London, Dec. 27, 1705.

   Sir

                  I could not have wondred at ye warmth you expressed your self with relating to ye request I was desird to make Mr. Grove on Curtis's behalf, did not my heart entirely acquit me of any ye least intentional wrong to'rds your brother Westrope in it, whose merit I'm no stranger to, and could have hopd you had not been so great a one to my nature, principles and practice, as to have thought me capable of meaning a prejudice, where I had so often told you all returns of favour were justly intended, and shall yet be punctually performd by me on all occasions that shall offer. This being ye naked state of my mind, it cant but think it self a little hardly usd to have its innocence made liable to misconstruction, for want only of Mr. Grove's shewing me the error I was ignorantly surprisd into before he exposd it any where else to my disadvantage; for had he undeceivd me in ye mistake I lay under (by misinformation) of his not dealing with any of ye Corporation, he woud soon have seen how sensible I had been at ye imposition aimd at on him & me by turning advocate for ye continuance of his kindness where twas so worthily bestowd. As ready as you are to conclude me in ye wrong, I cant help being as much concernd as ever to hear your health does not go right, knowing how much depends upon't; but I hope to hear that mends apace, now you know I'm not guilty of ye wrongs you feard, & that I heartily forgive you those you've done me in but believing me to be so. I only beg this general justice of my friends, that they never woud entertain injurious distrusts of my fidelity to'rds 'em till they find me tripping in any one instance, having never wilfully offended against ye sacred laws of gratitude. Since then all ye hardship of this case happens to fall on my side, I trust in your goodness to make me ye compensation of setting me right again in ye oppinion of those who may have been reasonably enough scandalizd at my seeming unaccountable part in this unlucky application. I shall conclude with letting you know I have not been able to see Sir R. Blackmore since I receivd your last; but when I do, shall let you know which of ye evacuations you mentiond are most safe & most proper for Mr. Grove, whose life is still as valuable to me, as if ye last false step in point of friendship had never happend towards his & your faithfull friend and neighbour.

258. To Sir Richard Cocks. London, Jan. 3, 1705.
    Sir
            You wrong my taste, as well as ye merit of your own letters, when you suppose me capable of being tired with them; and if my silence hath given occasion to so unjust a conjecture, let this assurance undeceive you once for all, that when I do not answer them, tis more because

Vol. I.   D D

I cannot return ye entertainment they bring (which is ever welcome to me), than that I woud not have them always continued & multiplied as far as your leisure can afford. The itinerary you last sent me was very agreeable, especially in that circumstance of it which honours me with being ye principal motive of your journey, a favour I woud have come to Town on purpose to receive, had I known of it. But there's one passage in it that woud prove a great allay to ye pleasure I found in reading of it, coud not I make (at least) as good a defence for my self in that matter as my accusers can, either for differing with me in that judgment of How & P, or imputing it to me as a fault that I did not implicitly concur with them therein. Appeals in equitable causes leave greater latitudes to mens minds in determining of property (one of ye most sacred trusts of peerage) than writs of errour do ; for in proceedings of ye latter kind we are bound up by ye strickt rules of law ; whereof ye judges being ye best interpreters, and sitting among us to inform and guide our judgments in points purely legal, & that then before us depending solely upon ye validity of form, & 10 of ye 12 judges being clearly of opinion that were ye judgment to be enterd again they coud not tell how to express it better than in ye very words whereon ye errours were assignd, and that this judgment run in ye very same terms that all others in ye like cases do, and that ye ablest of ye entring clerks can never find out more apposite words than those in dispute to secure their clients damages by ; after hearing this and ye admonition of my own conscience, which I thank God hath hitherto been so faithfull a monitor to me as to make justice ye first principle of my conduct, it was impossible for me to gratify those friends (even together with ye additional byass of my own leaning inclinations) at ye expence of my morality ; for coud I have been against How without hurting of that, I'm sure twas due to him from me for ye poor part he desird I might act in it of being absent, dispairing of that justice which such a request little entitled him to ; and to satisfy you farther how clear I stood of all interested regards in that cause, I at ye same time knew how ill I made my court elsewhere in what I did ; for whatever airs he may give himself in ye country, I believe his cake is growing as dough at St. James's, as in Glostershire. So now do you judge between me and our friends, whether they've not done me wrong for having been thus forced to do Mr. H. right. I wish nobody may contribute more to ruin ye reputation of our house & cause than I have done, being throughly persuaded that nothing can support both so effectually as never deviating from my old fashiond rule, that all other interests ought to give place to honesty. For if once ye partialities of partys come to confound ye distinctions of right & wrong amongst us, whigism becomes Felo de se, & at one stroak destroys its own essential professd principles of liberty & property ; & then where can ye injurd or oppressd find a sanctuary, let ye pendulum of power swing which way it will ? I was not insensible how dear I was to pay for my dissenting with them in this matter ; but being affraid of nothing so much as to be thought a dishonest man by my self, I choose rather to incur their displeasure than my own. O te felicem, Marce Cato, a quo rem improbam nemo petere audet. The subject which closd ye other sheet touchd me in so sensible a part that I'm sure you'l pardon ye length of ye apology as well as ye warmth of it ; since (to use your own words) injurys from friends make deeper wounds than from avowd enemies. But if swerving from them in a particular personal concern coud provoke them to load me with such heavy imputations as you imparted to me, what censures am I not to expect for ye publick protest I've impolitickly made against ye Regency (alias Expedient) bill ; wherein my shallow understanding differs so widely from theirs ; yet I do think tis ye falsest step that ever was made by any set of men, & I've so much charity for them as to wish ye consequences I have foretold about it may rather make me look like a visionary dreaming fool than a true prophet. The remark you make upon the mutual civilities, which have passd between ye A.B. of Quebeck & B. of W. and their inferiour ciergy as to ye succession of our Bishops, is very right ; but then it puts one upon

further speculations what they expect from ours in return; for ye Church
of Rome's policy is never to make any advances to'rd hereticks, unless they
find a previous disposition in them to deserve it. For my part it puts me
in mind of a passage at a late Westminster Election, where a wagg on our
side publishd ye bands of matrimony between ye Church of England and
ye Church of Rome, (believing ye candidates of ye other well affected to
Popery): whereupon a witty rogue started up & cryd, Hold, I forbid those
bands, for they're too nearly related already. I dont at all wonder at ye
little effect ye present young set of beauties made in you at Lord Mayor's
show, nature having been so very profuse of her favours & labourd so very
hard to frame an exact standard of female perfection in Sempronia,* that I
was not surprisd to hear you say they seemd unfinishd patterns of their sex
compard with those you have seen formerly, being born since she was made,
and compounded out of ye refuse of those ornaments which suited not with
ye excellence of her materials. Did you know as well as I do how much
her country owes her, you woud love and honour her as much as I do; for
tis ye glorious share she hath had in bringing my prophecies to pass concerning ye good and great turn that hath been given to our home affairs,
which hath endeard her to all true Englishmen, and particularly to your
most faithfull friend etc.

259.   To Mr. Norton of Ixworth.   Feb. 19, 1705.
      Sir

           The removal or continuation of worthy Justice
Taylor having been one of ye chief reasons which retarded ye alteration of
ye Comission of ye peace for our County, & ye Duke of Grafton having
honourd me from time to time with ye communication of all occurrences
relating thereto, I find my self obligd (at last) to let your self and Mr.
Calthrop know (with my service) that Sir Thomas Hanmer hath laid so great

---

* John Hervey's marginal note says L.M.., meaning the Duchess of Marlborough. S.H.A.H.

weight upon his usefullness to him in all ye affairs of both his neighbourhoods, and ye personal unkind air it woud have for his Grace to turn out ye
only man he pretends to sollicite or interess himself for, that I plainly
perceive it must necessarily occasion a domestick misunderstanding should
not his Grace sacrifice his own inclinations in this difficulty by indulging to
his father in laws request ; and this being ye true state of ye case, I know
twould make his Grace much more easy under this necessary compliance
were he to understand you two coud be tolerably satisfyd with his being
kept in. I'm sure no consideration but ye peace of ye family I wish so
throughly well to could have prevaild on me to turn a sort of advocate for
such a client, who is just as well thought of by ye rest of ye world as by,
Sir, your etc.

260. To Lady Gipps.
Madam
The adjusting of ye proportions which ye several
exchangd lands etc. are to be chargd with to ye Town rates & land tax,
shall either be now settld or deferd, as your Ladyship likes best ; wherein
that part assignd to Mr. Covells care was only to get ye ancientest men of
both parishes* to meet on Tuesday come sevenight in order to inform Mr.
Underwoods judgment what was just and reasonable to be done for both
sides therein ; for I shall desire no better umpire to decide between us than
himself, altho your Ladyships own agent, to shew ye sincerity of my professions for ye continuation of a constant good correspondence between our
familys, which I shall always be very carefull to cultivate on my part. But
if all reports are to be credited, tis impossible any friendships whatsoever
shoud prove longlifd ; for I do assure your Ladyship never any complaint of
ye exorbitancy of my purchase was ever yet or shall be made (unless by Mr.

---

* Horringer and Ickworth. See Diary 1705. S.H.A.H.

Covell, whose tongue I've no more command of than himself) by, Madam, your etc.

261.   To ye Duke of Marlborough.   London, May 21, 1706.
   My Lord
                     The fresh crop of laurels your Grace is gathering with so successfull a hand in Flanders, exceeding even that most plentifull harvest of em you reapd in Germany, must draw upon you ye farther trouble of receiving new congratulations from all your friends, as well as ye united thanks of all ye freed people in Europe. Accept then of my poor mite, my Lord, in both these capacities, as coming from a heart much more full of joy that ye man I'm bound & do wish best to shoud prove ye chosen instrument of providence to work such wonders by, & to have been so signally preserved thro all those imminent dangers you have run in executing its decrees, than for ye valuable benefits we or our posterity may now reasonably promise our selves from ye happy consequences attending all your victories, which have been so great & so amazing in all ye circumstances of them, that since even some of our contemporaries can hardly find faith enough to believe them real, how is it to be hopd but that so many surprising passages of your life must prejudice ye truth of your history by rendring matters of fact incredible to after ages? and what pity t'were they shoud not be believd then, since your Grace's known modesty restrains us from speaking of 'em now as they deserve; & by fearing to displease that eminent virtue in you force us to be injust to ye rest of your merit; but having been an eye witness with what a becoming decency, with how unaffected an humility, your Grace wore ye trophys gained at Hochstet, obliges me to say no more of those won at Ramillies than

      Thus Hannibal, his many conquests past,
      Found Fabius still to grapple with at last;

Fabius more great, with wiser conduct blest,
Vanquishd ye victor, & his pride represt.

I'm with all possible respect your Graces most obliged & most obedient servant, etc.

262. The Duke of Marlborough to Lord Hervey.

My Lord   Arzele, June 14, 1706.

I am favour'd with your lordships obliging letter of the 21st of the last month, and thank you for your obliging expressions on the victory the arms of her Majesty and her allies have by the blessing of Providence gaind over their enemies. By your known affection to the publick good, it is easy to guess at the satisfaction you take in our success; and I have had too many instances of your friendship to doubt of the sincerity of your kind expressions as to what relates to my selfe. You must give me leave to admire, since I cannot imitate, your most ingenious conclusion; and to assure you in plain prose of the sincerity wherewith I am, my Lord, your Lordships most obedient humble servant, Marlborough.

263. To ye Duke of Northumberland.   June 15, 1706.

My lord

The bearer hereof, my nephew Elwes, being ambitious of having a comission under your Graces comand, I coud not consent to his perfecting the agreement for it untill your Grace had seen him; and if you think him fit to pass muster for a horse officer under ye misfortune of his lameness, (which doth not in ye least disable him for such service,) I shall be throughly satisfied with ye choice he hath made of placeing himself under such a Collonel, of whose encouragement & protection (I have told him) he may assure himself, in case your Grace finds he hath merit enough to deserve it, (which I hope he is not quite destitute of,) & otherwise your Grace's countenance towards him shoud never have been requested by your etc.

264.   To ye Bishop of Lincoln.   Aug. 21, 1706.
    My Lord

Having made choice of a person for my two Vicarages of Methringham & Digby in your Lordships diocese, of whom I have so good an opinion that I doubt not but he will be very acceptable to your Lordship and serviceable to ye Church, I beg of your Lordship to give him any encouragement which your Lordship may think proper for ye ease of his expence in his admittance. My Lord, ye vicarages being seperately very small, & at a very convenient distance for an union, I have long desird and had a promise from ye late Bishop for a consolidation; which having not been performd, if your Lordship woud be pleasd to effect, I shoud look upon't as a particular favour; but, my lord, if it cant be done, I find it most adviseable, if your Lordship approves of it, for ye Incumbent to be presented only to Methringham, & to hold ye other by sequestration, & I hope your Lordship will do me ye favour to grant a sequestration to ye gentleman I have sent to your Lordship, & support him in ye possession of it. And since I am giving your Lordship this trouble, let me take ye liberty of mentioning Mr. Archdeacon Cawleys holding his Visitations again at Falkingham, notwithstanding Sleeford hath been ye place where they have been constantly kept, & that ye Chancel there hath been repaird with great expence according to direction, and a new inn built for his officers better accomodation. But if after this we must still loose ye benefit of them in favour of Mr. Wyns interest at ye other place, I must be allowd to think its done with a preference to one, who hath shewn himself on all publick occasions a better friend neither to Church or State than, my Lord, your etc.

265.   To Mr. Manwaring.   Yorke, Aug. 30, 1706.
    Sir

The voluntary confession you have made me of your fault looks so like repentance for ye unjust attempt, that, joynd with ye inclination (natural to all husbands under my circumstances) I ever had to approve & serve you, have together so readily obtaind forgiveness as to put me upon solliciting my nephews letter on your behalf as prothonatory, which I herewith send you unseald, that you may not only see how heartily I've made him espouse your interest, but also have it conveyd to his deputy by so safe a hand, that he may have no excuse of ignorance to plead, in case his principles or reingagements shoud tempt him to stand in need of one, for not punctually persuing ye directions of it in your favour. But had neither of ye other two ingredients stood advocates with me for pardon, yet through experience of your great and usefull parts to serve ye publick in such a capacity woud have gone a great way with me to have so far sacrificed my private wrongs to ye good of my country as to have given you all ye assistance on this occasion within ye power of your once injurd servant.

266.   To Dr. Covell, Master of Christs Colledg in Cambridge.

Sir   London, Dec. 7, 1706.

The honour you do ye air of Ickworth Parke by allowing ye influence of it any share in ye happy midwifry of your rural muse, must be more owing to your urbanity than to any real assistance her usual force or fruitfullness could find (much less stand in need of) in so barren a sollitude as reigns there. When ye University of Cambridge hath once seen ye ingenious coppy of verses you favour me with, their modesty will be so justly discouragd from attempting to send them up in suitable company, that I conclude we shall not hear from them, coud their affections prove near as zealous on this, as their prejudices lately did on a less justifiable, occasion; and therefore I beg leave to comunicate this single offering of yours (worth all ye panegyricks I have read before) to ye deserving subject of it; who, with all that beautifull stock of modesty he wears his unparalled successes with, cant but be touchd with some secret satisfaction to see his merit so well comended ; so very well that I cant help ending with this dystick :

Vol. I.   E E

> Thy verse from time secures ye heroes name,
> And makest thy self immortal in his fame.

I am, sir, with much respect yours etc.

267. To Lord Treasurer Godolphin.

My Lord   Windsor, June 25, 1707.

Since I had ye honour of speaking with your Lordship yesterday, Sir Hervey Elwes hath sent me word that he finds there is a grant of his office for three lives, passing in ye names of Henshaw, Frates & Polwheel. We were in hopes, my lord, ye Queen would not have been pleasd to give it from him, till she had first spoken with my Lord of Derbey, who could have acquainted her with such a series of unfortunate accidents which have attended my nephew thro out this affair, that I dare assure my self your Lordship would have disposed her Majesty's usual goodness & generosity to have had some consideration of him on this occasion; for as it was originally conferrd on his ancestors by ye bounty of the Crown at ye Restoration for their loyalty and sufferings in King Charles the firsts time, that circumstance alone might have inclind her Majestie to continue his present life in't, which was all his modesty woud suffer him to petition for, altho his and his whole familys strict adherence to all our Princes true interests ever since might have encouragd a more forward assurance (than any of my relations are owners of) to pretend to something better. But seeing this thing hath made so unexpected a progress, we must necessarily have recourse again to your lordships help, who, among ye many usefull talents you possess, are singularly eminent for giving sudden happy turns to any business which needs it; and therefore if your lordships active fruitfull mind can suggest any friendly expedient which may accomodate this poor young man under so unluckly an exigent, twill ever be gratefully rememberd by him, and added to ye large account of those great obligations I already stand indebted to your Lordships kindness for, by your etc.

268. To Lord Derby. Windsor. June 25, 1707.

My Lord

I'm very much concernd & surprisd to hear of ye great forwardness any grant of my nephews office is in, after being told her Majesty had been pleasd to answer, she woud do nothing neither one way nor other in't till she had spoken with your Lordship; which we rested safely in, knowing your Lordships friendly disposition to give her Majesty not only a favourable character of him, but also to lay before her the many unluckly accidents which had befallen him in ye whole course of this affair; for your Lordship can best tell how many weeks his petition for an exchange of ye life then in being for his own had been in your Lordships hands, which by reason of your abscence was never delivered before ye untimely death of Mr. King; that ye grant was orriginally made to his ancestors for their services and sufferings in King Charles ye firsts time; and that ye whole family have ever since acted with all zeal for ye true interest of our succeeding Princes; & especially since ye Revolution, to which we are chiefly indebted for all ye successes and blessings of this present reign; that altho he's now but young, yet I may modestly affirm to your Lordship I think him one of too great hopes to be discountenancd, sourd or thrown away for nobody knows who: that a very wise man said, Twas worth all princes thoughts that friends are not so easily or surely made as kept; tho' at ye same time I say this, I will tell your Lordship a very impolitick maxim of mine, that shoud this seeming hardship or any other future disappointment be able to work any alteration in him or his wonted affection to our present settlement & government, (which I know it woud not do,) he shoud ever after be disownd by your etc.   I hope your Lordship & Lord Treasurer will find out some way to help him.

269.   To Sir Hervey Elwes.   Windsor, June 25, 1707.

Dear Nephew

I wrote Sir Thomas Felton word by last nights post that I had askd my Lord Treasurer before he left this place for London, whether ye Queen had been pleasd to give him any farther answer in your affair; who told me she had not, unless it were that application had been made to her by other hands for ye same thing, but that she woud do nothing in't till she had spoken to my Lord Derby, which she hath not yet done; but I find ye matter hath been carryd very farr (in ye mean time) to ye prejudice of your pretensions, if ye grant cant be longer suspended than two or three days; & ye secrecy & expedition usd in preparing of it for ye Chancellors seal makes me expect little favour in preventing ye passage of it. However, I herewith send you a letter for my Lord Treasurer, & another for my Lord Derby, (which I woud first have you shew to Sir Thomas Felton, & if he approves them, then to deliver them as soon as you can where directed,) to see if it be possible to do that; and if not, I think your best way will be to inform your self for whom ye new grant is in trust, & to treat with them for a sum of money, either to hold it for your own life only, or to buy their interest wholly out, & to pass it your self for any three lifes you like best; for without money I fear it will never be retrievd out of these hucksters hands, who have so proggingly laid hold on't. The Duchess of Marlborough being unluckily gone at this time to Woodstock, nothing more can be done here by your much concernd & affectionate uncle, etc.

270.   To Mr. John Hervey at Thurleigh.

Dear Cousin   Ickworth, Nov. 18, 1707.

The undertaking I engagd in for ye redemption of my first wife her estate in Lincolnshire hath not only exhausted my purse, but taught me (tho too late) how much better money yields than land; which after taxes & repairs allowd never answers above 3 per cent; & therefore I can have no thoughts of making any farther purchases out right, especially at ye rates you mention, ye value of lands being so considerably fallen, that those estates in this country which I woud formerly have given 20 years purchase for now go a begging at 18, & I have actually refused to buy them so. But rather than Thurleigh shoud ever be possessd by strangers, if you care to treat upon ye foot of rent charges, for yours & Mrs. Herveys life, to augment your present revenue, I woud willingly run ye hazard of streightening myself for some years to make your self and my cousen easy, & to secure ye inheritance in ye same blood which hath enjoyd it for many generations. If this way suites your convenience, and meets with ye same disposition in your self to have one of my sons settled there after you, ye terms will not be very difficult (I believe) to adjust between us, ye value of lives being stated by every days experience in business. Whatever becomes of this treaty, I shall never fail to wish Mrs. Hervey & your self long and happy ones, being hers & your etc.

271. To Sir Richard Cocks. Ickworth, Nov, 17, 1707.

Your letter finding me at so great a distance from ye scene of business makes me less prepard to send you an authentick answer to ye question it contains ; but if resolving one part of it will at all enlighten you therein, I can assure you most faithfully that if there have been or are any such measures on foot as tend to ye prolongation of ye present Parliament beyond its stated legal period, ye conspirators (for I cant give those a milder name who woud attempt a breach upon so essential a part of our Constitution) knew my mind too well to intrust me with any secret of that kind. The report of such a project hath been indeed ye common entertainment of discourse in both my neighbourhoods this summer ; but I always treated it as a chimæra, and only bruited about by ye malice of ye Tories to blacken our friends ye Whiggs by an insinuation of their being become unnatural enough to destroy their own issue for ye serving a present purpose. Upon ye whole tis my humble opinion you may safely aply your self to ye task you mention; and if your friends will do themselves and you ye right they owe you in their next election, I dare warrant (as abandond a world as we live in) that ye trouble you give your self and them on that account will not be rendred abortive by any such dangerous experiment. There being such a dearth of men of worth and integrity, I shoud most zealously wish you all good success, had I not ye good fortune of being as I am already your etc.

272.   To Dr. Covell, Master of Christs Colledg in Cambridge.

Sir   Dec. 1707.

I know not well which I shoud first or most commend, ye charitable designs or ye ingenious turn of your last letter, for both are excellent in their kinds; ye former succeeded so well that it presently put King Davids thankfull interrogation into my mouth—Who am I, O Lord God, and what is mine house, that thou hast brought me hitherto? A question never to be accounted for by me but thro his own darling attribute of infinite goodness, shewing mercies to thousands in them that lovd him and kept his commandments, and so imputing my present prosperity to ye piety of my parents, being conscious of nothing in my self but ye frailties or omissions incident to humane nature. However, the full and lively description you have drawn of my happyness cant fail of fixing such indelible characters of gratitude in my soul as must necessarily make me resolve to live better for ye future, wherein I cant propose a better pattern than your self; & tho I thought to dispair of attaining ye perfection of my orriginal, yet constant imitation may gradually improve me, at least so far as—Deorum muneribus sapienter uti; a maxim you have as eminently surpassd most other men as in all other virtues.   My wife sends you her thanks for ye great share you allowd her in my felicity.

273.   Lady Hervey to John Hervey.   London, March 11, 1707.
My dear dear Angel

I woud begin with telling you how miserable you have left me; but I am sure if I told you half what I've sufferd since I saw you, your dear kind nature woud not be able to bear it; therefore I will say no more but I hope (which is the worst wish I ever gave you) you a little sympathize with me; but I am not alone in trouble at this time, for the whole Town is in an uproar. The first that I heard of it (which is a very good authority) was by Lady Herriett, who was with me this morning before 11 a clock, and told me she had been wakd by 3 by an express from the Fleet to Lord Treasurer, which said the French had passd them 24 hours before they knew anything of it, but that now they were making all the hast they coud after them, but feard they woud be landed in Scotland (which was the place they made towards) before they coud reach them, for the wind and tide were so fair for them they thought they might be landed before they coud receive the letters here. She told me Lord Treasurer had been up ever since 5 a clock, and several officers sent to as she supposd to prepare for Scotland. I need not tell you that I woud not have you name all these particulars, if you talk of the news. The Duke of Marlborough, Lord Treasurer and Lord Sand : went to Kensington at 5 a clock in the morning, and there was a Councel summond immediately, which mett between 7 and 8, and they say there is another this afternoon. The Queen is come to Town to go to the House to pass the bill for the Annuitys, but everybody expects a speech : she appointed 4 a clock, but tis now 5, and she is not yet gone; so I wont seal up my letter till it is late, in hopes of more news, for there is another express come in which no body knows any thing of; Lady Sunderland said it come to my Lord at one a clock. Lieutenant General Withers is gone or going post towards Scotland to command the troops that are coming from Holland. Mr. Stanhope made a motion to day in the House to pass an Act, that all vassalages of Scotland whose lords shall rise in rebellion, that if they

will quitt their service and come in to us shall be intitled to whatever lands
or tenements they hold under them, and have the full possession of them,
to them and their heirs for ever.   I am afraid I have not worded this right,
but I coud not get it in writing, so I hope you will understand it if I cant
get it more perfect.   I sent to my Papa to know this or any other news ;
but the Houses are both sitting still in expectation of the Queen.   I dind
with my Lady Orkney, and my Lord come out of the city and says that they
are all mightily cast down there, and all the funds and stocks mightily fallen,
and the Goldsmiths already refuse to pay gold, guineas are risen 3 pence.
All this bustle and the want of my dear Angel, who ever was and ever will
be my only comfort, sinks my spirits so much that I was not able to go with
the Du : of Grafton to the play, but I cant be excusd supping there, therefore
I will carry my letter open in hopes to hear more news there ; I suppose you
hear they have been upon the Suffolk coast.   You may see by the inclosed
I have been very industrious for news.   I think that is the best account I
can give you of the Queens speech.   I am now at the Du : of Graftons, and
Sir Thomas Hanmer has sent for the Address of the Commons ; if he can
get it, I'll put it in ; supper is upon the table, so, my dear dear, farewell.   I
long for to morrow to know how you passd your journey, and hope to hear
when you come back.

    274.   Lady Hervey to John Hervey.   London, March 13, 1707.

                  I am glad my dear dear Angel slept so long after
so tedious a journey, though it hinderd me of the pleasure of a long letter ;
but I must tell you that you added much to my present sufferings by having
a doubt that I wanted any experience to be certain how impossible it was
to live without my invaluable treasure in the same dear kind fondness I have
for 12 years been blessd with ; and tis my only pleasure now to think that I
have still so much of it, that if you knew half what I suffer by your absence,
this woud not come to your hands before I see you.   I am sorry I have no

news to tell you; for all this I am sure you must feel better than I can express it; but my trouble is so visible that people have taken notice of the tears in my eyes several times a day; it is enough to provoke Hoppy's witt, for he said, Come, chear up, Lady Hervey, the longest day will have an end, and this is but a short meeting. I was at Court last night, and thought her Majesty lookd a good deal out of humour; however, she was very gracious to me. Lord Sunderland recommended a parson for Hartis's living last night, and the Queen told him that she was engagd to Sir Thomas Felton, so I hope Mr. Barriatt is secure. He deliverd Bury address last night. I am to be with him to night to meet the Crimpers, so I hope to meet with some news there for you.   I am now at my Papas, but there is not a word of news, but they expect to hear of the French being landed; but I hear some good news for me, which is that Lord Ryalton comes to morrow, so that I am in doubt whether I shoud send this; but for fear my rival Ickworth shoud prevail, it shall go rather than my dear dear angel shoud ever have any disappointment in any thing that concerns your constant faithful E. Hervey.

275.   To ye Duke of Grafton.   April 21, 1708.

Your Grace having formerly done me ye honour to comunicate some of your thoughts to me relating to ye interest at Thetford, and it having been always my opinion that ye only way of setling it to ye satisfaction of both sides woud be to share it equally (for her Graces ease as well as life) between yourself & Sir Thomas Hanmer, and he being now at full liberty (which he was not before) to concur with your Grace, throughly disposd in every measure that may secure it accordingly, I hope your Grace will pardon me if (as a friend of your family) I take this opportunity of acquainting you that I humbly beg you will not think of entring into any new engagements that may frustrate so desirable an accomodation, foreseeing such consequences must attend any breach of this kind as I have always

Vol. I.   F F

studied to prevent, not more from my relation to him than as I am with all sincerity your etc.

276.   To Sir Thomas Hanmer.   Ickworth, May 2, 1708.
    Sir

I took ye liberty of giving ye Duke of Grafton ye trouble of a letter concerning ye subject of our discourse when you did me ye favour to be here last week; and his Grace having honourd me with an answer to it, I think my self obligd to let you know ye contents of it; viz. that it was always his desire that Thetford shoud be between your self and him; but when that was askd (for ye quiet of both sides) it was then rejected: however, he did not engage himself till he heard you was resolvd to serve for our County; that about two months since, despairing of your complying with ye partition, he unluckily engagd ye little interest he had; which I'm confident he woud be glad of any expedient honourably to retract; but you knowing how difficult (not to say impossible) that is for him to do so near ye crisis of this affair, I hope (considering all ye circumstances it hath been attended with) such mutual allowances will be made as may still preserve those decent correspondencies so near a relation requires; to which I'm in all cases (but more especially in this) so great a friend, that nothing can exceed it but ye particular esteem wherewith I'm your etc.

277.   To ye Duchess of Marlborough.   June 4, 1708.
    Madam

Your Grace having always done my wife ye honour to shew so much kindness in whatever she is concernd, makes me take ye liberty of giving your Grace this trouble, to let you know that soon after she had written to your Grace she fell into labour, and yesterday about noon was deliverd of a son, which dyed about two hours after he was christned. She is so well to day as not to dispair of having ye pleasure of obeying your

Graces commands in some appointment before ye summer passes, wherein my concurrence can never be doubted, since twould prove ye greatest satisfaction that can be proposd by, Madam, your etc.

278.   To Mr. Edward Milles.   Ickworth, July 12, 1708.

   Sir
                  Since Mr. Pemberton is resolvd to concur with me in such measures as my counsil shall think fit in defending our selves against Devenports suit, I hope he will in ye first place tell me ye naked truth of that agreement he made with Mrs. English her agents, whereby they were consenting to forbear ye trying of 3 causes, which they have been so long ready for ye tryal of, against his tenants; for if I go into ye discovery of ye whole estate lyable to ye pretended rent-charge, & in whose hands it now is, with ye true value thereof, (wherein I can give them better lights than any other person,) I shall expect (at least) to stand upon as equal termes with them as himself; for otherwise I shall only help ye enemy in performing to them what Mr. Pemberton promisd, without having any security at ye same time from them (as Mr. Pemberton has) that when that's done my tennants shall be at rest as well as his have been. I remember you was once speaking of their taking a new distress in order to bring in Mr. Fox upon his covenant, which I do not well see how they can also reasonably deny, supposing me willing to bring in all ye lands pro rata that are subject to their pretended grant; and unless I see Davenport disposd to show me ye same fair play he hath allowd Mr. Pemberton, and to make ye average fall as equally among ye parties concernd as may be contrivd by our Counsil, I shall attend ye worst that can happen to me from this stale demand rather than submit tamely to be their ass of burthen, and thus much you may tell em in treating of both the points afore mentiond is ye steady and ultimate resolution of your etc.

When I have receivd Davenports answer (by you) upon ye 2 main points,
I shall then send you mine to Pemberton.

279.   To ye Duke of Marlborough.   Ickworth, July 17, 1708.

   My Lord

                       The signal services your grace so frequently repeats
for ye peace & prosperity of your country, and ye common cause, (whereof
your Grace is not only the present tutelary genius, but your glorious
character and noble actions will even do everlasting honour to ye age we
live in) will not suffer those who are so zealously interessed in whatever concerns your Grace or them as my self to sit silent at a time when they
happen in such eminent instances as ye late battle & victory near Auden-
arde; whereby your Grace has sufficiently convinced ye French king that his
derniere resource in a General, the Duke de Vendosme, can no more reassure
ye lost courage of his beaten troops against those led on by your Graces
superior conduct than when they fought under ye command of his other
Marshals, Tallard, Marsin or Villeroy.

> Success so close upon thy troops does waite,
> As if thou first hadst conquerd fickle fate;
> Since fortune for thy righteous cause & thee
> Seems t'have forgot her lovd inconstancy.

I know no farther refuge he has left him, unless it be to play a second Pucelle
D'Orleans upon you.   But how vain a project must that prove? since we all
know you have vanquishd that sex as universally by ye excellency of your
person as you have ours by ye ascendency of your parts.

> Vieux tu des talens pour la Cour?
> Ils egalent ceux de la guerre;
> Faut il du merite en amour?
> Personne n'est plus gallant sur la terre.

Since then neither sex can any longer oppose you, we hope ye time is now come que votre grandeur acheverer d'enchainer le damon qui s'oppose a la paix de l'univers; which must be recorded to posterity as ye greatest atchievment that was ever brought to pass in any age by ye merit of one man.

> Tis you ye length of scatterd time contract,
> And in few years ye worke of ages act;
> Unparalleled in story is ye change;
> But nothing, where such virtue works, is strange.

That ye stern may still continue in those skilfull hands, which were ye only ones capable of preventing ye shipwreck which once so iminently threatend not only this State but all Europe, is ye sincere desire of your Graces etc.

280. To Mr. Wroth. July 24, 1708.

Since I received ye favour of yours of ye 13th instant (which this comes to thank you for), I have had an opportunity to acquaint my nephew, Sir H. Elwes, with the friendly contents of it; who is altogether uningagd, unless it be that having seen Mrs. Reeve several times, I find she hath so farr taken possession of his heart as to make him wish himself ye man that could touch hers enough to get leave to make his addresses to her; which if you could obtain, I dont doubt but she would find him answer ye character throughout which your kindness may have given her of him; whereto I must add that among ye few destind for happyness in wedlock one of those must be his wife, he being throughly qualified to make a woman so, according to ye best observation of your etc.

281. To Dr. Hutchinson. July 26, 1708.

Not meeting with you yesterday at Bury to show you ye inclosd, makes me now send it you, more to satisfy you that I had done my part than from a belief you had not already heard my Lord

Chamberlain had done his by ye hand you first employd in this matter. Your way being once made to Her Majestys ear, I shall have nothing farther left for me to do than to wish

> Di tibi dent annos, a te nam cætera sumes.

Yet should you at any time hereafter think that little credit I have may prove of any use to you, your known merit has a just title to ye best services that can be done you by, Sir, your etc.

282. The Duke of Marlborough to Lord Hervey.

My Lord   Camp at Helchin, Aug. 16, 1708.

I have receivd your very kind and obliging letter of the 17th of the last month, but assure your Lordship I know my selfe too well to take what you attribute to me otherwise than a mark of your real friendship, which I shall always value. If I can any ways contribute towards making us happy at home, and procuring a solid peace abroad, it is the utmost of my ambition, and with Gods blessing I hope we are now in a fair way to both. I shall then desire nothing more but to enjoy any share in a little retirement among my friends. Your Lordship will allow me to place you in the first rank, and believe me with great sincerity, my Lord, your Lordships most faithful humble servant, Marlborough.

283. To Collonel Whichcott.   Aswarby, Sept. 7, 1708.

Mr. Battely, ye present Alderman of Bury, having lately sent me inclosed certificates, desiring I woud acquaint some of ye acting Commissioners that Sir R. Davers doth insist upon a deduction of £8 per annum out of ye £40 per annum payable out of Forsksey to ye Hospital of Bury; & recommending it to my care to get it taken off, since they beleive the difficulty hath arisen from their laying aside Sir Robert to chose two relations of mine, who are both your friends; and seeing none of ye subscribd list who can be so able, or will be more willing, to get this matter redressd than your self; makes me take ye liberty of giving you this trouble, to beg ye favour of you that you woud inform your self, whether according to ye value of ye estate the present assessment doth not allow for ye £40 per annum issuing thereout for this Charity; & if you shoud find that ye £88..12 per annum mentiond in Clerks certificate of ye 9th June last shoud answer to ye full rack rent without any consideration had to ye charity, that then you woud please to take care that such abatement may be made in ye next assessment as may effectually exempt ye said Hospitalls revenue from any farther loss, & ye managers thereof from future trouble, which will be a peice of great justice to them, & shall ever be ownd as a most sensible obligation by your etc.

284. To Mr. John Turner. Dec. 7, 1708.

The Gazette of yesterday will shew you that neither ye violence of ye greatest cold which ever seizd me, nor ye joynt endeavours of other people to make Mr. Shepherd serve, could prevent ye zealous industry of mine to get him off; especially since I beleivd so unexpected an alteration (by your means) might tend to increase ye friendship between you two; & concluding at ye same time that so authentick a test of my readyness to comply with any of your desires would not (at least) diminish that betwixt you & your etc.

285. To Mr. Alderman Turnor. London, March 5, 1708.

The common loss we have sufferd by the death of my worthy father and your faithfull friend, Sir Thomas Felton, makes it necessary for me to acquaint you and all ye gentlemen of ye Corporacion, that yee may loose no time in thinking of a suitable successor to such a servant as he hath been to them.

> One who with hands unbribd and heart sincere,
> Twixt prince & people did a medium steer;

Preservd that ballance which supports ye state,
And made ye people safe, ye monarch great.

A man so religiously just to his word, that one coud not be more sure of the thing he had done than of that which he had once promisd ; one who never deservedly made any man his enemy; & if he had any, it might have been his (& is my) satisfaction that they were only such as had shewn themselves to be no friends either to ye liberty or laws of our country, whereof he was always a zealous patriot ; one—but whither woud my knowledge of him & ye fruitfullness of ye subject lead me—I'm afraid they've already carried me beyond the bounds of decency or a letter ; & therefore I must force my self to conclude with this general request, that yee woud cast your eyes on such a person as may in ye most essential qualities approach that merit which shone so conspicuously in that man, whom yee all along chose with so unanimous respect & kindness, at ye well-meant recommendation of him who can never forget those former favours done to their & your etc.

286.   Lady Hervey to John Hervey.   London, March 8, 1708|9.

I cant satisfy my self with sending only the news without saying something to my dear and everlasting love, though I am at this time very unfitt to write, and I believe (by our parting in the morning) you are as unfitt to hear me, upon the subject that takes up all my thoughts ; therefore I will leave it to tell you something of the visitt I had just now from the Dutchess of Marlborough, which was with so much tenderness and so many kind expressions that she coud not have done or said more to any child she has. I endeavourd to return it in the best manner I coud, for you as well as my self. At last we began to talk of my Papa's affairs, which I said I was quite ignorant of, there being nothing lookd into but the will, but I believed she coud inform me as to one particular better than any body, which was whether the Queen had given him any grant or lease of his lodgings, which he had often spoke of asking. She said she really knew

nothing of it farther than that Mr. Dunch had made some pretensions to
them as Master of the Houshold, but she thought it very reasonable that
whoever had them shoud pay the bills for what was laid out upon them, and
that she woud speak to my Lord Treasurer about them, and do me all the
service that lay in her power in that or any thing else ; which gave me so
fair an opportunity to go on with what I intended as I coud never have
hopd for ; but that stupid creature, the porter, took it into his head to have
me receive visitts, and let in my Lady Wems just in that minute, which sent
the Duchess of Marlborough away, but she told me she woud come again to
morrow, and every day that she went abroad. The other lady, I believe
was ignorant of my present condition, for she talkd to me of nothing but
seeing the Opera, and such impertinent stuff, which teazed and vexed me
so much, with what I felt before, that I coud answer her with nothing but
tears, that I believe she thought me mad. I need not tell you how bad my
head is, when you read this letter and see the blunders I have made ; the
greatest ease I can have to that and all my troubles is to be satisfyd you
take care of your dear and precious self, precious indeed to me, and never
enough to be valued by your poor orphan, E. Hervey.

P.S.—Remember me to Jack ; I hope he does his charge. Pray stay as
long as is necessary for your health and business, (particularly ye first.)

287.   My ever new Delight   Playford, March 9, 1708;9.
                        Even in affliction and adversity ; being the only
cordial to a mind oppressd with the loss or absence of everything that's dear
or valuable to it except little Jack, who, tho he makes a considerable article
in reckoning up my treasure when I am blessd with his dear mothers
presence, yet now affords me but small comfort, wanting her, especially in
this place where I want both those who heretofore made it so agreeable to
me; its neighbourhood hath shewn an universal respect by their attendance
at the funeral, where I had some satisfaction to see all things appear in that

        Vol. I.   G G

decency, order and ornament that coud be desird. I have had time this evening only to shew Sir Compton Felton the state of Mr. Talmash's trust, and the schedule of Sir Thomas's debts, which last seemd to surprise him, saying he did not believe he had ever owd a quarter of that sum, and with-all that the whole ought to be well lookd into. I mentiond the discharge of the servants, and the house still kept on at London, which I said pressd most at present; which I found he concurrd with me in, and told me he would gett to London as soon as twas possible for him, and do me the best service he was able; he is gone home, but intends to be here again in the morning to talk farther of these matters, the result whereof you shall have by the next post from Ickworth, and whatever I have to say by the post after that shall by God Almighty's permission be brought you by your most affectionate faithful friend & lover, Hervey.

P.S.—Give all the children my blessing, and a kiss to Nan, which I will repay to Jack for you.

288.   Lady Hervey to John Hervey.   London, March 10, 1708|9.

I hope this will find my dear dear angel well after his melancholy journey, which is hardly possible if you have felt half so much as I have done for you; for I was so ill on Tuesday night, (with va-pours, as they call them,) that I sent for Mr. Maltes in the morning, and told him I had as good be knockd o' the head as suffer such another night; so he gave me something to take, and I was better till 6 a clock this morn-ing, and then I was to the full as bad, if not worse; thank God I am something better now, but am in dread of night. I have changed my room, but find that nothing will change my uneasy mind but my dear and only comfort; yet, however, I must beg of you not to come a minute sooner than is convenient to your health & business. I have seen no body since I wrote last, therefore can tell you no news but that Lord Wharton is dangerously ill of a fever. The Dutchess of Marlborough sent me an excuse for not

coming yesterday according to her promise, but I believe Lady Month:
being brought to bed in the morning, and the Duke of Montague dying at
5 in the afternoon, might very reasonably hinder her; his death was very
sudden; he was taken with a shivering on Monday, but was well enough to
be abroad on Tuesday, but I know nothing more concerning him. Sir
Robert Davers declares he shant trouble his head about Bob being chose at
Bury; if they do it without his taking any pains, he says tis very well; but
he shall never concern himself with them again as long as he lives; this Mr.
Fox told at Mrs. Barrons. I have kept my letter open till nine a clock in
hopes of some news, but I have not seen any body since Tuesday but
Lady Dalkeith, who is just now come in, but can tell me nothing, so I must
conclude with wishing my dear angel a better night's rest than I fear will
fall to your poor ever faithful orphan, E. Hervey.

P.S.—Dear Angelica was mightily delighted with writing this bit of paper.
She looks in the bed and all about for you every morning, and will drink no
chocolate without you; thank God, she and the rest are well.

289. My ever new delight   Ickworth, March 11, 1708/9.

Altho the pacquet of news miscarried, yet amidst
that set of ill accidents which have lately attended me I had the good luck
to have your kind letter come safe to me by the Ipswich post, which this is
to thank my dear orphan for, and so farr to alleviate the sense of that your
new name and condition as to assure you most solemnly if my heart be
capable of any change towards you, the alteration must necessarily prove
to your advantage, since my mind is perpetually inventing how by fresh and
additional tendernesses it may the sooner make you forgett the fatal accident
which made you so; but for the same good reason you gave I shall not now
farther enlarge on this fruitful theme. Sir Compton Felton hath promisd me
to be in London, if the state of his health (which is very much broken by
those frequent fitts which attack his stomach) permitts, by the latter end of

the next week, and will in the mean time take care of discharging the family at Playford, which he seems disposd to do, by entertaining all the servants there in his own family; and for the horses which were there, I have brought them all hither, leaving an acknowledgment with him under my hand of my having receivd both them & those at London into my custody. He cursorily mentiond the arrears of rent the tenants were in, the quick stock upon the land in hand, and the money in Coleman's hands, with several other particulars, whereof he would enable himself to give the best account he was able at his coming to Town; after which he spoke of his bond for £500, and told me, his brother having alwaies promisd his daughter (being Sir Thomas's god daughter) £1000, he could not but think he designd that bond shoud make up the rest; to which I coud only answer that I knew nothing of his mind in that matter; he also took notice to me that the pavement for the new building I spoke to you of done since we were there was not actually laid, but that the stones were ready upon the place, and desird to know what he must do in that matter. Now considering you have an interest so near in reversion as that there is only your cousin Henry's life (which I take to be no very strong or long one, being the most alterd I ever saw, & going fast into a consumption.) between you and the inheritance, I dont think it at all adviseable for you to seem backward in doing any thing of that kind which your uncle may look upon as reasonable, altho in its own nature it should be found quite otherwise. I thought it my duty to offer him a lodging in my house, and the Burgesship of Bury, both which he peremptorily refusd, altho' accompanyed with great expressions of thanks for the offers. The town are at present so disconcerted in their measures as to their new member, that I cannot yet tell you where my friends will center, there being no less than 4 candidates on our bottom beside Mr. Davers on the other. Serjeant Weld, Mr. Maynard, Mr. Wroth and Mr. Turner (which last never communicated his intention or desire of standing till most of my friends had run upon the Recorder,) not only divide but distract my friends;

however, I hope so to contrive matters in the conclusion that the interest may be preservd entire, which thou knowest has cost me and thee so much trouble, thought, expence and uneasyness to establish. I am ever and entirely thy most faithful friend & lover, Hervey.

P.S.—I had not room in the other sheet of paper to tell thee, Jack eat more for his dinner to day than he had done in three at London; and that I shall hasten back to thee with all the expedition of a bridegroom, being more truly in love, and valuing thee more now, than I did or coud do before I knew thee as well as I do. I hope Tuesday will joyn us again, till which long time farewell. If any accident here shoud retard that purpose, you shall know it by Wednesdays letters, which nothing but necessity shall bring to pass. Every word you tell me of the Dutchess of Marlboroughs kindness to you would fill my soul fuller of gratitude and well wishes towards her, could it admitt of more. May her prosperitys increase till I think them too much, which would secure her a very large & long lease in them.

290. Lady Hervey to John Hervey. London, April 5, 1709.
I hope this will find my dear dear angel better after his journey than when he left me, which has been and is such a continual uneasyness to me that I hope you will relieve me by a letter as often as is possible; and when you have not time, (which I woud never take from business that must keep you a moment the longer from her that loves you with all her heart & soul,) pray let Will Carus send me word how you are without the least disguise, which I hope he has not forgot to do from Newport. I cant but be glad of this fine weather, though I am afraid it will make you unwilling to leave the country. I cant bear the thoughts of your being quite without wine, though the stock you left is so small, that I shall send you but a dozen bottles by the waggon to morrow, which will be at Newmarket on Friday; there is six of Annadea and six of claret, three of which is my Papa's that is seald. I was yesterday at dinner with the Duchess of Grafton,

where your dear health was drank by everybody but Madam Nerve, for which (amongst many things) I hate her for heartily; I went afterwards to the play with the Duchess of Marlborough, and from thence to crimp with her, which she told all the company she had much ado to persuade me to, and indeed I was very unfitt for that or any thing else but home, for I had cryd my eyes out after you were gone, and had like to have been guilty of the same fault of sending for you back again before you got to the Green Man. I have had a fall to day, but I hope I was more frighted than hurt, for it will not hinder me from being at the Duchess of Marlboroughs by and by, where I hope to hear some news for you. In the mean time I know nothing but what they said yesterday, that the French Ministers were gone back, and had rejected the Duke of Marlboroughs proposals, so that there was not like to be a peace this year. I can meet with no news but that they have carried it for the Treason bill by 23 votes in the House of Commons. My dear dear, good night.

291.   My ever new Delight   Newmarket, April 7, 1709.

Your letter, from which I hopd to have receivd some comfort to a mind never well at ease without thee, (and much less so now than ever, being more unable to bear absence the longer I have been blessd with the company and conversation of so valuable a rarety as a constant lover & faithful friend,) hath added to the present disquiet of it untill I hear the fall it mentions is attended with no ill consequence, which I desire to know without disguise by the next post. I thank you kindly for your care in sending me some wine; but alas! my spirits are too low to be raisd by any cordial but thy dear company. I had so many other things to think of before I left you, that I forgott to recruit your stock of wine; which Sir Henry Furnese would supply, if you woud signify your want. Lord Treasurer is fallen into an Ombre-vein here, which I never knew before, and it hath cost me 47 guineas; however, you shall still choose whither you woud have it on your immediate account or not, my chief business being to please you in every thing. And altho' the longer your letters are the more they please me, yet knowing how ill writing much agrees with your head, I had rather make a short one long by reading it over and over again than that you shoud feel the least inconvenience from any kindness shewn to your most grateful lover, Hervey.

P.S.—Dont let Angelica forgett me; remember me to ye rest of ye children.

292.   Lady Hervey to John Hervey.   London, April 7, 1709.

I am sure if my dear dear angel coud tell what I suffer in his absence, you woud not let me have that so weighty addition of your taking no more care of your self than to fast all day, (and I suppose read), which coud not but give you the pain in your head I hear you had; and if I had thought that Welch fool woud not have prevented that, he shoud never have been so happy while I am so miserable, and I shall now (if it be possible) be much more so, since you coud break your word with me the first day you were out of sight, when the last words I said to you was to beg you to take care of your dear and invaluable self. I know not a word of news, but they talk of an invasion, which no body believes. The Scotch are all mightily dissatisfyd about the Treason bill, and they say are all resolved to go home and come no more, because they see they are opposd in every thing. Thank God, dear Angellica has missd her ague once; she comes down and looks in your place every morning, and calls you, and then holds up her hands and says all is gone. The rest are all well; Jack has wrote you a French letter, which he says is all his own. I hope I have quite recoverd my fall, though I was very ill all day after it. I must again reproach you (which I never had cause for before) with useing me ill, which I beg you woud mend, if not for your own sake, yet for hers that loves you more than is to be expressd, my dear dearest life, your faithful E. Hervey.

P.S. Pray, my dear, let Will Carus bring an inventory of the kitchen things at Ickworth, and what is good or bad of them.

293.　　My ever new Delight　　　　　Newmarket, April 9, 1709.

I am just now taking coach for Ickworth, which once in my life I can truly say I'm sorry to go to, envying every body who went towards London this morning ; but as I am not like to see these parts any more till after Midsummer, necessity obliges me to settle many matters there, which, I believe, have already wanted my presence. However, I hope to bring all my business within the compass of your desire (which is always my chief aim) to be back on Saturday. I must beg of you to thank dear Jack for his French letter, which I am in too much hast to answer now any other way than by letting him know he and his brothers and sisters have all the blessings they can ask, or my poor piety or meritts can bestow. I wish the orthography, as well as the sense of it, were all his own, knowing the former not to be so correctly attainable at his age. As for sweet Angelica, I shall begin to suspect her good sense when it leads her to say all is gone, where her dear mother is to be found; in whom every thing worth seeking for has been observd to reside in all perfection by your most faithful lover, Hervey.

294.　　Lady Hervey to John Hervey.　　　London, April 9, 1709.

I give my dear dear angel a thousand thanks for his kind letter, which I waited for with great impatience till half an hour after six, to give me some relief to the additional trouble I was then in for poor Charles, who was taken very ill yesterday about noon; his first complaint was in his head, after that in his hipp, which we were not certain might not be his back, which made Mr. Maltes think it might prove the small-pox ; therefore he gave him a vomit, which did very well with him, and this morning he thinks it a rheumatism, for he complains sometimes in one place and sometimes in another; he has a fever with it, but Mr. Maltes tells me there is no danger, so I have not yet sent to Sir R. Blackmore till I see how to morrow is with him, and if there be any alteration for the worse, you shall hear from me by the coach, which will be with you a day sooner than the post; but I woud have nothing hasten your journey this fine weather, though I suffer never so much for the want of your dear company; yet I have this comfort, that you will find a great deal of benefit by the country air, and not being an eye-witness of all my spleen, which I am sure your dear and tender nature woud bear a larger share in if you were here.   I suppose the votes (or better hands) will inform you of all the particulars of the clause the Scotch has carried to be added to the Treason bill, which they say will hinder it passing. Lord Feversham died yesterday morning, and Mrs. Smith was married then. This is all the news I know, except this inclosd paper, which I heard Lord Sun: commend mightily, so I have teazed Mr. Hopkins till he has got it me, for tis not published, tho' it is printed. Mr. Manuring and one or two more is named for the authors of it. Lady Cornwallis has miscarried and been in great danger. I have sent to Sir H. Furnese to day about some wine, for fear you shoud want when you come to Town, which will be so happy a time for me that I shall want nothing but to repeat to my dear dear angel, how much I love and am entirely his faithful E. Hervey.

P.S. I believe Charles' illness will fix in a rheumatism, for he changes his complaints every hour, but I think he has not been in so much pain to day as he was yesterday. All the rest are well, and dear Angelica calls upon you every day, and then says Gone with her hands up.

295.   My ever-new Delight   Ickworth, April 11, 1709
            This park woud now be thought a perfect Paradise by any body but thy poor solitary Adam, who can never think any place has the least relish of one (with all his supposd partiality to Ickworth)

without the center and completion of all happyness, his constant consort, Eve.

> His better Eve, being by no crime accursd,
> More beauteous, yet not brittle as the first.

The nightingle has welcomd my arrival by more variety of harmonious strains than ever Nicholini's throat coud reach.

> With her sweet notes my plaintive sighs all night agree ;
> Of Tereus she complains ; but I for want of thee.

Our operas here being performd between them and the bleating lambs, with the shepherd's boy pipeing and singing as if were never to grow old, or be parted from the object of his love,

> With whom the babling springs now joyn their mone,
> And whispring oaks make vows for thy return.

And till that longd for season happens, I shall be so farr from finding the true contentment it has formerly afforded me, that at present it only feeds those melancholy thoughts thy absence ever gives me.

> Each bank, each bow'r, each cool inviting shade,
> That to our sacred loves were conscious made,
> Each flow'ry bed, each thicket & each grove,
> Where I have lain, charmd with Eliza's love,
> Wher'ere she cheard the day, or blessd the night,
> Incessantly are present to my sight.
> Wher'ere I turn, the landskip doth confess
> Something that calls to mind past happiness.

There's not a field but what's all o'er enamelld with cowslips, violets, daizies, primroses and wild emonies ; the lawns laugh with flowers of every kind.

> How can they be so fair, and you away?
> How can the trees be beauteous, flowers so gay?
> Could they remember but last year,
> How you did them, they you delight,

The sprouting leaves which saw you here,
And calld their fellows to the sight,
Would, looking round for the same sight in vain,
Creep back into their silent barks again.

But upon consideration tis no great wonder they shoud appear with rather more than their usual gayety.

For who can blame them now; since you've been gone
They're here the only fair, and shine alone.
You did their natural rights invade,
Wherever you did walk or sitt ;
The thickest boughs coud make no shade,
Altho' the sun had granted it ;
The fairest flow'rs coud please no more near you
Than painted flowers set next to them coud do.

And yet, amidst all these sweets of nature and the charms of solitude (so agreeable to my temper), I'm only more throughly confirmd in my former experience, that without the presence and participation of my dear partner, all other pleasures which are foreign to her must prove but a kind of gently killing punishments to one, who

Till his last hour all he can wish to see,
All he can love to look on, will be thee.

But no more of this, for fear I shoud infect you deeplier with my disease, ye spleen, for which I despair of any cure till Saturday, when I hope to possess again that sovereign remedy for all the wants and woes of, my dear orphan, thy most tender guardian, Hervey.

P.S.—Thank dear Betty for her letter. I hope Charles's ayles will prove only a great cold by playing till he sweated, and then drank or set still after it. Parson Grove of Chevington has desird me to write to you to know when the Queen touches next, he having a wife who wants it, and that you would lett Lady Isabella know your answer to this, of whom he will wait to know what it is, that he may bring her up, if it is yet time enough for this season.

296.   Lady Hervey to John Hervey.   London, April 12, 1709.
                              The pain I have sufferd in missing a letter by yesterdays post may truly be calld the breaking the bruised reed; for I thought the measure had been quite full before, and it was so near so that I could not hinder it from running over, (before Lord Treasurer, Lord Hallifax and Count Callash at the Duchess of Marlboroughs where I dind,) when the page (who I left at home for that purpose) brought me word the post was come in but no letter for me ; Lord Treasurer tryd to comfort me by telling me he thought he saw you writing a Fryday night at his house, and believd you had sent it by somebodys servant that had forgot or lost it ; indeed I had hopes of one by some of them ; and I think if after all these disappoint-ments I shoud meet with any to morrow, it woud be more than I coud bear; and for an addition, where I hopd for a relief, I sent to my Aunt Effingham, who expected a letter from you in answer to one she sent by Thursdays post ; but every thing was to add to my torment in the uncertainty of your dear and precious health.   Charles is very much better, but I think I am lamer than ever, for I can hardly go cross a room, and have not been able to get up to see him since Saturday, and then was ready to sound when I got up, though I am sure I was full half an hour a going.   I dont know a word of news, nor I dont believe I should be able to make you understand it if I did ; for I think my brain is quite turnd, but I hope it will not be necessary to write again before you will settle it with your dear presence, which is the only life, comfort & pleasure of your faithful E. Hervey.

P.S.—Since I seald my letter the post has just brought me your dear letter, which has given me such relief that I am in another world ; but I am so angry with the postman, I think he ought to be punishd.   I direct my letter to Newmarket because they tell me there is a match to morrow. I shall not write on Thursday except I hear by your letter to morrow that you come through a Saturday, which happy day is most impatiently longd for by, my dear dear, your E. Hervey.

297.　　Lady Hervey to John Hervey.　　London, April 26, 1709.
　　My dear dear angel

　　　　　　I have made all the enquiry I could about the Queen's touching, both by Lady Sunderland and Mr. Maltes. I find the first can give the best account of it, having several to get it done for ; and she says the Queen has said she will touch before she goes to Windsor, which they talk will be the beginning of May, but till her hand is well tis uncertain the time of her touching, but it may be at a days warning, so I thought it best to give you this notice, that they might order their affairs as they think fitt about coming to Town. I coud not sleep in two hours after you left me this morning, and my head is so bad I am able to say no more, but that you have left the most deplorable poor wretch that ever livd, but am in all conditions of life, my dearest treasure, your most faithfully & entirely E. Hervey.

298.　　My ever-new Delight　　Newmarket, April 28, 1709.
　　　　　　If my own inclinations (which are ever very strong) to stay with you had led me into rash resolutions towards securing that end, I'm sure your absence has punishd me more than my part of the crime deservd, since the breach of them was entirely owing to your own determination. But I beg you would never for the future put my health in ballance, where our mutual satisfactions are destroyd with regard to it ; since it is impossible for my body to be the better where my mind pays so dear for the means. I am sorry to send you the ill news of the Duke of Bolton's mare her being beaten by Countess, whereby I lost near 40 guineas,

but wherein you shall be no farther concernd than suits your convenience, notwithstanding the commission you gave me. Your not mentioning whither you would send the children down as you intended makes me not know very well how to order my relays for getting to you on Monday; but if they are not sett out by that time this comes to you, I think you had best send my chariot to Hockeril on Sunday, being resolvd to get through from Ickworth on Monday, whatever pains or difficultys it costs to thy most impatient fond friend & lover, Hervey.

> **299.**   Lady Hervey to John Hervey.   London, April 28, 1709.

I am glad to hear my dear dear angel got well to Hockeril, and I hope this will find you as well after the other part of your journey, and that you meet with more entertainment than you've left behind for poor me, who am at this time more miserable than I dare tell you ; but in order to my relief I send your coach for you to morrow with the four boys ; but I have mett with so many difficultys in the hiring another, that I must desire you woud send one from Bury, which I believe will be more convenient for you, because they may come out at your own time, and bring you any part of the way you like best. I hope to morrows post will bring me word when that welcome hour will be, which can have but one addition more to make up the perfect felicity of, my dear dear life & soul, your most constant adorer, E. Hervey.

P.S.—I have orderd the children to bate at Newmarket on Saturday, so I hope you will bespeak them some dinner.

> **300.**   Lady Hervey to John Hervey.   London, April 28, 1709.

I forgot in my letter to beg my dear angel to give Mr. Richar a charge about the childrens being ever sufferd to go out of sight of the house without somebody with them, for I think he does not trouble himself with any thing but their books, which makes me in great pain for them till Squire goes. We have had a melancholy parting, but that is no wonder, for every thing is so now that I have to do with ; but I hope now to be a little enlivened with dreaming of my dearest life, for I am just going to bed, so, my dear dear, good night, and God bless and love you but half so well as I do, and you are happy.

301.   Lady Hervey to John Hervey.   London, April 30, 1709.

I shoud be mightily concernd it my not saying any thing of the childrens journey (which I thought quite settled) should be a moments hindrance to the longing impatience I have to see my dear dear angel again ; but notwithstanding that, I cant but be very uneasy to think of your coming through from Ickworth ; but I hope you have changd that resolution, and that I need not despair of seeing you to morrow with some-body that comes then, which I hear several does, as well as to day. I find by your dear kind sympathy I need not tell you what this absence has cost me, but I hope to be rewarded soon with seeing my dearest treasure again in perfect health. I hope you will leave the boys better after their journey than you will find these here, for Herriett's ague is turnd to an intermitting fever, and Betty is not very well, which makes me indifferent whether the coach comes yet or not, if you have not hired it and make use of it in your own journey ; but if you do I think it will be much better to make but one charge and trouble of it, since her illness is not any thing that will hinder her journey, but that she will be rather the better for it. There is nothing talkd of here but peace, which they say is more likely now than ever, since the French Secretary is come to the Hague ; they say the Duke of Shrewsbury and Lord Townshend are to go Plenipotentiarys with the Duke of Marl-borough with the first fair wind. My head as well as heart is so much dis-orderd that I dare say no more, though I coud write till we meet and not tell you half the tenderness and passion my soul feels for you, thou eternal blessing and comfort of your E. Hervey.

302. To Carr Hervey. London, May 26, 1709.

My dear son

I have sent you ye great glass you desird for your bedchamber by this days waggon, & wish it may have ye honour of frequently representing ye most accomplishd young gentleman of this our (now) famous and happy island. The books I mention to you had accompanyd it but that I am not yet determind which will instruct you most with ye least reading, knowing you are engaged in a course of other studies which will not afford even ye most commendable industry much leisure to peruse authors of that kind. The reason of my giving Brittain ye epithets of famous and happy is because thro' a series of heroic actions performd in war we have thereby forcd ye enemy into such unexpected terms of peace as will (in all humane probability) transmit a lasting tranquility to posterity. That you may long reap ye benefit of that and every thing else that is worthy of a right wise and virtuous man in his generation, is one of ye devoutest prayers that can be put up to Heaven by ye heart and soul of your etc.

303. To ye Rev. Mr. Wyche concerning John Grix of Sleeford.

Sir London, May 18, 1709.

If you perceive any signs of grace in that flagitious miscreant who was once so void of all humanity as to destroy his own flesh & bloud, God forbid that I should break ye bruised reed or quench ye smoaking flax, by preventing his enjoying such a scituation of life for ye remainder of his days as may give him leisure to make frequent & usefull reflections on ye infinite mercy of his offended Maker, & from thence become so through & perfect a penitent, that with Mary Magdalen he may hereafter love much, because so much hath been forgiven. In hope whereof I recommend him hereby to those concernd to fill up ye vacancy you mention; but to be expelld with shame if ever he be found guilty of any ill example in the hospital; by which strict tenure you may let him know he shall hold this very favourable possession at your request from your etc.

304.   To Sir William Gage.   London, May 30, 1709.

I have had an opportunity of speaking to Mr. Bond concerning ye decree you mentiond, & hope twill be now settled to ye satisfaction of all the parties concernd; but there yet remains one circumstance relating to my part in ye execution of ye trust of Lady Bonds will which I desire may be forthwith adjusted, & that is as to ye custody of ye jewells, which ought formally to have been in my hands from ye death of Lady Gage till my cousin Julia her being of age; but that being now gone & past, ye next thing to be done is to procure an authentick order from your daughter to deliver them over to you, & that your receipt endorsd on her said order shall be good & sufficient discharge to me for ye same, & this I beg may go hand in hand with ye intended decree. I cant think it a very fair proposal in a widdower to exchange leaps, however you may command ye Turk for your present propose; & as to ye equivalent, that must be adjournd & settled according to ye next choice you make, whereby your bon goût I make no doubt will enable you to do justice in what you've offerd to your etc.   Charter house vacancys are so hard to obtain that I almost dispair of doing Mr. Brownsmith service that way.

305.   To Sir Thomas Hanmer.   June 9, 1709.

My wife & I consulting how to make our thanks most acceptable to the Dutchess of Grafton for ye great honour she hath done us, resolvd to give you ye trouble of conveying them; & I hope my Lady Grantham will do me ye justice to let her Grace know how zealously I stickled to have ye childs name Isabella, knowing so many excellent persons who have borne it. Your post is so punctual in transmitting letters upwards (having never faild of bringing me one of Mrs. Manleys), that I cant imagine how mine shoud have miscarried; but they can prove no loss in any sense to anybody, unless by missing of my last you might think me guilty of an omission in not acquainting you, who are so very kind a well-wisher to my family, with every increase that happens in it ; especially since its most allowable pride & greatest merit must arise from being a branch of that happy stem which partly producd your self, a consideration which gives a value to every member that augments ye number of it ; & nothing less than such an additional treasure (for so I count them all for that reason) coud compensate ye disappointment it hath occasiond by rendring ye mother unfit to partake of ye pleasure we promisd our selves of waiting on you in Wales this summer. The happiness (as you have goodness enough to term it) of your being preservd in my remembrance is a general right your vertues have entituled you to in ye minds of all who know you, & ye pleasing reflection of having so considerable a man for my particular friend is so continual a feast to my memory, that for ye sake of my own satisfaction alone tis impossible any distance or other accidents can ever suffer you to be forgotten by, Sir, your etc.

306.   To Sir Thomas Hanmer.   Aswarby, Aug. 22, 1709.

If sincerity is ye natural product of ye country, I'm sure Wales must more peculiarly abound in quite as rare & valuable a vertue, which is humility, to make you think it possible anybody can be a looser by your correspondence, much less me who can only deserve ye continuation of it but by reckoning (as he does) the unequal exchange of his letters for yours, ye most proffitable traffick was ever driven ; & since it enriches me without impoverishing you, I desire you woud not count me wrongly mercenary if I endeavour to carry on ye commerce, whenever absence gives ye opportunity. I hope ye near approach of Holy rood will soon put an end to our present distance ; & if ye Dutchess of Grafton (to whom my wife & I are most humble servants) & you will be so kind as to take this place in your way to Euston, we can do more than throughly make good what her Grace so rightly undertook to you for us when last at

Ickworth, that you can be no manner of trouble, since it woud prove ye greatest honour & pleasure tis capable of affording us. The friendly character you have given me of Frank Manley, & ye charitable inclination you shew to have something done for his family, shall quicken my importunity, as soon as I see Lord Treasurer at Newmarket, to bestow some post on him, that may both make my scheme for his industrious brother's Tom's advancement in ye world easy, & not be so difficult in its discharge as to endanger ye credit of my recomendation, which is a point ought carefully to be secured, as well for ye sake of his reputation as preserving ye interest of, Sir, your etc.

307. To ye Prince and Duke of Marlborough on ye Victory at Blaregnies.

My Lord   Aswarby, Sept. 7, 1709.

As it woud have been impossible for anything less than ye same powerfull providence working by ye same well chosen agents, Vigilance and Valour, to equal any of your Grace's former actions, so this last difficult decisive Victory of Blaregnies (being attaind by ye same ingredients) will (if possible) in some sort surpass them, since it must necessarily crown all ye other Herculean labours with ye most valuable of blessings, a safe and honourable peace to Europe; wherein our pious Queen & famous country may justly claim so meritorious a share (by your Grace's wise & skilfull conduct of her armies) as throughly to deserve that noble character Plutarch gives of Rome—that ye Roman Government servd as a sheet-anchor to ye desperate distresses of ye once drowning world. And ye generous disinterested one Salust gives the same people will be now no less their due — that ye Romans never fought to take any thing from their vanquishd enemies, but ye mischeivous power of ruining their innocent neighbours. The relief of ye oppressd & ye protection of ye helpless being works so Godlike, Heaven has apparently shewn its approbation of them by ye repeated successes & miraculous preservations of your person thro' ye whole course of those imminent dangers you've so prodigally exposed it to in bringing them to pass. And if Moses built an alter upon Joshua's single conquest of the Amalekites, which he calld—ye Lord is our refuge, sure all your narrow escapes from death, and (by them) ye worlds from bondage, deserve as gratefull a memorial. Ye history of your deliverances will make mankind find easy faith for that of Shedrech & his companions, theirs being scarce more wonderfull than yours, who have so often passd unhurt amidst all those destructive flames which ye modern Nebuchadnezzar has commanded ye most mighty men that were in all his armies to direct against you ; a promising presage your precious life is reservd to compleat those bountifull dispensations Gods infinite goodness has yet in store for this happy generation you were born in. For mine, my wifes & children's portion of those benefitts you've already done mankind, & ye many more we may reasonably expect in consequence of them, I know not how to acknowledge my sense of them better than to conclude in Tertullus's words :—seeing that by thee we enjoy great quietness, & that very great deeds are done unto this nation by thy providence, we accept it always & in all places, most noble Felix. I am with ye utmost respect, my Lord Duke, your etc.

308.   To Lord Orkney.   Ickworth, Sept. 21, 1709.

My Lord

I had sooner returnd your Lordship my thanks for the kind trouble you gave your self in sending us the wine which is extream good, but that I staid for an exact account of ye last battle, that I might at ye same time congratulate your Lordship upon ye eminent share I concluded you must (according to your constant custom) have had in ye victory ; which I am informd was in a great measure owing to ye seasonable service of 13 battallions, which were more imediately under your Lordships conduct ; a circumstance yet more glorious for you than that which fell to your last at Blenheim, tho' both illustrious, & both (thro' ye same good providence obtaind upon as safe termes as have been all along most sincerely wishd you by, my Lord, your etc.

309.   To Mr. Thomas Goodall.   Ickworth, Sept. 23, 1709.

This comes to acknowledge ye favour of yours of ye 20th instant, notwithstanding it brought me no better account of our affairs ; wherein I'm very unable to give you any advice till I can find out by what infusions matters have been sufferd to be carried with so unequall a hand against us ; the truth whereof twill be impossible for me to arrive at untill I can get to London ; but that my business here will not admit of till the sitting of ye Parliament ; & if by that time you (for I must own to you, I do not care to joyn with Mr. Rich in any farther applications, it being to his unparalleld conduct that our present & passd grievances are originally owing,) will shape out any way whereby my little credit may prove of any use to you & ye rest of your fellow adventurers, the opportunity shall be readily laid hold of & faithfully persued by their & your etc.

310.   The Duke of Marlborough to Lord Hervey.   Oct. 7, 1709.
My Lord

I know your Lordships congratulations & compliments on the late victory are such true effects of your zeal to the Publick and friendship to my selfe, that I cannot omit my hearty thanks for them, tho' I must at the same time own your kind expressions on that occasion are much above what I can pretend to deserve ; but I am sure no man can join more sincerely than I do in your good wishes, that the continu'd successes with which Providence hath hitherto blessd us may at last procure us the most valuable blessing of an honourable & secure peace, to the satisfaction and advantage of all well wishers to the Publick, in which I am sure your Lordship will have your share, and I shall have the pleasure of assuring you more frequently of the great truth wherewith I am, my Lord, your Lordships most obedient humble servant, Marlborough.   My most humble respects to Lady Hervey.

311.   To Sir Richard Cocks.   London, Dec. 31, 1709.

The defluxion of rheum, which some time since fell upon my eyes, provd a double affliction to me, having deprivd me of ye pleasure of reading ye usefull papers you sent me, and prevented ye return of my thanks for them so soon as I woud have done.   Had I ever forgot my self so much as to suffer the least abatement in my heart of that just concern which always possesses it for ye welfare of my native country, you might well suspect it capable of ye next great wrong of not remembring a friend for whom I have ye greatest esteem for his simpathizing so throughly with me in that laudable disposition ; but as I can faithfully assure you that no new honours or alteration of times etc. have wrought any change (unless by their increase) in those two only valuable qualities I dare own of being a zealous well-wisher to ye prosperity of this nation & those of ye same sentiments, so I must beg you'd do me ye justice to continue ye same favourable opinion you formerly conceivd of me in ye H. of C., altho' my best endeavours shoud prove fruitless in getting any of your bills past in ye H. of Lords ; for as ye former hath (as you rightly observe) many members who are sensibly interested against them, so ye latter hath but very few of my quondam acquaintance who have minded anything much of late besides bringing about personal schemes, which when effected, the Publick (they are vain enough to think) must do well of it self, without troubling their heads (that I can see) about mending or so much as securing it in its most essential vital part, ye Protestant succession.   I have more than once remarkd that those may be seemingly great and powerfull for a while, who serve their Princes's turn, or their own & their party's interests ; but they will be always and only truly so who make justice & ye safety and happyness of their fellow subjects ye prime principle of their conduct, and who inviolably adhere to that honest maxim, that all other interests ought to give place to ye publick good. Methinks, there's one obvious reflection, sufficient both to make & keep any men honest that have ye least love for virtue or ye real respect of those they have to deal with; which is that seeing all base and mercenary compliances never fail to end with the contempt even of those they have humourd, so ye noble resolution of ye steady & inflexible comes off rewarded with ye secret reverence of those they might (at first) displease by being such. But I fear the present pride and luxury of this kingdom, added to ye natural corruption of mankind, (which Blount calld self interest incarnate,) hath so blinded most mens understandings as neither to relish, nor so much as to discern, ye truth and lovelyness of this observation ; honesty being brought to that deplorable pass that ye integrity of both partys & their principles almost universally depend upon ye highest bidder; so that tho' I like ye draughts of all your bills extreamly well, yet alass! Quid leges sine moribus vanæ proficiunt? I must speak my mind as freely to you as Cicero did to Pomp : Atticus; who confessd to him that Cato's virtue (which he as much admird as I do John Doe's) was unprofitable to his contemporaries, & ownd that that divine man (for so he calld him, & he deservd ye name something better than his reverse, Louis ye 14th,) was quite out of fashion, proposing things which were too wise & vertuous, ill suiting with ye depravity of ye times he livd in ; & that when he spoke or voted in ye Senate, did both with that unbiassd, disinterested spirit, as if he had fancyd himself in Plato's Comonwealth, and not among ye dregs & refuse of Romulus's asylum. Catonem seculum suum parum intellexit. I wish my reasonable friend John Doe's endeavours to correct some of ye abuses of this age better success ; which if they meet with, I hereby promise him ye General will be so just as not to rob ye traveller of his material share in ye victory. Tis you who have made this character your own.

> Who from ye busy world retires
> To be more usefull to it still ;
> And to no greater height aspires
> Than what's attaind without an ill ;
> Who with good neighbours or his books
> Can think ye longest day well spent ;
> And praises God, when back he looks,
> To find that all was innocent.

And to make Sir Ralph Sadlers mine, viz. that he bequeathed to his prosperous posterity the blessing of Heaven on his integrity, becomes more and more ye cheif aim & utmost ambition of your etc.

I have coppyd your papers, & shall deliver the orriginals to ye hand you direct.

312.   To my Son Carr.   London, Feb. 2, 1709.
        My dear Son

Mr. Laughton's principles & practice are so much to my mind, that I have taken all ye care in my power to have them set in a true light. I have read your letter to ye Bishops of Ely & Norwich, & several other peers & gentlemen within ye walke of my conversation ; who cant tell which to like best, whether the reformation he so justly aims at, or ye description you make of ye opposition it meets with in a place where all things of that kind shoud first take place. However, they unanimously agree that you shoud send me ye reasons he has drawn up in vindication of so laudable (altho' ye present spirit of high Church may render it fruitless) an attempt. I cant conclude without making your tutor ye same compliment Philip of Macedon made Aristotle, when he wrote him word that he coud not well thank ye Gods more for having given him such a son as Alexander, than that it had pleasd them to send him into ye world at such a time as he might reap ye advantage of his instructions ; neither

shoud I grudge him so just a share in your future esteem as Alexander
afterwards paid Aristotle, when he answerd those who askd him, how he
came to prefer him even to his father, Quoniam a patre accepi ut viverem, a
praeceptore vero accepi ut bene viverem. Adieu. Yours etc.

313.   Lady Hervey to John Hervey.
Tuesday, 3 a clock. March 28, 1710.

This opera is done so early that I shall play at
Crimp after ; therefore I desire you woud ask Lord Treasurer and Lord
Carlisle, and, if either of them fail, the Duke of Bolton or Lord Ryalton. I
hope out of these four you will get me two, which is all I want besides your ·
self, without which nothing is complete to your E. Hervey.

P.S. Pray send me an answer to this, and how the Gaming bill has
gone.

314.   To Sir Richard Cocks.   Ickworth, April 25, 1710.

You must very much over rate mine, & no less
undervalue your own observation of things, to think my opinion of our
present circumstances worth your asking, since you sent me a more lively
description of them in that short letter you desird mine by than I coud
possibly represent to you in a much longer. Had I any thing to communicate worth your notice, our former correspondence has not kept you
such a stranger to my sentiments of public matters as not to know I have
for some time disapproved ye measures of several persons, from whose
conduct I expected wiser and better things ; but tis (I fear) as much too
late for them to recover those fatal false steps as my endeavours provd too
weak to hinder their being ever taken. I woud not here be understood to
arraign ye counsils which set on foot ye Doctors prosecution, for sure twas
high time to put some signal stop to such pulpit doctrines as must again
bring upon us ye sad necessity of more revolutions. The errors I mean were

Vol. I.   K K

the incredible (tho' not unaccountable) treatment ye motion met with from them for calling over the Protestant successors ; the longer continuance of that den of tyrants, ye Scotts Privy Council; & ye rejection of that most necessary bill for lessening ye exorbitant number of officers in ye H. of C. etc. ; all which were carried in such a courtly manner as throughly veryfied ye satyrical remark, viz., that ye parties had swapt principles. Tis to such as these that saying is applicable, Honores mutant mores, & not to your etc.

315.   To Mr. Barret.   April 27, 1710.

Hearing you are enterd into a very unjustifiable (as I understand it) concurrence with Mr. Mayer for ye Chaplainship to ye Court of Sessions, (that office being now become as much his right as it was formerly yours by virtue of ye Readership to St. Mary's Parish,) I hope you will no longer persist in your pretensions thereunto, if there were no other reason than that tis very unbecoming to see so warm an opposition maintaind between two chaplains of one who woud be glad to continue your etc.

316.   To Monsieur Masson.   Ickworth, May 19, 1710.

I cant believe any one, except ye same person whose morals coud give him leave to attempt ye seducing of another from ye service he was engaged in, capable of a double misinformation so much to my disadvantage ; for I do assure you I never intended to send my son abroad but with your self; neither did I ever think of offering you a less pension than four score pounds a year, & am very ready to make it a hundred since you insist upon that sum, & it may be twill prove to be a little better paid than ye other might have been, there being some people of a worse humour than they woud even represent mine, which is to be most liberal in promises, but very loose in performances; and since I find you are of opinion this is likely to be ye last Campaigne, & that ye confederate army will be one sight very well worth a young travellers observation, I have resolvd he shall remove from Cambridge to London ye beginning of ye next month, where I intend to meet him, & then settle with you his farther motions, which shall be regulated (with all other matters) according to ye advice you shall think fit to give your assured etc.

317. To Mr. Barrett.   Ickworth, June 7, 1710.

To enjoyn your resignation was what I never pretended to do; but I perswade my self you understand enough of my mind to know how acceptable twoud be to see an end of a competition between two, where I may naturally be supposd to have influence sufficient to put a stop to't; if therefore you woud let ye contest drop by using no farther endeavours to revive your title, twoud be agreeable to ye desire of your etc.

The note you gave Sir T. Felton for £32..5, dated March 30, 1708, is put into my hands to receive what's due upon it at your convenience.

318. To Sir Thomas Hanmer.   London, July 4, 1710.

The kind encouragement you gave me last year makes me lay hold of ye first opportunity to renew a correspondence so much my interest to preserve. This comes therefore to let you know that yesterday about 2 afternoon it pleasd God to bless me with an other son, and that his poor mother and he are both very well to day, notwithstanding it provd a cross & lingering labour. His coming sometime sooner into this corrupt & variable world than my wife reckond for will (we hope) be compensated by ye nearer prospect of seeing ye good company at Euston (to whom we beg our most humble services) than we hopd for, whose neighbourhood to Ickworth gives it one of ye most valuable recomendations to ye known affection of, Sir, your etc.

319.   To Mr. Secretary Boyle.   July 7, 1710.

The Duke of Grafton having desired of you to move her Majesty for a pass for Sir Henry Bond ; and least ye Queen may out of her wonted tender regards to justice scruple to grant ye same, for fear it may occasion farther prejudice or greater losses than to those persons to whom Sir Henry Bond stands joyntly bound with his brother to near ye value of £800 ; this is to let you know that according to ye best of my knowledge & belief in Sir Henry's affairs his going out of Brittain is entirely owing to ye unkind conduct of his brother, who by first absenting himself hath rendred Sir Henry imediately liable to ye severall prosecutions of those creditors who have advanced ye said £800 to his brother ; and that no other persons will be affected thereby.   I must now beg your pardon for this trouble, which had not happend but at ye instance of ye Duke of Grafton, & to assist an unfortunate gentleman, which is an office can never be easily refused by etc.

320.   To Sir Thomas Hanmer.   London, July 22, 1710.

I'm so very fond of believing that pleasing passage in your last letter, where you assure me of ye kind share you take in all things relating to our family, that I cannot forbear from troubling you again, tho' upon ye mellancholly occasion of ye last childs death, which gives my poor wife so much concern that I did not dare (till now) to leave her long enough to her own thoughts to write you ye news of it ; for my part I've brought my self (at least I think & hope so) to such a necessary pitch of resignation as to receive most (I will not peterize so far as to say all) dispensations of God's providence with that due submission which bcomes a Christian and your etc.

My wife and self are ye Dutchess of Graftons & Mrs. Ramseys most humble servants.

321.   To Mr. Progers.   July 29, 1710.

There having been a son of Mr. Lathbury's, a youth of virtue and learning, for some time at Cambridge, who was my son's Cizer till he (now) left ye University, whose education there hath been chiefly carryd on by a subscription of several gentlemen, which by death or otherways seems to decline; & he being a young man of very promising parts as well as of remarkable sobriety & application to study; Mr. Turnor of Bury, who hath eminently interested himself in his fortunes, and knowing how kind a benefactor you had been to his father, desird me to give you this trouble, to let you know that if you'l think fit to bestow anything on him towards his expences at Clare Hall, he will see it carefully expended for his greatest advantage. Knowing how right and reasonable this suit was, I coud not possibly refuse so charitable an office; wherein I am doubly warranted, both from ye share I have in it my self, & ye knowledge of your readyness & pleasure to do good; which are, I hope, sufficient to make any farther apology unnecessary from your etc.

322.   To Sir W. Gage.   London, July 29, 1710.

The reason of my not mentioning Sir H. Bonds & his brothers withdrawing was because I concluded news of that kind woud reach you soon enough, & I always avoid doing any thing that may unnecessarily disquiet my friends, or look forwardly officious to reveal a secret to other peoples disadvantage. I have taken all ye true care in my power to obviate every inconvenience that I foresaw might happen thro their misfortunes; as in ye first place to possess my self of all necessary powers whereby I may at any time do justice to your daughters (to whom my service), in case others refuse or neglect to do it. I hope they will receive punctually every quarter doubly what is due to them, that so in a short time ye arrear may be dischargd; and there is now ready in Mr. Pennes hands the Midsummer quarter, which he has direction to pay to them or their order upon their signing a proper receipt, the form whereof was agreed on before Sir Henry's departure. But my concern did not terminate in your daughters interests only. I have also had regard to your own by getting in your bond for £1500, which otherwise might have lain out, & been made use of hereafter to your prejudice; I obtaind ye custody of it on this condition, that I woud undertake to state and examine an account yet open between yee; & on paying or allowing ye ballance to deliver it up to you. These due precautions being taken, I hope ye part I had in facilitating Sir Henry's escape will be throughly justifyd, not only upon ye foot of an ancient friendship and ye endearment of having been fellow travellers formerly, but as a debt of charity & humanity to one left in distress as a sacrifice to his brother's creditors. If I have sufferd my self to do any thing that may prove wrong in it, I shall bear ye testimony of this conscience, that I did not (at ye time) with ye best foresight and reflection I am master of apprehend ye least inconvenience, much less prejudice, to any for whom I am intrusted. Coud I tax my self with any thing of that kind, every loss I suffer of my own woud teach me to read my sins in their punishment, & sit much more heavily on ye mind of your etc.

323.   To Sir Richard Cockes.   London, Aug. 8, 1710.

      The death of one son & ye imminent danger another* has been in (of no small hopes and value in my family) will I conclude be a sufficient excuse to a man of your humanity for not thanking you sooner for ye Papers you lately favourd me with. I am so throughly inclind to approve ye lawyers side of ye question as to ye Hannover succession that his argument cannot receive all those comendations it deserves from so noted a friend without suspicion of partiallity, & therefore shall wave particular panegyricks upon it, & only tell you that a worse head than that which dictated his speech may find a great deal to say on so fruitful a topick; for

---

* Marginal pencil note says, Jack.   S.II.A.II.

even I never thought of it (& that not seldom) but fresh reasons offerd themselves ye longer one's mind dwells upon it. Tis this is ye one thing necessary our for future peace and safety; this is ye main stock we must all graft our common hopes upon; this is ye liklyest expedient to prevent a storm; or if one shoud arise, (as tis usually observable ye deaths of illustrious persons are attended with remarkable tempests,) this is ye sheet anchor that can alone enable our labouring barke to ride it out, & bring at last those honest passengers securely into port, who have venturd their all on ye wise & necessary bottom of ye Revolution. Had there never been any poisonings, assassinations or other villanies practisd by ye immoral enemies of our peace, yet, as ye publick happiness depends upon ye precarious thred of one life, that single circumstance would make one tremble, when one reflects on ye necessary laws or frequent accidents of humane nature; & grieve one to consider that ye state being perpetual shoud be left to lean on any one pillar for ye support of its religion, laws and liberty; for should that fail (which as zealous a well wisher as I profess my self to ye P——t S——c, as I sincerely wish may never happen in my time) without her successor in this kingdom amidst all our factions and distractions which have taught most men to be changeable as ye winds & fluctuating as ye tides, such a prospect might tempt even a good man to fear what Cicero once said —Quem Deum etiam si cupiat opitulari Reipublicæ credamus? O! what a heavy load must lye on those consciences (shoud any fatal consequences attend ye rejection of it) who, when a Parliamentary overture was regularly made to fix this important point beyond most moral possibilities to defeat, either mercinarily opposed or (at best) artificially baffled it, equally exposing their own present reputations & our future quiet. Tacitus gives this character of such polliticks—Concilia callida prima specie læta, tractatu dura, eventu tristia. I pray God our modern ones prove not so. The Sacheverelian feaver is so altogether owing to ye scandalous measures which our bastard Whiggs have lately taken in this & other material particulars (some whereof I formerly mentiond) that tis with ye utmost injustice Sempronia's conduct is chargd with any share in ye ill consequences of them, she being one I still think (as Scaliger calld Picus of Mirandola), Monstrum sine vitio ; & such I doubt not she'l appear, when ye most industrious malice hath sifted every passage of her life ; & who may now complain, as ye late king did to Sir William Temple of his unfortunate scituation in ye affairs of ye world, who when others comitted ye faults he must suffer all ye blame. Lord Treasurer being this day desird to break his staff, & ye family falling into disgrace, you cant (& I hope you never did) suspect me of flattery ; & therefore for ye sake of truth and justice I will farther acquaint you that there has not been any true piece of old Whiggism practisd of latter yeares but has been principally owing to her influence ; that when ye place-bill was depending, after having heard many arguments pro and con on ye subject, (some having urgd ye danger & unseasonableness of altering ye prosperous train of things at that juncture,) leaving her own judgment undetermind, she made in my hearing this noble declaration ; that she implicitly prayd God woud dispose of that & all other matters so as woud prove best for Brittain. Had you patience, or I more room, I coud enumerate many more indearing instances of her steady adhærence to every maxim that can either procure or preserve ye liberty & happyness of this nation, even to deserve ye character Paterculus gives of Livia : Mater enim eminentissima et omnia Diis quam hominibus similior fœmina, cujus potentiam nemo sensit nisi aut levatione periculi aut accessione dignitatis. I know but one attonement left in store for our new schemists to expiate ye criminal counsil of laying aside her successfull husband & those other ministers under whose administration our affairs have wonderfully prosperd ; & that is to advise her Majesty as your lawyer woud do* ; which if they are wise or honest enough to give, & she blest enough to take, so as to make it her own act & deed, twill opperate

---

* Marginal note says, To send for ye P: successor. S.II.A.II.

like charity in my fond heart, & cover a multitude of ye Tories other sins with, Sir, your etc.

You never sent me word what became of your address, which I fear had too much of ye antidote in't to pass with so poysond a people.

324.   To Collonel Porter.   Aug. 25, 1710.

Dear Brother

Upon ye first rumour of a dissolution I wrote to know your mind concerning your next election ; and to acquaint you with their resentments at your last winters absence, which you have not furnishd me with excuses for. I need not tell you what coy mistresses boroughs are, & that they never were more courted than at present. Some are so enamourd as to desire I would assist them in making their addresses there, concluding by your cold attendance that you have given over ye pursuit. But my answer was, I had not yet heard from you, & that as long as you desird the little help I was master of, I coud not think of lending it elsewhere. Sir R. D. stirring again (as I am told) to introduce his son, twere very necessary your intentions shoud be known as soon as possible, that my friends may preserve their strength intire to oppose that interest, which can never prevail but when any breach may happen in mine. I'm going next week into Lincolnshire, intending to return hither by ye beginning of ye Fair, & shoud be glad to receive your instructions at either place, that I may proceed accordingly, being resolvd to act in this, as in all former occasions, with that sincere affection that has been ever borne you by your etc.

325.   To Mr. Alderman Wright.   London, Jan. 9, 1710.

Mr. Alderman

That I may be safe in every thing which passes between Mr. Gipps and me, I desire so cautious & prudent a friend as your self may convey my answer to ye paper he sent me (by Mr. Howard), signd

Vol. I.   L L

by himself as an acknowledgment of ye undeservd injury he had done me
in falsely charging me with treasonable words (more majorum) my heart
coud be as little capable of conceiving as my tongue of uttering them.   Tis
then that my unfitting nature for ye age I live in always inclines me to forgive, when any signs of repentance appear in those who wrong me ; but then
lex talionis suggests to me that Mr. Gipps ought to prevail with others to
do ye same by ye miller, who ought not to be sacrificed in ye cause ; &
when that just point is agreed, if Mr. Gipps will order ye following adver-
tisement to be inserted in some subsequent Gazette ; viz. I Richard Gipps
of—— in ye County of Suffolk Esq., do acknowledge that ye following words
I spoke of ye Rt. Honble ye Lord Hervey is for bringing in ye Prince of
Wales, and his Lordship said it himself, that if Sir Philip Parker lost ye
day at ye election for Knights of ye Shire for ye said county, that his Lordship woud make it his business to bring in ye Prince of Wales : were falsely
by me spoken, & are utterly untrue, having said ye same of his Lordship
without ye least reason or foundation whatsoever ; for which with all submission I humbly beg his Lordships pardon & make this publick acknowledgment : the same shall suffice to one who (tho' he owes no forgiveness to
that family) has grace enough added to his indulgent nature to pardon even
seventy times seven in an offending brother, when he reflects on ye many
frailties of your etc.

326.   To Sir R. Cockes.   Jan. 13, 1710.

          The iminent danger my eldest son has been in
from a pleuresy woud alone excuse my silence, did you but know (as I think
I do & hope not partially) how worthy he is of all ye concern my heart has
felt for fear of loosing him, especially since every day convinces me of ye
growing scarcity there is either of able or right principled men to keep up ye
credit or support ye constitution of our declining country ; but when to this
may be added ye unreasonable prosecution of your & my best friends, & ye

continual attendance their defence (tho vain in part) required of me, you will not wonder that I've no sooner thankd you for ye last papers you have sent, which if you will not favour me with ye orriginall, I beg you woud (as formerly) permit me to preserve a coppy of, having often met with those natural satisfactions in perusing them which most men experience in reading authors who represent most of their own thoughts to them in such advantageous turns of expression as make them afterwards more justly tenacious of those sentiments they had before espousd. Coud anything make me more in love with true old Whigg principles than I've always been, twoud be to find how capable they've been of forming a perfect patriot in your self, whose laudable example it shall be his utmost ambition to emulate, who is with great sincerity your etc.

327. My ever-new Delight   Newmarket, March 4, 1711.

Your two Jacks are as well here as tis possible for them to be anywhere without you, which I am become less able to bear than ever: when I've told you this truth, I know ye next satisfaction to you will be to know young Jack passd his journey as well as you could wish; and that I might be able to send you a particular account of him, venturd to make him my bedfellow, but was disturbd neither by his coughing nor restlessness, having slept soundly the whole night. As to his dyet, he eat heartily of the beef and butter at Epping, did the same of a fricassee of chickens at Hockeril, and of his own accord broke into the paper where the plum-cake lay on this side of Born-bridg, and having lookd over the horses we supped on mutton and were in bed before ten. I hope you'l in return send me as good news concerning your self, which I shall want to enable me to pass this short intended absence with tolerable ease. As to my return, I beg you will send me your undisguisd desires about it by Thursdays post; for according to them (let the consequences happen as they will) I am resolvd to regulate my stay here, every hour being a self denyal nothing could make me undergoe but the consideration of your welfare, which justly claims the first place in his thoughts, whose sole happiness so entirely depends on it as your most faithful friend's & constant lover's, Hervey.

P.S.—Kiss Nan and Hercules and all our children for me. God keep them and you in his safe & merciful protection.

328.   Lady Hervey to John Hervey.   London, March 4, 1711.

My dear dear Angel

It adds much to the trouble of your absence to find your journey attended with such ill weather, for I am sure it is impossible but that you and Jack must both have increasd your colds, and I am afraid it has added to the complaints you left me with, for I was not very well last night, nor am not better to day. Nurse Edwards calld to me in the middle of the night, Madam, you dont sleep ; shall I rise and get you something to drink ? Poor soul, as if her slops coud have been any comfort. But though it were possible I could want you more than I do, yet I beg if dear Jack and your dearer self find any good by the country, that you would not come sooner than is for your good and convenience ; but I shall be glad to hear by the next post what day you think that will be. I have no news to tell you but that the third Dauphin is certainly dead, and just in the same manner as all the rest have done, which makes every body conclude it is by poison. They say the King of France is very ill too, though they give out he is well, Lady Catharine Windham has miscarryd with her fright. Will and Harry walkd hither to day ; they and the rest (thank God) are all well, only the colds you left them with. Sir Richard Blackmoor tells me they at Chelsey are mending, and have rested very well in their new lodging, but I have very much repented sending them since the weather has provd so bad. I am glad to hear you and Jack got through it so well to Hockeril. Pray God continue to prosper you now and at all other times, is the constant prayers of your most faithful & affectionate E. Hervey.

P.S.—I am forced to send 3 packets, there are so many prints.

329.   My ever-new Delight   Ickworth, March 5, 1711,

If this place was incapable of making me easy when adornd with all the beauties of the spring, because the chief beauty and pleasure of it was absent, what an uncomfortable life must I now live, suffering the same absence in the most melancholy winter scene of frost and snow I ever saw here.   The greatest consolation I have is to think two days more will end my stay, unless your letter by this nights post (which Emmett has not yet brought after me from Newmarket) conjures me not to venture so early a return to London (as by Sunday next) for fear of unavoidable consequences; but I had rather live the life of Tantalus than continue any longer as I find my self, being more & more unable to live without you.   The next comfort is that I can tell you, Jack is as much the better for this journey as tis possible to conceive, his cough rarely troubling him either by night or day, and as that declines his appetite and sleep increases.   I had not time to tell you in the letter I sent you by Lord Ryalton, that I declard you paid the forfeit to Mr. Craven, (in case there was any bett depending between you on Duns match, none appearing on the articles,) so half that money (at the worst) will be savd you.   I have sett up for your dear letter (which is just now come in) till midnight, and am so uneasy to hear by it that you were not very well on Monday night, nor better yesterday, that I am resolvd to be with you (God willing) on Sunday, hoping my nursing and slops will do you more good than Mrs. Edwards's; till when adieu, my dearest, dearest, only love & pleasure.

330.   Lady Hervey to John Hervey.   London, March 6, 1711.

Shoud I make use of the kind power my dear dear angel has given me over his absence, I am afraid you woud think I made but an ill return to your generosity; but I am in hopes the cold weather will bring my wishes to pass without discovering how self interested I am as to that particular.   In the mean time I am glad you and Jack bear it so well;

for my own part I cant keep from getting cold by the fire side, and I am afraid shall increase it to day by being above stairs. I have not dard to let my prince come down since you went, but I have given your kiss to Sweet-face: none of my governesses will let me have her for a bed-fellow; they say she is so unquiet; I am glad you dont find Jack so; I hope tis a sign he is well. I thank my dearest for his particular account of him, but should have liked better to have heard more of your dear self. I had a letter to day from Squire, which says the children in the country mend very much notwithstanding this bitter weather; thank God, these here are well also; I cant say I am so, for my head achs sadly, and my eyes are so weak I cant tell you half what I have to say, for I think I coud fill a quire of paper, tho' I do not know a word of news; if I hear any before the post goes out you shall have it. The little oracle said yesterday, Papa would loose his match, though Lord Dorchester told me all the crack at Newmarket was for Hervey Dunn; but I am afraid it was but a Newmarket crack; however, if it proves so, they say their may be some good out of evil; this will be one to me, if it makes you weary of the place and brings you quickly back to ye longing arms of your faithful pining turtle, E. Hervey.

P.S. I have just receivd your dear letter with the welcome news of your coming home on Sunday; but I conclude Dunn has lost, though you say nothing of it. I have sent Katt: as you desired with all the money you left, which was 250£.

331.   My ever-new Delight   Hockeril, March 31, 1711.

Since I must necessarily trouble you with a letter by every opportunity which offers it self, I cant forbear acquainting you that the very best thing my present condition will allow me to say of it is that con-sidering the badness of the ways, and how fatal their consequences might have provd to your indisposition, I am (O that ever any concurrence of accidents shoud ever be able to make this declaration true) yet better able (tho but a little, God knows,) to support your absence than I coud the wounding reflection of my having ever been the fatal occasion of your doing any thing that might increase your uneasynesses, or render more difficult the re-establishment of a health on which my happyness so entirely depends. Twas upon these terms alone I coud exercise the most self denying philosophy that can possibly be put to the choice of a heart so fondly wedded to your company as is that of your most affectionate lover & faithfullest of friends or husbands, Hervey.

P.S.—The whole cargoe of boys are well. I am quite undone if you dont send my keys of my strong boxes after me, which you have upon your ring of keys, and which I forgott.

> 332. Lady Hervey to John Hervey. London, April 2, 1711.

It woud sound very odly from any body but me to my dear dear angel to say I am glad I am not with you, for I am sure I must have disappointed your journey if I had gone, besides the grieving your poor, tender heart to have seen me so ill as I have been ever since you went, I think in more pain than ever. I spent most of the day (Saturday I mean) upon a couch at Lady Sunderlands; she and Mrs. Dunch both said I gave them vapours to see me, and that they woud desire you never to leave me again; but for all this I venturd to Church on Sunday morning, but there was so great a crowd that I was afraid I shoud not have been able to have held out till it was over; I was something better in the afternoon, and went to Hide-Park with my Lady Dalkeith, but I bore the coach worse than ever; and was forcd to beg her to come out, for I had such a violent pain in my back, besides my other complaints, that I was not able to bear it, and so faint and dispirited that I coud hardly draw my legs after me, and my pain in my limbs so bad that I was forcd to have my legs rubd for half an hour; yet with all this Mrs. Dunch kept me there till almost twelve a clock, for she said she was sure I shoud go home and cry. Sir David was here this morning; he says bathing has had some share in this disorder, but it is chiefly fretting, and the over working of the medicine; to help the last he has ordered me to take it but every other night; the first is only in your power to cure; in order to it I beg to know when the last match is, not that I woud have you come till your business is done at Ickworth, for that woud be but to have a second parting, which I am afraid I coud not bear. Dear Sweet-face come to me just now, and seeing me very melancholy put her little arms about my neck and said, What's the matter with you, Mama, wont you go abroad? I told her I was not well: then she said, O, I know what woud cure you. I askd her what; she said, Papa to come to you, I know that well enough. This minute your dear letter is come from Hockeril, which is some comfort to my poor heart to hear you are got well so farr; pray God it may continue with every other good that can attend a mortal life, which shall be the constant prayers of, my dear dearest life, your most faithful & truly affectionate wife, E. Hervey.

P.S.—My pain is something better, and I am going to Lady Sunderlands; if I hear any thing before to morrows post you shall hear from me again; at least I will send you word how I do, as I beg you would do to me as often as possible.

333.   My ever-new Delight   Newmarket, April 3, 1711.

I have got so painful a crick in my neck by being in the cold high winds since I came hither, that I can hardly endure to hold it but in one posetion; and altho' the posture for writing is not it, I cant be half so uneasy in doing it as I should be in omitting what I know would disappoint you. I can guess a little by what I felt my self when I found never a line from you here at my arrival on Sunday night to let me know how you passd the rest of Saturday; but I comforted my self by concluding if you had been worse than I left you I shoud have known it by your own or some other hand. I hopd you receivd my letter from Hockeril, which

I do not mention by way of reproach, or if I do, tis with the same vein of kindness which must run through every thing that proceeds from a heart increasing dayly with love and tenderness towards you, such being the condition of his soul, who is with the utmost truth, my dearest life, your most affectionate friend and lover of near 16 years old, Hervey.

334. Lady Hervey to John Hervey. London, April 3, 1711.

I cant put up the prints without saying something to my dear dear angel, though I have had the mortification this morning of a boy coming from Newmarket without a letter; but it was some amends to me to hear you and the dear children got well thither, and I am sure it will be no less pleasure to you to hear that I am better to day upon not taking my medicine, and design to venture to Mr. Hescotes play with the Dutchess of Montague, Lady Berkeley and Lady Betty, who are mighty kind and compassionate to me at this time (when indeed I need it much). I hope you will thank Sir John for it; he setts out to morrow and will be with you on Thursday; (would to God he coud carry me in his pocket.) I did not think I coud have an addition to my trouble, but indeed I find the want of Sweet face is one; yet I cant tell whether it is envy or jealousy that she shoud be with you when I cant, and to be certain that you are pleasd with any thing in my absence, which can never happen to your faithful and constant E. Hervey.

P.S.—The train-bands have been all night in the Square, so that my fears are not yet over. Poor Mrs. Montague is dead. Jack was very poor when he went from hence, and I know he wont ask you, though half his pleasure will be lost if he has not money to bett.

335. Lady Hervey to John Hervey. London, April 4, 1711.

I have been better this evening, and been at Lady Betty's (where I am invited to morrow to dinner), but hear not a word of news. There is nothing talkd of but the Town being sett on fire to night, and papers thrown into peoples houses in several places to tell of it. However it is, I am fool enough to be afraid there will be some bustle; all the train-bands are out; they have been in the square all day, and tis the same in the city; but I will try to forgett it by going to sleep; so good night, my dear.

336.   My ever-new Delight   Newmarket, April 5, 1711.

You will see by the letter I wrote from Hockeril how sympathizing a feeling we both had as to being asunder at this time under your circumstances. May I never again experience the double load of suffering the one or apprehending the dismal consequences of the other; since next to privation your living in pain woud prove the most sensible affliction to me; if my absence has the least share in the cause of it, it shall be your own fault if the effect ceases not, for I will be with you any day you shall sett me, being a lover (though of near 16 years standing) whose passion to please and make you happy easily sacrifices all other considerations of business or convenience to that chief object of all my care & conduct in this life, your health and prosperity. Hervey Dun having been beaten yesterday, I must desire you to pay the 500 guineas in the chest to Chambers, that he may pay the bill I drew upon him for those stakes; never young horse gaind more creditt, (but you'l say, Hang him toad, what do I care for that, since we have lost our money;) for tho' them are ran too fast for him from first to last, yet he run very near her at the last, altho' upon extremity through the whole 6 mile course whipd and spurrd. Altho' this has made me very poor, yet Jack shall not be so, since he has gott so powerful an advocate. I shall not fail to thank Sir J. Germaine as I ought for his and Lady Betty's kindness & civilities to my dearer half. Since your heart is susceptible of envy or jealousy towards Sweet-face, I will not conceal a secret from you, which will afford you some revenge upon her for inspiring those uneasy thoughts in you, which is this; that really and truly I found not half ye pleasure in her without as with you; which amounts to the last demonstration that your presence is absolutely necessary to make me relish all other satisfactions in this world, even tho' they are such pretty and most agreeable parts of your self: therefore since you see the impossibility of my tasting any joy where you are not, shorten by your summons my stay in the country, if not for your own, for the sake of your most affectionate lover & friend, Hervey.

P.S.—The children are all well at Ickworth.

337. Lady Hervey to John Hervey. London, April 5, 1711.
My dear dearest life

How coud you be so cruel to me as to tell me you mett with any disappointment from me where love and tenderness were concernd; but I hope you are satisfyd by this time that it was to spare yours from having any unnecessary pain upon my account, which I knew a letter by Saturdays post must have done, for indeed I never was worse in my life than all that day. Last night I came home with an intention to supp with your son to take leave of him, but was in such violent pain I was not able either to eat or to sitt up longer than ten a clock. I had a very ill night, and am very faint and dispirited to day; however, Sir David (who has been here this morning) has desird me to go abroad, which I am easily persuaded to, for indeed I hate home (at this time) most heartily, so am going with Lady Betty Germaine to dine by Mrs. Chetwynds bed-side, broken bones being the fittest company for my broken and disturbd mind, though I hope mine is more likely to be sett right and sooner than I am afraid hers will be. Your son has been with me ever since I was up in order to take leave, which was a ceremony when it come to I was not able to perform; but that is a subject fit for neither of us at this time, so I will adjourn this in hopes to hear

some news either publick or private before night.   I am now lockd up in Mrs.
Chetwynds closett, but have heard no news, only that there has been an order
to examine all lodgers to find how many Roman Catholicks there are in this
town, and the account given in to the Secretarys office is 53,000, besides house
keepers and women and children ; this I heard Lady Essex Roberts tell, who
said she had it from one of the Secretarys.   Captain Elwes calld upon me to
desire I woud send your horses to Hide-park this morning for my Lord
Portland to see, that he had a mind to it, but I did not know whether you
woud like to have them go since there was nothing but boys to ride them,
and in such a crowd as a review some accident might happen ; so I sent the
page to my Lord Portland to say that the groom was gone out of Town,
therefore I coud not send them to Hide-park, but if he cared to see them in
the Square, either now or any other time, they shoud be sure to wait of him.
I hope I have done right, as I always wish to do in what relates to you ;
but sure you have not had the same thoughts towards me, else you woud
have taken more care of your self, and not have got such a cold ; but I beg
you woud have your neck irond ; Jack can tell Mrs. Fawsett how to do it ;
but I hope this warm day will relieve you without it, for fear you shoud not
have patience for that, any more than I have to bear the thoughts of Newmarket, which I now hate more than ever, and feel your absence more
insupportable to me every day then ever, being with all the truth and love
imaginable, my dearest treasure, your most faithful E. Hervey.

P.S.—Mr. Chetwynds brother goes to morrow, and has taken the whole
Packet boat, but he has promisd me to take care of your son.   I am better
to night.   I have had such a horrid pen and ink at Mrs. Chetwynds that I
am afraid you cant read it.

338.   My ever-new Delight   Newmarket, April 7, 1711.
          I thought I had so well explain the true source of

my disappointment that the mention of it woud rather seem kind than cruel to you, otherwise it should have been smotherd in silence, as I choose to do every thing that may possibly occasion you the least uneasyness. You will see by my last letter that your mind-setter is ready to attend you whenever you'l please to summons him, till when you may say to him, Doctor, heal thy own ; mine being as much broken (if not more) than yours can be, and which nothing can sett right but that sweet society it has been accustomd to with its dearer half. I thank you for your care in the receipt you sent me to cure my crick, but that is so well over that I wish all your pains as short a date. Could the fervent prayers of an ungrateful worthless sinner be heard, I'm in some hopes the vows I make on those occasions woud procure you a long and easy life, which from the continual experience of God's infinite goodness towards me & mine, I've an humble confidence will still come to pass. I throughly approve your conduct in the answer you sent about the horses, as I do the kindness you shewd in recommending poor Carr to Mr. Chetwynds care, which tho' very good news yet not half so welcome as what followd it, that you were better, when you closd your letter to your most affectionate friend & lover, Hervey.

P.S.—Dear Jack can ail nothing at this place, where he is so continually pleasd, as he'l tell you himself.

339. Lady Hervey to John Hervey. London, April 7, 1711.

How coud you trust me, my dear dear angel, with the power of naming the day of your coming; but I please my self with being certain that you woud not have venturd it without having (almost) as much mind to come as I to have you, for if I were to follow my own inclination, I shoud say, Pray, my dear, come as soon as you receive this; but when I consider cruel business which (I know) must be done, and that if you come away without doing it that must necessarily occasion another parting, which

(O my dear) if you love me relieve me from the fears of in your next letter, for I think, though it is intolerable, I can better bear this then another separation, since I hope it need not continue above 3 or 4 days after the matches are over to settle your affairs at Ickworth, for I find the Bath nor no other medicine can take effect without my dear and constant companion. I have orderd my lodgings to be got ready by the 26th or 27th of this month, so that to compass that I must set out Monday or Tuesday fortnight from hence, if you like it. I had a letter yesterday from Mrs. Burslem to tell me how sorry she was that she coud not go with me, but Mr. Burslem was so very ill that Fryday last they thought he woud have dyed; she said in the same letter that he had orderd several sums of money to be paid in to Mr. Chambers next week, so that I thought if I stayd a few days to see what that woud produce, it might be better than to pay that money you orderd in now, since you seemd to have a mind to keep it till you come to Town, and I find (upon sending to know what money he had in his hands) he has receivd near £500 since you went, as you will see by the inclosd account, which was a farther encouragement for me to stay till I heard from you again, hopeing that little Thief will perform better than that ugly toad Dunn. However, that in the mean time you may meet with no disappointment in the charging of your bills, I sent for Mr. Chambers's man to come to me (not being able to go to him), and told him that if your bills upon him overchargd the cash he had in his hands of yours, he need make no difficulty in the paying of them, for that I had your orders to pay him in more money whenever he'd let me know he had not enough of yours to answer with. I shall be glad if this method I've taken in your affairs prove to your liking; I am sure this long letter woud not if you knew how ill I had been to day, in the same manner I was 3 weeks agoe; upon going to rise this morning, I was ready to faint, and forcd to lie down again, and shoud have done so all day, but that Lady Sunderland beg'd me to come and stay with her, so Sir David has consented to it provided I lye upon the couch, which indeed necessity will force me to, I am so very faint ; but thank God this illness is some relief to my pain, for I am much easier of that. Lady Betty Germaine begs you woud give this inclosd letter, or send it back again if Sir John is come away ; she woud not have troubled you, but for fear it shoud be lost if he were not there. Pray, my dear, send me word the soonest day that you can come without suffering as much in your affairs as I do in your absence, which is saying the most that can be by your doating wife, E. Hervey.

P.S.—I am something better to night.

340.　　Lady Hervey to John Hervey.　　London, April 7, 1711.

I am now upon my Lady Sunderland's couch, and the Dutchess of Marlbourough by me, by whose order I write this second letter to beg you woud come to Town by Wednesday night, and bring every body with you that has any votes in the Bank. Thursday is the day of election, and she says it is a terrible reflection upon any body that can stay to see a horse race though there were but a possibility of having the Bank of England put into ill hands by it, and if the Tories get the better (as they threaten), Mr. Hopkins says you may all make use of your horses to run away. Pray send me word by the stage coach whether you will come, because if you do I woud not send my letters on Tuesday for fear they shoud be lost.

P.S.—I have a great deal more to say, but that they will all read my letter, so I cant, and they say I've wrote more to day already than you will have patience to read. [Pray come away that you may have nothing to repent of. S. Marlbourough.]

341.　　My ever-new Delight　　Newmarket, April 9, 1711.

I make Israel stay till I tell you by him what I

coud not by the coach, (that not yet running, or if it did comes from London on Mondays,) how unlucky I find my self to have an impossibility enjoind me by those for whom I woud at all times do every thing that were not so ; Thursday and Friday being the two very daies on which all my tennants are summond to attend me at Ickworth from all parts of the County to pay their rents and adjust their accompts ; beside, if I coud come when desird, I must necessarily make another journey hither to settle those and all other matters at Ickworth before I coud sett out with you for Bath, which I woud not retard beyond the day you have fixd of the 27th for any other consideration since your health is so nearly concernd, and that a second separation would I find agree with neither of us. If you can think of any expedient by which these difficulties can be surmounted, lett me know it by a messenger on purpose as soon as this comes to you, for there is nothing I woud not do to compass (if possible) what your self and the Dutchess of Marlborough seem to desire ; there being nothing I coud ever so much repent of as the appearance only of the least omission of any service towards one I'm so very much obligd to ; Dun's blindness and Thief's lameness being but small misfortunes compard with the present perplexity of mind, wherein these jarring duties have cast your most affectionate friend and lover, Hervey.

342.   Lady Hervey to John Hervey.   London, April 10, 1711.

Your dear letters being the only pleasure I can taste at this time, the post was yesterday doubly welcome to me when I saw two superscriptions with your hand ; but I must own the disappointment equald the pleasure when I found they were not both yours, though the other was from so dear a part of you as poor Jack. However, I must beg you to kiss and thank him for it, without discovering how ungratefully it was receivd. Lord Dorset told me yesterday at Lady Betty's (where I dind again) that he was the chief jockey at Newmarket, but I can gett no account from any body (nor you say nothing) what is become of Thief's match, nor how much you lost upon odious Dun. I forgot to desire you to pay Mr. Craven twenty pounds for me, which I lost to him upon that match.—Just when I had wrote so farr, Israel came with your letter, which was about twelve a clock, so I went immediately to Montague House to know what the Dutchess of Marlborough woud have me do, and whether I shoud send for you or not, but by great good fortune she was abroad and not expected home till night, so that I saved your creditt and your trouble too, which must have been a great deal to have taken so many journeys in so short a time, though I must confess before I had well considerd your inconveniences in it I was very glad to be employd in the sending for you, and not a little disappointed when I found I was not likely to see you to morrow night ; but the business you were to come about was the least consideration with me, nor I dont find that any body else makes much ot it but such zealous people as her Grace and Lord Sunderland, who has teazd me to death all day to send you an express ; if any thing coud make me do it, it woud be to know the day that I may hope to see you (without inconvenience), which I beg you woud let me know by the next post, it being so impatiently longd for by, my dear dearest life, your most tenderly affectionate wife, E. Hervey.

P.S.—I have been something better of my pain these two or three days, but farr from well in mind or body, God knows ; it woud be some ease to me to count the hours if I knew when they woud end, which I again beg you woud let me know. All the news that I can meet with to day is that Mr. Ha : is to be Treasurer ; this I had from good hands ; but they talk of other alterations which I cant tell you for truth ; it is that Lord Paw : is to have the Post office, Mr. Benson Chancellor of the Exchequer, Mr. Mansell Cofferer and a Lord, Mr. Padget the first of the Admiralty, and Sir T. Han : Secretary in the room of Lord Dartmouth.—Will Oliver forgot to send Milton word that I woud have no more meat come, so there has been one hamper spoild, and

Vol. I.　　N N

another to come to morrow that will be so to, as I conclude. Sir Charles Duncomb dyd last night. Pray look of your letters whether they are seald with the seal I always send to you, for I had like to have had a trick playd me.

343.   My ever-new Delight   Newmarket, April 10, 1711.

After having trusted you with so nice and tender a heart as I am pleasd you know I'm owner of, you need not wonder I shoud leave every thing relating to it in your disposal, especially in a point I hopd you'd determine according to its own desire. But since you've turnd the whole upon getting to the Bath by the 27th, I'll diligently persue every step in my business which may enable me to accompany you thither by that time, and shall be better satisfyed to sacrifice all the pleasures I promisd my self in seeing all the pride of nature opening it self day by day at Ickworth to your ease of mind and health of body than to see and taste the glorys of the spring. Tho' Thiefcatcher was so lame that he went upon 3 legs, yet I venturd to run him against Thief upon the contemptible opinion (you know) I always had of him, and beat him the last mile by dint of goodness, which extraordinary performance I can attribute to nothing but the virtue of those kisses I've seen you give him, which I experimentally know will inspire uncommon feates. You have acted most prudently touching Mr. Chambers's affairs, for now you need not part with your ready money, which it is good in uncertain times to keep a stock of by one. Let Lady Betty know (with my service) I deliverd her letter to Sir John as soon as it came to the hands of your most affectionate friend & lover, Hervey.

344.   My ever-new Delight   Ickworth, April 16, 1711.

The usual uneasyness which seizes me as soon as I am from you made me hasten from Newmarket to this Park, in hopes of finding rest where you have often heard me say my center was; but I'm so farr from feeling any of those sweet satisfactions I usd to tast here, that I can never hereafter allow that name even to this place when not blessd with thy dear presence: the most endearing circumstance it can pretend towards me at present is that I found all the pretty pledges of our love in perfect health, its good air being one of those meritts I hope you'l be much the better for at your return from the Bath. That I may be able to attend you thither by the time appointed, I shall loose none here, and have already talkd with Milton about her going away, who says she would be glad to be dischargd as soon as your convenience will admitt, her sister being very ill. And if I can be of any use to you herein, pray send your instructions, and they shall be persued. She tells me there are inventories of the linnen and bedding, but of nothing else except the utensils in the kitchen. Coud I deliver you from any care or trouble in this or any other of your affairs, my pains would be most abundantly compensated, knowing how necessary it is for the re-establishment of your health that your mind shoud not be burthend with any thing but how to love me enough. My dearest life, adieu till next Post.

345. Lady Hervey to John Hervey. London, April 17, 1711.

I was glad to hear by the coachman that my dear dear angel got well to Hockeril, and hopd the air curd your sickness as sleep did mine, which is a relief to all my sufferings, for in my dreams I have your dear company, without which no other pleasure can be tasted, nor any benefitt to be found at the Bath, which has determind me not to think of going till you come back, and I have wrote to day accordingly to tell them I will have my lodgings from the 3rd of May. Yesterday there was a drawing-room, when the Queen was so particularly gracious to me that it was taken notice of: for though there was a prodigious crowd and the table quite full before she saw me, yet she was not at rest till they brought me a stool over every bodys head and made them set quite close to her own chair; yet with all that I was forcd to sitt behind, where I had room but for one hand. All the news now is that Mr. Boyl will be declard Secretary in a very short time; there is nothing talkd of but changes, which are so differently reported that there is no credit to be given to them. I am going to dine with Mrs. Chetwyn, who is very happy, for she has sett her feet to the ground and walkd the length of two rooms with being led by 2 people. I will keep my letter open in hopes of some more news there. Poor Lady Betty Germain has lost her girl this morning, which I am extreamly concernd for, and makes me more uneasy for fear any of your Bury visiters shoud bring the small pox to Ickworth, for I hear it is very much there : if you love me, my dear, get out of their way, and dont let them come plaguing you and hindering your business, which if they do, to keep you an hour longer there, I shall never endure the sight of them again, I know very well, and I really cant bear it. They want straw here for your horses; I know nothing of the quantity, so beg you woud let me know: in the mean time I have orderd them to get what is necessary. My head is so very bad, I am afraid I have wrote and spelt worse than ordinary, but (according to custom) you must forgive and pity your poor forlorn E. Hervey.

P.S.—Betty Langley and her niece will go in the stage-coach on Friday; therefore pray send the chaise to meet them at Saxham corner. I had rather Milton shoud not be dischargd till I am there, because she may instruct Betty in the business. I have sent you the inclosd letter, not knowing but you might have a mind to enquire into it. I dare not direct your letters to Ickworth for fear you shoud miss of them. Not a word of news. My pain is something better.

346.   My ever-new Delight   Ickworth, April 18, 1711.

I have just now read your dear letter, which I sent for to Newmarket this afternoon. I fear by the complaint of your head you dont keep so good hours as I enjoynd and you promisd at our parting.

> If careless of thy self, of me take care;
> For like a ship where all the fortunes are
> Of an adventrous merchant, I must be,
> If thou shouldst faile, quite bankrupted in thee.

Therefore pray, my dear, give me at least the ease of thinking you are not the worse for my absence in point of regularity: I've uneasynesses enow upon my spirits which necessarily attend me whenever we are separated, without making that the occasion of more. My condition was prophetically described by him who said:

> What anxious thoughts,
> What kind perplexities tumultuous rise,
> If but the absence of a day divide
> Me from my fair belovd; vainly smiles
> The chearful sun, and night with radiant eyes
> Twinkles in vain; the region of my soul
> Is darkness, till its better star appears.
> What heavy toil, what torment to sustain
> The rolling burden of the tedious hours!
> The tedious hours are ages; Fancy roves
> Restless in fond enquiries, nor believes
> Eliza safe, Eliza in whose life
> My life consists, and in her welfare mine.
> Fear and surmise put on a thousand forms
> Of dear disquietudes, & through my ears
> Whisper ten thousand dangers.

which though I trust in God they'l all prove chimerical, yet the load of fear only is much too great an oppression for you to be but an accessory in;

wherefore once more be sure to do all things for the recovery of your health. I am glad to hear the Queen receivd you with such particular marks of esteem; but how shoud she do otherwise when she compares your conduct & character with the rest of her female train, and reflects on the publick professions she has made to countenance those only who approach nearest to those perfections you are the standard of. If she surveyd you with my eyes, Carbunconella must give place to you, as others have done to her. I shall take great care to prevent any infection coming from Bury by having as little communication with my friends there as I can possibly contrive; but were the small pox not there, nothing there or elsewhere shall detain me from you longer than Sunday come sevenight, that you may be attended to the Bath at the time fixd by your most faithful friend & constant lover, Hervey.

P.S.—The straw is not worth your care.   The children are all well.

347.   Lady Hervey to John Hervey.   London, April 18, 1711.

It woud sound very selfish and ill-naturd in any thing but a heart so tenderly nice as mine is towards my dear dear angel to tell you how rejoicd I was to hear you coud tast none of the pleasures of Ickworth without me; for it was from fearing that impossible to happen made me first hate the place; but your last kind confession has not only easd my jealousy as to that, but my fears of your staying there a moment longer then is absolutely necessary for your business, which if I shoud delay by any affairs of mine I coud never forgive my self; therefore have given Betty all the necessary instructions I can think of, if Milton must be dischargd before I come, which I am very unwilling to consent to for many reasons; but if it must be, all the trouble I will give you in it is to take my inventory out of the chest in my chamber, and have it compard with hers. I have given Betty the note of what has been sent since; but I beg you woud not let her go till I come if you can help it, for it will leave things in a strange confusion.

There is no news, nor nothing talkd of but the death of the Emperor, who they say the Court will go into close mourning for, because he was a friend of the Princes, and did so for him. The Duke of Montague went away yesterday, which made her Grace fit company for me, with her eyes swelld out of her head; she and Mrs. Dunch supd with me last night: to night we are invited to my Lady Whartons with the rest of that gang. I hate home so much at this time that the first that asks me is sure of me. I sent to the Dutchess of Marlborough to have an appointment with her, but she coud not, being in a hurry to go out of Town to day. Poor Betty is very melancholy for want of her brothers & sisters; I am glad to hear they are all well; that you and they may continue so shall be the constant prayers of, my dear and only joy, your ever faithful E. Hervey.

P.S.—If the evening produces any thing worth your knowing, I will write again by the post, for I chuse to send this by Betty as the safest and quickest way.

348. My ever-new Delight   Ickworth, April 20, 1711.

You have done me a greater injustice than I know you woud willingly be guilty of towards me, whenever you've been jealous of any person or thing this world affords; for believe me, (dearest of all pleasures,) I'm so uncapable of tasting any but those I derive from you that all beside are so insipid they scarce deserve that name. Did you but know how little entertainment this place has yielded me in your absence, it woud make you rather angry with than jealous of it. I've not seen a fine day since I came, which makes me hope the season has heard my wish, (knowing how beneficial fine weather is to your distemper;)

> Attend her, courteous spring, tho' we shoud here
> Loose by it all the treasures of the year.

I have receivd your key by Betty, but hope to spare you and my self the pain of routing in the inventory by persuading Milton to stay till your return, wherein my best rhetorick shall be employd to morrow. I intend to bring Jack with me, unless you countermand it in the interim. Woud it were possible to pack Sweet-face up too without hurting her, for she is really so much more agreeable than ever that, if it were possible, she is the only object capable of creating jealousy; but I believe were my sentiments for her duely distinguishd, the tenderest of them would be owing to her being your daughter and the sweet resemblances she bears to her mother, upon which account I hope you'l pardon the passion of her and your admirer, Hervey.

349.   Lady Hervey to John Hervey.   London, April 21, 1711.

How coud my dear dear angel (that always thinks so right) believe that my illness in my head (which they say is vapours) coud be from any cause but your absence; but I must give you the ease of knowing tis so farr from being what you guessd, that I never kept so good hours in my life, for I've always gone to bed at twelve and sometimes sooner; yet notwithstanding this, I was so full of pain when I wrote last that I woud say nothing of it; but I am much better now of that, but very ill still in my head, as the Duke of Kent (who is gone to day) will give you an account, for he playd at omber here last night, and I was so very bad that if my Lady Orkney had not been my half I coud not have held out. I was at home (though Mrs. Dunch dind with me) most of the day alone, which I spent in your closet reading your dear letters; though that pleasd me very much at the time, I believe it had not a very good effect upon my spirits afterwards, when I considerd I was like to be without their dear inditer so long, though my Lord Kent has promisd to gain me a day by joining his horses with yours, to come through on Saturday, if that will suit with your affairs. I beg you woud let me know whenever it is the post before, for if I shoud be abroad

or have any engagement, it woud vex me sadly ; as I was to hear that Jack
was at Newmarket of the Friday when you orderd him to go home a Thursday, and to make it worse he was at dice at the Chocolate house. I am sorry
I am forcd to make complaints of him, but to say the truth I think Will
Oliver as much to blame as he to let him ; but (by some storys I have heard
of him since you went) I believe he was quite as well pleasd with it, especially the play part ; this hint may make you enquire a little in to that
matter, if you think it worth your while ; for my part I think nothing so but
to consider (if that is possible) how to love you enough, and to be so blessd
as to make you as happy as this world and the entire possession of my poor
(but faithful) heart is capable of. Kiss Sweet-face for me, though I grudge it
her. I was at Mr. Dauls's yesterday morning, and he has desird me to sitt
once more, that he may mend my picture before the Dutchess of Marlborough
sees it. I woud be glad in this and every thing else to know your mind first.
He says he never heard of our being there, else he woud not have faild either
to have come or sent to know your commands. There is not a word of news
stirring, but I heard the History of the October Club commended, so have
given it to Mrs. Maynard to bring you ; if you will send on Monday night,
she will be at Bury by the stage coach ; or if you are at Newmarket then, I
have desird her to leave it there. I wish you good luck, and shoud be glad,
if you think there is a sure match, if you coud win my £20 back that Dun
lost ; I will venture to loose £30 more, and with that to win as much as you
can. My dear dear, farewell.

350.   My ever-new Delight   Ickworth, April 23, 1711.
                    Finding Milton very uneasy at the proposal I made
her of staying here till your return from the Bath, fearing (as I perceivd) her
absence from a sick sister might prejudice her more in point of interest than
our service woud compensate, I resolvd to prepare for her discharge, and have

Vol. I.   o o

employd this whole day in paying off her wages and the House-book, and fixing two inventories (one to be left with Betty, the other to be kept by you,) wherein are included all the goods sent hither since Milton came to this time. The inventory you referrd me to in your chest helpd us very little, being only an old one of Bury goods, with some entries in Will Carus's hand of some things sent hither in 1709; but I woud have you satisfyd that (I hope) this matter is as well settled as it coud be in your absence, and that there is not one thing tumbled or misplaced in your chest, which I know will be good news to you, considering whose hands the key was entrusted in. I am so fatigued with the business I have gone through within and without doors to day, that nothing but conversing thus with thee coud support my spirits enow to keep me out of bed, which I cannot care to go to till I have told thee how very welcome that passage in your last dear letter was to me, where you tell me nothing is worth your while but to love me enough (if that's possible), and to make me happy in the entire possession of a faithful heart. O my dear! the bare repetition of it is such a cordial to my mind that it has wholly unwearied me of my days work; ney, it has so endeard the labour of it to me, that I shoud gladly pass through such another to morrow, woud it shorten my absence but one minute from that kind soul, which has so amply anticipated its own wishes as to leave me never a one to make but that God woud please to continue your life and love, and to make me worthy of both. Your grudging Sweet-face* a kiss (which I gave her in your name) was due to the declaration she made Sir William Gage upon asking her, who she woud have for her husband? answering, My Papa.—Do with Daule just as you like best. I shall endeavour to retrieve your loss by Dun, and hope my genius will prompt me to do as much better for you as I love you much more than my self, being most entirely and only yours, Hervey.

* John Hervey's marginal note says, Nan.   S.II.A.II.

P.S.—On Sunday night expect me, but it is impossible before. I cant get from hence till Wednesday. I thank you for your History of the October Club.

351.   Lady Hervey to John Hervey.   London, April 24, 1711.

My dear dear Angel

I was very sorry to see by the list of matches in yesterdays Courant that there was not only a match on Saturday but Monday too, which has put me in some fright for fear you may be concernd in it, or a mind to see it. I fear you will think this very unreasonable in me after your kind indulgence to my fondness to punish your self for this ugly Bath journey, which I wont yet despair but that it may be put off, for I've been much better of my pain this three or four days, which I dare say you will be as glad to hear as I was to hear you coud not be pleasd at Ickworth without me ; I am sorry you had any other reason to dislike it, by this dismal weather, which the Duke of Grafton says you did not want, for he said he coud not make his horse gallop in any part of the park for dirt, though it was dusty every where else, (I told him I woud tell you.) Visc presents his service to you, and says you had best make hast to Town, for every body is so kind to me in your absence that he is afraid you will be forgot. I told him I always thought he was a sad lover, but now I was convinced of it ; but he is so farr right that if I coud tast any pleasure without you, my friends are all so charitable that they do what they can to contribute towards it, for I have been invited abroad to dinner every day since you went, and for every day to come of this week, and some suppers. Last Sunday the Dutchess of Shrewsbury invited me to dinner, but I was engagd, but she said she woud take no denial but upon a promise for next Sunday and to come to play there on Thursday ; this was all with wonderful expressions of kindness too long to be expressd in this paper, and I am afraid you will think most of this might have been spard, but I am like Sir Martin, when my hand is in I must go on though it is nothing to the purpose, and indeed nothing is without I coud tell you how full my heart is of you, and how much and dearly I love you, and am with the most tender affection faithfully yours, E. Hervey.

P.S.—Pray let me know by the next post the day and hour you will be in Town. The Game bill was passd to day. Next to you I long to see dear Sweet-face, but that is so impossible I dare not think of it. I have such a horrid pen & ink I am afraid you cant read this.

352.   My ever-new Delight   Newmarket, April 25, 1711.

I am gott thus far on my way towards thee, which I long so impatiently to be at the end of, that no matches or other consideration can tempt me to retard beyond Sunday next, altho' there are several made for Monday and Tuesday after, which I am glad of for no other reason but that they'l afford me several small sacrifices to my superior inclination. The good news your letter brought me this evening of your pains being so abated for 3 or 4 days that you dont yet despair but that the Bath journey may be deferrd, gives me a joy inexpressible abstracted from the consequence of spending this spring at Ickworth; for thy precious life is of so inestimable a value to me that the restoration of your health (could it be purchasd no other way) woud make me easily consent to a perpetual banishment from it for the remainder of my days, and think the bargain cheap. Your telling me any body is kind or charitable to you in my absence overcomes all my prejudices to them on other peoples score to that degree that it almost converts them into friendships; seeing therefore the force of my predominant passion for you, it ought to make you nice in suffering civilities from some, least it makes me unawares ingrateful to others; ney, I must confess it to you, (since I know you're too good ever to make a wrong use of such a foiblesse, if it ought to be so calld,) my fondness of you for the uncommon virtues you are so absolute a mistress of is grown up to the pitch describd in Othello.

> His soul is so enfetterd to her love
> That she may make, unmake, do what she list,
> Even as her appetite shall play the God
> With his weak function.

A good night, and Adieu till Sunday, till when and ever may blessings, such as my most zealous wishes for thee in their greatest extasies coud never reach, attend thee is the constant prayer of your pious petitioner, Hervey.

353.   Lady Hervey to John Hervey.   London, April 26, 1711.

It woud sound like affectation to any thing but such a tender sympathizing soul as you (or rather, I am blessd with in you,) to say I'm sure I felt (at least) as much uneasyness at reading your dear letter to hear of the fatigue you underwent that day as you had in the performance of it, and as a weighty addition to know that I was the cause of it. Sure, my dear dear angel, you coud not think of me when you did it, or why woud you tell me of it but by your self, which woud soon make up that and all my other sufferings by your absence. I am glad you have relievd me of my fears of your staying on Monday by saying I may expect you on Sunday night, though I must confess (till you told me how impossible it was) I had a little hopes of seeing you on Saturday, enough to hinder me from being engagd but upon condition to be releasd if you came, though I have been mightily sollicited for the Opera for the benefit of Pilota, who has a great interest made against her because she came from Hanover, and has so many Whigg friends, in which number she reckons me, and has been to see me, so I have taken a ticket and now promisd to go, being out of hopes of being better entertained. Yesterday I dind with Lady Dalkeith, and she and Lady Katt: supd with me after the Opera, which was as full as ever I saw it at a subscription, but that was by way of party, in order to get it empty on Saturday. I know this is sad enter-

tainment for you, but there is not a word of news, so you must be contented
to let me go on in this way, and tell you that I dind to day with my Lady
Orkney, where I met Mrs. Ramsey, who presents her service to you, and
says she longs to see you to tell you of a new lover of mine, that was the
whole discourse of the Dutchess of Northumberland's circle last Sunday, but
he is so extraordinary a one that I think I ought to give your mind the ease
of knowing he is with you ; but I will not let you lose her entertainment by
telling you any more ; I am to meet her again to night (with the Dutchess
of Grafton) at supper at my Lady Cornwallis's ; to morrow I am to dine at
my Lady Portland's, and Saturday at Mrs. Dunch's, and for Sunday I have
told you already. Now I have given you this account of the whole week, I
think I may bid my dear angel adieu till we meet ; till that long time, Fare-
wel.

P.S.—I still continue to be much better ; my blessing to Jack and the rest
of the dear children, if you are to see them any more ; I dare not name
Sweet-face, for fear I shoud be to particular. For God's sake take care of
the waters, for I hear they are very much out.

354.   To Sir Richard Cockes.   May 13, 1711.
                        The friendly office you intended me by your last
letter deserves my earlyest & best acknowledgements, which this comes to
pay you. I am very much obligd to ye gentleman, (or rather (I believe) to
your kind representations of both,) for his favourable opinion of me and my
son, who is so fortunate hitherto as to be in ye good graces of all who know
him ; and if ye comon rules of modesty woud admit of so much truth &
justice from me to him, I woud fain tell you as a well wisher to my family
he so far deserves their esteem & my affection that I know no vice he does
not avoid as unworthy, nor no virtue he does not practice as ye duty of such
a gentleman as Gods grace and his own happy disposition are concurring to

ye forming of; I mean one as much after his heart as he is entirely after mine. And that you may believe this is not said with any view to ye treaty you so kindly proposd ye overture of, I must acquaint you he was gone for Holland in order to his travels before your letter reached me at Newmarket; so that nothing can (at present) be farther done or said thereupon than that a most gratefull remembance of your well meant part therein shall always be preservd in his mind, who is with much sincerity your etc.

355.   To ye Prince and Duke of Marlborough.

My Lord   Aswarby, July 2, 1711.

The distinguishing civilities your Graces goodness was pleasd to honour my son with, when he waited on you at ye Camp to pay part of that duty which he and I so justly owe you, makes it necessary for me to give your Grace ye trouble of my earlyest and best acknowledgments for them, I must confess with some concern that I have hitherto been one of your unprofitable, well-wishing servants only, but hope he may live to discharge some of ye vast arrear your Graces friendship & favours have made his father so long your debtor for. It has been some ease to me in ye mean time to feel so very gratefull a sense of them as I have constantly done, since I've heard it quoted as a maxim in morality as well as in religion, (supposing an incapacity of better returns,)

> That thanks and gratitude pays all we owe
> To God above, or our best friends below. ·

Your Graces kindness has been so much more obliging as it coud not possibly be otherwaies repaid; and since I find my self equally at a loss how rightly to thank you for, as to deserve, it, I ought not to inlarge on a theme I'm sure not to succeed in, farther than to assure your Grace there is no one you ever did me but has made such indelible impressions on my heart, that I shoud esteem it as one of ye most fortunate occurrences which coud happen

to me in ye remainder ot my life, woud Providence bless me with any effectual opportunity of shewing your Grace that, tho' you may have many more
usefull, yet in ye world you cannot have a more sincere & faithful etc.

My wife is your Graces most obedient servant.

356.   To Sir Hervey Elwes.   Aswarby, July 16, 1711.
     Dear Nephew

                    I always told you, ever since I knew in how ill a
condition your grandfather left you and as often as those circumstances
became ye subject of our discourse, that there were but two expedients to
make you easy under them ; either to sell your mortgagd lands, or endeavour to redeem them by a wife's portion. I cant but think, had ye latter
been your aim, you coud not in all this time have missd of a fortune (with
your youth, person and estate,) sufficient for that purpose ; and since I find
it is not, I know of no other ressource but to look out for a purchaser, which
as trade and credit now stand, will prove as difficult a task as ye other.
You are like to prove a double sufferer by delay, as taxes & repairs have been
borne by you in ye interim, and as ye value of land is year by year decreas-
ing ; I can therefore still think of no better advice to give you than my
former, which is to come to a speedy resolution either to proceed in one or
t'other, and to put either you can first attain to into an imediate execution ;
and in ye mean time to let Mr. Guidott know you are determind to sell rather
than pay £6 per cent ; and to shew him ye sincerity of such intention send
him a particular of ye estates you woud alienate, desiring him (if it lies in
his way) to procure you a purchaser for them. I hope there is no mistake
or difference between you as to ye payments I made on your account for
interest, having paid her Grace £250 on ye 10th Sept. 1709, & £250 more on
ye 12th January following to ye D. of Marlborough by a bill of Coggs's,
which he desird me to take. If you can tell me of any way in my power how

this heavy burthen of yours may be made lighter to you, it shall be readily pursued by your etc. My wife and I give our services to your sisters. If you'l come hither yee shall be all welcome.

357.   To ye Earl of Albemarle.   Aswarby, July 3, 1711.
    My Lord

My son was too proud of and well pleased with ye honours your Lordship did him at Tournay to let me be long ignorant how very much he and I have been obligd to your Lordships kindness for them.   Your Lordship cannot add a greater favour to those you have already done me than by your Lordship's or my Lady Albemarle's (to whom my wife & self are most humble servants) honouring us with some of your commands in this country, which, as it woud afford us an opportunity of discharging part of a just debt, woud be paid with pleasure by, my Lord, your etc.

358.   To Mr. Masson.   Aswarby, July 5, 1711.

I hope my son continues well, and that he receivd ye letter I last directed to him at ye Hague, as I have yours from Brussels of ye 27th past, wherein I'm glad to find how very kindly he has been receivd by all my friends at ye army, (for which I have sent my particular thanks to ye Duke of Marlborough & my Lord of Albemarle;) & am yet better pleased with ye account you sent me of his right behaviour upon those and all other occasions.   May Minerva (by which I mean God's all sufficient grace) attend on him as closely throughout his travels as she did Ulysses, & then you'l find him feed so plentifully on Mercury's salutiferous herb Moly as to avoid all Circe's fatal enchantments.   He who seems so blessd by nature as to have few or none evil inclinations to subdue, has ye transporting prospect, both for himself & those who have or are to have any interest in him, of being able to carry on and end his life with that sweet tranquility

    Vol. I.   P P

and indolence of mind, which ye best & wisest men in all ages have chiefl
aimd at by an innocent and honourable conduct thro ye world. He i
hitherto, God be praised, likely to make that shining part of Brutus's char
acter his own :—his life was gentle, & ye elements so justly mixd in hin
that nature might boast to all ye world & say, This was a man. One wou
think he had chosen Sir Philip Sidney for his modell, who was sweetly grave
familliarly obliging, of an equal temper, & such strict moralls that he taugh
England ye majesty of honest dealing and true interest of being sober an
religious ; who lookd with usefull curiosity into men and things, and s
happy in all he said or did that he seemd born for every thing he went about
Such, if I am not partially deceivd, are ye promising materials your skill &
care have ye encouragement to work upon, and I make no doubt but you'
improve them accordingly. Shoud I overvalue his meritt or overlook hi
faults, I depend intirely on your sincerity (in friendship to us both) to shev
me my mistakes & to rectify his errors whensoever they appear. It may b
I have been guilty of a great one in revealing my thoughts so farr concern
ing him ; but if you think so, correct it with your prudence by letting hin
know my mind no farther than you find his can well and wisely bear it.
had never venturd to disclose my sentiments of him or to him but as he gav
early marks of that laudable disposition Quintilian declared for in a youth
mihi detur ille puer, quem laus excitet, quem gloria juvet, qui victus fleat
But by this time tis possible I may have said too much of him even to you
& therefore will conclude with telling you there is little news here but wha
has been occasiond by a reigning mortality among our great ones ; ye Duke
of Rutland, Bedford & Newcastle being dead on one side, & ye Duke o
Queensborough & ye Earle of Rochester on t'other ; Mr. Vice-Chamberlaii
Bertie dyed also suddenly last week. These accidents remind me of thank
ing God for Carr's health & safety, & to pray for ye continuance of both a
ye second blessing Heaven can bestow on his affectionate father and you
most assured friend, etc.

359.   To Sir William Gage.   Aswarby, July 23, 1711.

Dear Cousin

You coud not have made use of a much more attoning reason for disappointing my wife & me in ye pleasure we promisd our selves of seeing my Lady Gage and you at this place than by letting us know twas occasiond thro business tending to so agreable a purpose as shortning ye distance between her neighbourhood & ours, which I cant but humbly hope will have ye same good effect upon our friendship too, since we have gradually found (as you told me) she is one of those rare and valuable acquaintances who—si propius stes te capiet magis, and that we may (at least) promise our selves ye more yee know of us it will not fright yee farther from us. This being the state of our case, I depend on your good offices to make our future correspondencies (which with no small uneasiness to me have been too long interrupted) as intimate as has been always sincerely wishd for, both as I've ye honour of being descended from a Jermyn & as I am your etc.

My wife is a servant to you both.

360.   To Francis Hayes, Esqr., at his Chambers in ye Inner Temple.

Sir   Aswarby near Sleeford, July 23, 1711.

The fee-farm rent of four pounds per annum issuing out of a mesuage and lands in Pinchbeck, (formerly Capt. Thos: Ogles, &) which you lately purchasd of Sir Robert Dashwood (who constantly paid ye same) or his heirs, being again in arrear ever since Ladyday 1705, I hope you will give order for ye speedy payment of it to some one agent or tennant of yours in these parts, who may at ye same time be directed by you to discharge it yearly as ye same shall grow due hereafter, that you may have no more troubles of this kind from your etc.

361.   The Duke of Marlborough to Lord Hervey. Aug. 20, 1711.
     My Lord

I have the favour of your Lordships letter and am extreamly pleasd to think it was in my power to shew any civilities to Mr. Hervey. You are too kind in your acknowledgements, since they could no ways deserve those you make me; you may be sure I shall always be glad to embrace any opportunity that may offer to shew my friendship to Lord Hervey or any of his. I will not trouble your Lordship with what passes here; you will see it in the prints. We have overcome many difficulties, and I hope shall succeed in the siege notwithstanding the enemy's superiority; it will be of great consequence to the Publick. Pray make my compliments to Lady Hervey, and believe me with much truth, my Lord, your Lordship's most faithfull, humble servant, Marlborough.

362.   To Sir John Newton.   London, Aug. 23, 1711.

Being removed out of Lincolnshire into Suffolk & thence hither, your letter of ye 14th instant did not reach me till yesterday, which makes mention of a former one I never receivd, otherwise you shoud not have faild of an answer to both. I am not a little concernd to find there shoud be any concurrence between us for Willoughby, since it might probably have been prevented either by letting me know your mind or asking me my own before I was actually engaged in ye purchase of it; altho' I never made it any secret that I woud endeavour to lay it to ye rest of my estate (which almost surrounds it) & is (at least) as convenient for me as it can be for any other person, having procurd a particular of it several years since when I heard it was to be disposd of, which I have now by me; so that I cant imagine upon what grounds any assurances coud be reasonably given that I woud not bid for it as well as others, since I was an original dealer for it in Sir S. Barnardiston's time; & being considerd only on that foot I cant but think my self free (since you own £8500 is ye utmost ye estate is worth, & that I have already bid £8400 for it,) in case more is offerd for it hereafter to do by others as is done to, Sir, your.

363.   To Mrs. Felton.   Bath, Sept. 1, 1711.
Madam

I hope this last fit of ye gout has given Sir Compton Felton less pain than usual, since it occasiond me so great a pleasure as a letter from you, wherein you so well acquitted your self as no modesty but your own woud have apprehended a censure from ye severest critick; if you had any thing to fear from me twas want of taste; but ye merit of it was sufficient even to secure applause from a discernment as gross as mine.   I beg leave to give my humble service to my Lady and Sir Compton Felton, & that you'd let them know, if they like Ickworth venison, I've left order with my Park keeper to obey any order they shall send for more at this or any other time.   I hope to get thither by Bury fair, which if you like well enough to bear with ye inconveniencies of our lowly Lodge for ye time it lasts, you will be most welcome to my wife, (who is a faithful servant to all at Playford,) and if possible more so to, Madam, your etc.

364.   To Mr. Battely.   Bath, Sept. 1. 1711.
My good friend

Your kindness has done my birth day more honour than it deserves in remembring of it, unless some part of ye remainder of that life you so cordially wish ye continuance of may prove of some service to you, whose friendship has increasd with them from ye first to ye last; in ye mean time I return you wish for wish with equal zeal that perfect health, prosperity & longevity may attend you, not only as my particular friend but for ye publick good, as you have done and will still do many right and use-

full things in your generation ; among which I think ye putting Dr. B——
out may be reckond, wherein I doubt not your influence had its wonted share,
as well as in substituting one more worthy of authority in his place, who I dare
say will never abuse ye power he's intrusted with to punish his innocent neighbours & colleagues, whose only fault was having more zeal than ye then
magistrate coud bear. I hope your new elect will also act like a new convert
with extraordinary zeal for ye right interest of Bury. As to ye other matter
you mention, as soon as I get to Ickworth, (which I hope will be in three
weeks,) whatever is necessary shall be imediately orderd by your etc.

365. To Mr. Hervey, Minister of Methringham.
Sir   Bath, Sept. 10, 1711.

As you have only acquainted me with ye hard-
ships you lye under from ye arbitrary power of ye Chancellour's Court, without mentioning ye proper remedies that may be taken for redressing them,
(to which I am an utter stranger,) I know not what more to say at present
than that if there be any legal course to be pursued, whereby they may be
certainly removd, let me know it from some authentick person throughly
versed in ye proceedings of those venerable Courts, and you shall find me
as ready as you can wish to see justice done you. I cant conclude without
desiring you woud in a most particular manner give my service and thanks
to Sir W. Ellis for all his kindness and favours towards you, & that you woud
let him know I have thought my self doubly unlucky this year, to miss of ye
satisfaction I promisd my self in his conversation both in Lincolnshire and
at this place, ye hope of meeting him here being one of ye chief comforts
expected to make it agreeable to your etc.

366. To Mr. Jodrell.   Bath, Sept. 10, 1711.
I herewith return you ye Decretall order, wherein I

can observe but two things which want amendment; ye one is that it does
not appear ye Church has receivd much more advantage than any of ye land
owners (proportionally) by ye inclosure; ye other that you allow no time
between ye Vicar's demand and his making distress, which is usually from
20 to 40 days. When these are rectified, you may proceed to ye passage and
enrollment of it. I desire if any thing has passd or shall hereafter be done
relating to ye play-house affair, that you woud from time to time communicate ye same to your etc.

367.　To the Duke of Marlborough.

My Lord

Your Grace's last self surpassing scheme, which
so dexterously duped the Mareshall de Villars out of his non plus ultra lines,
& shewd him they were no more impregnable to your transcendent genius
than Boncham was relieveable by his superiour army, has equally demon-
strated your mastery in stratagems and a most through knowledge of ye
Carte du pais you are acting in. Non alium ducem opportunitates locorum
sapientius legisse, said Tacitus of Agricola; but how much more justly
applicable to your self? since nothing but ye nicest & more criticall learning
in that necessary science of your profession coud possibly have enabled you
to undertake & succeed in a siege where, tho you foresaw ye enemy might
probably post themselves almost within cannon shot of your approaches, yet
rightly judgd they woud never be able (thro ye precautions in your power)
effectually to disturb either them or your convoys. If ever mortal man was
blessd with so skillful a prudence as (under Providence) to secure events,
you are he; whose veneration for your virtues and ye many signal services
they have brought to pass for ye publick good increases proportionally as you
continue still to exert them for ye peace & prosperity of a people, who if
they shoud not all prove so worthy as they ought to be of their severall

shares in your universal benefits by ye utmost affection and thankfullness towards ye author of them, so black an ingratitude woud only serve to brighten your character, and indear you more & more (if possible) to all true lovers of their country; among whom permitt me to claim not ye last place, being with a most sincere respect your etc.

My wife is your Graces most humble servant, and joyns in all congratulations.

368. To Mr. Carr Hervey. Bath, Sept. 17, 1711. (his birth-day).

My dear son

Twenty yeares time has now gradually increasd ye joy I first felt for ye blessing this happy day afforded me, since each of them have passd in such agreeable progressions of your improvement as my best prayers (thro' God's grace) have fervently desird for you. I have long since observd you wise enough to know our years renew in vain unless we become better by them, and that a long life must prove rather worse than never to have had a being when not spent in virtuous and praiseworthy actions. Yours is so well begun that I may with all modest assurance hope it will be prolongd not only for your own, but mine, your countrys & familys sake; for I see nothing in you yet but what gives each a hopefull earnest of your proving ye just & general pride of all. May your autumnall fruits surpass even ye blooming promises of your spring; & may all your travels & studies tend more towards making you a good & wise than ye most learned or politick man that ever was. Then you'l make that noble figure described by Sir Thomas Brown :— stand magnetically upon that axis where prudent simplicity hath fixd thee, and let not ye ocean of temptations, tho' nere so brightly baited, invert ye poles of thy integrity; and that all sorts of vice may become uneasy and even monstrous to thee, let repeated good actions and long confirmd habitts make vertue natural or a second nature to thee;

and since few or none prove eminently virtuous but from some advantagious foundations in their temper & natural inclinations, study thy self betimes, and early find out what degree in true meritt thou art capable of. They who thus timely descend into themselves, cultivating those noble seeds which nature hath planted in them, and improving their virtuous dispositions to perfection, become not shrubs but cedars in their generation ; and to be in ye indifferent form of ye best of ye bad or ye worst of ye good will be no sort of satisfaction to them.—I so throughly approve Mr. Masson's scheme of your travells, that I enjoyn your staying at Venice no longer than ye beginning of ye year, otherwise twill not be possible for you to avoid ye heats, and get to Hannover time enough to stay so long there as I woud have you, and be at home so early in ye winter as I expect to see you. When you are at Venice, be sure to make your Mama's and my compliments to Seignor Cornaro in ye best manner possible, and let no consideration prevail with you to stay longer there than till ye beginning of ye year, because twill frustrate my project as to ye latter end of your travells. Give my service to Mr. Masson, and let him know neither he nor you write so often as you promisd, which is a sensible disappointment to me, since there's no passage relating to your health or journey but whats most welcome to your most affectionate father.

369. The Duke of Marlborough to Lord Hervey. Oct. 28, 1711.
My Lord

I cannot enough thank your Lordship for the favour of your letter upon the success of our campaigne. I hope every body will do me the justice to allow I have done all I coud to serve the Publick ; but the kind things you are pleasd to say on that subject must be intirely owing to your friendship. Our campaigne is now happily over, and the troops marching to winter quarters ; but I shall be obligd to stay here

Vol. I. Q Q

three or four days longer to give the necessary orders upon this frontier, and then design to hasten to the Hague in hopes soon to meet you and Lady Hervey in perfect health. In the mean time I pray you will assure her of my humble service, and believe me truly, my Lord, your Lordships most faithful, humble servant, Marlborough.

370.   Lady Hervey to John Hervey.   Ickworth, Nov. 1711.

I found such a dismal sight when I come of your poor daughter that struck me to the heart; but as soon as I coud recover my self I spoke to her, and she talkd of Newmarket and our going to London as sensibly as ever she did in her life, and told me what a load of things Mr. Batteley had given her since I went; just as she was speaking they brought more things, and she said, Do but see now how many more they have brought me; but I have promisd her she shoud take nothing but what was absolutely necessary, and she is very well satisfyd. I sent for Mr. Battely, and have got him to give her such a kind of mixture as Jack took, ... I have put him in mind of giving her a strengthening glister, which she is just now going to take. Pray God it may have the success that is most heartily prayd for by your faithfull E. Hervey.

P.S.—The postilion is so very ill, I was afraid I shoud not have got home with him; therefore I desire you woud send the boy that rode before to be here between 8 & 9, that I may either come to you or send him back as this night proves; she is now in a quiet sound sleep; pray send me word what you woud have done to night by the boy in the morning. I have reckond my money, and I think I am pretty sure Mr. Cottons is 148 or 138, I cant be certain which till I've time to think a little more.

371.   My ever-new Delight   Newmarket, Nov. 1711.

A thousand thanks for thy dear letter, altho' it

brought me not so good news as I wishd, neither of your self or poor Bell.
I have sent Cunningham to have it in your power either to go or stay as you
see occasion ; pray flatter me not and let me know the truth, whatever it is,
if you find her not well enough to come your self. Mr. Cotton's card made
your debt £148. The Duke of Bolton won only one game, but no party by the
night. Our common stock lost 16 by betting, and I lost 6 for you at bassett,
much to the displeasure and disappointment of so zealous a well wisher as
your most constant, faithful friend & lover, Hervey.

372.   To the Dutchess of Marlborough.   Jan. 2, 1711/12.
          Madam

                      Having often endeavourd unsuccessfully to find an
opportunity of speaking to your Grace on an unhappy subject which still lies
heavy at my heart, forces me at last to take this liberty of begging your
Grace woud not deny that relief to one, who, as he acknowledges himself
ye most obliged, so you shall ever find him ye most faithfull of all your
friends & most obedient of all your servants.

373.   To Mr. Alderman Wright.   London, Jan. 24, 1711/2.
          My good and steady friend

                      If we have any one among us so very unreasonably
variable as not to be retain'l unless he be indulgd by two complyances,
either of which will inevitably sap ye very foundations of that honest interest
we have with so much care and industry establishd, I desire we may rather
run ye risque of loosing such a friend than be sure of entertaining two such
vipers in our bosom as will not fail to prey upon ye vitals of that power which
are to give them birth to its own destruction ; above all things, therefore,
avoid falling into any such fatal snare, let ye motives seem never so specious.
Were not my poor wife in hourly expectation of being brought to bed, I woud

have been with you as soon as I had learnd ye Recorder's death.   But that's
too important a circumstance to admitt of my taking such a journey at
present.   If our friends woud be so wise as by an unanimous adherence to
any one person shoud throw cold water on Sir R. D's pretensions for his son,
ye consequence of shewing such a spirit early woud be that he, dispairing of
carrying that favourite point, might be induced to sit passive as to ye moving
for a new writ this session, (which I've employd a friend to persuade him in,)
and then you might honour my son with ye vacancy at his return from his
travels, he being of age on ye 17th of Sept. next.   But this hint I leave to
be improvd by you as occasion offers.   I have repeated your answer to Mr.
Warren to ye Duke of Marlborough & Prince Eugene, (who were both together at my house,) & they both agreed twas ye best thing has been said
on ye occasion.   My hearty service to all true townsmen concludes this from
your etc.

   374.   To Mr. Samuel Battely.   London, Jan. 26, 1711.
     My faithfull friend

              I so entirely approve of ye choice our Corporation
has centerd in for successour to Serjeant Weld as Burgess of Bury upon ye
publick account, that were your reasons as opposite as they are agreeable to
all my private views and interests, I could not but applaud it.   You may
have forgot, but I never can, how long since my opinion was the town coud
not pitch upon a more proper person than your self to represent it, and I
think my self doubly happy that the Body has now furnishd me with an occasion to shew how sincere my sentiments were on that subject; for tho'
there was a project to protract ye motion for a new writt in case our friend
shoud find his cake dough for his son, yet I'm so throughly satisfyd with ye
wise and seasonable turn our town has given to this important election,
(whereon ye improvement or destruction of ye true and honest interest of ye

place so absolutely depends,) that I hereby relinquish and disclaim all other expedients, and shall accordingly promote ye motion (instead of obstructing one) for a new writt, whereby you may be returnd to Parliament, where such honest, unbyassd, disinterested members as your self were never more wanted than at this time to take care of ye publick; since not only ye fate of Brittain, but of Europe, rests upon ye resolutions which may be taken upon ye present conjuncture of affairs, wherein the family and fortunes are involvd of your etc.

375.   To Mr. Hervey.   London, Jan. 29, 1711/12.
    Dear Carr

      Mr. Masson's of ye 15th instant (N.S.) from Venice is just now come to my hands; wherein he acquaints me how sensibly the news of your dear sister's death has afflicted you, notwithstanding all ye prudent precautions I desird him to use in the breaking of it to you. I hope your consideration for me will enable you to bear her loss so as I may meet with no additional sufferings to those just and natural ones I have already felt by being deprivd of one of ye most dutifull and faultless children any parent was ever blessd with ; or if that shoud prove insufficient, there is yet a more powerfull persuasive than my sake, which is that you woud remember twas God's will it shoud be so ; & (believe me) ye earlyer you can learn that necessary, tho' difficult, lesson of resigning yours entirely to his, the more pure and uninterrupted will those pleasures prove which he may intend you shoud enjoy in ye course of your life; & ye more easily & with less reluctancy will you part from them when his Providence sees fitt to withdraw any of them. Lett us take St. Jerom's advice : Non mæremus quod talem amisimus, sed gratias agimus quod talem habuimus; imo habemus, Deo enim vivunt omnia, et quicquid revertitur ad Dominum, in familiæ numero computatur : since (in his sense) you'l find she's not (even now) quite lost

to us. For my part, considering ye thorough progress she had made in all
piety and vertue, I shall always reckon it a particular honour & blessing
she ever was a member of my family ; & when I reflect how little inviting
this world must have appeard to a soul so well prepard as hers was for a
better, instead of lamenting I think we shoud rather (on her account) congratulate death (as Cowley did her great uncle Herveys).

> O happy Bell ! ta'ne from this wicked age,
> Where naught but malice & hypocrisy does rage ;
> A fitter time for Heaven no soul ere chose,
> The only blessed place, now free from those.

The having been taken away in ye prime of her life may seem to superficial observers ye most comiserable circumstance in her case ; but those
who can penetrate to ye bottom of such dispensations make truer estimates
of such exchanges, and rightly represent them thus :

> He that surveys ye world with serious eyes,
> And strips it of its gross yet weak disguise,
> Will find tis injury to mourn her fate ;
> They only dye untimely whe dye late.

Besides, si munera cœli bene computamus, diu vixit ; so that I shall close
all my arguments & exhortations to you with that comfortable conclusion my
most dear and pious father rested in upon ye death of your most excellent
grandmother Hervey : Mortua obtinuit plurima quæ meruit.—   I
thank you for your letters, (which I find no fault with but that they are too
short & come too seldom,) particularly for those passages relating to L.P.,
which I shewd to D.M., who read them with pleasure to find your friendship
and mine so firmly fixd to him in these trying times. I'm glad to see your
conversation lyes so much among ye best men you meet with; tis a sure
mark of your right taste, & no small one of theirs. Serjeant Weld dyed

suddenly of an apoplexy last week, so that Bury is unprovided of a Recorder & a Burgess. Mr. Turnor sollicits to supply ye former vacancy, and I believe Mr. Battelly will accept ye latter as your trustee till your return, which he has already kindly signifyd to be his only purpose in medling with it. Inclosed is a letter from your cousen Baron, & the coppy of an Epistle dedicatory which Doctor Garth desird I woud send you, designd as you will see (to his new edition of Lucretius) to ye Elector of Hannover, but is not to be printed with it for prudential reasons. I'm afraid tis not correct, being transcribd by Will: Oliver, who you know is no criticall Latinist. Once more I desire Mr. Masson (to whom my service) & you woud let me hear twice a month from you between yee, which is no unreasonable request from so affectionate a father as yours etc.

376. To ye Rt Honble the Lady Isabella Turnor.

Madam   London, Feb. 12, 1711/12.

It has given me no small concern (at a time too when few things can give me much but that for my poor wife's safety) to find that Mr. Turnor has not given you ye satisfaction you expected from my kindness in his pretensions to ye Recordership of Bury. He seemd contented with what I told him relating to it, which had your Ladyship heard, I need appeal to no better judge whether more coud have been desird or said considering ye nice situation I find my self in with respect to that affair; which is so entirely ye Corporation's peculiar, that they might justly resent any invasion of it by my recomendation, unless they themselves woud first have signifyed nothing woud be done therein without such nomination from me; which they have been so far from doing (notwithstanding what his brother has heard of that kind) that I was earlily & (as I thought) prudently precautiond not to meddle in it without being first applyd to by them; and whenever they'l ask ye question, who I think ye properest person for that place, or who woud be most agreeable to me, or most serviceable to the true honest interest of all our friends, it woud be readily answerd by his and your etc. My poor wife holds out still, tho' Tuesday was her full reckoning; she's your Ladyship's servant; you shant fail of hearing when she's brought to bed.

377.   To Mr. John Wright.   London, Feb. 9, 1711/12.

I have been all along so truly sensible of your steady, disinterested adherence to my personal as well as ye publick service, that I shoud be extreamly concernd any circumstance so necessary to the preservation of both as your continuance in ye Corporation shoud prove a barr to your succeeding poor Mr. Craske in case we shoud be so unfortunate as to loose him. You can weigh ye influence & difference of such an alteration so well, and are of so right a publick spiritt, that according as you'l find ye ballance turn with respect to ye whole, I know ye determination may be entirely left with you by your etc.

My wife & I are Mrs. Wright's humble servants.

378.   To Mr. Alderman Turnor.   London, Feb. 12, 1711/12.

I have written to my Lady Isabella by this post, & because I woud avoid troubling you with repetition, will therefore referr you to that letter for a present answer to yours, wherein you'l find my case as to ye Recordership truly stated, & thereby discover my inclinations to serve your brother in it to be as sincere as you your self woud have them, they only wanting such an opportunity to exert themselves as may furnish me with a just excuse for medling in a matter out of his proper province, who will always shew in every thing that is so how much he is your etc.

My wife & I are Mrs. Turnor's humble servants.

379.   My ever-new Delight   Newmarket, April 3, 1712.

Unless it be when you vex me with setting up and destroying that health I must alone depend on for my happiness; this is to let you know both your Jacks are come well hither, and that we found Lady Thigh so too, who is more followd by all the men in this town than the brightest beauty ever was in London, except one, who I've often thought might have been yet more so, had she not gratefully prizd the humble purchase of one sincere heart before all the vain conquests of that kind, for which obliging choice I must not only owe but will for ever pay her all the constant love and services of a life long devoted to make hers as easy and as blessd (if possible) as she has done her most faithful friend's & lover's, Hervey.

380.   Lady Hervey to John Hervey.   London, April 3, 1712.

I am very impatient for to morrow's post to hear how my dear dear angel past his journey, and how he does after it, for I am afraid having so little sleep the night before may have disorderd you, for I thought you were a little hot when you went. In the next place I shall be glad to hear how Jack does, as I believe you'l be to know your dear little image is well; she told me she was come to stay with me now Papa was gone, and indeed she has kept her word, for she has not stirrd from me to day but to eat her dinner. My cough is better, but I am so hoarse I have quite lost my voice, which made me very unfit to entertain so much company as I had yesterday, for I think I hardly ever saw more in any place in my life, and all of the best sort. The Duke of Marlborough stayd above half an hour after he had done play, (talking to Monsieur Bothmar and some other of the Foreign Ministers,) which I was much surprizd at, for I thought there was some of the company which woud not be very agreeable to him, especially the Dutchess with the Gold-key, but he talkd as easy to her as if

Vol. I.   R R

nothing had happend, and stayd till past eleven a clock. But all this has not produced a word of news for you, so that you must content your self with the prints and knowing that Lord Dorchester was made a grandfather last night by Lady Kingston's being brought to bed of a son. If Colonel Butler and you have any accounts between you while you are at Newmarket, you may settle it as is most convenient to your self, that is by paying him any goldsmiths bills that you receive (for they talk so much of their breaking that even Sir Francis Childe is suspected, but Mead very much,) as far as 88 guineas, which I have in keeping for his share of our bank, besides the 50 Lord Ashburnham owes.—My heart is so very heavy to day that I cant help hiring a horse to go to Chelsea to know how poor Miss Harriot does, though I sent last night and she was pretty well. I wish I coud as easily satisfy my self about my chief treasure at Newmarket, and then my self woud be the messenger to tell my dear dear angel how much and dearly I love him, and how entirely I am his faithful E. Hervey.

331.   My ever-new Delight   Newmarket, April 5, 1712.

I hope my last letter put you at ease as to both your Jacks getting well hither, and this may satisfy you of their continuing as much so as is possible without you ; your absence makes this place so tedious that I am almost indifferent whether Ladythigh wins or looses on Monday, (altho' he is twice matchd with the same horse,) since the consequence is to be never making another match if he looses, and then I shall be sure never to be parted from you on such frivolous occasions, where none of the promisd pleasures ever at all answerd the pain. I am glad Sweetface is so throughout like me as to like your company better than all others, and am much pleasd to hear Harriott is better, who possesseth no small share of my affection, notwithstanding my heart allows Nann so Benjamin-like a portion of my kindness.—I must thank you for the hint you sent me

as to Colonel Butler's share in your bank, which I have not yet had an opportunity to make any use of, having not venturd twenty guineas at any thing,
nor will not till Monday is over.—I desird Sir William Gage to let you know
my poor Cotton colt not only won the Queen's Plate, but such immortal
honour with it by beating all the horses of his age the 3rd & 4th heats,
after having run the 1st & 2nd upon extremity also, that his name is changd
to Ickworth, since he's become so great an excellence in his kind.*—I hope
your hoarseness has left you by this time as well as your cough; I'm sure it
woud did you keep as good hours as I have done, having never been out of
my bed at twelve since I left you. I woud say much more to you, but your
son is going to sweat Union, and asks me if my letter is not long enough till
next post, so that I must till then deferr the rest to please him, at the ex-
pense of his satisfaction who is entirely and only yours, Hervey.

382.   Lady Hervey to John Hervey.   London, April 5, 1712.

Sir William Gage has just sent me the good news
of my dear dear angels being well, and that you won the Plate, of which I
wish you more joy than I am able to feel for any thing in your absence, which
I think I bear worse (if possible) then ever, being every day more and more
engagd by new proofs of your kindness, of which your dear letter yesterday
is a witness, and that I may be sure not to forget it by sitting up to hurt my
health, I have given over play, though I am afraid you'l think I have not
been very regular when I tell you my cold is still bad, though much better,
yet I venture to the Opera, because poor Pilota has great faction made
against her. The Dutchess of Grafton and Sir Thomas Hanmer is to sup
with me after, which forces me to finish my letter now, and not without some
difficulty, they are talking so fast about me, for I am with Mrs. Dunch sitting for her picture; she presents her service to you, and wishes you good

---

* Pencil marginal note says, This horse I gave to Sir Thomas Hanmer.

luck on Munday, and so does Lady Ann Hervey; she says she has bought
Mr. Hervey's bett of him on purpose to bring you good luck, for she never
lost a bett in her life. They tell me all the company comes on Tuesday,
and that it is very necessary you shoud all be here, which makes me hope
I shall hear by Monday's post that Ickworth and this fine weather wont carry
it against us all, but in particular for her sake that longs to see you with the
last impatience, being with all the tenderness of a grateful heart, my dear
dear life, most faithfully yours, E. Hervey.

P.S.—The children are all well, and little Hercules increases in beauty
and strength every day. There is not a word of news. I have kept my letter open till now in hopes Sir Thomas Hanmer coud tell me some news, but
he says he knows none but that he is going into Holland with the Duke of
Ormond; he presents his service to you, and says he shall be glad to receive
your commands; he tells me he goes in no publick character, but only for
his own inclinations; but it seems to me as if there was some mystery in
it; when I know more you shall hear it. It is now so late I must make use
of the proffer Lord Kingston made me to carry this, being past eleven a
clock. The Dutchess of Graftons being here makes me write in such a hurry
that I am afraid you wont be able to read it.

383.   My ever-new Delight   Newmarket, April 6, 1712.

No less reason than your express desire coud have
prevaild with me to send you any piece of news so disagreeable to you as I
know that of the loss of Ladythigh's match must prove; my greatest comfort is that as it is the first great match the Duke of Rutland ever won, so it
shall be the last (upon my word) I'll ever make.—Had I not appointed my
tenants to be at Ickworth on Friday & Saturday next, you shoud have seen
me sooner than Sunday, which now is not in his power who in all conditions
preserves the same love & tenderness you can wish in the heart of your most
faithful Hervey.

384.   My ever-new Delight   Newmarket, April 7, 1712.

Remembering how damping a disappointment I felt on Sunday when I opend the news pacquets and found no letter from you, (tho' twas soon relievd by Lord Kingston,) I give you this second trouble, least the first I sent this morning by the coach shoud miscarry. I am loath to repeat the ill news you'l there find of Ladythigh, and that I cannot see you till Sunday at soonest. Shoud Mr. Battely not recover, I must necessarily spend some time at Bury to settle his successor at Bury, which, as matters stand, is of the last consequence to my interest there. I go from hence to morrow for Ickworth, and must therefore desire you to direct Thursday nights letters thither, and since the accident of Mr. Battely's death may retard my return to you, (which woud effectually continue the series of my ill luck,) I desire you woud not want both me and the entertainment which I know play affords you at the same time. If you have occasion for more money than I left with you, I hereby desire Mr. Chambers woud give you creditt for as much more as you shall need till I come back, when my Bankstock shall furnish me wherewith to repay the whole. I once more desire you woud make use of this expedient, as you woud shew me you believe the offer & request sincerely made you by your most faithful disconsolate companion and constant lover, Hervey.

P.S. Jack is very well, but so dejected upon being beaten yesterday that he coud not endure the Warren hill after the match was over, but retird home.

385.   Lady Hervey to John Hervey.   London, April 8, 1712.

Coud I ever tast any pleasure in the absence of my dear dear angel, I shoud think the uncommon heaviness at my heart lately were an ill presage for Ladythigh, since you assure me my chief concerns are well by your dear letter of yesterday, which was indeed dear to me in another sense, by meeting with a great disappointment in your not sending me word when you will come back, but I rather hope it was Jack's impatience that hinderd you telling me than that you were not yet resolvd.   However, I was so near seeing you yesterday at your match that nothing but the crossest accident in the world coud have hinderd me, which vexd me so much that I believe it was the chief occasion of my being so ill all day, for I wakd in the morning with the same disorder I did when I was last ill of the cholick, which frighted me so that I believe I was the worse for it, but I had a very good sleep after, which made me something better, and it went pretty well off without any of the consequences I apprehended, (though I have it still upon me to day.) I venturd a little while in the evening to Mrs. Chetwynd's in hopes to hear some news for you, but there was nothing talkd of but your match, and the nine new Lords that they said were to be declared last night in Counsel, but I coud not hear any of their names but Jack Berkeley.   All the talk on Sunday night was of the Pretender's being given over with the small-pox, and my Lady Lindseys being brought to bed of a son, and also of an extraordinary good peace we are like to have that will satisfy every body.   I have sent Robinson to the Stage-coach in hopes of a letter to know how Ladythigh came off, which I've had a world of messages to enquire after to day, and am very impatient my self to hear ; the little prophet said you woud win.—The wind being contrary hinderd Sir Thomas Hanmer from going to day.   I dind with him to take my leave, where we drank your health, and Mrs. Ramsey desird you woud bring some lap-wings eggs when you come back.   I wish only for their wings, and then it shoud not be long before I gave vent to a heart full of love and passion to the only dear object worthy of that and more than can be expressd, though not beyond what is felt for you by your faithful E. Hervey.

P.S.   Thank God the children are all well except Harriott, and she is much as she was.

386.   My ever-new Delight   Newmarket, April 10, 1712.

        You mention a cross accident which hinderd me from seeing you here, but did not name what it was; I give my self the ease of thinking your disorder was not great, since it sufferd you to go to Mrs. Chetwyn's the same day it attacked you; and if my disappointment was occasiond by any other cause, I shall hate it as long as I live, since my impatience to see you increases daily, and especially with the prospect of be ng kept longer from you than Sunday, which I foresaw and foretold you must necessarily happen in case poor Mr. Batteley's life shoud be despaird of by Friday night's letters; in which event all my friends at Bury have engagd me to appear there to secure a successor, which I hope will prove Sir H. Elwes, and in order to it he is to lye at Ickworth on Friday night, and if the news comes of Dr. Batteley's death, (which is every post expected,) then I am to carry him with me to Bury on Saturday, and have a meeting of all our stanch friends either at the Bushel or the Angel, where I purpose to propose my nephew to them; and at the same time intend to promote Mr. Turnor's pretensions to the Recordership, which he expects and without which he can never hope to attain it. Could we be sure of such a peace as you speak of, (that will please everybody,) I woud leave both the last mentiond points to take their fate; but as matters stand at present we must take care for a new good House of Commons, or all will be lost both at home and abroad. Were any less consequence concernd, nothing shoud prevent my seeing you on Sunday, nor even this neither, unless the last necessity compells your reluctant lover and fond fool, even to an habitual impossibility of living either pleasd or so much as easy without you, Hervey.

P.S. Jack has eat (after sweating Ickworth who won the Queens plate) 2 cutts of plum pudding, 3 cuttlets of mutton and two whole pigeons.

387.   Lady Hervey to John Hervey.   London, April 10, 1712.

I never thought a letter from my dear dear angell coud have given me any thing but pleasure, but I have had a great deal of disquiett from that of yesterday, by your telling me Sunday was ye soonest day I must expect you, and even that upon the uncertainty of Mr. Batteleys health, who I doubt is too certainly in a very bad condision, tho' yesterday they thought him better. Mrs. Batteley has sent me word to day he is as bad as ever. Endeed, my dear, it is imposable for you to immagen what I suffer by your absence, especially since your last disappointment in Lady Thigh, which I cant but fancy has had some agravating circomstance attend it, if what they say hear was true, that it was no match ; but I hope you did not lay more money of it sence you went, tho' they hear report a vast sum that you have lost. I am afraid it will do Jack more hurt than ye country air will do him good, if he thinks you will keep your resolution to make no more matches. If you dont come or send for me by Sunday, (which I beg you woud do if you think of staying,) I shall not be able to resist ye Duke of Grafton's compasionet offer to bring me & Kattern to you next week, tho' it woud be no smale uneasynes to me to leave poor Harriatt such a dismale sight as I found her to day, (the Dutchess of Grafton being so kind to cary me to see her,) tho' they tell me she has mended this three last days ; but I see so little of it in her looks that I shoud be very glad Dr. Garth might see her (from ye succes he had with Sir Hervey Elwes) if you aprove of it, being the never failing good genious to me & mine ; that I may ever prove so to my everlasting love & pleasure, will be the constant prayers & indeavers of your faithfull wife, E. Hervey.

Sir Thomas Hanmer went yesterday with the Duke of Ormond.

388.   To Mr. John Craske, Town Clerk of Bury.

Newmarkett, April 29, 1712.

I have by this post written to Mr. Gibson, not only

recommending ye prompt payment of ye bill for £30 which you say will be tenderd to him by Mr. Alderman's friend on Thursday next, (for which reason I sent your letter directly to London,) but also ye remaining £5..6..4 due from Mr. Bond, which I have done in ye strongest most persuasive terms words can express, and whereof I flatter my self ye Alderman will find the fruit to his content.—As to ye important business of a new Recorder, whereon I lay so just a weight as to believe ye continuance or ruin of mine and my friends interest in a great measure depends upon ye right or wrong choice shall be made of one, I have allways readily ownd my approbation of Mr. Turnor whenever my opinion was askd of that matter, and as oft as such opportunities have offerd (which were neither so early nor have been so frequent as my wishes suggested) I have as constantly taken occasion to tell all my best friends (for their sakes as well as my own) that they could not pitch upon a properer person than Mr. Turnor, all respects & relations being duely considerd; and of that mind I hope and desire to find all those who are friends & well wishers to your faithfull servant.

I desire you woud present my most hearty and affectionate service to all true friends.

389. To ye Lady Bond. Ickworth, May 19, 1712.
Madam

I am sorry to hear by Mr. Penny how ill your Ladyship has been; I hope this fine season will hasten your recovery, since your health is doubly necessary at this time to your family. I have done all in my power to bring Sir H. Bond back to you, but find some people so perverse that no arguments will take any place with them, tho' never so unanswerable. In this class is Cooper ye butcher, who (notwithstanding Sir R. Davers's sollicitations) sent me word he woud rather loose all his debt than sign ye licence. Mr. Caters answer is he knows better things

Vol. I.   S S

than to do it, but says he shall shortly be at London, and will then waite on your Ladyship. Mrs. Pearle is also advisd to refuse unless fully assurd her money shall be paid at ye end of ye two years. Mr. John Cook is now at London, as is also Mr. Stafford, at both whose returns ye licence shall be tenderd for their execution. Mrs. L'estrange is at Norwich, whether ye instrument shall be sent after Mr. Cluff & Mrs. Newson have subscribed it, who both live 10 miles distant from Bury. All who have yet signd it are Mr. Wroth for Lady Castleton, Mr. Cook ye carrier, and John Millegan; but of all ye disappointments I have met with in this affair none surprizd me so much as Lady Dovers not doing of it, especially after what Mr. Penny wrote me word she had by letter promisd your Ladyship; but all my servant coud say of the great use her example woud be to induce ye other creditors to do ye like, she sent him home as he went. As to Mr. La Ferriere, I think it woud prove a troublesome precedent in ye course of this bussiness shoud your Ladyship comply with his demand of paying ye costs of his suite comenced against Sir H. Bond, for others in that circumstance (and there are severall) would expect ye same indulgence, and that woud amount to a greater summ than I know where to raise; beside if Lady Cranmer sticks out, that & all ye pains will be lost which have been and shall yet be taken by your etc.

390.   To Mrs. Ramsey.   Ickworth, May 19, 1712.
      Madam
                Nothing less than ye cause of modest merit reduced to its accustomed circumstances coud possibly have prevaild with me to give you this trouble, to desire you woud employ ye powerfull persuasions I know you are so great a mistress of with Mr. Ryley (to whom I beg you'd give my humble service) in favour of Mr. Morris, whose condition is so throughly comiserable, and he so right an object of both your goodnesses,

that did you know him and ye true state of his numerous family so well as I do, you woud thank me as much for helping you to so just an opportunity of exerting your benevolent temper as I shall think my self bound to do you for undertaking it, whatever ye success proves, since in all events I am un-alterably Mrs. Ramseys constant admirer.

391.   To Mr. John Hervey.   Aswarby, July 31, 1712.
        Dear Jack
                        It gave me a double satisfaction to read ye lively description you sent me of ye sweet delights a country life affords ; since nothing could enable you to paint them so very well as you have done but a mind early blessd with wisdom enough to prefer such pleasures which are innocent and virtuous before all others, that, not being so, yeild ye fatal dealers in them ye melancholly fruits of diseases, and repentance only in ye conclusion.

> Trop heureux qui peut acquerir
> Le bon gout de la solitude,
> Et qui fait tout son etude
> D'y bien vivre et d'y bien mourir.

You'l find Cicero thought nothing more worthy the employment of a wise & honest man than husbandry ; some have placed ye summum bonum in it ; Virgill gives ye followers of it ye title of fortunate ; & Horace ye epithet of blessed ; the Delphick Oracle pronounced one Aglaus a most happy mortall, who having a little farm house in Arcadia never cared to stirr from it unless to do some service to his neighbours, his contentment keeping him a stranger to those evills a publick course of life exposes most men to ; and Simile (one of Adriens ministers) retiring to a country life seven years before he dyed, orderd this for his epitaph : Here lyes Simile, who tho' he was old never lived but seven years of his life.

> The Gods themselves ye rural life approve,
> And kindly guard that innocence they love.

Pomponius Atticus tho' fitly qualified to make a considerable figure in ye world, yet rightly chose the quiet, solitary part in life, constantly declining all publick offices of power or profitt: and tho' Balzac had acquaintance & interest with ye top favourites at Court, yet being by nature none of ye obsequious flatterers and by principle far above practising the mercinary maxims & manners of ye age, and having seen and known ye world throughly, indulgd his better genius and retird into ye country, where he was wholly taken up with ye more valuable entertainments which good books, full leisure, & conjugal endearments afforded him. The mention of ye latter naturally leads me to ye taking notice of an omission in your catalogue of (us) farmers felicities ; for sure Horace's pudica mulier & his dulces liberi are two most necessary ingredients to compleat them. You alone (had not God blessd me with other corroborating proofs) have given me such sufficient reason to esteem ye last article essential to my happyness that yours is now become so to my own. I therefore congratulate not only you but my self, and that better part of me your tender mother, on ye just opinion & right choice you seem to have made towards it; we shall earnestly pray that those forward seeds of goodness we have long observd in you may kindly ripen to ye production of as plentifull a harvest of all ye cardinall and other virtues as ever any humane soul brought forth, that you may prove a steady promoter of your country's prosperity, and a faithfull subject to your Prince, and a blessing and ornament to ye family of your etc.

392.   To Mr. Hervey.   Aswarby, Aug. 5, 1712.
        Dear Carr.

I am at last got hither from sweet Ickworth to perform my annual office for you & my family of auditing ye Steward's accounts, & rideing over the grounds, & surveying ye buildings, & taking care that the one be not impaird by ploughing & that ye other are kept up in good order. This Lordship with ye house and gardens upon it is so very valuable a branch of this Lincolnshire estate that it woud be ye greatest pity shoud it ever happen to be dismemberd from it ; yet that woud be ye consequence shoud it please God by any accident (which I trust in his infinite mercy to avert) to deprive me of you (tho' of age) before you have by deed conveyd it to me & my heirs in case you shoud dye without issue male of your own ; for Mr. Scrope & his children would otherwise inherit it before me or any of your six brothers ; which is what I am sure you are too well a wisher to ye name of Hervey not to prevent by any act in your own power. I have therefore prepard a Lease and Release for that purpose, which I will send to meet you at any place where you'l let me know you shall be about or after ye 17th of September next (our stile) ; for you must be sure not to sign, seal and deliver them till after ye day of your coming at age, since otherwaise they'l be void in law, and so frustrate both our intentions. Let Mr. Masson (to whom my service) & L'oyseul be two of ye three witnesses which are to attest your executing ye deeds ; & let Mr. Newton, if he be with you at ye time, be ye 3d witness ; or, if he shoud not, my Lord Herbert or any other English man of credit or public notary will do as well. I'm ye more sollicitous to preserve this house & land in your name & family, because there's so plentiful an estate to attend it, which since God has blessd us with ye honest attainment of, & ye Queen has been pleasd to enoble our blood, I hope ye whole will be enjoyd intire by you or whoever else ye Divine Providence intends it for after me.—I sent Mr. Masson sometime since a full account from Mr. Beronger concerning ye bill in dispute, and finding you have not receivd hall ye letters I have written to you & him, I sent a duplicate of it by a succeeding post. I dont wonder my letters miscarry, since neither of you have sent me particular directions how to address them. I knew no better for my two last, nor for this, than as you

see, To Rome, at large.   I shoud be glad, at ye same time you send me word
where ye deeds are to meet you, that you'd tell me how you have laid out
ye rest of the time you intend to spend abroad, & by what time I may hope
to have ye pleasure of seeing you again, which no consideration coud make
me consent to defer a month longer but your advantage, to which I will
sacrifice my own satisfaction so far as that if ye peace proceeds, (which ye
misfortune at Denain will necessitate,) you may return through France, &
when you have seen every thing worth your observation there to pass ye
winter at Hannover, (if you cannot possibly dispatch ye whole before,) where
I woud have you know and be well known by every body.   If ye season has
been as moderate with you as here, you might have left Rome sooner than
in most other years to persue your travells homewards, having felt no heats
this summer to hinder any journey at any time of ye day with us.   I conclude you have all publick news in print, otherwise I woud send you that ;
but for ye other, I must reserve ye comunication of those particulars and my
own thoughts concerning them till your return, which is wishd for & expected
with all ye impatience natural to a most affectionate father.

Dear Mama, who has a just esteem & value for you, sends her good wishes
for your safe return, & desires you not to forget her fanns & ye flowers.
Your sisters, Betty & Nann, are both here ; ye latter is on small ornament to
your Pallazza.

393.   To Mr. Masson.   Aswarby, Aug. 16, 1712.
                    Yours of ye 30th passd (which I receivd but this
morning) has put me into a state of ye utmost uneasyness and impatience
for my dear & valuable son, till I hear from you again, my mind being uncapable of that releif it wants but from knowing his recovery, which you
give me hopes of proceeds without any check or threatning symptom of a
relapse, the prevention whereof must be (under God's mercifull Providence)

his & the physicians cheif care ; the best security against one will be ye use
of an abstemious dyet upon ye return of his appetite, & ye keeping good &
regular hours, both as to eating & going to bed, and not to read or write much
(if either at all) till his strength be perfectly re-establishd ; & since tranquility
of mind is necessary to co-opperate with all ye former towards a through
cure, I desire you woud let him know it shall always be his own fault if that
is ever interupted by any thing that depends on me longer than he'l comunicate ye cause of it, since I am very ready to remove not only ye present
(and especially because you confirm my own belief that no ill use has or
will be made of an addition) but all future ones of this or any other kind,
hereby empowering you to make such farther allowance for his cloaths as he
shall desire.   As to his return, I think ye shortest & safest way home must
now be chosen, which I leave intirely to your prudence and experience, with
this strickt caution only, that you do not let him begin it till there are visible
marks of his being well able to bear those journeys you know he must
necessarily undertake in ye route you shall at last resolve on.   That God in
his infinite mercy (wherein I solely trust in all difficultys & distresses) woud
direct you for ye best, that he may come back in health & safety to me, will
in ye interim be ye continual, fervent prayer of his most affectionate father
& your thankfull friend.

394.   To Sir Richard Cocks.   Bath, Sept. 15, 1712.
            The frequent removals I've lately made from one
county to another, with ye necessary bussiness I have always to dispatch in
Lincolnshire and Suffolk, left me no leisure to read over ye manuscript you
favourd me with till I came hither ; which I have now done, but with a very
uncommon effect upon me in perusing what you write, since I must own my
usual pleasures were allayd with pain, & my constant profit mixd with
knowledges I woud forget ; for tho' my mind was entertaind with many

agreeable passages, lively characters, usefull observations, solid reflections, and ye whole picture of ye times it treats of painted with such masterly stroaks as must afford ye reader most sensible satisfactions of one kind, yet as ye whole course of your history runs almost parallel with some more recent transactions, an affectionate Briton could not reflect on ye miserable consequences those High-church principles produced without applying to ye present what Cicero's presaging heart suggested to him, when ye Roman affaires were at as dangerous a crisis. Hæc quæ sint eruptura timeo. For as our knaves have revivd and found fools enough to espouse the same senseless, imaginary fears of ye Churches danger, which first rung the allarm-bell and was afterwards improvd by those religious incendiaries into that dreadfull conflagration which set all France on fire ; and as our modern ingineers are remarkably busy in working up ye like combustible ingredients to so tindery a consistence as that one spark may put our world into as furious a flame ; woud not so resembling a conjuncture almost tempt a desponding patriot to ask Tully's question :—Quem Deum, etiam si cupiat, opitulari posse Reipublicæ credamus ? The sole ressource (if any) that remains must be to get her M— to read ye story of ye League, (books of history being, as Alphonsus of Arragon rightly observd, ye safest and sincerest Councellors of Princes,) by which she'd quickly find how fatal it has ever been to place such men at helm as ought rather to sit at ye oar ; one especially, who, if guilty (as is supposed) of having advisd ye late unprecedented creation, has given a more than Guiscardian wound to ye constitution of his Country, and for which (as twas said on Clodius's intrusion at ye mysteries of Fauna) it is impossible to guess what punishment ye Gods will think fit to inflict, since none has ever dared to commit so great a crime before. Sure he never read or must have forgot Tacitus's remark :— Consilia callida primâ specie læta, tractatu dura, eventu tristia. I can recollect but one maxim he coud ground it upon, which is ye oracular saying mentiond by Aristotle, that some men shoud call danger to their releif in danger, and endeavour to save themselves from one evill by another. He who has once abandond modesty must be heroically impudent, and not do things by halves, must conclude with Cataline, ye ills he has done cant secure him but by doing greater. But let such know their subtilties sow thornes, which when grown up have often obliged ye authors of em to walk barefooted upon: thus Machiavell's Borgia and Pope Clement ye 7th prickd their own feet. I'm only concernd those just and royal intentions he has ye execution of shoud be so ill seconded, and that ye present measures are capable of being so artfully disguisd, as to deceive one I have been so signally obliged by into future uneasynesses; for Rentivoglio shews how Cardinall Granvills dexterities (falsly so calld, since honesty is ye only good policy in my books,) provd Philip ye 2d's intanglements; & D'avila observes that Henry 3d grew weary of ye perplexing projects and unsuccessful intreagues his secretary Villeroy's teeming brain engagd him in. May ye same satiety soon seize ye heart which his hypocrisy has deluded before it be too late for her and our peace; may that Scriptural passage be prophetically fulfilld in him, that ye triumphs of ye wicked shall be short, and ye joy of ye hypocrite but for a moment; they that have seen him in power shall say, Where is he? and may his rage against ye best & usefullest Englishmen prove, like ye Devil's, only so great as it appears, because his time is to be short. But whether is my zeal transporting me? Woud not one believe he had either neglected or disappointed me? You, I hope, who know me, will easily credit me when I assure you, neither; for when a man aims at nothing more in this world than to deserve some small share of that noble epitaph of Lord Grey of Wilton, that having livd to most of ye useful purposes of life but to that of self-interest he dyed etc—, he never exposes himself to any such refusalls as commonly occasion private resentments. I have on ye contrary rejected overtures that have been made me of entring

Vol. I.   T T

into bussiness, having learnd (as Sir W. Temple did) by living long near Courts and public affairs I am unfit for either.   He found ye arts of a Court were contrary to ye sincerity and openess of his nature, and ye constraints of continuall attendance too tedious for ye liberty or leisure of his life or humour ; that ye advancements of men's fortunes being ye cheif end of waiting there, he never minded that, having as much as he needed, and, which was more, as he desired ; wherefore he coud never perswade himself to go to service for nothing but bare wages, nor think of advising where he knew twoud prove to no purpose.   He understood ye modes of a Court were to talk ye present language, to serve ye present turn, and follow ye present humour of ye Prince, how variable soever it happend to be ; of all which he found himself so utterly uncapable, that he coud never speake what he did not mean, nor serve a turn he did not like, nor follow any man's humour wholly against his own ; besides in above 20 years experience he had seen more than enough of ye uncertainty of Princes, the caprices of fortune, the infatuations of ministers, the violence of factions, ye unsteadyness of counsells, & ye general corruption of manners, to part with that sweet independance in a declining which he woud not barter for any other thing in ye flower of his age.

> If ere Ambition shoud my fancy cheat
> With any wish so mean as to be great,
> May Heaven thenceforth from me farr remove
> The humble blessings of that life I love.

Impute not then ye unusuall gall my pen has dropd to any less provocation than ye public sufferings, which are increasing to that irretrievable pass that tho' I can truly affirm—me natura misericordem, patria severum, crudelem nec patria nec natura esse voluit—yet that mans politicall sinns are grown already so irremissibly great that Cataline or Rome must perish ; for as if ye violation or rather extinction of our constitution woud not have been sufficient to perpetuate ye erostratical memory of his ministry, he has also sacrificed ye faith of treaties, and hazarded ye safty of our allies to so gross a degree as to seemingly incurr Virgil's character of Curio :—

Vendidit hic auro patriam, dominumque potentem
Imposuit.

For according to ye most candid interpretation that can be put upon ye (yet known) terms of peace, ye ballance of power will be as much broke abroad in favour of France as it has been at home to ye prejudice of both of ye peeres & people ; wherein these have justly reapd ye fruit of their own folly by having acted so contrary to all ye virtue, wisdom and fortitude of their forefathers ; who by ye most surprising slavishness and corruptest conduct that ever either were guilty of in any time have wickedly converted that glorious series of successes with which Providence had favourd us into curses rather than blessings by ye dangerous use is going to be made of them.   Quid aliud talis populus agebat, nisi ut cum eum Deus perdere adhuc fortasse nollet, tamen ipse exigeret ut periret? said Salvien of ye scandalous Christians at Carthage when beseiged by barbarians.   I have written with thus much freedom and length from ye great greif and indignation of my soul to behold ye degeneracy of ye present age ; but at ye same time that I am easing my own mind by pouring part of its pains into a friendly bosom, I forget ye contagion must catch so publick-spirited an one as yours, which I woud by no means impart to it, knowing how very uneasily the thoughts of these things have set upon ye heart of your most faithfull friend & servant.

I shoud be glad of a coppy of your History, & yet more so to meet ye author of it anywhere.

395.   To Mr. Hervey.   (Carr.)   Bath, Sept. 17, 1712.
My dear son

The sight of a letter writ with your own hand was

a surprizing satisfaction to me after ye cruel anxieties I had sufferd during ye doubtfull state of your health; but as no joys in this life are or ought to be possessd in purity, it was not a little allayd when I read that ye impatience of your piety to relieve an afflicted parents pain had put you upon transgressing your physicians rules; which has cast me into fresh fears least writing sooner than was safe for you may have occasiond any return of your feaver, which I hope God's goodness has prevented, since ye motive was filial duty, to which he has annexd his blessing. In full confidence whereof I congratulate you on your inheritance to Aswarby by his gracious protection of your life to this day. O! let us never forget his mercy to us both in your miraculous recovery from so dangerous a distemper, and may his all sufficient grace continually attend you to ye very end of those days he has farther allotted you; that so by ye strictest imitation and persuit of those perfections which are in him, you may become as eminent a proficient in every practical vertue as humanity is capable of attaining, and all ye world allow—

> This, this is he, in whom does mixd remain
> All that kind parents wishes can contain;
> His love to's friends no bound or rule does know,
> What he to Heaven, all that to him they owe;
> As never more to man by Heaven was given,
> So never more by man was paid to Heaven;
> And all ye virtues were to ripness grown,
> Ere yet his flow'r of youth was fully blown;
> All autumns store does his rich Spring adorn;
> Like trees in Eden, he with fruit was born.

As to ye route of your return, I still leave that intirely to Mr. Masson's prudence & experience, (to whom my service and thanks again & again for his great care in your sickness;) and for ye passes, I have used all ye diligence possible to procure them since you first mentiond them, which was but in your last, that did not come to my hands till last Saturday. My remoteness from Court, and ye present paucity of my friends there, has renderd it more difficult than formerly; but I have got Mr. Vice-Chamberlaine Cooke who is here to write to ye Duke of Shrewsbury at Windsor to ask ye Queen's leave for them, and that ye Secretary of State may deliver them to Mr. Godfrey (Milles) my agent at London, (Mr. Beranger being in Kent,) who I have orderd to despatch them to Messrs. Cliffords, that they may forward them to meet you according to your directions on ye confines of France. And for your going to ye Court of Hannover, tho' I shoud be extreamly well pleasd to have you known there, yet as ye plague seems to have infected severall of ye neighbouring countrys thereabouts, I must desire you woud deferr paying your duty there till a more convenient season, not only for that reason, (tho' that alone woud determine me,) but as my impatience to see you again daily increases to that degree that I can no longer live easily till you return in safty to your etc.

396. To the Duke of Marlborough, on ye death of Lord Godolphin.

My Lord   Sept. 29, 1712,

The same affectionate zeal which gave me so pleasing a share in every circumstance of that prosperity which has attended your Graces influential merit, naturally interesses me to bear a proportionable part in all such adverse accidents as may befall you; and therefore cannot avoid giving your Grace this trouble to condole with you on ye loss of so usefull a friend and so agreeable a companion as my Lord Godolphin; so intimate an union as I had ye happyness to be a witness of between yee, even verifyed that difficult definition of friendship—Amicus est una anima duo corpora ferens—and created a commerce in life of all others to be ye most envyed; but tho' Seneca must be allowd to have said with great reason—

Nulla est pretiosior possessio bono veroque amico—yet I know your Grace's present greif cannot make you forget you have a much better part of your self still surviving; and that he also informs us—Nemo infelicius eo, cui nihil unquam evenit adversi, non licuit enim illi se experiri—; and as your Grace is one of those superior Genius's which Providence takes a pleasure in guiding to perfection, it seems to have sent some late tryals on purpose to shew ye world your Grace can govern passions as successfully as armies, and that it has blessd you with such excellent wisdom as to be capable of converting misfortunes into fresh ornaments more brightly to adorn ye only unfinishd side of your most noble character, by bearing fortunes frowns as gracefully as you wore her favours.

> Thou only unconcernd hast let thy country see,
> It has ungratefully disgracd it self, not thee.

One woud have thought your Grace had gatherd lawrells enough to sit down in quiet (at least) under the shade of them, since your unnatural enemies coud not have done so under their own vines without those successes, which have both enabled and emboldend them to carry on their laudable scheme without your Grace's farther (felo-de-se) services; whose malice seems as monstrously malignant as Virgil's bees, who rather than not sting—vitasque in vulnere ponunt—; and may that be their fate after having out livd their criminal councils just long enough to inheritt ye mortification of seeing & feeling this comfortable truth for your Grace universally confirmd :—Si magnus vir cecidit, magnus jacuit; non magis illum putes contemni quam cum ædium sacrarum ruinæ calcantur, quas religiosi æque ac stantes adorant. Among whom none pays so great a reverence to those divine qualities your Grace is endowd with, nor remember ye invaluable benefits they've performed for us and our posterity with so growing a gratitude, as your Grace's etc.

I beg leave to let ye Dutchess of Marlborough know how due a sense I have of her just sorrow on this occasion; & that she woud do me ye right to believe she has not in ye world a more stedfast friend or more obedient servant than my self.

397.   To Mr. Hervey.   Newmarket, Oct. 30, 1712.

Dear Carr

Mr. Massons of ye 11th & yours of ye 14th instant, both from Florence, came together last night. I have by this days post written to Mr. Beranger desiring he woud take ye earlyest care to furnish you with such credit as Mr. Masson mentions, both at Lions and Paris, which I hope you'l find effected at your arrival in each place to your satisfaction. You will have (as I told you before) ye advantage of my cousen Hanmer's conversation & countenance at Paris, of both which I have beggd of him to afford you as great a share as he can possibly contrive, as I also do of you that you would not fail to improve so lucky an opportunity into ye establishment of such a friendship as I very much wish to see between yee; for tho' all your political principles may not tally so exactly as I woud have them, yet I know he's blessd with so tender a nature, so excellent a temper, and his morals so pure, that you can follow few better examples in ye future conduct of your life, since by ye exercise of those happy qualities his has been one continued uniform scene of sobriety, prudence & universal civility. Pray thank Mr. Masson from me for ye very best and most welcome news I coud learn, which is that you have so thoroughly recoverd your strength that I may expect to see you in perfect health at your return.—The deeds I sent you were calculated for a precautionary provision only, to prevent Aswarby's going into another family, in case it shoud have pleasd God to punish me by taking you into another world; but whether they have been yet executed in a legal valid form, neither you nor Mr. Masson have explaind, since yee only tell me you have signd them, whereas they ought to have been seald and deliverd (as well as signd) as your act & deed in ye presence of two or more credible witnesses, and that too since ye day of your being at age, which was ye 17th of Sept. last according to ye computation of our Church of England. Your pass to come thro' France was sent to Messrs. Cliffords to be by them conveyd to Turin or elsewhere, according to ye advices they shoud receive from Mr. Masson where to meet you, which I hope they'l do as opportunely as your convenience can require, that so I may ye sooner be made easy in seeing you again, which is most impatiently desired by your etc.

398.   To Sir Thomas Hanmer.

Dear Cousin

Your resolution to leave us being suddenly executed, we concluded consequently your stay would prove but short; wherefore I deferrd giving you any trouble of this kind in daily hopes of your return; but finding that uncertain, you must now give me leave to interrupt your pleasures at Paris with this short enquiry after your health; and at the same time earnestly to recommend my son to your countenance and conversation when he arrives there from Italy; which are two such valuable advantages that I ought to found my claim to them in Bithynicus's words to Cicero :— Si mihi tecum non et multæ et justæ causæ amicitiæ privatim essent, repeterem initia amicitiæ ex parentibus nostris etc ; since I desire you would alwaies consider him (as well as his father) in the double relation of your friend and kinsman; and hope you'l find him not unworthy of his share in either. If he has contracted any wrong or awkward habitts, or should be surprisd into the commission of any faults incident to the frail feaverish condition of one and twenty, I throughly depend on your wonted kindness to correct them, which he'l be wise enough (or else I know him not at all) to love and thank you for as much as your most faithfull friend & most obedient servant.   My wife is very much your servant, & your good & honest godson [Tom] begs your blessing.

399.   Dear Carr

Mr. Masson need run no risque at all in staying with you at Paris, if he will gett my cousin Hanmer to make use of the credi he has to procure leave for him to remain with you only so long as you shall stay there, which I desire he would apply to him for in my name, & am sure he will not refuse to use his interest in a matter where yours and mine is so much concernd. I dare say the Duke of Shrewsbury (to whom my service) would not decline interposing his good offices should they be wanting in this affair, did you request it ; and (considering ye known terms of Peace) France may well give us such a point as this into ye bargain, and have no dear pennyworth of it neither ; I am sure ye warr has cost me above £40000, and I know of nothing but this small convenience that will accrue to me in return. I should be glad to hear you are safely arrivd at Paris, and to know how long Mr. Masson proposes you should be there, and which way will be best for you to take to go from thence to Hannover, being very desirous (as impatient as I am to see you) that you should go and be known there for some time before you come home, especially if you hear ye pestilental distemper is ceasd which they once apprehended was getting into their neighbourhood, whereof pray lett Mr. Masson inform himself with the utmost care and exactness, and send me ye best account he can gett, of which and all other he has been most surprisingly spareing ever since September last. Altho' I hope your own wisdom has renderd all cautions of this kind superfluous, yet I must conjure you to observe a more than ordinary care in your conduct while tis under ye inspection of so severe a judg as Sir T. Hanmer, that he may not only write over a character to your advantage, but think you capable of business, (if you should live to like it better than your ffather,) and recommend you to it accordingly ; but I must thus farr prejudice you as to any resolution of that kind, that you would find the track of publick employment made too dirty for men of clean hearts and hands to travel in, and that ye wise and honest choose rather to decline ye road of it by retiring to a private life of honour and innocence, seeing those only greedy of preferments fill those stations which such as do not naturally seeke them are alone fitt for.—Your Mama desires, if you have not brought ye flowers out of Italy which I mentiond last summer, that you would ask ye Dutchess of Shrewsbury where they are to be had, either at Paris or in Italy, and to gett some time enough to bring with you when you return to your impatient & most affectionate father.

400.   To Sir Thomas Hanmer.   London, Jan. 20, 1712.
    Dear Cousin

The constant experience I have had of your good nature made me justly conclude your kindness would prevent my desires of affording my son your assistance and advice whenever you found he wanted either ; and if he seems to need no admonisher, it must be owing to his copying your conduct, which I recommended (of all others) to his imitation.— The little box you mention has had a place among the most precious goods in my possession ever since you trusted me with the custody of it ; and I cant forbear telling you, I was so farr worthy your confidence on that occasion, that it has slept ever since with my last will, whereof I took the liberty to nominate you co-executor with my wife ; and if you'l forgive me that freedom, I'm rather to thank than pardon you for yours.—You may be sure I faild not to acquaint your happy Godson [Tom] with the welcome distinction you made between him and the rest of my little family ; who being pressd by me for a genuine answer of his own suitable to so particular a favour, (like him who undertook a definition of the Deity, desiring longer and longer time for the solution,) at last ownd with a sigh, he could think of nothing near good enough to say to or of such a man as you are. This being both my first wifes & his birth-day, I alwaies observe it with a double distinction,

as it producd one of ye best women, & as he is ye grand & God-son of two
ye worthyest men I ever knew.—Your intended journey into Italy is yet
unknown to ye Dutchess of Grafton, & shall be still a secret for me till she
learns it from your own information ; but in ye mean time I desire this may
be none to you, that wherever you go my best wishes will attend you,
that you may meet with all ye satisfactions you propose to your self in it,
& that you may return in safety to your declining country, which claims &
wants your assistance, & to those friends who rightly value (& consequently
regrett ye loss of) your conversation ; among whom none will more impatiently expect you than your etc.

401. To Mrs. Crispe. March 28, 1713.
Madam
The most welcome part of the panegyrick you are
pleasd to make on the melancholly letter I sent for your perusal, consists
more in the relief and conviction you allow it has afforded you than in all
the other commendations it can pretend to ; which, joynd to your desire of
reading more on the same subject, has encouragd me to expose an other of
them to the same affectionate correspondent ; whereby you, who have been
a wittness how amply God all-mighty has since rewarded my resignation to
his then seeming most severe will, by unexpectedly repairing my ruind happiness in substituting a successor so worthy of engrossing the tenderest affections she once justly held in my heart, may see
I livd to shew his power who once did bring
My joys to weep, but since my grief to sing.
That such may be the issue of your present sorrow shall be the prayer of,
Madam, your most faithfull servant.

402. Lady Hervey to John Hervey. London, Aprill 2, 1713.
My hoarsness is so increasd that this woud be the
only way we coud convers weir my dear dear angill now with me, which I

wish to God you weir, for then I coud feel no uneasynes, tho' I have now a great many, & the absence of your dear & valueable self increases them all . I cant help doing my little rivell some good offises by teling you that she askd me twenty times yesterday, where abouts do you think Papa is now ; & she told all ye company that came to see me that my Lord was gon to Newmarkett; & if any body went to play with her, (which Lord Lansdell did for one,) she told them, pray dont teas me, for Papa's gone, & I am very much out of humour. I hope the account of this artles affection will sattisfy you instead of news, for I dont know a word but that ye peace will be signd before this day senett, & that the Queen certainly intends to go to the house then. I am not likely to hear any thing more, sence I am not well enough to see any company to day but Lady Burlinton and Lady Sharlott to play at omber; so, my dear dear, (for the present) adue to this imperfect conversation, but never from the thoughts, tender wishes & inclination of your faithfull E. H.

I long to hear how you passd your jurney. I thought you woud like to read Mr. Maccartneys letter, so have sent it.

403. My ever-new Delight   Newmarkett, Aprill 3, 1713.

Our frind Jack & I passd ye jurney as well as coud be expected, ye one disappointed by your injunction (to ye last degree) that he shoud not ride Union his match, & ye other feeling no true sattisfaction in any place where you are not with him. That state of mind has this day receivd ye farther improvment of Ladythighs having been beaten by Scarr, tho' Ben Cooper has told me since ye match he is sure my horse would have won, had not they calld him back after he was started & gon a good way before him down ye hill, which made him pull up, & ye other rider George perceiving so he then clatterd after him, & made it a match by running on, when Ben was forced to put my horse into a fresh rate, which by that time he had done ye other was got before him, & as it was provd so hard a match on ye flatt that George was forced to jostle within 12 score of ye ending post. You may wonder how I came to run it, but I was determind to it since I came by seeing Scarr had a big leg, which I hopd to disable him quite of, but at least to save ye next forfeit by it, which is not unlikely to happen accordingly, for he went lame out after rubbing.—I am very much obligd to your rivall [Nann] for her distinctions even in absence, which in one so young must proceed from a wonderfull fund of affection. I sett much the greater value upon it as she must derive it from you; at least I'l give my self the pleasure of thinking so, that I may love you both the better for it, & by that thought banish all others that woud intrude to lessen ye happiness of your most affectionet & faithfull lover, Hervey.

404.   Lady Hervey to John Hervey.   London, April 4, 1713.

It was no small disappointment to me not to hear by yesterdays post that you got safe and well to Newmarket, for I was in hopes (you talkd of going out so early) that you woud have got time enough there just to have told me that, which woud have been a great ease to my mind, and indeed, my dear dear angel, it is impossible for me to tell you how much I want that when I am from you; I think I am now more sensible of it than ever, but that is no wonder, since I am so much longer acquainted with your worth and merit, which has always shewd it self so particularly towards me that I know you will be glad to hear my cold is better, but these cold winds make my rheumatism pains very uneasy to me, and I find my self weaker and fainter upon going abroad than I expected. I venturd yesterday to prayers, but I shall do my devotions to morrow without any hazard of getting cold, for Lady Betty Germaine has a Sacrament at home, where she gives me leave to come, and has invited me to dinner afterwards. I am going now to prayers, and then to the Dutchess of Cleveland to meet our newsmonger in hopes to hear some particulars of the peace, which Mr. St. Johns brought signd (yesterday) by all the Allies but the Emperor; he is to have a 1000 guineas for a present. The great guns were let off and the bells rung, but I heard of no bonfires or any other expression of joys.—I am now at the Dutchess of Clevelands, who presents her service to you, but our gentleman has disappointed us, and I cant meet with any body that knows any particulars about the peace, nor when it is to be proclaimd, though I've sent to every body I coud think of. Your 3 Westminster boys are gone to day to be confirmd by the Bishop of Rochester; all the rest are well. Pray God keep you and dear Jack so this bitter weather, which is the constant prayers of your faithful E. Hervey.

P.S. Tuer was at the Temple with Mr. Hays, but he says he cant pay the money till you send a new receipt, for the taxes must be just double what you have allowd them.—I hope you have got a rider to your mind for Union; pray remember my ten G: with Mr. Craven, and ten more that I go with the Duke of Bolton of Hackwood, and if you like the match make it up fivety for me, and twenty apiece upon any other match.

405.   My ever-new Delight   Newmarkett, Aprill 7, 1713.

I must begin this letter with ye good news of Union's having repaid ye losses of Ickworth and Ladythigh, who tho' but a galloway beat Babylonion upon rate, & made so fine a figure over ye flatt that Jack woud have become him much better than ye rider your injunction forcd me to substitute in his place. Could you imagine ye mortification it provd to us both, how he dreamd of the disappointment every night by saying in his sleep, Pray lett me ride him,—& after that—I will, I will; you shant refuse me, etc.,—you would never think of preventing any thing of this kind more; & endeed now tis over & I have indulgd your tenderness on this occasion, I must beg of you for ye future so farr to intrust him with me as never to over-rule what my caution (which is sufficient for both your & his security) shall think fitt to allow of this kind. His working brain coynd & urgd a hundred Jesuitisms in order to evade your request to me at parting; but I pay so pious a regard to every promise I make you (& especially in absence) that no part of his persuasion (which did not want for rhetorick neither) could ever shake ye firm resolves I had taken to gratify your (give me leave to call it) weakness for this once, since it tends to nothing but effeminacy, the very worst of education; his age, strength & stature is now at such a crisis that you must determine to be content to see him live a shrimp or risque something to inable him to commence man. I'm of council for ye latter, & hope I've not lost so much ground since your declaration about my Mahometism (should I have provd of that persuasion) as not to bring you over to my opinion, which beforehand bribes you so to do by being strongly byassd to favour every circumstance wherein your true interests or satisfactions are concernd, they being ye chief drift and aim of every thought of his heart who is most entirely yours, Hervey.

I am glad to hear your cold & hoarsness is better. I shall take care of your betts, & acquaint ye Duke of Bolton what you go with him. I beleive it will be difficult to gitt any more mony bett on ye first of these matches; but what can be done shall be by your faithfull H. Pray, my dear life, when you have read ye inclosd, seal it up, & send it with my servis to Sir Thomas Hanmer, desiring he woud take care to have it conveyd to Paris by ye first opportunity, otherwaies Carr may be gon from thence before it getts thither; this will be (for Sir Thomas's comfort) ye last trouble I shall give him of this kind in all probability.

406. Lady Hervey to John Hervey. London, April 7, 1713.
My dear dear angel
Jack cant be more concernd for not riding Union's match (which I am glad you gave me the ease of knowing he did not) than

I was to hear Ladythigh was beaten, for I think loosing a match in such a
manner vexes one more than 3 woud do in a fair way; but I woud fain have
Scarr new namd and calld Trickster, since I find he is never to run without
one; but I hope these disagreeable accidents and the more disagreeable
weather will hasten your journey hither, since it is impossible for me to come
to you, which I did fully design, but am so farr from that that going to sit
still in one place is all I am able to do in a day; for Sunday, tho' I went
only to my Lady Suffolks and my aunts, and to take leave of Lady Bell
Bentinck, I came home so very ill that I had like to have fainted before
they coud get me to bed; yesterday I was better and playd at bragg at the
Dutchess of Somersets, and am to pass this evening with the Dutchess of
Cleveland, where if I can meet with any thing you shall hear from me again,
but the publick affairs are kept so private that no body knows any thing of
them. I was told by one that was here this morning (you may guess who) that
they look at Court as if there was some mistery that was not as it shoud be,
which makes it doubtful now whether the Parliament will sit on Thursday.
As for private news I know none, for I have not had strength nor spirits
enough yet to go to Mrs. Chetwynds, which is the likely place to meet with
it, though I hear they have been full of quarrels there of late: one was
between Ma: Rosengrance and Mr. Gage; but the other was the most
material; for my Lord Stairs and Collonel Carr haveing lost a good deal of
money to that bank, my Lord desird 2 deals more, but was refusd, upon
which he grew pretty warm, and they say made severall reflections which had
been better let alone; however, I have heard nothing of it since.—We went
into mourning on Sunday for a sister of Mr. Harrisons and 2 other cousins;
therefore if you will give me orders who shall make them, I will bespeak
you a black sute, for you cant go abroad without, and I find by the list the
matches end on Saturday for this meeting, and sure no body can stay for

the stir of an easterly wind, especially if it brings such weather as it does here, for this day it has raind, snowd and haild ; if I could believe you coud find any good by the country in such an unnatural season, I woud not be so self interested as to desire you to come back, but as it is I must again repeat that I find it more impossible than ever to live without the greatest blessing (and the greatest that ever was given to mortal) and pleasure of my life, thou dearest treasure of your faithful E. Hervey.

P.S. Pray send me word if you find my letters are opend, for they tell me they do it to all. All the blots at the latter end you must excuse, for they come by being interrupted with messages of invitation to go to the French Ambassador's ball, which is given to the Dutchess of Grafton, but I have refusd, next Thursday.

407. My ever-new Delight   Newmarket, April 10, 1713, 9 at night.

For fear you might have heard of our being over turnd in our journey hither by any other hand but my own, I write this to let you know none of us got any harm, and have sent it by the coach, which will convey it to you near two days sooner than the post, to prevent any uneasyness you might be under on my account. I am in truth so fatigued that instead of supping with Lord Dorchester, (who invited me with the rest of the Coach-company,) I am going to bed, in order to be up in the morning to write again to thee, that being my chief pleasure whenever absent from the source of all his satisfactions, who is & ever will be without division or remission thy most affectionate Hervey.

408.   My ever-new Delight   Newmarket, April 11, 1713.

I hope the news of our being over thrown in our way hither did not outrunn my care to let you know by the flying-coach that none of us got any hurt. I will now acquaint you with some good, which is that Flanderkin won the Queen's Plate, but with more strife and diffi-

Vol. I.   w w

culty (and consequently more honour) if possible than Ickworth did this
time twelvemonth ; and to add to our satisfaction in the success, I must do
Jack the justice to tell you tis the universal opinion here that had he not
venturd to comptroll my orders in the riding for it, the prize woud have
been carryed off by Mr. Fagg, whose horse beat mine the second heat, and
might have done so the third had my horse run it away from start, (as I
orderd, knowing mine to be more master of the weight than his,) but Jack
seeing we were sure of having the speed, chargd Jack Faussett not to run till
the last mile, which being ground Flanderkin run best in beat the other
about two lengths at last. Did I not know this boy to be as much my little
rival as Nan can be yours, I woud not have been so particular in a relation
of this nature after your late declarations of enmity to this sport and place ;
but since I am enterd upon his praises I must not conclude them till I have
told you he has given me as exact an account of all my betts and the stakes
to be taken up etc, as if I had been here my self, endorsing each paper and
parcel of bills or mony with more exactness even than his father, who you
know is not very loose or careless in the main about such affairs.   The use
I woud have you make of this narrative is to thank God (as I do most fervently) for the pleasing prospect you have not only in him but the rest of
those fine children God has blessd you & me and my family with ; which
ought to furnish us with continual themes for thanksgiving to his goodness,
and to beg his grace may attend them through the whole course of their lives,
which is the very best wish can be made for them by you (their dear original)
or your and their most affectionate well-wisher, Hervey.

>   **409.**   Lady Hervey to John Hervey.   London, Aprill 11, 1713.
>   My dearest dear

                    You left me in so il a state of body & mind that
I never laid my eyes together from ye time I saw you tell 7 a clock, counting

how many days it was likely to be before you coud come back, & reflecting upon my own weak condision, that I fear will hinder my coming to you so soon as I could wish. Wether it was thees thoughts or no I cant tell, but I was wors yesterday then I had been for some days before, & still continue so; however, I made it my bisness to pick you up some news; in order to it I sent to Mr. Porter to call hear to tell me what was done at ye Hous of Commons, which I had but an imperfect account of yesterday. I cant say I know much more now, but that Mr. Pitts (not our cousen) movd for the thanks to ye Queens spech, which he made such work of that the nonsence of it makes it worth reading, so that I have begd the perteculers of it in writing, (which I hope to gitt time enough for ye post;) he was seconded by Sir Thomas, who they say begun with ye old reflection upon ye late Minestry, but ended with saying he thought it improper to return thanks for ye great care the Queen had taken to gain so good & advantagious a peace for us & our Alies, (which was ye first motion made,) while ye greatest part of the house weir so much in the dark as to the perteculers what those advantages might be. I dont know wether I use ye same expressions, but this was ye sence of it. Their was yesterday another debate upon ye same matter, where Mr. Stanup disird only that ye word hope might be aded, which was by thanking her Majesty for ye great care etc, and for the advantages they *hoped* might be received from it to us & our Allies; upon which their was a division of 49 & 231, where Mr. Ham showd himself by voting with the majorety. Young Poltney they say was very warm in ye debate; Mr. Manly upon answeiring of him (by mistake) calld him my Lord; upon which he rose up & said he was oblidgd to that gentelman for the honer he did him, but he did not know that ever he had made interest to be a lord, nor he hopd he shoud never be thought worthy to be put into the next sett that was made.—I dind to day with ye Dutchess of G——n, where J hopd to have heard some news; but all I can meet with is that ye Commons have voted an address to be presented to her Majesty to lay before them all ye perteculers relating to ye peace with France & Spain, & alsoe what conserns ye Allies. Ye news to day is that France is agreed with ye Em—-r ; the Duke of Ormond is Lord Livtenant of Norfolke ; the Lords & Commons have been with there address to day ; if ye latter comes out time enough Sir Thomas has promist me to send it to you. I am afraid you will think me a very lame news writer, but you must take ye will for ye deed in that as in every thing els relating to your dear self, sence I must always fall short of what is wishd towards you by your faithfull E. Hervey.

410.   My ever-new Delight   Newmarkett, Aprill 14, 1713.

Your last letter gave me no small uneasyness from ye discription you therein gave me of your health, till Mr. Holloway relievd me a little by telling me he saw you at ye Oppera on Satherday last ; so that I look upon some of ye strongest expressions & worst of the circumstances relating to it intended only as a lame legg to beg a short return in this interval of sport between ye meetings, which you need never contrive for me, my own inclination ever preventing even your own wishes on all such occasions ; but I have dedicated that time to ye dispatch of a very necessary business, which is to receive ye rents and adjust accounts with my Suffolke tenants, which must now be done with more than ordinary exactness, since ye present audit must be the foundation for Will : Oliver to connect ye subsequent ones by ; besides there is ye intended kitchin garden to be laid out at Ickworth, which will never be tollerably executed in my absence ; yet notwithstanding this & a great many other considerations which require my stay in these parts, should your next letter still beg on, my bowels have such particular yearnings towards you that twill not be in my power to resist the innocent pious fraud, since my own pleasure is doubly concernd in ye relief, whatever I may pay for it in my affairs ; but then I must leave you again on

Munday, being concernd against Windam ye 22d instant, & having a match of my own ye 24th, and every parting (tho' I know it is not to be very long) renews such a fitt of maloncholly in my mind as none but I that feel it can imagine; then ye roads are so very bad as well as ye weather that ye jurney is scarce compassable in a day; you who know me & my love can never wrong your own meritt & my value for it so farr as to suspect these negative reasons are urgd with any design to excuse my coming; if they have any meaning beside thier own visible ones, tis that I would shew you these nor any other obstacles shall ever prove prevalent enough to oppose or defeat any disire of yours, especially when founded upon so endearing a bottom as giving a mutual satisfaction between thee & thy most tenderly affectionate frind & lover, Hervey.

I thank you for your news, as I desire you woud Sir Thomas Hanmer for ye address he sent me, as also for his right endeavour to save ye dignity of ye House of Commons, as I would have done that of ye H. of P.—, by not blindly & implicitly thanking her Majesty before she had thought fitt to lett them know for what.—Jack is very well, but so inamourd with ye pleasures of this place that he has no spiritts (comparatively) any where else; we weir at Ickworth but 24 hours, & it raind incessantly ye whole time, so that I coud do nothing.

411. Lady Hervey to John Hervey. London, April 14, 1713.

Tis always a great pleasure to me to hear from my dear dear angell, but yesterday your letter was doubly wellcome to me, for tho' I had it under your own dear hand (Saturday night) that you got no harm by being overturnd, yet I could not help being uneasy tell I heard from you yesterday that you weir not ye wors for so fatigueing a jurney as I am sure you must have sufferd, & your telling me you went to bed instead of suping with Lord Dorchester confirmd that beleife. I hope you weir not a sufferer with him in his match Saturday, but that you took ye oddes (which I hear weir very high) both for your self & me. Tis a mighty pleasure to me that any part of me can give you so much sattisfaction as you express to recieve in dear Jack; I hope in God it will never lessen by ye want of my prayers for ye continueance of that and all the other blessings he has bestowd upon me, cheifly ye inestemable treasure of your dear dear self. I told Sweetface how much Jack had gaind upon you in her absence, which I repented, for she took it so much to heart that her culler came & ye tears into her eyes with this expression : I am sure Papa dus not use to care for him so much, for he always beat him about ye room with his hankercheif when he vext me. I sent your proxey yesterday ye muinett I receivd it, but I hope this bitter wether will make you take it away again (for this vacant season at Newmarkett), which makes me bear ye increas of pain it gives me in my limbs with more patience. It has snowd ever since 7 a clock last night, and is very likely to do so much longer, for the wether is colder than ever it has been yet; however, I long so much to see you, & find it so imposable to live without you, that shoud not hinder my being with you next week, if Sir David (who was hear this morning) had not positively forbid me with teling me severall terable accedents that might happen from ye jurney, but I believe he made it ye wors, seeing me so much sett upon it, tho' I must confess I found somthing of what he foretold yesterday upon going out with Lady Thomond in her spring coach ; he has so convincd me of the danger it will be for ye young child to go yett that I desire you woud not send ye horses tell you hear from me; if you shoud go to Ickworth, (which I am still in hopes you wont,) pray tell Lady Issabella that I thought Mr. Turner had understood me that I depended upon Mrs. Syer for a house-keeper, els I woud have sent to her sooner ; but I cant take her till I come my self; pray dont forgitt to send this message by W. Olever if you dont go your self, for she writ to me about it. There is not one word of news, nor nothing spoke of but Mr. Addisons fine play, which I am to go to this day with ye Dutchess of Cleveland, Lady Ann Hervey & Lady Thomond ; we shall be free from the croud by being in ye stage box, els I durst not have venterd. If I can meet with any thing before I come home, you shall hear from me again, tho' I grudg the time this long letter will take you from your bisness to read, for every moment is an age tell we meet to ye impatience of, my dearest life, your faithfull E. Hervey.

If tis not very inconvenient to you, pray, my dear, come to me.

412.   My ever-new Delight   Newmarkett, April 16, 1713.

Had your complaints been continued & increasd as ye rain & watters are, I woud have venturd through them rather than not have seen you ; but finding you were well enough to be at Cato ye same day you wrote your letter, has determind me to go & take care of my affairs at Ickworth, where my presence is more wanted than you can imagine, having Westley and Tuddenham both in hand, & ye latter wholly unprovided of sheep, & so out of repair that a years rent wont make it good, beside ye watters are so extreamly out that I fear it will not be possible for us to gitt from hence through Kentford this afternoon as I intended. W. Oliver coming through last night tells me that it then took horses up to ye mid-rib at passing only near ye bridg, so that were you to have given ye decisive vote on this occasion, (whose inclination is chiefly consulted & generally governs my conclusions,) I have judgd it woud have decreed as I have determind, especially too sence I could not have gott to you (if at all) till Fryday, & must have left you again on Monday ; & in ye mean time might have done that which, whenever it gives you ye least uneasyness, costs me more pain and repentance than any thing but sin shoud produce in any soul, feeling so true a tenderness towards you as to gitt ye better of all its other sensations to that degree that ye most exquisite pleasure looses its property &

degenerates into pain, where you may possibly be ye worse for't. This last passage naturally reminds me of answering your question about opening your letters, which I cant perceive have been so, & I hope ye same by this; but if it shoud, what would the curious enquirer be ye wiser or ye better for it, unless it could convert them to ye practice of so pure a conjugal correspondence as none of her Majesty's chief ministers are famous for, but which I hope by God's grace & blessing they shall ever find carryed on to ye heigth of happiness between thee & thy most faithfull of frinds & most constant of lovers, Hervey.

I had heard to much good of White-rose to lay any mony for you against him. I will tell Lady Izabella what you desire; kiss dear Nan for me.

413.   Lady Hervey to John Hervey.   London, Aprill 16, 1713.

I am to well acquainted with your love & tenderness towards me to let you have ye uneasyness of mising a post, if ye watters or any thing els has prevented your coming as Mr. Hays sent me word you intended, & hearing by Lady Godolphin that my Lord is expected to morow makes me conclude you will once more keep him company, and I have ye satisfaction to believe this jurney will neither hinder ye bisness nor pleasure you proposd at Ickworth by building; for sure this wether hinders every thing of that sort, & will I hope make you not regrett giving the pleasure of your company for this short time (as you have already prepard me for) to her that longs to see you with the last impatience, & loves you with all her heart & soul, which I hope to tell you before you read this.

414.   My ever-new Delight   Ickworth, Aprill 17, 1713.

I ever found this place my center of rest when you was with me; but alass! tis so much alterd by your absence that most, if not all, of its meritt towards me (formerly) I now feel was wholly owing to your making me pass my time so pleasantly in it; the place had no share in ye sattisfactions I tasted here; twas your presence alone made me so easy & happy, & till you return to it I despair of being either. I hope Mr. Charlton's servant brought you my letter, which was just going to ye post-house as he calld upon me; I chose rather to send it by him, because it containd mysterious passages relating to so sacred a passion that vulgar eyes (had it been opend) would not have found faith enough to have believd practicable or possible. I knew it would please poor Jack, & therfore shewd him that part of your letter which related to him & dear Nan, whose interest in me (next your own, & in this like it too) is so well establishd that nothing can shake or abate it, which I desire you would tell her in such a manner as to make her understand it, & then she'l be happy too. Pray dont lett Fell forgett me, for as he is another pretty part of your self, I can find love enough for him too, & make as many more subdivisions of my heart among ye rest as is consistent with & flows from that paramount passion your virtues clame & have created in ye gratefull soul of your most tender lover, Hervey.

415. Lady Hervey to John Hervey. London, Aprill 18, 1713.

My dear dear Angell will see by my last letter how much I reckond upon your coming, therefore it will be needless to tell you how great the disappointment was, nor indeed I coud not if I woud. From eleven a clock I begun to listen to every coach that came near the door; I believe my maids and I were a hundred times at the window; my aunts came to see me, but I believe they were quite tired of me, for every question they askd me was answerd with—I begin to think he wont come, it grows so late —but notwithstanding this impatience to see you, it would be no small addition to my trouble, if I thought there needed any art to bring it about, when it was in your power; so that what I told you of my health was just

Vol. I.   x x

the state of it at that time, but the being at the Opera was no signification to it, for I had Sir David's leave for any thing but going
in a coach.   These two or three days I have had my old distemper
upon me, which you know is more dreadful to me then any thing
else, and I believe the apprehensions of it when I feel it makes me the
worse, and the weather being so bad makes Sir David not dare to
give me physick yet, but I believe I must be forced to do it next week ; in
the mean time he has ordered me the Bath waters warm.   I wish I coud give
you any better entertainment, but there is not a word of news.   I have been
at work all this morning with Lady Pembroke; she tells me that both Houses
are adjournd till Tuesday, and that my Lord Ferrers had desird all the Lords
might then be summond, for he had something of moment to communicate
to them ; but I hope you are told every thing of this kind in a better manner by the minutes, which I desird my Lady Cornwallis to put my Lord in
mind of to get sent to you.   Mr. Hays calld here yesterday to know if you
were come to town, and was very well paid for his visit, for we made an
appointment to play in the evening, and he dealt and won above £300.   I
shoud have had a share among the sufferers, but that I more then savd my
self by going in the bank.   He had abundance of punts, the table full of
ladys, and 7 or 8 men playing over their shoulders, and he won of every
body but Lady Ann Hervey ; but last week Sir John Germane was just the
reverse of this, and quite undid the Dutchess of Cleveland and me with going in the bank ; Lord Stairs won £250 for his share besides all the rest, so
that I had resolvd to play no more but that Madam Rossengrance persuaded
me to try Mr. Vichetty, which I did, but was determind to venture but £20,
and with that I won 90, and I hope that has turnd my luck again, for I have
not lost since, therefore I hope I shoud not make yours worse if you bet
£20 for me, as you do for your self, of all the matches to come, which I am
glad to hear are so few, for the Duke of Bolton told me last night there was

none after Wyndams till his match that day sennight; so pray give me the pleasure as soon as you can of knowing when I shall see you; when I receivd your letter yesterday and reflected upon the conveyer of it being come without you, there was two verses I coud not get out of my head the rest of the day.

> So have I seen the lost clouds pour
> Into the sea a fruitless shower;
> And the rude sailors curse that rain,
> For which poor shepherds pray in vain.

I wish my memory woud serve as well for some of Mr. Addison's play to repeat to you, for I never met with any thing before that outdid expectation except your dear and perfect self, whose merit is beyond whatever my fond heart coud wish or imagine, and farr beyond what can ever be deserved by your (only in that unfortunate) faithful E. Hervey.

P.S. Miss Ann has a cold, and Charles is much out of order, and the little boy has such a sharpness in his blood that his ears and under his arms is so raw, that he is not yet able to be coated; the rest are well. Whebster servd me such a trick yesterday when I had orderd him, while I went to make a visit, to set the table for cards and get me a good fire against seven a clock that the company was to come, which he was so farr from doing that when I came home and some of the company with me, I had not a spark of fire, and the room as I left it after dinner, and never set eyes of him till nine o'th clock. I woud not have troubled you with this but that you are with his mother, that she may chide him.—Meat rises so much that your butcher woud fain be off his bargain; I tell you this only because you spoke of buying stock, and thought knowing this might be of use to you.

416. My ever-new Delight Ickworth, April 20, 1713.

I must for ever hereafter distrust my own judgment, if with all the care and caution I took in consulting your inclination

in the main I at last determind contrary to it, when I took the resolution of
coming hither; for I concluded the circumstance of the waters (which might
have swallowd both your Jacks together) being joynd to the consideration
of doing my business here, beside our common fears of my doing yours if I
had gone to London, woud on the whole have made you vote on the same
side of the question; otherwise I might have spard my self the repentance
I have since felt for doing it, as I assure my self your good nature woud the
aggravation of letting me know more than once how disagreeable a disappointment it provd to you, since absence alone is sufficient to make me as
miserable as I need be for a yet greater fault. The poetry you quoted in
your last was so well applyd that I am sorry I cant put my case into rhime
too; but Mr. Ironside has stated it so well in prose, that tho' you may have
read it lately I cant help repeating it on this misjudgd occasion. Says he
—Virtue is so farr from being alone sufficient to make a man happy, that
the excess of it in some cases (as in love, when joind to a soft and tender
nature,) may often give us the deepest wounds, and chiefly contribute to
render us uneasy etc.—And again—In this last passion it often happens that
we so entirely give up our hearts as to make our happyness wholly depend
upon another person—which God knows I have done to that unlimited
degree as to incurr his censure by it; but he cant condemn my practice more
than I do his opinion that that's a trust for which no humane creature however excellent can possibly give us a sufficient security; since thy virtue,
kindness, prudence & piety have so throughly confuted it that he woud with
shame retract it, did he but know thee half as well as thy most affectionate
friend and lover, Hervey.

P.S.   As to my return, name but the day in your next letter and I'll comply
with it, whatever becomes of things here or at Newmarket, where I am going to morrow. I was yesterday at Bury; Lady Isabella says Mrs. Syer is
secured till you come into the country. Ladythigh is to run again on Friday,
if no body be wiser than Ben Cooper, which is not yet certain.

417.   Lady Hervey to John Hervey.   London, April 21, 1713.

Sure, my dear dear angel, you had not receivd my letter on Friday night when you wrote to me, for you must find by that how much I expected your coming, and consequently woud have condold with me for so great a disappointment, though I cant (very sincerely) do so with you for the pleasures of Ickworth not answering your expectation; but to confess the truth I rather rejoyce at the uneasyness you feel upon this occasion, (hoping they are now near an end,) that we may both resolve never to put our selves into the like circumstance for the future; for I find as time increases my passion towards you it will make absence more insupportable. This fine day woud tempt me to remove this evil by coming to you, if I coud have got Sir David's leave (who has been with me to day), but he will not hear of it, and I am so terrified with my old complaint that I submit to any thing. I am to take the purging waters to morrow, but he has given me leave to go in the evening (in a chair) to the Dutchess of Richmonds, who has sent to me to come and play at Omber with the Spanish ambassador. I dind on Sunday at the Dutchess of Graftons with the Duke of Ormond, where I was invited to the Duke of Grafton's wedding, which they hope to compass next week; it is to be at Chelsey at the Dutchess of Beauforts, but my going is a secret till it is over.—I believe you will think I might shorten my letters, when I have not a word of news to tell you but that there is a Drawing-room to night, which is a rarety enough to be reckond news; I am to go with Lady Burlington.—Miss Ann's cold is well again: I told her your message; she said, Pray present my duty to him, and tell him I am glad with all my heart he loves me, and I long to see him and kiss him a hundred times; but she is mistaken if she thinks so much time woud be allowd her by, my dear dearest life, your most faithful and tenderly affectionate E. Hervey.

P.S.   Charles & James are much as they were; dear Fell is prettyer (if possible) then ever, and is so farr from forgetting you that he looks for you every morning in bed. I hope to hear by to morrows post when I shall see you, for I cant bear it any longer. I am just going to poor Lady Betty ; Sir John has sent me word she is in labour. I wish I had some of the stuff the Guardian speaks of to day, and then I know where I woud soon be.

418.   My ever-new Delight   Newmarket April 23, 1713.

I have not time to write to my niece Ame and Mr Reynolds ; must therfore desire you to shew her the inclosd letter, and to let her know I see no reason against the alteration proposd, in case the whole Essex estate (when the purchase of the value of £5300 is added) be settled on her son without taking out the 2 farms of £18 & £20 per annum comprizd in the first agreement, which Mr. Reynolds says may be obtaind ; and indeed ought to be consented to, because that part of the settlement on the son is not so compleat as the rest. And as to Trustees she is the best judge ; but if she woud know who I think proper, I think her brothers or my brother Porter and both or either of the Reynolds's very fit to be namd ; which she may settle with my brother Porter, with whom she must conferr, and to whom my answer by her must be conveyd to this alteration.—And now, my dearest life, since your repeated complaints extorte a notice from me, (which is contrary to my maxim never to indulge a valetudinary mind with pitying or entertaining it with discourses of its ayles,) I cant conceal the continual disquiet from you which your old distempers return has given me ever since you first mentiond it ; . . . but the Duke of Bolton's account was so unfairly given that there are no less than 4 matches between this day & Hackwoods ; and Wenn's being the Munday after I cannot possibly see you before that time ; when if Mr. Meggot will get the deeds ready, he shall not be delayd by me, who, with all the impatience of a bride-groom, I will defy to long more for that day than, (my now much dearer,

more valuable treasure to me than I coud imagine when thou wert my bride,)
thy most faithful friend and constant lover, Hervey.

419.   Lady Hervey to John Hervey.   London, April 23, 1713.

        I was in hopes to have had a great deal of enter-
tainment for my dear dear angel from the expectation every body had of this
days diversions by the Peace being proclaimed, and a great ball that was
to have been at the French Ambassadors; but it is all ended in nothing, for
the Court does not go out of mourning, nor there is not so much as a Drawing-room, which is a great disappointment to me, for I had such success
there last Tuesday that I believe I shall be a great courtier.   I did what I
never did in my life, won a £170; every body got something, for the bank
lost 600, though there was but six deals, and I the deepest player; the Dutchess of Cleveland won above a 100, but we had both sufferd the day before;
but I was mightily dampd when I came home, where I found a great deal
of company (from the Play, besides those that came with me from the Drawing-room,) which told me of more matches that were made; but the Duke
of Bolton relievd me a little by telling me he thought that which was made
for his horse woud not be run, because the Duke of Rutland woud not lend
his mare; and I conclude your having made another is a false report,
because you say nothing of it in yesterdays letter, where you trust my
generosity beyond the power of practice when you leave it to me to name
the day of your coming , which I beg may be the first time you have 3 days
vacancy (from pleasure and business) to rest you in town; yet sure if you
had but two, the journey woud rather do you good than harm this fine weather;
but if you dont think so, I beg you woud not come, as much as I long to see
you, which is more then words can express; I hope to morrow's post will
tell when I shall be so happy.—People begin to be mightily discontented,
for they say the Queen wont lay the terms of Peace before the House of

Commons, yet so blind are they to go on with the supplys without it, though
they said) they had once resolvd against it, and they say there is but a 150
thousand pounds in the Treasury of the civil list, and not one creature belonging to it paid a farthing, as I was told to day by one of the number,
(you may guess who ;) the same author told me that the French ambassador
had been at the bank to invite the Governours to dinner, but they all hid
themselves, he only catchd two, Sir W. Sea: and Sir James——, and carried them home with him. Sir John Germain is mighty happy with Lady
Bettys being well brought to bed of a son; Lady Kingston and Lady M.
Montague have both daughters.—I woud fain fancy my self necessary in the
removing your goods from Newmarket; if you think so, pray send me the
coach as soon as you can, (if you dont make use of it yourself,) and I will
steal from Sir David, for I am satisfyd, let him say what he will, the body
can never be well while the mind is so much otherwise, as is at this time
your poor disconsolate pining turtle, E. Hervey.

Thank God the children are all well, only Charles and dear Felle have had
ill nights, one with his swelld face and neck, the other I hope is only his
teeth.

420.   My ever-new Delight   Newmarket, April 24, 1713.

The next pleasure to being with you is to hear of
any good fortune which attends you in my absence; pray dont let me loose
any meritt towards you, (since I've so little, and you deserve so much,) and
therefore remember the 100 g. I left with you may have been (considering
the zealous wishes that went along with them) the foundation of your good
luck; at least be so just to me as to think so, since nothing ever prosperd
with or pleasd me but I attributed it to your good genius. The Duke of Bolton must have some design of brewing ill bloud between us, otherwise he
coud not misrepresent matters to you as you describe; for tho' his match is

not run with Creeping Molly, nor have I made any, yet there are three matches depending before Hackwoods, so that there are not even the 2 vacant daies you mention, or else I woud have seen you before Tuesday sevenight. As to your stealing away from Sir David, I had rather loose all the rest of my goods than you, & therefore shall not send the coach for you, but will endeavour to get the household stuff (that Mr. Hawkins will not have) to Ickworth without you, tho' I am very inexpert at such affairs ; and in return to your kind intended theft I must tell you how farr I deservd it, that I went to Nelson my self to know if he had any horses to carry me to Hock-eril, and I woud have sent my own away immediately on the receipt of your letter (which was after 8 a clock), but he having none I coud not possibly go one day and come another, as was designd by him that loves and values you more and more from every day he has spent with you, and longs more & more to be with you every minute since he left you, and who can neither dispatch business or tast any pleasure till he be happy in seeing you again, being solely and entirely thine in all senses, Hervey.

421.   Lady Hervey to John Hervey.   London, April 25, 1713.

I obeyd all your orders to Madam Ame, but she was afraid her memory woud not serve to follow all your directions with my reading of it to her, so I gave her Mr. Reynolds his letter and a copy of what concernd her in yours. The want of my constant comforter put me into such a passion of crying that I was resolvd to endure it no longer, but sent Robbin Wildman to see for a set of horses for me against this morning ; but alass ! how uncertain are all designs in this world, for the very thing that causd me to take the resolution has prevented the accomplishing of it by increasing my pain to a greater degree than I have felt these twelve months, which joynd with some other accidents that have attended me since my lying-in makes it impossible for me to undertake the journey. I woud not

Vol. I.   Y Y

have renewd your trouble with these complaints of my body, if it had not been necessary in the letting you know (the farr greater) distress of my mind by your absence.—Now all my ill boding dreams are come to pass, for just as I had wrote this Mr. Maltes comes to tell me my little boy, James, has had a fit, which they woud not tell me till it was over, and he is now in a quiet sleep; I have sent for Sir David in hopes he may prevent a return of them ; I think it was a very odd fit, for he was only convulsd of his left side, and that very strong, in his eye, mouth, hand and leg; he neither turnd pale nor black, but mighty red.—Sir David has been here, and gives me great hopes that the child will do well; he has orderd him something to purge him, and drops and powders for the fits, and in case he has another he is to bleed with leeches, which I have great hopes he wont, for tis now above five hours and he has only had a little starting, but at present sleeps very quiet again ; in which interval I wish I had any news to tell you, but I know not a word, nor have not any hopes of seeing any body to day to tell me any, for I dont know a mortal that is not gone to the Play that coud get places, either in boxes, pit or gallery. I was to have gone with the Dutchess of Bolton ; though it is allways as full as it can hold, yet there is more rout to day than ordinary, for my Lord Treasurer and Lord Chancellor are to be there; tis I find made a mighty party business, for my Lady Cooper told me three or four days agoe I must needs be there ; but why I cant tell, for both sides agree in liking of it, for the Torys say Cato is meant for my Lord T., and they are in the right (after what they have done) to think they can put any thing upon this poor nation. Mr. Booth acts so perfectly well that he seems to be that very Cato which he represents; he had a compliment with 50 G. sent him on Thursday night at the Play ; it was said to be by the Duke of Or— and Lord Bu—, but I heard by one that gave a guinea towards it that it was a subscription. I coud not have held out with this long account of the Play but that (I thank God) my boy is finely well, and has not had another fit; if anything worse happens I will send a messenger on purpose; therefore dont be uneasy and add the weighty addition of your troubles to one that has at present her share, but is in all states of mind with a most tender affection unalterably yours, E. Hervey.

P.S.—That you may be satisfyd how things are mended, I must tell you I have given the porter order if any body comes to see me from the Play to let them in. Mrs. Dunch has been here these 2 hours, but can tell me nothing; if I meet with any body that goes to Newmarket a Monday you shall hear from me again.

422. Lady Hervey to John Hervey. London, April 26, 1713.

If I coud ever be tempted to break my word with my dearest life, it woud be upon this occasion, not to bring you into this scene of distress; but when I promisd to send you word if any thing worse happend, I did not in the least expect there woud, for he was then to all appearance perfectly easy, and had been so for some hours before, and continued so all night, till between seven & eight a clock this morning I was alarmd again with another fit; they have continued upon him ever since with very little intermissions; when he is half an hour (or indeed but a quarter) without one the next is with greater violence, so that I am afraid there is but very little hopes of him, for I dont find that either the bleeding, blistering, or purging gives him any relief; tis plain it is from his head, because it always begins in his eyes and mouth, and Sir David (who is now here) thinks, if it is, there is very little hopes, but if its from any other cause he may recover. I am able to say no more; my dear, farewell.

423. My ever-new Delight. Ickworth, April 27, 1713.

As to what concerns the child, God's will be done; if he is to live and become healthful and easy to himself, let us trust in God's

goodness, (which hath most abundantly shewd itself in our favour, both by
bringing us together at first, and since been continued by a series of miraculous mercies for eighteen years ;) if he must suffer pain & sickness, his providence (we shoud wish) will prevent it ; and in this safe determination let
us rest it.—Your own case has given me much more anxiety by letting me
know your pain is increasd to a greater degree than you have felt this twelvemonth, which alone woud have determind me to come in this messenger's
place had I not got cold (I know not how nor when), which set my left kidney
into labour with gravel yesterday, and for the time it lasted (which was
about 5 hours) cost me a good deal of pain ; but by taking a turpentine
glyster, and some oyl of sweet almonds, with dicodium at going to bed, I
am now as well as ever I was in my life, the same God be praisd who I
hope & trust will ease yours likewise. It was in the same place where I
was taken with that painful crick in my side last October, which rubbing with
hot cloaths removd, and being now so perfectly well and at ease again makes
me hope this might be nothing else : however, I am advisd not to venture on
a journey so immediately after it for fear fresh cold may cause a return of
the pain ; but that I had much rather do than that you shoud think of one
in your much worse circumstances to undertake it, which by all that's most
binding between us I conjure you not to think of as you tender my quiet and
your own safety, whereon my welfare so entirely depends that could I not
assure my self what I have said is sufficient to secure you from coming
hither, I coud not sleep a wink, eat a bitt, or feel an easy moment in the
mean time till I can come to you my self; which if you woud have me do
sooner than Tuesday noon next, let me know by this messenger, and your own
time shall be complyd with by one who is day by day more and more your
most faithful friend & tender lover, Hervey.

P.S. Dear Jack is well and did me great service in my pain, tho' he
increasd it by seeing how much it affected him.

424.   To Sir Compton Felton.   London May 9, 1713.

Had you ever signifyed the least desire to have a coppy of the inclosed account before, you need not have given your self or Mr. Snelling a second trouble about it ; neither would your letter of the 17th past have remaind any longer unanswerd than all your former ones, had there been any passage in it that required or but seemd to expect one; and to multiply unnecessary troubles upon you, I thought not so reasonable as ye omission of them ; and as to Mr. Wanley ye part he has acted has been so farr from being criminal that the Bank has paid and he receivd the dividends as they became due purely out of respect and service to me during your inability to sign ye powers that were sent you from time to time for his receiving of them as formerly, and since you see how punctually they are placed to your account, I hope you'l rather approve than condemn his officious zeal to serve my son, since these sumons might have lain unreceivd like the other dividend due from Fells's estate etc., which, tho I sent the instrument to be signd for the receiving of it above a year since, is not (that I know of) to this day paid. Whatever I receive for principal and interest mony due upon Mr. Timperley's mortgage over and above the £1101..7..3 which I was forced to find at very short warning to pay off Mr. Talmash's creditors, shall have credit given for it in my account, or paid to your order as soon as I can gett it ; but when I shall see my own again or it God knows, tho' the circumstances of that security are without precedent, to have an arrear of above 5 years accrued before Sir Thomas Felton's death, and not one penny of that or the growing interest in above 4 years since dischargd, and at last not told with any certainty when I am to expect interest or principal, so that the last remedy must be employd which has been most carefully avoided by your most humble servant.

425.   Dear Carr   Ickworth, June 25, 1713.

I'm glad to find you so ingenuous as to confess I had just cause given me to suppose you much to blame by staying so long at Paris after my repeated orders to the contrary; but I'm so strongly inclind to think you as perfect as I wish to see you, not only toward me but every other relation in life, that I'm much readyer to acquitt than I was to condemn you, feeling a yet greater pleasure in the one than I did pain (tho' not a little) in the other; and therefore will give you ye earlyest relief of knowing your apology of ye 16th instant from Namur, confirmd by Mr. Masson's of the 28th from Hannover, have fully restord you to my good opinion.—You being at last arrivd where I alwaies intended you should spend most of ye time I could spare you from me, I depend on your prudence to make ye best use of that which remains to ingratiate your self with a family so wisely designd by our laws and immutably destind (I trust) by those of God's providence to succeed our good Queen in ye throne of these kingdoms. The Elector bears so bright a character in ye world, that you'l find him one of those few who has as much reason to love truth as most other Princes have to fear it. Justitiæ cultor, rigidi servator honesti, is so peculiar a part of it, that strict honour and the publick good are ye first principles of his conduct in government, which he has practisd to such perfection, together with all other royal virtues, as have universally indeard him to all his subjects, and therby verifyed two of my maxims : Nil est tam populare quam bonitas, and that Honesty is ye best policy. O that for the sake of poor mankind all other Princes would believe and rule accordingly! I hope it wont be long ere you are able to inform me whether a present of horses would be acceptable or not, and, if any, what sort will be most welcome ; Mr. Masson wrote me word such as are proper for a breeding-studd would doubtless prove so, by which I understand Mares and Stallions. You may take the liberty to acquaint his Highness (with my most dutiful service, if you find it proper, because I'm wholly unknown to him, unless Baron Bothmar has been so just to represent me as one of the most zealous well-wishers to his title and family,) that as I am a breeder I have of all sorts and sizes, and that, if he'l please to tell you what kind he likes best, I should be very proud of ye honour to please him. You knew a horse well enough before you went from me to describe ye turn, size etc., so as that I may judg pretty near what will best suite his Highness's taste.— As to fixing any time for your return, that depends so much upon what reception you may meet with and ye advices I may from time to time receive from you and Mr. Masson, that no resolution can be yet taken of that kind, as impatient as 2 years and 3 months absence has already renderd your most affectionate father, Hervey.

426.   To Sir R. Cockes.   Ickworth, June 30, 1713.
            I was never owner of vanity enough to give my self ye pleasure of thinking I was at any time of much signification in ye service of my country; and finding by my late endeavours that I'm (at present) renderd wholly useless to her have with ye quieter conscience taken Cato's wise advice to his son Portius :

> Lett me advise thee to retreat betimes
> To thy paternal seat ;
> Where all thy frugal ancestors were blessd
> In humble virtues & a rural life ;
> There live retird ; pray for ye peace of Rome ;
> Content thy self to be obscurely good ;
> When vice prevails & impious men bear sway,
> The post of honour is a private station.

and am come hither accordingly to enjoy those innocent satisfactions this place affords; among ye chief whereof I reckon that leisure I find here for conversing this way with you, and thereby enabling me to discharge ye debt of thanks I owe you for ye excellent draught you some time since sent me of an Act will execute it self. I am so farr of ye penner's mind that if we are to be undone, I think ye shortest way would prove ye best, as twould sooner putt us out of pain: Sed ita lenibus uti videbantur venenis, ut posse videremur sine dolore interire; a method of all others I most apprehend, because ye slowest poysons make ye surest work, their sly approaches being seldom suspected till antidotes are ineffectual. I remember Fontenelle in his ingenious dialogues of ye dead introduces Junius Brutus telling Augustus that, if he had not first personated ye patriot, he could never have destroyed ye Roman liberty; and there's never so much danger as when a mercenary people can be so farr deluded as to believe they are going to be made rich & happy by ye very men & measures which are bringing ye reverse upon them; which shews there is as discernable a lunacy in states (in some certain conjunctures of time) as there is in private persons, and how incapable ye men of this degenerate age are of Cato's noble council to his country. men :

> Remember, O my friends, ye laws, ye rights,
> The generous plan of power deliverd down
> From age to age by your renowned forefathers,
> (So dearly bought, ye price of so much bloud ;)
> O lett it never perish in your hands,
> But piously transmitt it to your children !

Even our Popish ancestors were wise & honest enough, notwithstanding ye enslaving system of that religion they professd, to leave us just such an invaluable legacy ; and can Protestants be such ignoble, treacherous executors of their Trust as, instead of fulfilling ye donors will by perpetuating so beneficiall a foefment to all posterity, basely connive at, ney corruptly make court to, those who dard insolently advise such unprecelented steps as have renderd ye inestimable bequest precarious. O! (says Cato's son in the Play I equally admire ye hero and the author of,) is there not some chosen curse, some hidden thunder in the stores of Heaven, red with uncomon wrath, to blast the man who owes his greatness to his country's ruin? Well, what-'er becomes of him or us here, we have the sweet consolation of having done our duty, and that tho there is no discrimination in this world between the servile and sincere, ye vicious and the virtuous, yet there will be a state where (as my said divine poet makes my diviner hero speak)

> the firm patriot there,
> Who made ye welfare of mankind his care,
> Tho still by faction, vice & fortune crossd,
> Shall find his generous labours were not lost.

And there I hope to meet you if I am not to be so happy as to do so this year at Bath, where I'm to be about ye beginning of next August, unless prevented by a journey to Hannover, (where my eldest son at present is,) which is not yet finally determind by, Sir, your most faithful friend and sincere servant, Hervey.

427.   To ye Revd. Mr. Priest at Antwerp with ye Duke & Dutchess of Marlborough.   Ickworth, June 20, 1713.

Your letter gave me a much greater satisfaction than I hopd to meet with in my retirement out of ye world, by letting me know I still live in that part of it I ever most valued, ye Duke and Dutchess of Marlborough's remembrance and esteem; ye continuance of whose kindness towards so useless a friend as I have hitherto been is ye only errour I would have them remain in thro' your preaching and ministry; and sure if ever a pious fraud was laudably practisd, tis where so great a charity is concernd as making one man happy without injuring ones neighbour by

Vol. I.   z z

being so. O! how that passage charms me, where you say his Grace has often repeated things so much to my advantage as allowing me a most faithfull friend to him and a disinterested promoter of my country's good; as Cicero told Brutus: Cum a Catone nostro laudabar, vel reprehendi me a ceteris patiebar. How valuable is praise from that person who deserves more himself than ever mortal meritted from mankind since our Saviour; ney, Pliny said twas becoming a sort of God in ye world to protect ye innocent and relieve ye oppressd; and Seneca's sense of such benefitts as he has done Europe was, Homines ad deos nulla re propius accedunt quam salutem hominibus dando; and mine of those he has done ungratefull Brittain is ye same Crassus had of Cicero's, (& which every just or gratefull member of our Senate must acknowledg,) that we are obligd to him, not only for preserving us Senatours and free citizens, but for ye security of our lives and fortunes, and that he never lookd on his wife & children, or thought of ye then well alterd condition of his country, but all reminded him of Cicero's meritts; who too, like him, may well complain—nos non vitia sed virtutes affixerunt. But even Collier, ye non-juror, (by principle a slave,) could ask this free question; How many great and good men have been ruind by being over-chargd with meritt? what banishd Themistocles, and sent Belisarius a begging, but having done too much for their unworthy countrymen? And Monsieur Rochfaucault truly observes, Le mal que nous faisions ne nous attire tant de persecution et de haine que nos bonnes qualites: to which sort of illustrious offenders Mr. L'Abbee de St. Real administers this comfortable reflection: C'est une consolation bien douce et bien flatuse de pouvoir se persuader qu'un merite trop eclatant a fait tout notre crime, et qu'on auroit ete plus heureux si l'on avoit ete moins digne de l'etre. An application might in ye strictest sense be made by any modesty but his own, whose just character is

> The various virtues which in Marlbro' shone,
> As once ye glories which did Moses crown,
> Dazled ye crowd around, but were to him unknown.

But whether would ye contemplation of his good qualities and ye very ill treatment they have mett with lead me, should I persue ye one or enter farther into ye other than saying, Sure nature contrivd ye ferment and rising of ye bloud for such occasions as these? which nothing can allay but thinking he must certainly be designd by Providence to be one of those magnanimi heroes nati melioribus annis, which you may waite with greater patience for than any body, since that tedious interval of time to others will be most agreeably shortend to you by ye daily conversation of two persons, who were not only ye greatest ornaments of this country, but who do honour to ye age they live in, & who in ye kind civilities (you say) they shew you do ye same to your etc.

428.   Dear Carr   Ickworth, July 17, 1713.

As thro-bred English horses are allowd to surpass most of ye same species, and having now such an opportunity of furnishing ye Elector with much finer ones than I can hope may happen again, (since I'm disposing of my running stable,) and as King William had done me (more than once) the same honour, I was thereby tempted out of pure respect to make the offer of them by you, which since it provd so unlucky as to occasion any difficulty, I wish had n'er been mentiond. I'm willing to impute the motives of their refusal to ye causes you conjecture, especially since you have given me ye ease of knowing with what civility and kindness you are receivd at that Court, and think there's nothing farther necessary to be said on this subject but to make it clearly understood that I've desisted from my intended purpose merely upon ye intimation you were desird to send me about it. This being so there will be no need of Mr. Massons meeting Jack, his journey to you being disappointed by it also; and as to your own homeward, I desire whenever you find ye least beginning of satiety appearing toward you, you'd take your leave in the most dutiful manner; and in ye mean time to take all proper occasions of letting them know how justly proud I am of ye distinguishing honours they have been pleasd to shew you, as well as your Mama and me in thier gracious enquiries after us, and how glad I am they so farr know me worthy as to have been a most constant, zealous promoter of every measure that originally introducd or could since any way strengthen ye security of their succession; wheron everything that's precious to a free, Protestant poeple entirely depends. When once you quitt Hannover, I hope you'l make no stay any where by ye way, both as your presence will be necessary here in order to be chosen into a new Parliament, and as my impatience to see you daily increases; which I know will prove sufficient reasons (without more that might be added) to determine so good a Briton and so dutiful a son to make haste home to ye most affectionate of fathers.

429.   To Lord Chancellor Cowper.

Ickworth near Bury, July 22, 1713.

I am very much obligd to your Lordship for ye trouble you have given your self about my medal, which if any servant of your Lordships will leave with my goldsmith, Mr. Chambers, in Fleet Street, I shall have it as I go thro London for Bath, where I should be glad to do your Lordship any service.—As to ye *trust I reposd in your Lordship, had I not thought my honour & conscience quite as safe in your custody as my own, I could never have resolvd to dispossess my self of either for a moment; but as I knew both would be under the direction of a

---

*Marginal note says Proxy.—S.II.A.II.

sounder judgment, I reckond it rather a meritorious duty toward the
Publick than any neglect of one to retire and place them where they would
be employd to more advantage for my country, a motive alwaies most
prevalent with your Lordship's most obedient, faithful servant, Hervey.

430.　　To Mr. Hervey.　　　　　　　　　　Bath, August, 1713.
　　　Dear Carr

Yours of ye 28 passd found me here this morning,
and was very welcome, as it brought me ye pleasing relation of those
Princes lovely characters where you are, and of their continuance of their
great civilities & condescentions towards you, which I hope you'l take care
to deserve as far as you are able on all occasions, & by a blameless
behaviour gain the honour of their joyning in that harmonious chorus
which ye rest of ye world sings in your fond father's ears: Tum uno ore
omnes omnia bona dicere et laudare fortunas meas, qui gnatum haberem
tali ingenio præditum. You will find by ye last letter I wrote to you from
sweet Ickworth ye confidence I place in your penetration & prudence, since
I therein left ye time of your return to your own choice & observation,
notwithstanding ye approach of our elections to a new Parliament. For I
took such care before I left Suffolk to secure yours at Bury (with my brother
Porter), that unless I am much deceivd you'l not meet with one negative
there, (whatever he does,) altho' neither of us shoud happen to be on ye
place when they chuse their representatives. However, shoud ye least ray
of ye satiety I mentiond begin but to appear, take your leave in ye very
best manner & hasten homeward, where when arrivd you may either spend
ye remainder of this season with me in ye diversions of this place till Bury
fair, (where we are engagd to meet ye 2 Dutchesses of Grafton and my
Lady Cornwallis,) or else go directly from London or Harwich (where you
shall first arrive) to Ickworth, and so sollicite your election your self till I

can gett from hence, which will not be before ye middle of September, by which time I hope in all events to see you, being impatiently expected by your most affectionate father.

431.   To Doctor Friend.   Bath, Aug. 15, 1713.

I think my sons ought to be indulgd in their request for having chosen so powerfull an intercessor, especially since you say they will want ye security of being under my eye during their next vacation ; and therefore you may please to let them know they may go by ye first coach after your dismission of ye school ; ye time of their return too is wholly left to your appointment, that they may think themselves yet more obligd to take pains in acquitting themselves well of those exercises you think fit to set 'em.   Jack is truly sensible of all your kindness towards him, & particularly for ye remembrance of your last good wishes, which are returnd you with all affection and sincerity both by him & your humble servant.

432.   To Richard Minshull, Esqr.   Bath, Aug. 1713.

Since you have once thought fit to give your attorney order to proceed against me as well as ye other Lords concernd, (notwithstanding your repeated professions of shewing me some distinction,) I shall be very farr from desiring you to countermand it or expecting any favour from you, requiring only ye justice of your believing, that whatever I determine on this as on every other occasion shall be thought (at least) to be warranted by as nice rules of honour as any body can pretend to dictate to, yours etc.

433.   To Sir H. Elwes.   Bath, Aug. 1713.
          Dear Nephew

I hope this will find you well at Stoke, & tho' not with the addition of ye £2000 you wanted, yet with your increase of health your own imagination only made you think you stood in need of from ye help of Tunbridge waters. The horse you mention is ye weakest of all ye string, & therefore most unfit for ye deep country you are to hunt in. The properest in my opinion is young Wenn, who has both strength and hardiness, besides being the very best horse in nature (not excepting his brother Ickworth) of his speed. I have refused 3 score guineas for him of one that was at Wordwell on purpose to see him from Hide Park Corner; if you like him you shall have him for 100 guineas, not payable till you get a wife with £10000 portion, which without this circumstance is heartily wishd you by your affectionate uncle etc.

434.   To Mr. Masson.   Bath, Aug. 25, 1713.

      I dont at all wonder that you never receivd my letter expressing that satisfaction of yours, which it seems by your last of ye 18th you are still without; for most of mine (as I hope severall of yours have had ye same fate, since but two from you have come to my hands in ten weeks that you've been at Hannover,) have miscarried, Sir Thomas Hanmer having sent me hither a letter of mine to Carr, which was returnd to him from Paris by ye gentleman to whom he intrusted ye care of delivering it to my son; but tho' mine to you might have lost its way, yet that I wrote to Carr about ye same time woud have put you to all ye ease you not only desire but which I find you deserve, since I therein repeated my content with your conduct, notwithstanding I had met so many unintelligible appearances to allarm me. The contagious distemper which has hoverd so long about Germany very much perplexes me in ye orders you expect as to Carrs coming home; for I woud willingly spare him till ye removall of ye Court to Guevre, if you think ye credit he is in can increase, or that ye friendships he has contracted may be more firmly cemented, without running the risque of catching a pestilential disease, which shoud it approach ye quarter you are in, I woud have you leave it instantly without further direction from me. I'm so true a lover of my country, and have so great a regard for ye happyness of posterity, that I scarce know which transports me most, to hear by Carr how wonderfully well qualified all ye princes of that illustrious house are to make these nations blessed, (& especially ye surprising insight ye Electoral prince (he tells me) has into all our national interests, both forreign and domestick,) or to know from you how very much my son is esteemed by those who must be sound judges of merit by possessing so much themselves; more particularly ye Elector himself, who, Carr tells me, has been so gracious as to receive him with a countenance uncommon to his usuall reservedness. Let him be sure to leave so good impressions at parting as may not wear out before their meeting again, by which time virtue may hope to be better rewarded than I have hitherto observd it; & unless he can arrive at honours by passing thro' her temple, they shall never be wishd him by his affectionate father and your etc.

435.   To Sir Thomas Hanmer.   Bath, Aug. 27, 1713.

Altho' I commonly repeat in each succeeding letter every material article in my former ones which go beyond sea, yet I am nevertheless obligd to you for ye trouble you have given yourself about that which you returnd me hither, & am glad of ye oportunity it has given me to let you know with what a secret satisfaction I received ye welcome news of your having so wisely refused ye insidious offers of those, who woud dexterously make use of your rising reputation to support their own declining credit and authority, which were founded upon such destructive unprecedented measures as even this vile degenerate age will shortly blush to think they've borne with ye authors of so long. The chair of ye H. of C. of G.B. is the only publick post I coud at present congratulate you upon, since there I'm sure you may maintain that noble figure my friendship wisheth, & my great opinion of your virtue expects from you, of acting with that strict impartiality between prince and people, that those mortall wounds which have been given to ye bleeding constitution of this country by ye ambition of some and ye corruption of others may be so far closed again (for they can ne're be wholly heald) by your retrieving conduct, that arbitrary power may not hereafter be tempted to try its way thro' those fatal clefts that must and will remain. If I have gone too far in anything I've said, impute it to the transports of a most fervent zeal for yours & my country's service, which challenges all the world to shew a man who can surpass me in that sincere affection for both, which has not only been professd but I hope practisd by yours etc.

My wife & I are very much ye Dutchess of Grafton's most humble servants, & hope to see you at Bury Fair.

436.   To Mr. Richard Hovell, Alderman of Bury.

Mr. Alderman   Bath, Sept. 9, 1713.

I have had ye pleasure of receiving many marks of a most distinguishing affection from ye Corporation of Bury; but none ever made so sensible an impression on my heart as this last kind proof they have given me of their friendship for my family by chusing my son & brother Porter for their representatives in ye approaching Parliament; & as in his absence I shoud contrive to make my due acknowledgments as acceptable to them as possible, I desire you'd do me ye favour to convey my most gratefull thanks to them for it till he can pay them personally, which I have by this post orderd him not to delay, altho' he is treated with such particular grace and civility at Hanover that I was loath he shoud leave it on a less occasion than coming to receive your instructions against ye next

Vol. I.   A A A

Session ; wherein if he acts not with all ye tenderest regard to your true interests in particular & the nations in generall, may they ever after reject him, as I hope they will those who woud attempt to disturb so incontestable a right as ye select numbers of your burrough has hitherto enjoyd without any interruption, which as long as any justice remains, or Carr & I worth a groat, shall be supported against all opposers or invaders by him & their & your etc.

I desire my service to all those who are for maintaining your right, & none other.

437.   To Mr. John Crompe.   Ickworth near Bury, Nov. 23, 1713.

It being near ye time of ye Auditt you gave me notice of in August last, I must desire ye favour of you to acquaint ye Dean & Chapter (with my service to both) that my present tennants lease expiring at Michaelmas last I find I shall not be able to get more for ye future than ye former accustomd rent of £160 per annum for ye whole estate I hold of them, unless I lay out such fresh sums for severall improvements & repairs insisted on as I can never resolve to bestowe again upon ye premises, my last expences not being at this day reimbursd which I was drawn in to make upon ye advance of the last 12 yeares rent; and as ye reserved rent and pension to ye Chapter & Vicar amounts to above forty pounds per annum, I cant see any just or equitable reason or custom why more than a years clear profitt should be set for my fine, that being ye known common rate for all renewalls on ye foot of my tenure. By ye Chapter-order passd Nov. 28, 1684, it appears the persons then interested therein thought fitt to impose no larger a sum for eight years on my father than ye present lessors do on me for seven. And as you very well know I paid but £140 fine anno 1700, I hope ye worthy gentlemen concernd will not treat me worse ye longer I continue their tennant, for if they persist in their resolution of doing so,

I musti n time grow weary of being only their collector, which in that case would be ye sole benefit or business remaining in this affair to their or your etc.

438.   To Mrs. Anguish,
   Madam

The account you gave your self ye trouble to send me of my Lady Poley's death was receivd by my wife and self with all ye just concern due to ye loss of so good and common a benefactrice as she happily provd to both of us, since we always lookd upon her as ye providential means of bringing us first together. We most sincerely condole with my Lady Effingham & Aunt Felton on this sad occasion, & desire to know if they intend to bury her at any place in this country, that we may prepare ye neighbourhood as well as our own family to pay her our last respects, which shall be observd with more than ordinary affection by their dutifull nephew & your etc.

439.   To Mr. John Crompe of Rochester. Ickworth, Dec. 7, 1713.

Since it appears there was no more than £160 fine set for 8 years in the year 1684, and but £140 fine for 7 years anno 1700, I hope the Dean and Chapter will consider whether after having paid 4 shillings in ye pound taxes for 25 years (beside their reservd rent & ye Vicars pension) for ye whole estate, and having been at great expences in repairing and improving it, they will insist on making me pay more now than my predecessors did before this long and burthensome warr; for if they finally resolve to treat me so, I am as firmly determind to dispose of my lease, which as I am in their mercy for ye present renewal of, so when my term in being is once made up 21 years again, I shall be very glad to sell it at a Markett price, either to one of their own body or any of their friends or favourites, which I cant but think must be ye drift of those who aim at fixing such heavy constant fines as must make it not worth ye longer continuance of your etc.

440.   The Duke of Marlborough to Lord Hervey.
My Lord   Antwerp, Dec. 7, 1713.
                    My satisfaction is too great in seeing my selfe so agreeably rememberd by your Lordship in sending your son to see me, (who has all the good qualities that you can wish,) that I do not know how to thank you enough for the honour that you and he have done me ; but I am sure I shall allways value your friendship in a manner that will never permit me to neglect it, and if ever I appear ungrateful, it is for want of power to return the many obliging friendships which I have receivd from you as they deserve, and as the esteem that I have for you makes me wish I coud, who am with all the truth imaginable your Lordships most faithful and most humble servant, Marlborough.

441.   To His Grace ye Duke of Marlborough.
My Lord   Ickworth, Dec. 26, 1713.
                    The honour of your Grace's letter made my son more welcome to me than any other thing he could bring with him, as it not only gave me the pleasing assurance of your Grace's kind remembrance, but as it also confirmd to me by ye most authentick authority (what I next wishd to know) that he was master of any qualities worthy your Grace's notice and approbation.   One good one I can answer he possesses in perfection, which is the utmost sensibility of all your Grace's and ye Dutchess of Marlborough's great goodness and civilities to him at Antwerp, which he woud have given your Grace the trouble of his thanks for, had I not undertaken to make but one of both our acknowledgements, wherein we joyn

with ye sincerest gratitude, hopeing we may live to shew your Graces that all your favours (tho' many & substantiall) to me and mine have not been altogether thrown away. Had every body your Grace has been a benefactor to the same just sentiments of your meritts towards them, your noble mind need never have felt the generous pain of pitying your enemies folly & ingratitude, nor your friends have endured ye mortification of mourning your absence, which every month increases to such a degree of impatience in my heart that it now makes more ardent vows (if possible) for your return than formerly for your success & safety, wherein I trust they'l prove as effectual too, being put up with the same affectionate devotion by your Graces etc.

442. To Sir Richard Cockes. Ickworth, Dec. 28, 1713.

My son being, I thank God, returnd in safety to me, and his popular reception at Bury over, (which far exceeded his pretensions or my desire,) I have carefully discoursd with him on ye subject of your petition, whose opinion thereupon from six months conversation with men of most esteem for good sense and experience in business, and who are thought to be best acquainted with ye Elector's thoughts on such affairs, is that whenever ye comparison came to be made between ye point in question and pushing ye Pretender as far off as possible, he alwayes seemd more desirous ye latter might be urged and insisted on in ye ensuing Parliament than that ye other shoud be proposd, yet not that they could not prefer your expedient to ye other considering both as they are in themselves, but as they look upon the other in ye present ticklish conjuncture liable to fewer objections; as in ye first place they depend upon having yet so great a majority of the people of Brittain on their side, or at least who woud be against altering ye establishd succession, that things must (at worst) remain as they are till a demise, and believe their most powerfull enemies can no other way be able to hurt them than as far as themselves may furnish 'em a handle to alter ye disposition of ye people towards them by some act of thiers obnoxious to misconstruction, and thereby made subservient to ill purposes; and apprehending any such overture of invitation may afford ye ill-willers to it such an occasion, I perceive they are prudently cautious how so tender a motion is to be touchd at this time, concluding such incendiaries will not be wanting, who woud blow up a party spirit by representing ye House of Hanover as carrying on designs with ye Whiggs, and aiming to set themselves up at ye head of a faction here in opposition to ye Queen ; nay, tis more than probable their clamours woud not stop here, since tis experimentally true there is no calumny too black for some men to insinuate when tis to serve their vile purposes, nor any too absurd to be believd by many, especially when joynd with ye fatal influence of party interests. These with many other considerations not fitt to be communicated by letter, (since few, if any, pass unopened,) must make me suspend sending you any farther judgment about it till I'm better enlightend by talking with Mr. Schutts and my other friends (who now with confusion wish they had treated this matter as I woud have had them,) as soon as I can get to London, when if any thing occurs worth troubling you again, you shall not fail of hearing more on this most important subject from, Sir, your etc.

443. To Sir William Gage.   London, Jan. 14, 1713/4.

The rightest return I can make to so kind a desire as you signify of having Hargrave and Chevington pass into my family will be to contrive you should lose as little time as possible in disposing of them, and therfore I take the first opportunity to lett you know 21 years purchase is a greater price than I can give for any estate I ever knew or heard of in Suffolke, and if any body can be found who will, I shall equally acknowledg the offer of pre-emption as if they had actually become the possessions of yours etc.

My wife & I beg our services to Lady Gage.

444.   Dear Jack   London, June 18, 1714.

Could you know with how surprizing a concern I receivd ye unexpected news of your having taken upon you to make ye least delay or dispute in complying with any injunction of Mr. Laughton's, you would (I'm confident) have spard us both ye uneasyness your disobedience must have occasiond, more especially in a point of ye most dangerous consequence to your character in ye University; noscitur ex socio being an observation as old as society it self; and as custom is calld a second nature, so should reputation be reckond a sort of second life, & guarded accordingly. Example is so infectious that our first and chiefest care should be to find out & frequent men of ye most sober & virtuous conversation, since we insensibly fall into ye imitation of ye manners of ye company we consort with, and gradually become ye very men whose images at first frighted us. I know nothing of Mr. Finch, neither is it very material to ye matter in question whether he really is ye man you or Mr. Laughton takes him to be; his prohibition alone ought to have been sufficient to determine your duty, & if any affront arises out of this procedure, tis not any you can be deemd capable of towards Mr. F, who are not yet supposd to be in your own disposal, but rather to that safe & wise authority you are placed under, whose faithfulness & friendship towards us both in this prudent precaution (should it prove only such) will be here after approvd and acknowledgd by your riper judgment; and in ye interim know that an entire submission to his reasonable rules is made ye standard of your obedience to your etc.

445.   To Mr. Turnor.   London, June 26, 1714.

Dr. Friend, ye master of Westminster School, having been informed that Mr. Randal intends to remove in some short time from Bury, has recommended Mr. Kinsman, one of his assistants, to

succeed him; who he assures me is every way qualifyed for that employment; but I not knowing whether you & ye rest of ye Governors might not
have Mr. Lathbury or some other person in your views to supply that
vacancy whenever it happens, could give him no other answer than that I
would communicate his proposal to your self & my other friends concernd
in that Trust, & lett him know ye result of your determination therupon,
which is hereby desird by your friend & servant, Hervey.

446.   To my daughter Ann.   July 12, 1714.
    My dearest child

Tis now just seven years since it pleasd God to
bless me and ye world with the most amiable & valuable creature in thee
that ever his omnipotence yet produced. May ye same singular favour
which was shewn in forming thy bodily beauties so superior to all others
still attend thee in framing thy soul to a yet greater degree of perfection,
which ye same attribute of ye Deity can alone bring to pass; & when both
are compleated according to ye dictates of my best wishes in their most
fervent ecstacies, mayst thou under ye divine protection enjoy ye utmost
happiness this vale of misery ever afforded ye most favourd mortal, till He
in mercy shall call thee to that sweet society where thou shalt eternally
sing praises to that beneficient Being, who in his infinite goodness hath
made thee what thou art, so full of every principle which tends to ye most
consummate virtue, that my prayers seem already throughly answerd,
having often beggd

> May Heaven preserve her from ye fall uncursd,
> To shew how all ye sex were formed at first.

and has left me but one petition more to make at ye throne of grace, which
is that after dear Mama (from whom you derive most of your meritt) and I
have livd to see you inheritt all her virtues & become ye standard of female

perfection here on earth, we may all meet in Heaven & there joyn in Halelujahs with thy angellick voice (which has often charmd me with even Bell-piacher etc.) to ye merciful author of our common bliss for ever. In ye mean time kiss brother Felton & dear sisters for me, & love (as he does thee) thy most affectionate father.

447. To Mr. Seaton, London, July 20, 1714.

Your irresolution upon coming into and your abrupt departure from my service, joyned to the small signification (it seems) you have been of to my son, either in his studies or other attendance on him, must of course have made me very indifferent as to the loss of you, altho a little more warning was due of common decency, that I might have provided one wholly to my own mind to putt in your place; but as that is now impracticable I must leave it wholly to Mr. Laughton's care and judgment to substitute such a one in your room as may better answer ye future expectations of your etc.

448. To Doctor Friend. Ickworth, Sept. 5, 1714.

Having enquird into ye state of Mr. Randal's case since my coming hither, I find he is resolvd to try his interest with the Governors, whether he may not continue in the mastership of Bury School, notwithstanding ye living he lately accepted of; which depending entirely on their favourable construction of a statute, I already perceive ye result will be that ye majority of them will never vote a vacancy on this occasion, whereby I shall be deprivd of one wherein I might have shewn how much weight your recommendation of Mr. Kinsman would otherwise have had with, Sir, your friend & servant.

I desire ye continuance of your care & kindness towards my sons.

Vol. I.   B B B

449.   Copy of my son Carr's letter to ye Prince.

Monseigneur   Sept. 14, 1714.

Si je n'avois pas eue autant d'experience que j'en
ay eue de la bontè de vostre Altesse royale, je ne pourrois point esperer de
pardon de la libertè que je prend en luy addressant celleci ; effectivement
c'est une hardiesse qui n'admet d'aucune excuse, a moins que le transport de
joye ou nous nous voyons a present ne puisse rendre tout permis ; c'est dans
cette esperance seule que je prendray le courage d'assurer vôtre Altesse
royale que ma joye en particulier est si grande qu'elle ne me laisse rien au
monde a desirer exceptè le seul bonheur de me voir plus immediatement sous
les ordres et la protection de vôtre Altesse royale, et aupres de sa personne;
si vôtre Altesse royale m'honoroit encore de son souvenir, et daignoit
m'accorder cette requeste, je ne serois plus capable d'aucune autre de plaisir
que celuy de ne pouvoir jamais assez exprimer mon contentement et ma
reconnoissance; ce que pourtant je tacheray de faire continuellement par le
zele et les soins que je ne cesseray jamais d'employer en m'acquittant de
mon devoir. De quelque maniere qu'il plaise a vôtre Altesse royale de
disposer de moy, je ne pourrois jamais oublier les honneurs que j'en ay desja
receu, et je supplie tres humblement vostre Altesse royale de croire que je
suis avec le plus profond respect etc.

450.   To ye Rt, Honble ye Lord Bathurst.   London, Oct. 15, 1714.

The veneration I have ever retaind for the memory
of my most worthy uncle Hervey has been so justly gratefull that your
Lordship could not have contrivd to please me more than by the generous
present you have made me of his picture;* which not only claims my

---

* There are two portraits of this Uncle Hervey at Ickworth. The whereabouts of a third by Lely,
of which there is an engraving by Tompson, is not known. In the missing one he has his hand on a bust.
A picture of Aunt Hervey by Vandyke is also missing.—S.H.A.H.

earlyest acknowledgements, but to be rememberd by me even after some kind chance may have furnishd me with an opportunity of requiting it ; and as so welcome an occasion would afford me a satisfaction next to that your Lordship has already given me, I beg your Lordship would not refuse to accept ye prettyest horse I ever bred in all my life for any use, till I can shew by more convincing proofs how much your Lordship has oblidgd, my Lord, your Lordships most obedient faithfull servant.

The horse shall attend your Lordship when & where you'l please to appoint.

451. To Sir Compton Felton. Jan. 29, 1714/15.

You must conclude I was not a little surprisd to understand by Colonel Norton that after you had chosen to referr me to Mr. Webb as your counsel to peruse the settlements I had made, and had promisd by Mr. Redgrave in case he approved them to do what lay on your part towards vacating the securities I only enterd into for those ends, that now, when so much time and expence had passd in persuing your own method, I must be obligd to begin a new one ; which as I can construe to be with no other intention but to make me loose more time and put me to farther unnecessary charges, and that you seem at last resolvd to force me into Chancery by one Bill, I am determind to take this opportunity to require your answer by another ; why you have not yet thought fitt after so many repeated requests from my wife and me to order the delivery of one of the parts of the deed of the settlement made by Sir Henry Felton on Sir Adam Felton's marriage with Lady Munson, the custody whereof you will find is as uncontestably my right as to have my estate freed from those incumberances, sence every circumstance for which they were originally imposed has been more than strictly complyd with for the benefit of your niece and her children by your humble servant.

452.   To Dr. Hutchinson.   London, March 15, 1714.

I delayd troubling you with my compliments of congratulation upon the honour I some time since knew the King designd you till I could do it with infallible authority. My Lord Godolphin is the person to whom I believe you are principally indebted (next to your own personal meritt) for this marke of his Majesty's favour; all that I shall say of my share in it is that your pretensions receivd no prejudices (at least) by the repeated recommendations of your faithfull friend to serve you.

END OF VOL I.

www.ingramcontent.com/pod-product-compliance
Lightning Source LLC
Chambersburg PA
CBHW030952110726
47900CB00004B/1238